LEGENDS

of the

CIRCLE

To Dr. Ken & Janet

Happy Reading!

—STEPHEN J. GALGON—

LEGENDS OF THE CIRCLE

ISBN 978-0-578-32953-6

This is a book of fiction. Names, characters, places, and incidents are either the products of the author's imagination or are used fictitiously. Any resemblance to actual persons, living or dead, events, or locales, is entirely coincidental.

Legends of the Circle is published in the United States by
MJE Publishing, 2021
www.mjepublishing.com

This book is available on Amazon

Editing & Book Production: Harvard Girl Word Services
HarvardGirlEdits.com

For my grandparents
Frances and John & Josephine and Tom:
The real legends.

"Man kills without ceasing,
to nourish himself;
but since, in addition,
he needs to kill for pleasure,
he has invented the chase!"

—Guy de Maupassant
The Diary of a Madman

PROLOGUE

1924 — San Francisco

Those in power make the decisions that shape the world. They take society into their hands and mold it, bend it, and finesse it until it is as they believe it should be. They do it for themselves, in the interest of maintaining their positions of influence. And they do it right under our noses. Without even a hint of wrongdoing or impropriety, under the guise of "the greater good."

But sometimes, inadvertently, the decisions they make spare the common folk. In those decisions ignorance truly is bliss. No one knew this better than William Randolph Hearst, unarguably the most powerful man in America. At the age of 61, Hearst controlled the news and its cycle in a way that makes modern cable news organizations pale by comparison, and was, in many ways, the driving force behind American public awareness. If it wasn't in a Hearst newspaper, it probably didn't happen. And conversely, it *only* happened if it was reported in a Hearst newspaper. Look no further than the Spanish-American war. Hearst's power was in his ability to shape the narrative in a way that best suited him. Control what the public knows; control what they think. That's a power politicians only dream of.

Famously, even with the world at his fingertips, Hearst had an ever-present insatiable appetite for more. It was a side of him no one, not even his wife or mistress, could understand. The life of a wealthy man has its advantages, yet power and influence do not necessarily fill a man's base needs. That's something all the money in the world cannot buy.

Hearst had friends, confidants, kindred spirits even, but these men were off building their own empires around the world and their interactions were limited at best. Hearst liked listing them in his head just to remind himself of how small, yet elite and driven, his circle was. There was Harold McCormick, making a name for himself in the airline business in Chicago. Sir John Ellerman, accountant turned fellow newspaperman across the pond, with a knack for recognizing, and exploiting, undervalued commodities. Samuel Insull, busily creating electric power grids and forging the path for giants like AT&T. Hearst never spoke about his friendship with Andrew Mellon, but having a friend rise to the office of Secretary of the Treasury was, let's just say, mutually beneficial. Then there was Pierre Wertheimer who created his own empire in fragrances with the help of a new partner named Coco Chanel in France, and Frank Baumgartner off in L.A. somewhere making millions in wines and spirits. There were those like Henry Ford who spent all their time making the country smaller by insisting we get places in a great hurry, if you asked Hearst, but who could complain where there was so much money to be made. And his list wouldn't be complete without Rockefeller, who was busy just being Rockefeller. After all, no one can stop an oil man.

Lately, nothing engaged Hearst's predominant sense of ennui; not his mistress, accommodating as she was, not his many children, not building upon his massive properties. His fortune gave him access to every door in the world, yet he felt like a jockey whose horse wouldn't leave the starting gate.

It was in late 1923 that Hearst took to his study where he sat for days, breaking only for food and drink. Once he started putting words to paper, the idea erupted like a geyser, relentless and liberating, from his depths. Two days after completing his manifesto, after time to attend to business, his women, and logistical details, he pulled out a sheet of his highest quality embossed bond and wrote.

> *My friends -*
>
> *The time has come to ask, What's next for the illustrious few – for the ones able, willing, and bold enough to step into the future by virtue of the right to the consummate freedom we have earned? Meet me at San Simeon on the 1st of March. Tell no one of your plans. Come prepared to be set free! - WRH*

He finished off each letter with his personal blue wax seal: a capital "H" encased in a circle. To Hearst's eye the smear of the wax on the paper resembled an ice-cold flame. He would be surprised if even one of the men declined. Friends or not, one accepted Hearst's "invitations." Or suffered the consequences.

And so it came to pass that the 1st of March, 1924 found William Randolph Hearst setting the stage. San Simeon's unfinished Doge's suite and balcony was the obvious choice for the meeting. Inspired by the Doge's Palace of Venice, once completed, Hearst's Doge's Suite would be like no other. Priceless works of art were set aside from his personal collection, including Tintoretto's portrait of Alvisius Vendramin from the late 1500s and Bernini's stone sculpture of Apollo and Daphne, dating back to 1619. The room would be decorated with the finest blue silk and a painted ceiling designed by the finest craftsman to emulate the ornate chambers of the Doge's Palace in Italy. Elegance, luxury, and decadence oozed from every carefully considered element from wall coverings to furnishings.

To welcome his guests, the 61-year-old magnate personally arranged nine leather chairs in a circular formation in the center of the room. In between each chair was a small wooden accent table. Each one catered to its specific guest; a personal humidor fully stocked with each guest's cigar of choice, a drinking glass, and a bottle of the man's preferred liquor. Next to each glass, a gold letter opener rested on top of an envelope sealed with the familiar blue wax "H," the name of each recipient scripted in beautiful calligraphy.

Hearst was not a patient man, nor one prone to nerves. Months of planning, researching, scheming, however, hung in the balance. Still, you don't get to be William Randolph Hearst if you didn't know how to direct the fluttering in your stomach to your advantage, to welcome the anticipation of something so revelatory, so revolutionary. So *right.*

He, William Randolph Hearst, was about to change the world.

• • •

After Hearst's eight guests had been personally greeted and partaken in the exorbitantly priced champagne that was waiting for them, there was the usual repartee regarding life and business. Hearst's heart pumped with the exhilaration of knowing how difficult it was for each man to feign an air of indifferent curiosity. Hearst was at the top of his game. Unstoppable.

Hearst waited for expectancy to reach the point of near irritation before picking up his champagne flute and tapping out an attention-grabbing *clink* with his platinum ring, allowing the fine crystal to carry the sound for several seconds as the room quieted.

"Gentlemen," he began. If not for the fact that everyone in the room had heard Hearst's voice previously, and were mindful of his sensitivity about it, they might have giggled aloud at its high-pitched incongruity. "Thank you for coming. I'm sure you are curious about the nature of this meeting, but have no fear. All will be revealed in due time." The eight men listened, attempting to hide their annoyance with respectful attention. They were not men who liked to be kept waiting, or in the dark, though Hearst would never admit his theatrical cloak-and-dagger nonsense was bordering on childish. He extended his glass to the right. "Shall we retire to the Doge's Suite?" He strode from the room into the corridor, assuming they would follow.

William Randolph Hearst waited for no man.

The men did not look at each other as they exited the room, uncomfortable at being told what to do and preferring not to see that discomfort reflected in the eyes of the others. Inside the palatial suite, they automatically reached for their signature drinks and cigars. One reached for the gold letter opener as he sat down.

Hearst remained standing. "Enjoy your drink and your cigar, but please wait to open the envelope," he said, and waited for the man, whose face had creased in belligerence, to rein himself in and return the letter opener to its place of rest on the side table before continuing. "What I have to say may shock, or even disturb, some of you. But before I begin, I must insist that you agree to secrecy regarding the content of this meeting." He looked at each man in turn until he received his nods of commitment, which were tinged with both interest and, now, distrust. These were not men used to committing to things they had not personally devised.

"I apologize, gentlemen," said Hearst, sounding all but apologetic, "but I will require a verbal agreement from each of you." He looked at Andrew Mellon to his left. "Andrew? Care to go first?" Andrew Mellon took a moment before saying, albeit reluctantly, "I agree." His statement seemed to loosen the tension and the rest of the men soon followed suit, ending with Harrold McCormack, on Hearst's right.

"Thank you, gentlemen," Hearst said. "All of us have qualities in common, namely that we are incredibly wealthy, we are titans of our industries, and we have immense power as a direct result."

There was some general shifting and preening at Hearst's statement. It was well known that the more important the man, the more smoke he produced. Considering the clientele, the oxygen in the room was a commodity, like subjecting oneself to a relatively benign Cloquet fire.

"But," Hearst continued, "what if I told you we each have one more thing in common? Something that ties us together—in a way, almost like family. Something only a handful of people outside this room could possibly understand. Certainly, very few could possibly know what it feels like to have the weight of the world on their shoulders. Corporations, employees, even whole governments, all depend on us to direct their lives. So I ask you: Where does that leave us?"

The question hung in the air for several uncomfortable seconds. "I'll tell you where," Hearst said, "it leaves us rich, yes. Powerful, yes. And *alone*. Because, as they say, gentlemen, it's lonely at the top. Families, play things, all the little *asides*...while they have their place, who among us can say he is truly fulfilled? Who else but we, the chosen few, can truly grasp the raw need for purpose...excitement...the thrill of the chase?"

The silence in the room was becoming unbearably weighted, but Hearst surged on, energized. "Face it, gentlemen. We are an elite enclave that deserves more. More of everything we have built, owned, and controlled." He looked at each man in turn. "In fact, what we really deserve is to feel alive again."

Hearst waited for his words to sink in for another lengthy moment. The budding hunger in the room was palpable.

Finally, Rockefeller spoke. "Exactly what are you proposing, Hearst?"

Uncharacteristically, Hearst let the interruption slide. "What I propose, gentlemen, is that we do something daring. Something beyond bold. Something we may each have secretly considered, but never spoken of aloud." He paused, reveling in the tension that was stretching to its breaking point.

"And now, gentlemen, it's time. You may open your envelopes."

• • •

Each envelope contained one solitary piece of paper. On that paper was a list of names. Each name had a strange pseudonym next to it.

William Randolph Hearst – Mr. News
Mr. McCormick – Mr. Fly
Sir Jon Ellerman – Mr. Paper
Mr. Mellon – Mr. Treasure
Mr. Insull – Mr. Power
Mr. Wertheimer – Mr. Scent
Mr. Baumgartner – Mr. Vino
Mr. Ford – Mr. Motor
Mr. Rockefeller – Mr. Oil

"Gentlemen," said Hearst theatrically. "I welcome you... to the Circle."

The room buzzed. The men looked at the list, each other, and finally, back at Hearst, who waited for silence before speaking again.

"Listen carefully, gentlemen, for as of this moment your lives will never be the same. From this moment on, within the metaphorical walls of this organization I call the Circle you will go by the name that has been assigned to you. As you can see, my name is Mr. News. I expect you will each appreciate the care with which your name was selected to serve as homage to your lives of dedicated work."

"Randolph," sputtered Frank Baumgartner, "what is this? Another social club? I don't have the time to join another damn club. I don't even have time for the tennis club—for which I'm paying astronomical dues."

"Mr. Vino," Hearst said, his voice clipped. "Be assured. This is no social club. And please, I must insist you call me Mr. News."

Baumgartner rolled his eyes ever so slightly. Hearst noted it, but chose not to address it—for the moment. As the men would soon see, any misgivings they had became irrelevant the moment they had agreed to be here. "The Circle," said Hearst, "will indulge our deepest desires. Again, it is obvious that we have all the money and power to buy whatever we want. So, what is the one thing we do not have?"

Several heartbeats passed, no man daring to break the silence.

Hearst let it hang until the tension became unbearable, then said, "I'll tell you what it is, then. The ability to preside over life and death."

The room stilled.

"That's right, gentlemen. In the Circle, we will do one thing. We will hunt."

"Bull," said Samuel Insull gruffly, "I can go on safari any time I please, hunt whatever I want." He looked around. "We all can."

"Have any of you heard of Richard Connell?" Hearst said, his voice now expressing irritation at the mens' lack of vision. "No? Well, Mr. Connell has written a most intriguing and inspiring short story called The Most Dangerous Game. Allow me to read you a passage." Hearst withdrew from his side table a copy of the novella and opened to a marked page.

> *"'I wanted an ideal animal to hunt,' explained the general. So I said: 'What are the attributes of an ideal quarry?' And the answer was of course: 'It must have courage, cunning, and, above all, it must be able to reason.'"*

He paused to scan the faces of his colleagues, waiting for light to dawn. Henry Ford was the first. "You're not...you *can't* be serious."

"No, Mr. Motor?"

Ford scoffed at Hearst's use of the moniker. "Just to be clear. You're actually saying you want us to hunt...*people?*"

"That, Mr. Motor, is precisely what I am suggesting."

Many of the men were aghast. Or at least good at the pretense. A more cutthroat group had never been born.

"I don't know about the rest of you," said Ford, throwing down his letter, "but I'm done here. Hearst? You're insane."

Rockefeller and Baumgartner stood up as well as if to join him.

"That's quite far enough, gentlemen," said Hearst. "Please take your seats."

The room stilled once again. Men used to running the world don't take kindly to being ordered about.

"I said," said Hearst. "Take a seat."

Ford and Rockerfeller shared a long silent glance, a mutual understanding that it was better to indulge Hearst than to cross him. Shaking his head, Ford sat down heavily. Baumgartner followed suit.

"What exactly are you suggesting, Hearst?" said Insull.

"Not suggesting, Mr. Power," said Hearst. "Simply stating a fact. It's all very clear, really. The beauty of the Circle is in its simplicity. Circle members do one thing: they hunt. People have lost their raison d'etre, don't you agree? The thing that drives us all to feel the true essence of life. Something we have lost simply by having everything we want. Members of the Circle are offered the chance to replenish that excitement in their lives and rejoice in the knowledge that they have lived to see another day. They will be grateful for the opportunity, rather than expect each day to follow another with the same bland palette of the day before."

"Let's just say we were interested," Ford replied eventually. "About whom, precisely, are you suggesting we hunt?"

Hearst looked at Ford, then around the room. "Why, I should think that would be obvious by now. Each other, of course."

Instantly the room exploded in collective outrage. The men were at the door in seconds.

Hearst let them reach the locked door, benevolently gifting them with time to assimilate the situation.

It was Mr. Baumgartner who spoke first, his face pale, cheeks blotchy. "You can't be serious, Hearst. Open this door. I insist upon leaving this instant."

Hearst held open his hands. "That might not be your best option, Mr. Vino. Seeing as of the moment you leave this room you will be both the hunter *and* the prey."

Baumgartner fell back into his chair with a thud. "But..." he sputtered, "you can't possibly...."

"I can," said Hearst. "And I have."

Baumgartner re-lit his cigar with shaking hands.

"Wouldn't you all like to know that your lives mean more than work? Wouldn't you like to experience the thrill of the hunt and the glory of the kill? And not some poor unsuspecting animal, but a man. A man who can challenge you, who can fight back."

From the back corner, still in his seat, Wertheimer spoke up. "I'm in," he said.

"You're what?" said Andrew Mellon. "You're actually agreeing to this...this...lunacy?"

Wertheimer sneered. "Take a look at your life Mr. Treasure. Can you honestly tell me you are fulfilled by the average trappings of life? Your family? Your job? This is a chance to have purpose again." He turned to Hearst. "I supposed you've thought this through? Ground rules need to be established."

Hearst nodded, pleased. "Of course, Mr. Scent. I have been working on that myself, but go ahead, I'm listening."

"First of all, there would need to be more than nine of us, or this endeavor won't change the world, it will just kill us off one by one."

"Agreed," Hearst conceded. "We'll need to recruit additional members. Like-minded individuals, so to speak."

"That wouldn't work," Samuel Insull insisted. "We need members that *aren't* like us. Common men. But why would any common man choose to risk his life to be a part of such an organization?"

"Why, wealth, of course, Mr. Power," said Hearst. "Access to limitless wealth in exchange for their willingness to enter into our little game of life and death."

The men that had remained standing gradually returned to their seats at this suggestion. A conversation ensued, a long conversation. Each member ultimately succumbing to their new monikers over the hours they spent discussing, formulating, and deliberating.

This is how the Circle's bylaws were established. How the Circle's safe houses and furloughs were instituted. It wasn't until just before daybreak that they reached an accord. Hearst stood and raised his glass, "To the Circle!" he announced.

"The Circle!" the men replied.

"To Hearst!" Wertheimer added. "To Mr. News!"

"To Mr. News!"

The sun rose on a new day. The dawning of the Circle had come.

PART I

January, 1959—Mason City, Iowa

Roger Peterson held a cigarette in his hand, hoping no one else realized it was just for show. He stood awkwardly in the middle of the room surrounded by men playing either shuffle-board, on a table that had to have cost more than a year of his salary, or poker. Others were arguing about the placement of the television antenna to catch the best reception on the baseball game. He felt invisible, and yet somehow knew he stood out like the sore thumb he was.

Not that he didn't know exactly what was doing. Well, as much as he could. Still, he wished he hadn't eaten so much at dinner. The heaping plate of lasagna sat like a lump of putty in the pit of his stomach. Like his wedding day and his first day of flight school combined. But back then he hadn't taken a young wife with dreams bigger than the state of Iowa into account.

Piloting was the dream, but so was making the dough that came along with it. PanAm, TWA...those guys traveled the world and got paid a pretty penny to do it. Dwyer Flying Service, on the other hand, was much, much further down on the scale. He was tired of inching along, hoping for a big break as the bills piled up because there wasn't enough work for all the pilots competing for them. Tiffany offered to work at the stables not far from where they were living, but he'd stomped out that idea fast. No wife of his was going to work to put food on their table. That was *his* job. It was up to the man to provide for his family. And if his mother ever got wind Tiffany was working? Yeah, he'd never hear the end of it. How he was a loser just like his father. And he'd rather be found dead than let his stepfather step in with his—

"Mr. Peterson."

Roger had been so lost in his thoughts his forgotten cigarette had just about burned his fingertips when he heard his name. Grinding it out in a nearby ashtray, he searched out the source of the voice, a tall, older man in a fancy suit who looked like once upon a time he could lift a tractor with one hand. Dressed to kill. Figures Roger's clothes said only that he was dressed to do exactly what he was doing: standing there looking foolish.

The older man gestured to Roger to join him at his round table in the far corner. As Roger moved to oblige his host, he felt the weight of the room descend upon his broad shoulders. His normally calm hands felt clammy. His collar suddenly felt tighter. The same people who moments ago were perfectly content to see through him were now sending daggers his way. That's when Roger realized he was surrounded on three sides by men who were herding him like border collies to the chair opposite the giant of a man in the la-de-da suit.

"Welcome to the Circle, Mr. Peterson," he said. "I'm who you will come to know as Mr. Black." The voice was cultivated, unaccented. No twang or any other tell. Roger reached for the man's extended baseball mitt of a hand and was enveloped in a firm handshake.

"N—nice to meet you, sir," Roger managed through the lump in his throat.

"I understand you already know a bit about our organization."

"Yes, sir."

"No need for formalities here young man. Mr. Black is fine."

Roger nodded.

"Which leads me to my second question. The first being how you heard of us, of course, but revealing that may have ramifications, eh, boys?"

The men chuckled. Roger didn't get the joke.

"So, second question, Mr. Peterson. *Why* did you seek us out? We aren't your typical club. Not that membership doesn't have its obvious perks...."

Mr. Black's implication did not go unappreciated, but Roger was too far in to quit now. He cleared his throat. "The...the bank's about to foreclose on the property. Bills are piling up. I can't afford life insurance and, well, my wife...she deserves a better life. I heard that the Circle can help me give that to her."

Mr. Black was tapping his fingers on the table, making Roger twitch. Was he waiting for more? "Plus," he added, "I don't think being poor counts me out of wanting to live my life to the fullest. Like each day was my last. Do you?"

It was quiet for a moment. Shoot. Too much? Without a rule book, Roger was flailing aimlessly.

"Young man," said Mr. Black finally, "There is something you should know. Very—very—few people in your position find their way through our doors. You may think you know what goes on here, Mr. Peterson, but let me explain this to you in plain English so there is absolutely no misunderstanding. You are *already* one of us. By virtue of the fact that you have accessed the privilege to walk through these doors. You are *already* a member of the Circle. *There is no turning back.*"

This pronouncement came as no surprise. Still, Roger felt the room spinning at the ferocity of the speech.

Mr. Black went on. "Until your dying day, Mr. Peterson, you will be hunted. That day could be tomorrow, and it might well be at the hands of any one of the men behind you. Or it could be many years from now—unless or until you survive to the age of 60. One way or another, the wife for whom you joined in order to provide the life you want her to have, will only be able to share a fraction of it with you. Are we perfectly clear, Mr. Peterson? You...belong...to...us."

Roger nodded, not trusting himself to speak.

"However, as you stated so aptly, we also belong to you. The collective fortunes of every member, dating back to the Original Nine, are at your disposal. So, by all means, do take care of your wife and family. They will no doubt be requiring such assistance in the future."

Roger took another hard swallow. He'd prepared questions, and now had to search the recesses of his mind to locate them. "So, um," he said lamely, "I assume there are rules."

Mr. Black's mouth tightened a bit. "Why, yes, Mr. Peterson. And they are quite simple. As a member of the Circle you will be required to hunt another member to his death. Let me state that again. *To. His. Death.* And, just as you are hunting him, a member of this chapter will be assigned to hunt you, and your hunter, and so on. And so goes the circle of our existence. If you manage to kill your target, your reward is a 30-day hiatus. You might think of it like a vacation from eligibility. For 30 days you are free to do as you please. If you manage to strike first and defeat your hunter, 48 hours of additional free time is yours as well."

Of course Roger already knew the rules, and knew Mr. Black knew he did, but hearing them under these circumstances made them so much more real. Like a prison sentence without the possibility of parole. "If your hunter or your target is terminated—by someone other than you, that is—you will be notified by way of an official Circle envelope." Mr. Black held a blue envelope up for Roger to see. "All Circle business is conducted in this manner, and there's no need to worry. We will always find you."

Mr. Black set the envelope down and looked Roger in the eye. "Remember, Mr. Peterson, there is no escape from the Circle. There is no turning back. If you do happen to have a change of heart and attempt to leave, try to run…you will be simply relocated to another one of the Circle's chapters in one of the 50-plus countries in which we currently operate."

Comradery, nostalgia, the thrill of new prey to hunt... fear? Whatever it was, Roger was officially in. For life.

Then, as if echoing his thoughts, Mr. Black said, "This is your life now, Mr. Peterson. Welcome to the Circle."

2

May, 1959—Stapleton Academy, Maine

Her face was obscured, but he could tell she was smiling. Through the clear water he could see her sitting on the edge of the dock, her legs dangling over the side, her toes delicately touching the water. She looked happy, so he was happy. He began to propel himself to the surface. *Uh-oh.* His leg had become tangled up in some form of lake vegetation. Mild panic passed through him, but he was a strong swimmer, and reached to remove the entanglement.

There was nothing there.

Shock and horror overtook him. He flailed his arms hoping she would see him, or the disturbance beneath her. But she never looked. His panicked scream released bubbles into the water that took only moments to reach the surface. A surface that was quickly retreating. He wasn't stuck. He was being pulled. Farther and farther down into the depths. His vision of the surface, of her, faded from view. Instinct told him to keep fighting. He struggled harder, kicking his feet, swimming with all the strength he possessed. Yet down he went. There was no avoiding it. He was going to die.

The voice confirmed it. *Let go,* it whispered. *Just let go.*

• • •

Warren Nichols woke with a jolt. Angry. Breathing heavily. Drenched in sweat. Bed sheet tangled around his leg. Another dream. Another visit from Peter. The same message as always. *Let go.*

"Damn it!" Warren spoke into the darkness. In all his years with Peter, Warren had lost track of all the times Peter had whispered the same thing. *Let go.* But Warren knew better than to ever truly let that happen.

Warren first met Peter when he was six. He remembered the exact date. September 17th, his parents' anniversary. He'd marched over to his parents, the proud bearer of a drawing he'd done. The stick family portrait was their anniversary gift, and he'd worked hard on it all morning. When his mother waved him away to continue her phone conversation in that sparkling laughter he trotted over to his father, who simply reprimanded him for crumpling the newspaper he was reading.

Dejected, he'd moped back to his spacious bedroom and tossed the drawing into the wastepaper basket. *Who cares what they think?* said a voice. *I like it.* Warren looked around. His au pair was nowhere to be seen, and the housekeeper was still in the kitchen. And the voice was young, like his. A classmate calling from outside? Not that Warren had many friends who came calling. Or, really, any friends at all.

The voice spoke up again. *I'll be your friend,* it said.

A friend? Someone to talk to? "Sure," said Warren, excited. "But where are you?"

I'm right here, said the voice. *I'm always with you, even though you can't see me.*

"Why not?"

Why not what?

"Why can't I see you?"

Well, duh. Hellloooo...I'm in your head.

Warren thought about it. Made sense, he supposed. "Well, then, what's your name?"

I...I don't know, said the voice. *I don't think I have one.*

"Then what should I call you?"

Whatever you want, I guess. I mean, since I'm in your *head and all.*

Good point. Warren looked around the room for inspiration, realizing he'd never had the chance to name anything before. He'd never even had an actual pet. His eyes landed on his New York Yankees baseball cap. A souvenir from one of his parents' many trips back east. Not that they went to baseball games. It had come from some store at the airport. He had all sorts of things from airport stores, a last brief, passing thought before his parents boarded their next plane for their next destination or were returning from it. Warren wished he could have gone with them to New York. Maybe they would have taken him to Yankee Stadium where they'd eat peanuts and Cracker Jack. Warren knew all about Yogi Berra, even had his baseball card. A few of them, in fact. He had no one to trade cards with, but he still collected them. Warren wanted a name like that. Special, different. He picked up a card from the box where his decks were stored and turned it over. Lawrence Peter Berra. "Peter," he said. "I'll call you Peter."

Not a bad choice, said the voice. *I'll take it.*

"I'm Warren," Warren said, unnecessarily, but politely, as he'd been taught. Warren took his crumpled drawing from the trash and flattened out the folds. "Do you really like it?"

Sure, Peter said. *Can you make one of the two of us?*

"I don't know what you look like."

What do you think I should look like?

Warren tore off another sheet from his sketch pad and dragged his green crayon across the paper carefully, starting with a stick figure of himself. Then, with his red crayon, he made another figure, this one a tiny bit taller. The two figures were holding hands and looked virtually identical aside from their color and the minor height differential.

Am I the red one? asked Peter. *Why am I taller?*

"I'm not sure," said Warren. "But I think you should be."

Peter shrugged—or Warren imagined he did. *Fine with me,* he said.

"Can we be best friends?" asked Warren hesitantly.

We already are, said Peter.

• • •

Warren had never needed his parents' approval again. With Peter's arrival came the constant support he needed, and was better than any board game or tennis racquet.

Then Peter had changed.

Finally calming after his dream, Warren tried to get comfortable again on the top bunk of the same metal-framed contraption they called a bed that he'd slept on for the past year and a half, but it was impossible. Outside, the night was calm, with only occasional gusts whistling through the tiny opening in the boarding school window. In the dim light Warren studied the place where he lived. He had no photos or posters. Two identical desks on opposite walls each contained various papers, pencils, and school paraphernalia. Other than the occasional squeak from the bunk below when his bunkmate, Patrick, turned in his sleep, it was dead quiet.

Warren was tall for his age, already about six feet, attractive even with the fading adolescent acne and patchy scruff on his chin to remind you he hadn't yet reached the age of consent. It wasn't his imperfections or his height that didn't sit right with people, though. It wasn't anything they could pinpoint. Yet Warren knew he scared them.

It was his temper that had landed him at Stapleton. Well, Peter's temper, really. Forcing him into one too many brushes with the law. Association with the "wrong crowd," according to his parents, conveniently attributing his fits of rage to some kind of birth defect rather than attempt a brush with introspection. As long as Warren was not around to do any damage on their turf—well, out of sight, out of mind, right?

What would they say—what would all those shrinks say—if Warren told them it was all Peter's doing? It would only land him somewhere worse than Stapleton, that's for sure.

At least there were no bars on the windows or doors locking them in. But only because that would be admitting Stapleton for what it was: a jail for miscreants set in the wilds of a frigid nowhere. The fact that Warren and Patrick's room was not the most welcoming of environments was irrelevant. Each one of them, every single student at Stapleton, was from a wealthy family ill-prepared to deal with its "wayward offspring."

The Nichols felt nothing but relief at leaving the parenting to someone else. Warren was an inconvenience to their work and social lives, one that took too much time, too much energy, and far too much attention. Early days, he was more of an accessory, paraded around and shown off by his mother, dressed in finery for ogling. When cute and silent morphed into youthful impertinence, the hired help was engaged to "deal with him." Long before Warren was a teenager, his parents were done. By that time, he barely noticed. He had Peter.

Master puppeteer Peter encouraged Warren to skip classes, then skip school altogether. Warren considered saying no sometimes, feeling slightly uneasy doing those things, but when your oldest friend, someone who's smarter than you are, funnier than you are, and always has the best ideas, wants to go have some fun, you listen. Eventually, the school had also had enough of Warren. The staff was used to rich kids with big attitudes, but this particular smart-ass, a "borderline sociopath," as described by the teachers, was too much. Even if his parents had funded the new science lab and library.

The Nichols travelled. A lot. They learned of Warren's expulsion while on Safari in Africa, and resented the intrusion. Although even they had to admit, if only to one another, that ditching classes was the least of it, because it seemed their dear son had first attacked several classmates, and then his math teacher, in a bloody encounter in front of multiple witnesses.

Stapleton Academy in upstate Maine was the last stop before military school, which was too highly visible for the Nichols' social network. Not only was Stapleton clear across the country, but an institution well known in such circles for its "inclusivity." In other words, easily bribed.

Tonight, Warren's attempts to fall back asleep were abruptly interrupted by a dense thud on the door. Warren looked at the wall-mounted clock. 3:41. No one came knocking in the middle of the night unless there was an emergency. So far, there had never been one.

Mr. Pembroke, the headmaster, stepped inside.

"Mr. Nichols," he said, "I need you to come with me."

• • •

Warren held the black receiver in his hands suspiciously. That jerk Pembroke had refused to impart any information on the way to his office and Warren was pissed at being taken from his bed in the middle of the night, even if he hadn't been sleeping. He took the rare moment in Pembroke's quarters to gather some embarrassing details to share with his.... He didn't know what to call them. No one had friends at Stapleton.

"Yeah?" he said into the phone.

"Warren Nichols?"

"Yeah."

"Warren Nichols, son of Victor and Helen Nichols?"

"*Yeah.* What do you want? It's 4:00 in the morning."

"Mr. Nichols, my name is Orville McCoy, I'm your fa—"

"Dad's lawyer," Warren interrupted. "I know. So what? What'd they do now, enlist me in the army?"

Peter laughed. They shared the same sense of humor.

"No, Mr. Nichols, they did not enlist you in the Army. You can't legally—"

"Whatever," said Warren. "Just get on with it."

McCoy went quiet for a moment, then said, "Mr. Nichols, I don't know any other way to tell you this, but your parents were in a car accident tonight. Um...I'm afraid neither of them made it."

Warren's eyes widened ever so slightly. "Made it?" he repeated. "What are you saying?"

"I'm saying....I'm sorry....but they were both killed. The road conditions...they shouldn't have been where they were apparently.... But you know your parents. Ever the risk takers...."

Warren wasn't listening. His parents were dead. *Dead.*

McCoy blabbed on. "They were on their way back from Napa Valley. In the '56 Stingray. The red one your father covets—um, coveted—so much. You know the one."

"Who the hell cares what they were driving," Warren snapped. Although he hadn't known his father owned a '56 'vette, let alone coveted it.

The lawyer waited a beat. "Right," he said. "Sorry. It seems the car careened off the road and down an embankment. No one found them for several hours...and by then it was too late."

Warren's eyes stung, but he said nothing, aware that Pembroke was hovering in the room like a circling vulture.

"Mr. Nichols," said McCoy. "Are you alright?"

"I'm fine."

"I've sent a car to pick you up, Mr. Nichols. It'll take you to the Portland airport. I've already informed your headmaster."

Silence.

"Did you hear me, Mr. Nichols? I said—"

"Yeah, I heard you," said Warren.

Another silence.

"Well, then, I suppose I'll see you when you get home," said McCoy. "And again, I'm so sorry for your loss."

Warren hung up the phone.

"My condolences, Mr. Nichols," Pembroke offered.

Warren looked at him. "Can I go back to my room now?"

Pembroke's eyes widened, but opened the door and stepped aside.

Good riddance, Peter said as they left.

Warren had to agree. On both counts.

• • •

Unlike the rest of the world where trees budded and birds sang, springtime in Maine was still under cover of snow and mud. All the fresh air made Warren want to vomit. Once airborne, after the three-hour ride to Portland, he tried to remember the last time the family had been together, but he'd hardly seen his parents in years, choosing to spend his holidays at school where he could roam as he pleased with only a skeleton staff stayed to supervise, more interested in partying themselves than overseeing the "leftovers." This damn double funeral would put him front and center to withstand the scrutiny of his entire extended family, small as it was, plus the collection of his parents' "close friends," business associates, and hangers-on. A long flight on a private jet would be luxurious, however, especially after his long stint at Stapleton.

Aboard the plane, Warren tilted back his seat as far as it would go. Might as well enjoy the ride.

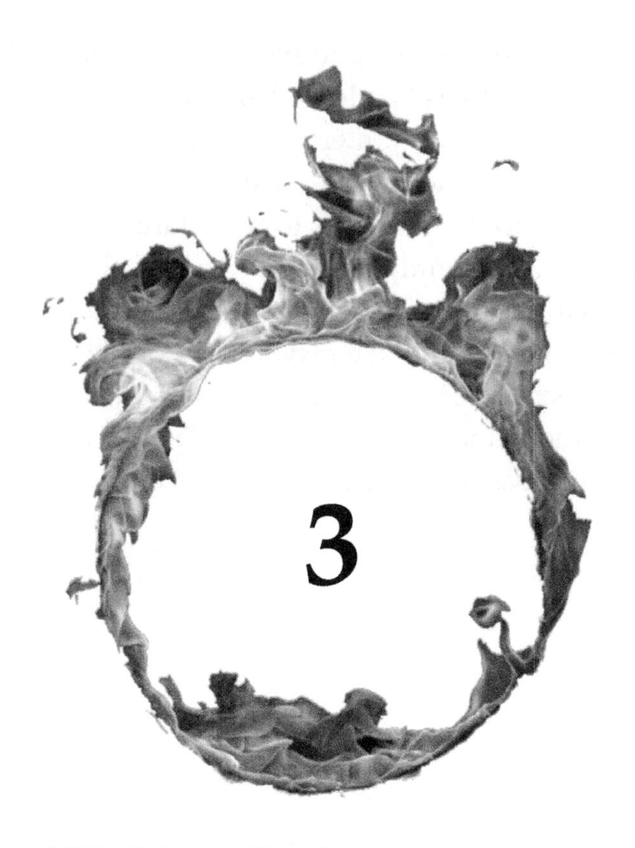

3

January, 1959—Mason City, Iowa

Apparently, Mr. Spade had killed his first target with—what else?—a spade shovel. For two weeks he'd been making Roger with his intrusive staring. Well, his picture had, anyway. Roger's first target. A man he had now seen at the safehouse on numerous occasions. The guy who drank bourbon when they played cards and swirled it around in the glass when he was bluffing. Spade's dossier stated he was worth close to 200 mil. After surviving the Korean War, he'd bought out some company in Des Moines and a year or so later another company that made engine parts for some government program that was supposed to put an American into space. After the launch of Sputnik, the Space Race had seen the net worth of Mr. Spade's company increase tenfold. America was space-obsessed, and Mr. Spade had been reaping the financial benefits since.

Apparently, there was no Mrs. Spade, no little baby Spades running around. Not even brother or sister Spades or parental Spades. Perfect Circle fodder.

Roger placed the photo back into its blue envelope, tucked the packet back in its hiding place behind the loosened wall tile between the toilet and the bathtub, and picked up his razor. To this point, his wife hadn't found his secret compartment. If she had, there was no way she'd be keeping quiet about it. He'd offered to take on bathroom cleaning as his chore of the week to ensure the tile stayed put. Tiffany was no slouch. She didn't know why he made the offer, but wasn't about to look a gift horse in the mouth.

"Are you still in there?" she was asking now. She could be right outside the door or in the farthest room, the kitchen, and it would sound no different. The house was that small. It galled him that he had access to all the money in the world, but no way to explain how he got his hands on a deed to a sparkling new palace of a house without raising suspicion. What good was it if he couldn't spend it?

"Out in a sec, hon," he called back. He quickly washed off his razor, dried his face, checked the envelope was fully hidden and the tile in place. Tiffany wasn't the nosy type, nor the best housekeeper, but still..... He opened the door. "It's all yours."

"Having more of those deep thoughts, huh?" she said.

"Only about you, sweetheart, only about you."

Tiffany smiled. "Right answer," she said.

It wasn't a total lie. All Circle-related thoughts involved her, didn't they? That's why he'd gotten involved in the first place. After flying that client a few months ago, the one who'd chartered Roger's plane to fly him away from what had turned out to be something other than the campsite Roger had been led to believe it was.

His first clue was the blood on the guy's pant leg. When Roger offered first aid, the guy asked for whiskey to go with it. The lie—that he'd caught his shin on a piece of metal—was obvious. Didn't matter to Roger either way. Clients don't pay their pilots to ask questions.

After the right amount of booze, the guy's lips were so loose Roger couldn't have kept him from spilling the beans even if he'd wanted to. Turns out the "campsite" was really a kill site. And the "hunting" the client had done was of the human variety. Endless money to burn. Did Roger want in on the action?

Naturally, he didn't believe a word out of the guy's mouth at first. But he'd had plenty of time to think about it once the guy slipped into Never Never Land. To think about what would happen when he got home that day and Tiffany would be washing their clothes by hand because their washing machine had broken down for the third time that month. It got him wondering. What if the guy wasn't talking out his ass? What if he really *was* part of something like...like that?

Tiffany grabbed him by the half-Windsor knot and kissed him. "Don't you forget those thoughts when you come home tonight," she said.

Tonight? Shit, tonight.

"I won't be home tonight, remember?" he said, as if they had already discussed it. "I have that flight out to South Dakota. It'll be too late for the return trip until the morning."

Tiffany let go of him. "Oh."

"Come on, honey. Don't be like that. It counts as overtime, and you know we need the money." *Oh, and by the way, I may have to kill someone.*

Late night and overnight "flights" allowed him to spend a lot of extra time in the safehouse, studying his target, staying—well, safe. His job with Dwyer Flying Service had become superfluous, but he hadn't been able to bring himself to touch the Circle money yet. He was planning to surprise Tiffany with a new washer and dryer that he'd claim was an Employee of the Month prize, as if there was such a thing. Although the Dwyers had been good to him, taking him on as a young kid and giving him a start. He'd tell them he was leaving when the time was right. In the meantime, being in the air was a hard freedom to give up.

"I don't remember your telling me about that," Tiffany pressed. She was obviously confused. With good reason. He hated that he obviously had a hidden talent for lying to the one person he'd sworn never to deceive.

"Must have been that night we splurged on that bottle of wine."

"Well, my mind *was* on other things that night, Mr. Peterson," she said with a sigh.

They'd been trying to conceive for close to seven months. By their friends' standards, way behind schedule. He was 21, she was 23, so what was taking them so long? They should be as fertile as, well, two healthy young people should be. "As good an excuse I can think of, Mrs. Peterson," he said. "Besides, it's only one night, I'll be back by 3:00 tomorrow. And you've got Kasey to keep you company." Kasey was their beagle, originally a hunting companion for Roger until he'd started his job at Dwyer. There was no time for hunting anymore; not for pheasant, anyway. Kasey had become a lap dog, but Roger still felt confident her powerful howl could scare off pretty much anything. Kasey looked up from her bed on the floor at the sound of her name. When she saw no food on offer, she went back to her nap.

"Well, looks like it's just the two of us again, huh, Kasey?" said Tiffany to the sleeping dog, who let out a snore.

They both laughed. "I'll be back tomorrow," Roger said. With a quick kiss to Tiffany's forehead, he grabbed his overnight bag, slung it over his shoulder, and headed out the door.

"Love you!" Tiffany shouted at her departing husband.

"Love you, too."

"Fly safe!"

"Always do," he said, hoping she wouldn't hear the wistfulness in his voice.

4

May, 1959—Atherton, California

Orville McCoy, as expected, was waiting in the family's 1949 Bentley when Warren deplaned. McCoy had been with the family since long before Warren was born, and just looking at him made Warren feel like crap.

As the car wound its way through the countryside, Warren considered his options. He could play the model son—he was a good enough actor when he made the effort—and pay homage to parents who had never once expressed an iota of love for him....

Or not, said Peter.

Warren slid a glance at McCoy, who was a lot thinner than Warren remembered. He must have shed at least 50 pounds since their last encounter, probably 10 years ago. His slicked-back hair was thinning, styled in a pathetic comb-over, and much more salt than pepper. The lawyer was old as dirt, and the stress of having clients like his parents had likely taken its toll. Warren might have felt sorry for him if not for the healthy retainer he'd received for the better part of a couple of decades that paid for his manicures, Italian shoes, and lavish lifestyle.

McCoy had allowed Warren "time to grieve" during the car ride, but Warren knew it was a temporary reprieve. Then he would be face-to-face and forced to confront the reality of his parents' death.

Sure enough, McCoy turned to him when they were nearing his parents' estate. "I'm sorry to have to do this now, Mr. Nichols," he said, "but time is of the essence" Warren shrugged; there was no reason to pretend he and McCoy had any kind of relationship, although being called "Mr. Nichols" was slightly weird "and we have some paperwork to go through." He gestured to a large file folder at their feet.

Warren had no inclination to indulge McCoy's need for speed, but it looked as if he might not have the choice. All he wanted was to be done. Done with McCoy, done with everything. At least for the day. He shrugged.

"Shall we go inside?" McCoy said, his hand on the door handle.

Stay in the car, Peter said, *make him work for it.*

"I'd rather stay here," said Warren.

McCoy got red in the face. He wasn't used to being spoken to this way. Finally, though, he nodded and proceeded to make Warren the sole heir of his parents' considerable fortune.

Some members of the family would be surprised, given Warren's exploits, but McCoy was not. Warren wasn't either. They were his parents. Parents left money to their children, even wayward ones, didn't they? Did he feel lucky? He supposed he did. Before his and Peter's mishaps at school he'd been told he was being groomed to take control of the family business, but there hadn't been any mention of that for years. Not that he'd ever shown the slightest interest in learning any other trade. Disinterest was the only avenue he'd cultivated.

"Mr. Nichols?" McCoy was saying. "You do understand the implications of what I just told you, yes? You are the *sole heir* to your parents' fortune. All they owned—their assets, their homes, and the company. You and I have a lot to discuss. There are plans to be made. People are already wanting to know what you'll do. There are shareholders to consider, and almost 5,500 employees wondering how long they will have their jobs."

Warren nodded. *Nod and smile, tactic of the rich.* Say nothing, reveal nothing. Keep 'em guessing. He was thinking about how the last time he'd seen his parents was two years ago, a quick lunch on their way back from another extravagant European getaway. Barely long enough to buy him a meal at a local restaurant, bemoaning the establishment's lack of sophistication and class. They'd hardly said a word to Warren, which was fine by him. He had nothing to say to them, anyway. After their brief stopover to refuel the jet, which he suspected was the real reason for their unannounced social call, they'd gone on their way. For Warren, it was as if the visit had never happened.

When McCoy finally stopped yapping, Warren got out of the car and stretched. He looked up at the tall columns by the front door. Made from the finest Italian marble, they reached 20 feet up to the second floor. When he was small, Warren played outside to stay close to his mother, who loved lilies. His mother had planted the beds all along the walk "all by herself." At least, that's what she told people. In truth, she pointed and directed and prodded while the landscapers toiled. Warren's antics got in the way of progress, however, and soon he was relegated "somewhere else" to play. Over time, as Warren watched her care for the lilies, his fantasies of demolishing them grew.

Man, these have got to go. Peter said.

Warren walked up the steps, leaving McCoy, who was still in the car stuffing papers back into his briefcase, and methodically began ripping lilies from their stems, yanking their roots from the ground.

The staff of Nichols House watched with wide eyes. When the butler went to intervene, McCoy stood by the car and held up his hand to stop him. The kid was clearly distraught. Or at least he hoped that's all it was.

Finally satisfied, Warren shook off the dirt and wiped his hands on his khakis.

The housekeeper stepped out. "I'll just clean this up," she said. Miss Stacy had been with his family for over a decade and had practically raised Warren in lieu of his parents and after the au pair had been dismissed for dallying with Warren's father. At the time Warren hadn't understood what that meant. Now he did.

Miss Stacy had risked her employment when she'd voiced her disagreement with his parents' decision to ship Warren off. The boy she knew was nothing like the hooligan he'd become at school. Time away from his family was the last thing he needed. Her disagreement would have gotten her fired if she hadn't been so competent and the Nichols so disinterested in making any staff changes.

She was significantly underpaid, but the Nichols' were hardly there, so in exchange they'd offered her room and board for herself and her daughter, Vivian. The job was a means to an end for Stacy, and if it meant scrubbing floors in return for the luxury of sending Vivian to the local schools, so be it. Being the biracial daughter of a black father and white mother was not easy, and Vivian's father had died in the Korean War when she was just a toddler. That meant many days of loneliness for Stacy Chambers, but none of regret. She'd done what she needed to do for her baby girl. Living at the Nichols estate was one of those things.

"Let them be, Miss Stacy," Warren said, going up the stairs. "I prefer them right where they are." Miss Stacy said nothing. She'd never admit it, but Warren knew she'd despaired of his mother Helen's lack of interest, and hence her flower beds, almost as much as he did. The move was symbolic for both of them.

"Warren!"

He'd recognize that voice anywhere. The one that could take his rage, his anger, and his arrogance and strip it away with nothing more than a word. The only one that could ever keep Peter from showing up when he was uninvited. *Vivian.*

Vivian was running down the staircase to greet him, her soft tawny skin framed by jet black hair, shorter than he remembered, tight curls bouncing and gleaming, brown eyes, penetrating and knowing.

"I'm so sorry," she said as she reached him.

Who knew what love really was? Warren sure didn't. But if it wasn't what he felt for Vivian then he didn't want to know. She was his best friend and confidant, the person who knew more about him than anyone in the world. She was the one who could break him down and build him back up with nothing more than a look. Leaving his parents had been painless. Ripped from Vivian? Devastating. It was Vivan's letters to him, which he'd read and re-read and secured behind a drawer in his desk at Stapleton, that had kept the voice inside. Had kept the voice of Peter at bay.

5

January, 1959—Mason City, Iowa

Mr. Spade wasn't as naive and oblivious as his potential killer believed. He'd known he was Mr. Peterson's target since they had first sat down at the card table a few days after his initiation. Compliment or insult, he wasn't sure. Was this the Circle's way of implying this new recruit would easily get the best of him, or did they think Spade should be the one to take out the neophyte quickly since he'd brought so little to the organization?

There was no time for these questions now—or ever, really. The Circle had its reasons, or it didn't. It was all just a crapshoot. How to avoid becoming the victim of this new recruit was what mattered. No one wants to get offed by a beginner, even if you weren't there afterward to deal with the flack. It's like losing your spot in the lineup to some rookie. Wally Pipp, anyone? If you weren't already dead you'd die from mortification. At the pun, Mr. Spade chuckled inwardly. Word games helped pass the time.

Spade sat, sipped his bourbon, and pondered all the information he had about his presumed hunter. As prey, he wasn't provided with a dossier for Peterson as he had been for his previous targets. Like Mr. Goode, also a new recruit, who had joined the Circle at the advanced age of 52, only eight years until potential "retirement." Maybe he'd been trying to game the system. A decent enough guy, a great storyteller, always regaling the group with tales of his adventures in the African jungles or the Amazon rainforest, famous and infamous acquaintances.

After each kill, Mr. Goode played homage to "his good friend" Chuck Berry by playing "Johnny B. Goode" in his vanquished foe's home. He often carried the 45 around with him for just such occasions, and had insisted on having the song added to the jukebox in the safehouse so he could celebrate his successes after the fact. A little over seven weeks ago, after Mr. Goode's demise, Mr. Spade had had that song ceremoniously removed to a few chuckles, a few requests for details, and a few polite murmurs. Circle members tended toward the circumspect, if nothing else.

Spade chose to keep his kill details close, however, almost like personal keepsakes to relish. For him and him alone. Although he didn't mind sharing the fact that he had gotten the drop on Mr. Goode while attending a fundraiser for Hubert Humphries Presidential campaign in Wisconsin. How he'd ambushed him in his car and choked him to death with Goode's own seatbelt. He'd had a good laugh over the fact that seatbelts were an option that cost extra and how without them he may have gone on to live another day.

But Mr. Goode was sloppy. Mr. Goode had become arrogant. Mr. Goode's easily exploited public rituals had taken him down.

Mr. Peterson, though, was an interesting case. The man appeared to have no interests or rituals, public or otherwise. No previous kills from which Spade could derive information. There was nothing that indicated Peterson hunted with a stomach for the up-close-and-personal, as Spade did. He'd pegged Peterson as a sniper, not a get-your-hands-dirty kind of guy. He hoped that assessment was correct.

As Spade took another slow sip of his bourbon, wouldn't you know it, the object of his musings walked through the door. Time to make sure his oblivious act was in place. He rose from his comfortable chair languidly and moved to a barstool to greet the man who was plotting to kill him with a warm smile.

"Mr. Peterson, so good to see you, young man." Calling him "young" was not an exaggeration. Peterson was by far the youngest member in this chapter. Another notch in the "he doesn't belong here" category.

"Have a seat, my boy. Drink?" Spade raised his glass to the bartender and pointed to Peterson. Drinks would be in front of them before both men were seated.

"Sure. I could use one," Peterson said, eyebrows drawing together at the offer.

"Tough day with the missus?" Spade asked. Wedding rings weren't as much a faux-pas as stupid, revealing a very important detail about a person. Unmarried men were far more unpredictable. Married men always had somewhere to be, didn't they?

Spade had a child himself, one he cared about very much, and never ever spoke of. From a local woman on one of his jaunts to Europe many years earlier. He and Yvonne had spent his entire furlough together in Paris before he'd been forced to return to the States. While Spade was back in America killing his friends, she'd given birth to a son she named Gérard. He hadn't even known about the boy until about two years later when he returned to France on another furlough. He'd searched for Yvonne until he'd found her. Her and the boy. And had not been prepared for the feelings that had arisen. The little boy looked just like him. Gérard was curious, playful, and exuberant, and Spade had missed almost two years of the child's life. Spade had spent every subsequent furlough with Yvonne and Gérard since then, aware that their existence must be kept 100% hidden. No phone calls, no letters, no pictures. Nothing that could put them in danger as a result of his...circumstances. Yvonne didn't like it, didn't understand it, but she put up with it. They were always on his mind.

"Nah," Peterson was saying, "I just don't like lying to her about where I go."

The kid was young *and* dumb, sharing information like that, information he should keep to himself.

"Well, it's not like you can tell her where you are."

"Trust me, you don't have to remind me about that."

"It is...interesting...how often you are here," said Spade. "A young man like yourself. With a beautiful wife and all. How do you manage to get away for so long?"

There was a shift in the air. Peterson clearly hadn't liked Spade's question and was stalling by attending to his pilsner. At least he knows not to share everything, thought Spade. Maybe he'd be more of a challenge than he'd thought.

"I was a pilot," said Peterson. "Still am, I guess. It's not unusual for me to be gone a few days at a time. Sooner or later I'll convince her that I hooked a job at a bigger airline, which'll mean more time away."

"Brilliant," Spade said without sarcasm. Convenient way for Peterson to keep his wife in the dark about his other life.

Peterson was still talking. "The money will convince her that I'm not lying," he said. "I can keep that up for years," he added unconvincingly. "At least, that's the plan."

"Cheers to your surviving that long," Spade said, making sure to add a smile. He offered his glass and the two clinked and sipped some more. "So, you can stay here for hours on end...study us, right?"

Peterson looked confused. Was he that lame not to have caught on yet?

"Well, if you were after *me*, I'd know about it," Spade said, planting the seed. "I have a sixth sense when it comes to that kind of thing. If there's one thing I learned in Korea, it's how to know when you're being watched."

Peterson's eyes were gazing directly into the mirror behind the bar. It was time for Spade to send his point home. "And it's obvious that you, young man, have been tasked with killing Mr. Slugger."

Peterson gagged on his beer. Spade obliged with a pat on the back and waited for the information to sink in. Mr. Slugger, the man who beat his first victim to death with a Louisville Slugger baseball bat, was no more Peterson's target than Mr. Black. But had Spade convinced Peterson that Spade wasn't onto him?

"Don't worry," said Spade in a whisper. "Your target's name is safe with me. Just glad I haven't lost my mojo."

Peterson looked ill. He coughed again, then nervously cracked his knuckles. "Remind me never to go after *you*."

And there it was. Peterson's tell. So obvious it was painful.

"No promises there, pal," Spade reminded him. "The odds aren't exactly in our favor, you know."

It's what made the game so exciting. The law of averages. Ultimately, at some point or another, if you survived long enough, every member would be assigned to every other member. That's what made new recruits like Peterson so valuable. Half the membership of the Circle was likely to die at any point. Given that reality, it was a miracle they had so many chapters. On the other hand, given human nature's lust for killing and devastation, maybe it wasn't.

Peterson was quiet.

"One day at a time, Mr. Peterson. Just live one day at a time," Spade said, giving him another quick pat on the back. "Best of luck with Mr. Slugger, too. And rest easy, I won't divulge what I know. Wouldn't be sporting, now, would it?"

Peterson only picked up his beer and took a long drink.

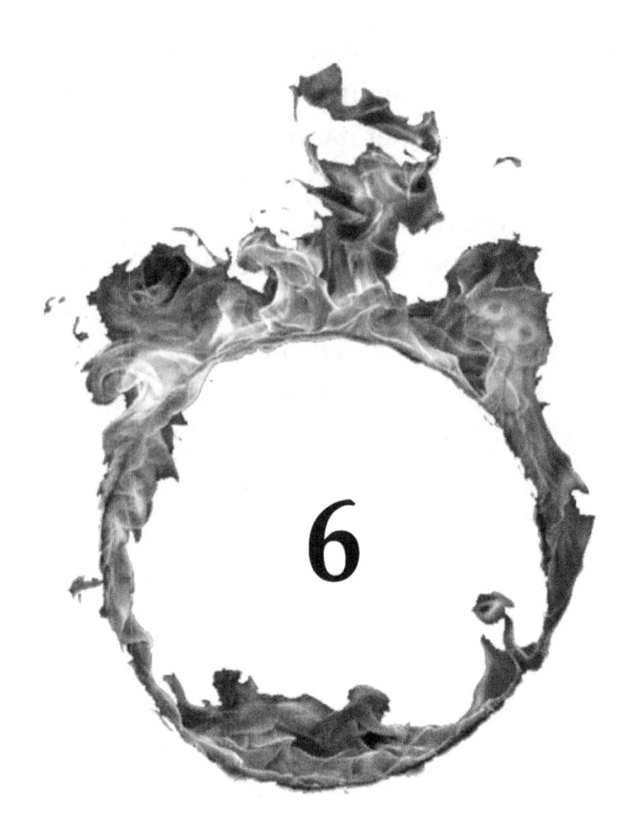

6

May, 1959—Atherton, California

The wake was finally over. Warren was drained from walking the fine line of the bereaved child and stoic patrician son for an entire week. The Nichols had money. Money brings other money out of the woodwork. Business associates, employees, friends, rivals. Warren tepidly greeted them all, keeping his face blank and his eyes red by rubbing at them every chance he got. The top-of-the-line caskets had been closed. No one had the audacity to ask why given the nature of their deaths. The truth? Warren didn't want to see them.

He went through the motions, receiving handshakes and the occasional uncomfortable embrace from people he barely knew, even indulging some stories about his parents. Everyone there seemed to know his parents better than he did. He accepted condolences from the rich and famous, too. Doris Day, John Wayne, Rock Hudson...even Steve McQueen had made the trip despite being in the middle of shooting *The Magnificent Seven*. His mourner's affect was tiresome, but Warren was enjoying his newfound notoriety. Who knew the Nichols had so much clout?

There was one man there who defied categorization, however. A Mr. Black. That was it. No first name in the guest book, no address or contact information. For some reason, Mr. Black seemed oddly more interested in Warren than in the funeral itself, too, which both interested and annoyed Warren.

The church service the following day was much easier. Fewer prying eyes. In all his years living at home, he couldn't remember a single time his parents had taken him to church or celebrated any Christian holidays other than Christmas. He hid his disdain at the charade behind dark sunglasses.

The priest meandered on for far too long in Warren's opinion, but he did learn a bit about his parents from the eulogies. He'd never known his mother worked in a factory making bullets during WWII. Why would she have kept that from him? And why hadn't he ever known that his father was rejected from the armed services despite attempting to enlist multiple times. All this time he'd thought his dad used some loophole or connection to avoid service. Most surprising, though, was hearing that when the board of Nichols Inc. had voted down the idea to donate to the war effort, his parents had donated 25% of their personal earnings. Why keep that a secret? And why did they have so much passion for things like that, and none for their only son?

Warren removed his sunglasses to wipe away his first actual tear and noticed Mr. Black had returned. He was in a pew off on the far side of the church, apparently alone, sitting respectfully, listening to the words the priest had to offer, but looking in Warren's direction. It caught Warren so completely off guard that he hurried to put his glasses back on and turned away.

The cemetery was a repeat performance, and Warren was weary of the relentless theatre. He positioned himself between the two burial plots and placed his obligatory rose on each casket just before they were lowered into the ground with a sigh of relief. Mr. Black was there again, among the mourners standing in the back.

I don't trust this guy, Peter said.

Warren agreed. He turned to Orville McCoy, who had stuck irritatingly to his side for most of the past few days' events, and whispered, "Who's that Mr. Black guy? How did he know my parents?"

"Your parents knew a lot of people," said McCoy with a shrug.

"I feel like he's watching me," said Warren, "and I don't like it."

McCoy took another look at Mr. Black. "I've never heard of him but that doesn't mean much. I guess I could have my people look into it. That is, if you really want to know."

"No, it's fine," Warren said, but he was creeped out about it. He felt a hand on his shoulder and turned to tell McCoy to forget about it, but McCoy had gone.

• • •

"Mr. Nichols," Mr. Black said, putting out his hand. "Let me say how sorry I was to hear of your loss. This cannot be an easy time for you."

Mr. Black's expression was appropriately consoling, but felt empty. Warren didn't like feeling how he felt—intimidated. Perhaps even afraid. Why, he could not say.

Stand up, Peter said. *Don't give him the satisfaction of looking down on you.*

Warren agreed. He stood to minimize the height differential, pleased to see he was the taller of them by an inch or two. Judging by the crow's feet, Mr. Black was considerably older than Warren had originally thought, although well preserved. Warren broke the stare from his penetrating icy blue eyes first and regretted it immediately. "Taking it moment to moment," he said, his programmed response these days.

"I'm sure," Black said. "I suspect you've wondered at my connection to your parents. Because the fact is, I didn't. Know them, that is. I'm here to meet *you*."

"I don't follow," Warren said. An understatement.

"Here," said Black. "My card. I have much to discuss with you, but not now, not until you're ready." The black card was emblazoned on the front with a flaming blue circle.

"What do you mean, when I'm ready?"

"When the time is right. Believe me, you'll know."

"I don't appreciate riddles, Mr. Black," said Warren, but he was curious.

"Apologies, Mr. Nichols," said Black, looking anything but sorry. "But I can provide answers to the one question that's been nagging at you for years."

"Oh, yeah," said Warren, "and what question would that be?"

Mr. Black leaned in close, close enough that Warren could smell his aftershave. It made his stomach churn. He suddenly felt frozen, like prey waiting for the panther to pounce. Mr Black pressed his lips close to Warren's ear and whispered, "What does it feel like to kill a man?"

What the…? Peter said.

Warren's eyes went wide. He wanted to protest, tell him that it was Peter that had these desires, not Warren himself, but he had no time to respond. Mr. Black had already turned his back and was walking away.

7

February, 1959—Mason City, Iowa

"Hello?"

The shrill sound of the clanging telephone woke Roger from a deep sleep. He was still tired, trying to catch up after a long day of flying for the Dwyers and looking over his shoulder for potential assassins. Navigating a double life was taking its toll. He was feeling groggy and annoyed as he stumbled to the kitchen to the wall phone to put a stop to the torture.

"Roger, thank goodness."

"Mr. Dwyer?" Dwyer rarely called him this late.

"I need you to fly out to Hector. As soon as you can."

"North Dakota?" said Roger as if Hector Airport were the moon.

"Just got the call to do a quick out and back. It's easy money, Rog, and you're the best we've got."

"Really?" said Roger, suddenly awake.

"No," said Dwyer. "But the only one I could reach."

"Fine," said Roger, irritated at being duped. "But you owe me."

As if. Dwyer owed no one. It was his personal creed.

Roger looked out the window. Damn. The weather had taken a turn for the worse. "Doesn't look too good out there," he said unnecessarily.

"Weather briefings'll be ready when you get here."

Yeah. Thanks for your concern. He looked back down the hall. Tiffany was now awake and stumbling her way to the kitchen, shrugging into her robe.

"What's going on? Is everything okay?"

Roger pressed the receiver to his chest. "Everything's fine. Dwyer needs me to fly out to Hector."

"Hector?" She sighed, resigned. "Oh, well. Fly safe. Love you." She pecked his cheek and went back to bed.

"Peterson, you still there?" Dwyer barked.

"I'm here. On my way."

"Attaboy. See you soon."

Important clients in the middle of the night. His big chance to make some important connections. He'd flown to Hector Airport dozens of times. He could do it with his eyes closed.

• • •

The bleak evening sky and the dark car provided all the cover he needed to watch his would-be killer sprint to his truck and take off in a hurry. Mr. Spade revved his motor and followed.

It was about half an hour to Mason City Municipal Airport. Spade parked a ways off as Peterson stashed his truck close to the hangar, then opened his door and quietly shut it behind him. He crossed the tarmac, staying low in the empty lot. Peterson and another man, probably his boss, were in the hangar attending to a plane prior to takeoff. The plane was small, adequate for shorter excursions. The front end of a locomotive with wings. Better him than me, Spade thought, then listened in on the conversation

"Make sure you check that equipment twice, Rog."

"Yessir, just finishing up now."

"Good boy. The weather briefings are on the desk over there."

"Copy that."

It was now or never. With Peterson in the cockpit messing around with the machinery, and Boss Man out by the tail attending to the rear of the plane, Spade snuck into the office. The weather briefings sat on the desk. He glanced through them, removing the final two pages, the ones with the phrases *limited visibility, adverse flying conditions,* and *air travel not advised at this time.*

Spade had not planned to eliminate Mr. Peterson tonight, not like this. He preferred the close encounter too much. Tonight was all about surveillance. On the other hand, when opportunity knocks, answering usually proves the wiser trajectory. Spade made his way back to his vehicle, started the ignition, and pulled out of the airport. On the road, he passed some kind of van or small bus headed toward the airport. In his rearview mirror, Spade saw it turn into the gates of the runway.

Damn. Passengers. Not part of the plan either. Spade pulled a u-turn and followed the vehicle back through the airport gates. Killing Peterson was one thing, but collateral damage was unacceptable to the Circle.

Three men exited the bus, extended handshakes to others still inside, then removed their bags and started for the plane inside the hangar. Before the vehicle pulled away, one of the men knocked on the passenger window. "Have fun in the storm, dude. It's gonna be a doozy."

The window rolled down. "At least we'll get there," said the guy inside. "You couldn't get me into a plane in this weather for anything."

"Chicken."

"Idiot."

"I hope your bus freezes up."

"Yeah, well I hope your plane crashes."

The window rolled back up to the sound of laughter and the bus spun off toward the gates.

Spade swore. He hadn't adhered to his plan and now he had to get back in there and put those damn pages back. Although why anyone would be stupid enough to fly in this weather.... Clearly, Peterson had some kind of death wish. Which was funny when you thought about it. But either way, Spade would not be responsible for the death of three innocent, if delusional, tipsy passengers.

As the men boarded the plane, its motor roaring into life, Spade made it back to the office and was about to slide the pages back where they belonged when the door handle turned. There was no chance to replace them now. He crouched down behind the giant metal desk just as a hand reached in to grab a few papers off its surface.

"You almost forgot these," Boss Man called out over the din, and shut the door again behind him.

Spade couldn't hear Peterson's reply over the motor of the plane and his own breath.

He waited until Boss Man was busy with the hangar doors before slipping out of the office and into the cold, dark night, silently praying that Roger Peterson was the best damn pilot in the sky.

May, 1959—Atherton, California

Two hundred nine. Million dollars. That's what the Nichols fortune amounted to. Not including the controlling shares of Nichols, Inc., the company his grandfather had built from the ground up long before Warren had come into the gene pool. At almost 18, he had little interest in any of it. Except the money.

McCoy had been droning on for such a long time Warren feared his eyes would close from the ennui.

Finally, McCoy's oration seemed to be wrapping up. "So, Mr. Nichols, per your parents' wishes, everything will remain in trust until your 18th birthday."

Wait. What? 18th birthday? That's not for months, Peter said.

"That's not gonna work for me," Warren said. "There's no

way I want anyone touching anything until I'm at the helm." Warren liked the sound of that. As if he were the captain of a ship about to save an entire fleet.

McCoy stared at him. "That may be so. But it's really not up to you, Mr. Nichols. You're still a minor. As such, you cannot come into possession of these funds until you are a legal adult. The trust will continue to manage the accounts until that time. They will make all decisions on your behalf—and, as always, in the best interests of the company."

Warren knew virtually nothing about the running of a company, but that wasn't the point. "Yeah, and who's to stop them from making a bad one?"

"*I* am," said McCoy flatly. "I am your representation in these matters. Your parents paid quite a large sum of money to my firm to make sure their interests would be protected. As their interests are now your interests, our agreement will continue until you turn 18. At that point, the decision to remain with our firm will be up to you."

There was a lot of money at stake. Life-changing money. And everyone knew lawyers were the money-grubbingist ones of all. McCoy was as transparent as glass. There was no love lost between them, that's for sure. Still, Warren couldn't change the date of his birth. He'd have to settle for the terms of the trust until the reins were his. He chose to say nothing.

McCoy set about packing up his papers, and Peter directed Warren's thoughts to the business card still in his pocket. The one from the mysterious Mr. Black.

February, 1959—Clear Lake, Iowa

"Don't you worry back there, boys," Roger shouted over the propeller. "You're in good hands."

It wasn't a lie. Roger felt alive, the way he always felt at the controls of an airplane. The challenge of potential bad weather would only test his skill. His course was charted out in detail, and he guided the plane to the northwest and into the eerie glow of icy snow until it reached his pre-established height of 800 feet.

His passengers weren't the talkative types. Fine with him. To be honest, they looked like they'd been through something, though hard to tell what. One of them looked more sick than tired and the other two were close to comatose. Roger checked the time. Almost 1:00 AM.

When the control panel's alarm system sounded, Roger calmly banked hard to the right, surprised by the strong wind gusts that were forcing the plane downward.

The passengers, startled by the sudden lurching of the plane, came to life and began to shout as if it would help navigate the plane. The sick guy was groaning.

Roger kept his eye on the panel to identify the cause of the problem. Red lights were flashing from multiple sources. *What the – ?* He pulled down hard on the control stick, but it was as if the plane had a mind of its own.

Roger felt the adrenaline rush through his veins. The plane wasn't responding. It was impossible, yet it was happening. To *his* plane. *His* flight. The plane he checked and re-checked before every single flight.

Defensive. He'd have to go for defensive. He looked up, but all he could see was a wall of white. Damn snow had come in earlier than expected. *A lot* earlier than expected, according to the report.

What now? I can't slow this baby. Not with this lousy visibility.

He reached for the radio, but it was too late. They were in the middle of nowhere in a white-out with an out-of-control aircraft.

His passengers screamed as they began to plummet.

Roger had often wondered how he'd feel at the time of his death.

Now he knew.

• • •

The plane struck the ground at close to 200 miles per hour. It cartwheeled across the field over and over and over, finally coming to a screeching halt as it stretched a barbed wire fence almost to the breaking point. Two of the passengers were violently thrown from the fuselage to the left. The third was launched over the fence into the neighboring cornfield. All of them died on impact. Peterson's body lay at the center of the wreckage, his hand on his heart where he kept the picture of Tiffany.

10

November, 1959—Atherton, California

He'd hardly call himself a trendsetter, but Warren was one of the first kids in his school to go crazy for Jack in the Box and now the chain was making its way up and down the west coast. He was a sucker for French fries and that was all that remained from the fast-food dinner he, Stacy, and Vivian were sharing at the small table. Just the three of them. He traced Vivian's elegant hands in his mind as they dipped into the bag, brought a fry to the ketchup, and then to her mouth in graceful movements. Bewitching him. There was little Vivian did that he didn't find intoxicating.

Only one more day before his 18th birthday. At midnight he'd become one of the richest men in the country. The last few months had gone by in a blur. He'd been excused from his final exams and had his personal effects shipped to him from Maine. Money talks; Stapleton had even tossed in a diploma to be done with him. Since his untethering, Warren hadn't given his previous life another thought, and had been free to plan for bigger and better things.

He hadn't heard from Peter in a while. All these years, and Peter had never shown up when Vivian was around. At first, Warren was hurt, but Peter insisted that he and Vivian could not coexist. Warren didn't mind, really. He didn't tell Peter, but having Vivian all to himself was what he craved. He'd hardly missed Peter at all lately. Sure, he missed him to talk to in that guy-to-guy way, but when Viv was around, he felt calmer. Less angry. It was a strange Catch-22.

"Are you sure this is how you want to spend your 18th birthday eve, Warren?" asked Miss Stacy, breaking into his thoughts. "Doesn't seem all that celebratory."

"I'm sure," he said. "There's no place I'd rather be."

"But we don't even have a present for you," said Vivian. "I hate that you won't let us get you something."

"Like I need anything," said Warren.

Vivian conceded the point. She was a senior in high school, only a few months away from graduation herself. Ever since he'd been back they'd been flirting with each other, flitting around like moths. Until the other night it had been entirely innocent. Casually touching hands as they reached for the same glass, sneaking glances at each other as they lay by the pool. With Peter on some kind of hiatus, Warren was afraid for the first time in years. Of the potential rejection, the vulnerability he felt. Of what would happen if the possibility of being with Vivian disappeared.

It was as they'd sat watching *Alfred Hitchcock Presents*, a bowl of popcorn between them on the couch, and their fingertips had met, that things shifted. Warren hadn't pulled away. Neither had she.

Moving the bowl to the table, Warren had slowly reached for her. Vivan had brought his hand up to her cheek and leaned into it, breathing in deeply as he ran his thumb along her soft, smooth skin. She bit her bottom lip—all the encouragement he needed. He leaned in toward her. Their lips met. For a moment they sat like that, lips pressed together, chests heaving, hearts pounding, until Warren forced himself to break away. "Are you sure, Vivian? Are you sure you want this?"

"I'm sure," she said.

Warren wanted to remember every detail of that moment. The electricity in his veins. The feel of her soft, salty lips against his. The lavender essence wafting from her hair. The feel of her arms wrapped around his neck and his hand adventuring down her back and along her side as it traced her curves to her hips.

A scream had brought them crashing back to earth and they jumped apart. *Alfred Hitchcock Presents* had resumed. They looked at each other and laughed nervously. After a moment, they returned to the show by mutual consent, although now they were holding hands, pressed side-to-side.

Warren was pretty sure Miss Stacy knew what was up, even though she'd said nothing. How could she not notice the way Vivian was drinking from Warren's cup and sharing his fries rather than eating her own? He didn't know if Miss Stacy's silence was a good thing or a bad thing.

"Well," he said when they'd finished, "there actually *is* something big happening tomorrow. Because I've made a decision."

"A decision?" Miss Stacy asked, "about what? Seems like a lot of decisions are headed your way these days now that you're an adult in the eyes of the legal system."

"True. But this one might be the biggest. As soon as I'm in control of the company...I'm going to sell it."

Miss Stacy raised her eyebrows.

"You're selling it?" Vivian said. "For real?"

Warren nodded. "I don't want anything to do with the life my parents planned out for me. And once it's sold and out of my life for good, I can focus on what's most important." He looked at Vivian, who blushed and looked down.

Miss Stacy considered the two of them. "Well," she said, "it's a big move, but I'm happy for you. I know you were never interested in running that company. Nor were your parents, for that matter, if truth be told. Just remember, Warren, once it's gone, it's gone. Are you sure you want to take such a big step so soon?"

"I know it's a big decision, Miss Stacy, but I promise I've thought this through. I need to put this behind me. I can't do that while I own the company."

"How much do you think you can get for it?" Vivian asked.

"Vivian! That's none of our business," Miss Stacy said.

"That's okay," said Warren. "I don't mind. But I don't really know.Whatever it is will be worth the clean slate."

"Well, then," said Miss Stacy, "I say this calls for that celebration we were talking about. Why don't you two go on to a movie or something?" She gave Warren a wink.

Warren got the message. So did Vivian. "How long have you known, Mom?"

"Way longer than the two of you, apparently," Miss Stacy said with a laugh. "Besides, the Warren Nichols *I* know is honorable and respectful and would never betray my trust."

"*Moooom....*" Vivian said.

"Never, Miss Stacy," Warren said.

"Then off you go. Have a good time. I'll take care of this mess."

Warren stood. "I'll get it, Miss Stacy. You're done taking care of my messes."

• • •

"I like this new Warren," Stacy said to Vivian as Warren walked to the trash bin.

When Warren returned he had an envelope in his hand. "There's one more thing I want to say before we go." He handed the envelope to Miss Stacy, who looked at him, confused.

"It's for you," said Warren. "Go ahead, open it."

Stacy removed the single sheet of paper from the envelope and gasped.

Vivian peered over her shoulder. "Mom, what is it?"

"I—I can't believe it," Stacy was saying. "This is a deed. It's the deed for the house!"

"What?" said Vivian, "what do you mean?"

"I mean, Warren just gave us the house. The Nichols' house. The whole thing. As a gift."

"Paid in full, effective tomorrow," Warren said. "You shouldn't have to feel like you borrowed our address. It's yours now, and always will be." He couldn't look at Vivian. Not yet. Not until he'd finished. "I think there's something else in there," he said, pointing at the envelope.

"What else could there be?" said Miss Stacy.

"It also doesn't go into effect until tomorrow, but it's all yours," Warren said.

Stacy took out the check and tears welled up in her eyes. "Warren, you can't do this. We can't accept it. It's...it's...."

"Enough for anything you could possibly need."

"Warren," said Vivian, taking the check from her mother. "This...this is a joke right? No one just gives someone 10 million dollars and a house for no reason."

"There's every reason in the world," said Warren. "I'm not giving you anything you don't rightfully deserve. You're my family. I love you both. That's all there is to it."

It was the first real generous gesture Warren had ever made. Sure it was big, but what was the point of having it if he didn't get to spend it the way he wanted to? Grand gestures, when made for the right reasons, changed the world. He was counting on it.

11

February, 1959—Mason City, Iowa

The usually calming cup of morning coffee tasted like acid in his mouth. Spade couldn't even manage a second sip as he read the *Mason City Globe-Gazette's* headline.

FOUR KILLED IN CLEAR LAKE PLANE CRASH

He'd barely slept since returning home from the airport, waiting on the couch until dawn for the paperboy to drop off the morning edition. And there he still sat, a blanket draped across his shoulders, as he read the same limited details for the umptheenth time. The article cited the relative inexperience of the pilot, poor visibility. And the kicker: "adverse flying conditions."

It only got worse from there.

Buddy Holly, Ritchie Valens, and J.P. Richardson, the Big Bopper. The three passengers. All dead.

It was inconceivable to him that he'd caused the deaths of three civilians. Three national icons. And all because he'd pushed the limits. Let his ego get the best of him. The national media would be all over it—and so would the Circle. The Circle avoided media attention at all costs. The organization would not be happy with him. Not happy at all.

Where do you hide from the organization that can find you anywhere?

12

March, 1959—Paris, France

The floor of reddish square tile was thoroughly scuffed from many years of the foot traffic purchasing fresh produce, toiletries, and canned goods. Today, the boy in a dingy white apron had already scrubbed the dirt from the tile and was now stocking the shelves slowly and methodically. A young woman aptly navigated the labyrinth that was the corner market with a basket in one hand with her nearly three-year-old son tightly gripping the other. She was fair-skinned with soft, welcoming brown eyes and auburn hair that fell between her shoulder blades. The boy was big for his age, with big eyes that peered out from beneath the wisps of hair that fell across his forehead.

The woman was hoping this trip would be a quick one. Bread. Fruits and vegetables. Fresh pasta. Cheese. Milk. Eggs. Shampoo. Toothpaste. In and out before her son had a mood change. Today, so far, he was smiling, announcing each item he recognized, pointing and asking, *"C'est quoi?"* for items he didn't. *"Adorable!"* exclaimed strangers. His mother nodded, but moved on. Her son was already much too aware of his own power. Of how to manipulate others to offset any trouble he happened to stir up.

"Bonjour, Yvonne, Gérard," said Celeste, the store's owner, as she placed the woman's items on the counter. "You have been a good boy today?"

Gérard flashed a smile and nodded. He knew this game.

"Alors, then, do you think Mama would let you have *un petit gateâu*?"

Gérard's eyes went wide.

"Yvonne, ça va?" Celeste asked.

"Of course," Yvonne said. "Gérard, what do you say to Tante Celeste?"

"Merci, Tante Celeste," Gérard sung, and snatched the cookie from Celeste's hand.

"Merci, Celeste," said Yvonne. She gestured to the boy stocking the shelves. "Charles has gotten so big." Yvonne had been coming to this market since Charles was a toddler. Celeste and her husband Henri were like an older brother and sister to her, checking in on her frequently. Being a single mom in Paris wasn't easy, and they never judged her.

"Oui," Celeste tsked. "If only his work was as good as his appetite."

The two shared a chuckle as they watched Charles for a moment. "He wants his own money to buy comic books," she said with a long roll of her eyes. "He wants money for useless things like that, he works. It's that simple."

Yvonne nodded.

"Time is moving faster than I would like, though," Celeste added with a sigh. "Be careful you don't let that happen with this sweet boy."

Yvonne turned to Gérard, "You will not grow up too fast, my love, will you," she said.

"Non, Maman," said Gérard, still busy with his cookie.

"Oh!" exclaimed Yvonne as the cathedral bells chimed 4:00. "I must get home and start dinner. Give my love to Henri."

"Oui, oui, Yvonne, a bientôt."

Outside, Yvonne loaded her few bags into their Radio Flyer wagon, leaving room for Gérard when his legs inevitably tired on the walk back. The sun had not begun its descent for the day and its warm glow kissed her face between the buildings as they walked up the city streets. The trees that lined the block were beginning to show signs of budding and soon it would be springtime in Paris, her favorite time of year in her favorite city.

Their apartment was brick and surrounded by a red cast-iron fence. Long stalks of ivy cascaded up into the corners where the light refused to shine. Yvonne ascended the half dozen stairs to the main entryway, a sleeping Gérard on her hip. They both knew he was faking, but she went along with the game until it was time to deposit him on the landing and retrieve her groceries from the wagon. They lived two flights up behind a peeling white door. *Numéro six.* Her lucky number.

Her friend Madeline lived one more floor up, on the top floor, which was unmercifully hot in the summer due to the black paint on the roof, but quieter, something Yvonne envied. Her own neighbors were eccentric artists with muses who were known to visit at odd hours, day or night.

She pushed her key into the lock and then stepped back when she saw the door was open. Had she forgotten to lock it? That wasn't like her. She gave it a little push, feeling unsettled. The only people who had a key, besides Celeste and Henri, of course, were her neighbors Nicholas and Rina, but they were out of town for the week and would have left a note if their plans had changed. Marie, Yvonne's nanny, was also off today tending to her own grandchildren across the city.

So why was the door open? She'd made it a fun ritual, locking the door, a ritual she shared with Gérard where they sang a silly song as she put in the key, turned the lock, and tested that it held. She put Gérard down, took his hand, and held it tightly as she considered her options. They lived in a lovely neighborhood, but all it took was one act of desperation.

"Wait here, *mon cher,*" she told Gérard, and picked up a heavy bottle of olive oil from her bag.

She pushed open the door and looked around. Nothing seemed disturbed. Yet noises were coming from the kitchen. *Cooking* noises.

Slowly, Yvonne crept toward the kitchen taking in the tantalizing scent of sauteing onions, garlic, and mushrooms. Disconcerted, yet curious, she peered around the door. The familiar room looked as if it had been through a tornado. Pots and pans everywhere. Cabinets open, cutlery scattered about. When she saw the man's back, she took another step inside with the bottle of oil held high, but at the same time thinking that no one cooking in her kitchen producing smells like that could be all bad. Could they?

When he turned from the stove and their eyes met, she gasped and dropped the jar of oil, which cracked on impact. He was wearing her *"J'adore la cuisine"* apron and had a skillet in his hand.

He took a step toward her.

13

November, 1959—Atherton, California

What better way to celebrate than with ice cream? Warren was driving his father's 1950 Ford convertible, navy blue with a wave of white that broke in from the front fender and ended at the base of the door. Warren reminded himself that in a matter of hours it would be *his* 1950 Ford convertible. Miss Stacy was sitting in the back "so the lovebirds could sit together" in the front. Vivian's head was leaning on Warren's shoulder. He was in heaven.

Rachel's Ice Cream Shoppe was one of Vivian's favorite places. The sleek exterior, accented by pulsating neon signage, drew in teens in multitudes, as if their very existence depended on cars, ice cream, and canoodling. Which it probably did. Warren finally found a parking spot and followed Vivian and her mother into the restaurant where they located a small table in the corner.

He looked at Vivian. "Vanilla malted, right?" It's what she always ordered.

"Nope. Not today," she said. "Today we're celebrating. It's the banana split for me!"

Warren laughed. "And for you, Miss Stacy?"

"Hot fudge sundae for me, Warren, please. With plenty of nuts and whipped cream."

"You got it," said Warren. "I'll be right back."

He navigated through the crowd to the counter to place their order. Most of the kids were his age, but he felt decades older. Not that he'd ever fit in, even before the death of his parents, before his new responsibilities. Other teenagers—besides Vivian, of course—seemed like they were from another planet.

"What the hell are you doing back in town?"

The voice brought back a tidal wave of memories Warren had thought were long gone. His longtime rival, Lance Cashman. Lance was a bully from way back. When Warren was still going through his scrawny stage, Lance had become Mr. Star Athlete. Warren had taken his share of torture, too, until Peter convinced him that fighting back was better than being bullied. Today, Warren was pleased to see that he had filled out to the point where Lance was no taller and no broader than he was.

Lance was a true cliché. He and his pals wore jeans and white T-shirts with cigarettes rolled into the sleeves and tucked behind their ears. Still, Lance was the reason Warren had been shipped off to Maine. It was his fight with Lance—the fight Warren had *won*—that had gotten him expelled, arrested, and sent away.

Well, well, well, said Peter. *I see we're finally gonna get the chance to finish this asshole off.*

Peter? Here? Now? *What are you doing here? I'm with Vivian!* Peter never came around when he was with Vivian.

You know exactly what I'm doing here. Don't be an idiot. We can take him, buddy. Make him hurt. Real bad.

"No," Warren said, talking to Peter, but realizing from the confused look on Lance's face that he'd spoken aloud. Warren had never, ever, replied to Peter in public. Shaken, he composed himself and pressed on. "Well, well," he said, "Lance Cashman. What, 20 and still hanging around teeny-boppers?"

"Screw you, Nichols," said Lance. "Heard your folks took a drive off a cliff."

"You might want to learn to read, Cashman," said Warren. "Get your facts straight."

"Who the hell cares, anyway?" said Lance. "All I know is that you're here and you're not welcome. Doesn't matter how much dough they left you, you're never gonna be welcome here. You're nothing but a punk in fancy duds. So get lost. Now. Before I finish what we started last time I saw you."

Yes, please, said Peter. *Let's finish it. Once and for all.*

"Shut up!" said Warren, frustrated with Peter's ongoing intrusion.

"Really?" said Lance. "And who's gonna make me, Nichols, *you*?"

Warren didn't know what to do. Peter was egging him on. *Don't leave me on the sidelines for this one. We've been waiting a long time for this. It'd feel so good to take this guy out, I promise. The best you've ever felt.*

Suddenly Lance laughed. His buddies joined in, though the joke was unclear. "Guess you're just too chickenshit, huh, Nichols? Look at this jerk," he said to the room. "Nothin' more than a pansy. Afraid to fight. Come on, guys, nothin' here. Nothin' here at all."

Lance laughed again and turned to go.

Chickenshit? Did he say chickenshit?

I think he did, Warren told Peter.

He tapped Lance on the shoulder. "Not so fast," he said. "In fact, I'm all for it. Finishing it, that is. As I remember, you had a bloody nose, your left eye was swollen shut, and you had a fat lip. If the cops hadn't shown up when they did, everyone would have seen you cry."

Lance's face twisted and he moved in fast, pushing Warren hard to the ground. A hard slap to the side of Warren's face made Warren see red. Morgan and Jeff, Lance's lickspittles, whooped and moved into position behind their leader seamlessly, as they had countless times before.

"What's going on here?" Stacy demanded, edging through the crowd with Vivian.

Warren stood back up slowly and dusted himself off.

"It's nothing, Miss Stacy," Warren said. "Just a little misunderstanding. Isn't that right, fellas?"

Lance backed off. "Sure, sure. That's it. Just a little clumsy today, that's all," he said, "right, guys?"

Warren forced himself to nod, and turned to Miss Stacy to speak.

"I'll be back with our ice cream in a minute," he said, begging her with his eyes to understand. "Really, it's nothing."

"Come on, Mom," Vivian finally said, "let's go back to the table." Miss Stacy gave Warren and then the boys one more long look before nodding and turning away.

Warren found himself turning to Jeff, always the weak link. "Hey, Underwood," he said, his cold, penetrating stare intensifying his next words. "You can walk away or we can let this go down. But no matter what your friends here do to me, just know I'll be coming for you. *You.* And I won't stop until you're on the ground. Is that a risk you want to take?"

Jeff's eyes widened in response to the threats coming from Warren's mouth. *Peter's* words. *Peter's* threats. It was as if Warren had no control over his own speech. For a moment, he hesitated. If Peter could break through and speak for him, what did that mean? What else could he do?

Jeff, clearly shaken by the unexpected direct threat, looked to his Alpha for a sign.

Lance, unwilling to tangle with Miss Stacy, a beloved member of the community, shook his head no to Jeff, who let out a sigh of relief.

Warren nodded once, returned his hands to his pockets, and headed to the counter to place his order.

• • •

"You guys see that," Lance said to his friends, gesturing in Warren's direction across the room.

"See what?" asked Morgan.

"Looks like our boy Nichols has a case of jungle fever."

They watched as Warren kissed Vivian's hand, fed her from his spoon, and laughed at something she said."Disgusting," he said.

"That's just not right," said Morgan.

"No," said Lance. "It's not right at all. And someone ought to step up and do something about it."

• • •

Something's not right, Peter said. *You feel it?*

Of course I feel it, said Warren, annoyed. He felt it all the way into his bones. He felt pulled in too many directions, too. There was Peter, who'd shown up unannounced and hadn't left. There were three guys chomping at the bit to take his head off. And there were two ladies with him who were looking at him with concern on their faces instead of the happy smiles that were supposed to be there.

Warren, Vivian, and Miss Stacy had finished their desserts

and were on their way back to the car. Warren reached into his pocket. "Here," he said to Miss Stacy. "Get in the car. You and Vivian. Put up the top and lock the doors."

Miss Stacy stared at him.

"Please," Warren said. "You have to trust me."

Miss Stacy blinked once, took the keys, pulled Vivian to her side, and did as she was told. When Warren turned around, Lance and his goons were only feet away.

Warren sighed. He'd hoped it wouldn't come to this.

Peter was thrilled. *Finally,* he said, *a chance to do the right thing. To settle the score with these assholes. We've been waiting a long time for this. Let's do it.*

Warren tried to block him out. "Look," he said to Lance. "There's nothing to see here. I don't want any trouble."

"Nothing to see?" Lance sneered. "Really? That's not what it looked like to me, not with the pretty little darkie there."

See, said Peter, *what did I tell you? The jerk isn't gonna let it go. Don't you think it's about time you listened to me? Man up!*

Warren's hands fisted. It was too easy to forget his promise to let bygones be bygones when the bygones were racist jerks. And when he had his best friend egging him on. "Just thanking my housekeeper and her daughter for their services," he said tightly.

You're kidding, said Peter. *That's what you're going with? A lie? Like some pansy?*

Warren felt sick to his stomach. It was another case of speaking before he thought. The shame ate at him.

Morgan moved in. "Looked a whole lot more friendly than that, wouldn't you say, Lance? Like our boy here likes monkeys."

Suddenly there was a click and Lance held an open switchblade.

It's time to let go, Warren, Peter cajoled. *It's now or never. Let go….*

Warren closed his eyes and took a deep breath.

14

March, 1959—Paris, France

"Don't you dare come any closer," Yvonne said. "What are you doing 'ere, in *my* kitchen—wearing *my* apron?"

"Now don't be like that," the man said. He put down the skillet, turned down the gas flame, and was by her side before she had time to blink. He took her in his arms. She fought, but it was useless. He was strong, like an immovable boulder.

Eventually, she stopped fighting. "I hate you," she said.

"I know you do," he said. "But I love *you, mon amour*."

Yvonne began to cry. "It's been so long. I'd almost given up 'ope that you would return this time."

"Shh, my love, shh," said Spade. "There, there. I've missed you, too, but I'm back now. And look at you." He dried her tears with the tail of the apron and gazed upon the love of his life. Her long brown hair. Her soft brown eyes. Her warmth.

Her curves, and the way they felt in his arms. "Beautiful as ever. *Magnifique*."

Yvonne leaned in, kissed him hard, and then punched him in the nose.

• • •

Yvonne packed a wallop. When Spade opened his eyes, she was standing over him holding their son, scowling. The woman's allure tripled with that fire in her eyes. How long before they'd be able to act on that heat?

"You 'ave a lot of nerve," Yvonne hissed, "pulling a stunt like this. I might 'ave called the police. Did you forget that I am the single mother of a toddler? That—what do you call it—breaking and entering—is a crime 'ere in Paris as well as in America? And 'ere you are...cooking me *les champignons*! And 'ow long 'as it been? I can tell you 'ow long. *Exactement.* To the day. That I 'ave not 'eard a word from you. Not even a phone call."

"But you love mushrooms," Spade protested. But she was right, of course. And he recognized how reckless it was for him to be there after the fiasco in the States with that stupid Peterson and the plane. "I'm sorry," he began soothingly. "You're right, I shouldn't have shown up so unexpectedly. But now that I'm here, let's not waste any precious time, *n'est-ce pas*? I've waited so long to see you...you and little Gérard here."

When he felt Yvonne relax slightly, he continued. "Remember that restaurant, back before Gérard was born? The one overlooking the Arc de Triomphe. Where we first met. Where you ordered this very meal and said you'd never tasted anything like it before. I procured the chef's recipe. I wanted to surprise you."

"A French chef just 'anded over 'is recipe to an American with a sad story?" Yvonne said, but he could tell she was weakening. And that she'd been practicing her English. A sign that she hadn't given up "'ope" after all.

"Well, the 1,500 francs helped, too."

Her response was not what he'd hoped for.

"Fifteen 'undred for a mushroom recipe?! What, *est tu fou*? Do you know 'ow far I could stretch 1,500 francs? The nanny alone—"

"Yvonne," Spade broke in. "Wait. Stop. You don't understand. I'm not crazy—well, not in the way you mean, anyway. Things have changed. You're never going to have to work again."

She looked at him suspiciously. "What do you mean? What 'ave you done, Thomas?"

"The details can wait. I have bigger news. I'm here to stay. I want us to finally be a *normal* family. My business in America is done." *If you could call it that.* "I have enough money for us to live comfortably for a long time. I'm not going anywhere... that is, if you'll have me."

It was a life he never thought he'd have. One he never thought he deserved. But now that he had somehow found it, he would fight to the finish to never let go.

"*Alors,*" said Yvonne. "That is a very nice speech. But there are some conditions."

"Of course."

"Gérard comes first. You fail him, you fail me. Then out you go."

"Agreed," said Spade readily.

"*Deux*. This is a one bedroom that Gérard and I share. *Gérard and I.* The couch is yours. No funny business."

What exactly did she mean by funny business? She couldn't possibly be implying that they wouldn't be—but he sensed that would have to wait. He sighed. "Is there a three?"

Her lips turned up. "*Naturellement, mon amour.* That you learn not to burn the mushrooms."

15

November, 1959—Atherton, California

The concrete bench was cold and hard. Jail Cell Interior Design 101. Warren got up to pace off the few feet, running his hands over the bars and along the filthy walls until he'd completed his course and sat down again.

He'd screwed it up good this time. Lawyer or no lawyer, money or no money. He may have thrown the first punch, but against a knife? But was there even a chance of someone with his record claiming self-defense—*three against one had to count for something, didn't it?*—or would they take one look and throw away the key?

The fight played over and over in his head. He didn't know exactly when he'd stepped over the line from attempting to diffuse the situation to boiling point of no return. Was it the look in Lance's eye when he spoke about Vivian, or when Morgan made the crack about her color? Whenever it was, Peter was ready, as if he'd been lying in wait for exactly the right moment. All he remembered was Peter telling him to *let go.* This time, unlike in the past, Warren had listened. The next thing he knew he was in the back of a police car in handcuffs.

Now that it was over, as he sat there waiting for McCoy, he was surprised to realize that he didn't like the feeling of that kind of letting go. Of surrendering to Peter. All those years he'd taken those small steps, done Peter's bidding, reveled in the mayhem that ensued from his actions. And now, here, alone with his thoughts, revelling had turned to revulsion.

He couldn't forget the way Stacy and Vivian looked at him as he was being taken away. Like he was some kind of monster. A monster to be reviled, afraid of. Aside from the occasional slamming of a door somewhere in the building, the clock on the wall outside the cell ticking off the seconds loudly was the only sound. *Tick. Tick. Tick.* Like the hammering of a gavel against a block.

He'd been locked up for hours after being searched, photographed, and processed. He'd been fingerprinted a long time ago after one of his earlier brushes with the law. 12: 28 AM. *Happy birthday to me.* He'd been sure today was going to change his life, but not like this. Why hadn't he been a big enough man to walk away? Why did his anger always get the better of him? He wouldn't apologize for standing up for what was right, but he was the one sitting behind bars while the two other guys were at the hospital eating Jello and whining that they'd been afraid for their lives.

There was a loud clang. "Nichols," said a cop opening his cell door. "Your lawyer's here."

Orville McCoy walked in, briefcase in hand and sweat on his brow. The man was a loser, according to Peter, but even he'd have to admit that he was Warren's only chance.

He shook his head. "Mr. Nichols," he said. "I find it difficult to express just how disappointed I am at this turn of events." He nodded at the cop, who closed the door and backed away slowly.

"The police say you almost killed two men. They want you for attempted murder."

"That's not what happened," Warren protested angrily. "Ask anyone there. I was defending myself."

"It doesn't really matter if you were defending yourself when the police find you with a knife to a man's throat, does it?" said McCoy.

A knife to a man's throat? Is that what he had done—*Peter* had done? Warren felt ill. He didn't want to show it, but it scared him to death that the fight had happened like that—and that he didn't remember. How could he not remember?

"Does it?" McCoy repeated "Does it really matter that they're the ones with the stab wounds and you have nothing more than a few bruises and scrapes? I'd say yes to that, Mr. Nichols. Which is why all I could do get bail set for a million."

"Just pay it," Warren said, again hoping the lawyer bought into his bluster. "It's mine now. I'm 18."

Son of a bitch could easily give you your money, Peter said.

Not now, Warren screamed in his head. *I can't listen to you now.*

"It *might* have been yours now, Mr. Nichols, but I'm afraid there's been a snafu."

That got Warren's—and Peter's—attention. "A...a snafu?"

"Well," said McCoy, sighing, "yes. You see, the trustees met to discuss the situation and felt that freezing your account would be prudent until this whole thing...blows over."

This guys a con artist. He's got your money! Do something!

I said, shut up!

Warren blinked. "What are you saying? Are you telling me I have to deal with this on my own?"

You're not on your own! Peter said. *I'm right here.*

Warren's head was swimming. He needed to concentrate and Peter wouldn't let up.

"I'm willing to defend you, Mr. Nichols," said McCoy with another annoying sigh, "but I'm afraid you're stuck here for the interim."

"You're telling me I can't get out on bail? That's insane. I can't stay here."

"I'm afraid you have no choice. The housekeeper and her daughter will make good witnesses, but there's no guarantee this will play out in the same manner your other 'misadventures' have through the years."

Before he left he turned with an unexpected parting shot. "Do you know why you were *really* sent to Maine, Mr. Nichols? Because it was the only way to get you released with a guarantee of no time in juvenile detention. To finish school as far away as possible from Atherton. And it was made possible only on the backs of your parents' good name. Your parents, Mr. Nichols, are gone now. They can no longer protect you. And I don't know how long I'll be able to either."

Warren had told McCoy where he could stick his lawyerly ass, which was still billing at hundreds of dollars an hour, but it didn't have much substance given that at the time Warren truly had the short end of the stick. A really, really, short stick.

Depleted and depressed, he sat on the thin mattress on the cot attached to the wall of the cell. It didn't seem to matter that Lance had pulled a knife. All that mattered was that he'd done the stabbing and appeared unreservedly poised to slit another man's throat.

You happy now, Peter? You got me sent to prison-school in the frozen tundra and now here I am in a real jail cell.

Peter only laughed.

October, 1961—Paris, France

Annette de Garmeaux's decision to move to Paris had been a difficult one. She'd wanted to spread her wings and experience life, but her parents hadn't seen it that way. To them her departure was an insult so grave that when they stated their final pitch—ultimatum, really—they made it clear that if she left them behind in Rouen to "tend to their orchard alone," they would under no circumstances welcome her back ever again. The Amish had a phrase for it, apparently; *under the ban*.

Annette discovered how serious they were when her mother informed her by telegram that her father had recently died and that the funeral had been three months prior. As far as Annette was concerned, she'd had no family to speak of for years, and that telegram was simply the nail in the coffin. Literally. She'd even legally changed her name from Annette de Garmeaux to Yvonne Finck when she'd had Gérard.

Annette was her past. Yvonne's future was all that mattered. Gérard, Thomas, and their dearest friends, Celeste, Henri, and Charles.

After Thomas' return to Paris, he and Yvonne were wed in a small ceremony surrounded by their close friends. The ring bearer and best man for both the bride and groom, little Gérard, stole the show. After the local priest performed the ceremony, they celebrated with a fine meal at the restaurant overlooking the Arc de Triomphe, the site where they'd shared their first date. They made sure to order the chef's special *champignons*.

The photo Yvonne held in her hand was so much more than a pleasant memory. It was a symbol. The five most important people in her life all together. Sitting at a round table at their de facto wedding reception. Toasting with champagne, and grape juice for *le petit*. Celebrating Yvonne and Thomas' love. Every day she looked at that photo before tackling the day's responsibilities and it brought her renewed strength.

It was a way to attempt to soothe the impact of the nightmare going on around her. To think herself somewhere else while the unthinkable was going on outside. The fact of the matter was that she was scared for her life and that of her family. It was days since the curfew was enacted, but the crowds just kept coming back. Night after night they grew larger and larger. Sooner or later they would be right in front of their own apartment. Something terrible was going to happen, she just knew it. The police had already raided their block. They'd taken away 11, or was it 12, Algerians. Off to the centers until this whole mess was sorted out. She hoped it was soon. This police presence had an all too familiar feel to it. Apparently, her beloved country had grown tone deaf.

She looked at Gérard, innocently playing with his toy train. Still just a boy, she thought, one day this would be nothing more than a distant memory. Or was she lying to herself? How much would a five-year old really remember when it's all said and done? The stillness of the city. The palpable tension thickening with each passing day. *I'll see to it that he doesn't remember,* she promised herself sternly, and returned to her dinner preparations. A good meal always helped wash away the troubles of the day. The bare refrigerator, however, reminded her that once again she'd disparaged leaving the house for fear of the chaos outside. The time had come when she could avoid her errands no longer. She tossed out the rotten vegetables and mentally constructed her list. She supposed she could call Thomas, but no, she was an adult. She could handle it. "Gérard," she beckoned. "Get your coat, *mon cher. Vite.* We're going to the market."

"Oui, maman," Gérard said, rising to his feet obediently, putting his train back into the drawer near the window and scurrying off to do as he was told. Such a good listener, he made his mother very proud. She knew God had big plans for him.

She looked outside. It was nearing dark; they needed to move quickly to make sure they would be back by the time the curfew came into effect. *"Dépêche-toi, mon amour,"* she called into the hallway. "Hurry."

"Oui, maman," the little voice called back again. In a moment he was at her side, holding her hand.

The walk down the Rue Poissonnière was a short but nerve-racking one. People could be heard, but not seen. Yvonne needed to get to the market and back before things took an ugly turn. Should she turn back? No, she would not let Gérard feel her fear. *Keep going. Breathe. We're almost there.*

Gérard skipped ahead, letting go of her hand to jump up to reach a low branch of a small tree. She missed how they used to travel with their Radio Flyer. How she envied his innocence. Gérard arrived at the intersection of Grands Boulevards before she did and waited as he had been taught to do in the past. But this time he wasn't as eager as usual to cross the street and visit with Tante Celeste and Oncle Henri. He also wasn't looking back to see how far ahead he had gone. He stood motionless. *Something's wrong.* Yvonne felt it in her gut. Her pace quickened until she was by his side.

The mob was about 200 meters up the block and marching away from Yvonne and Gérard's position. The market was close, visible from their location, but didn't feel nearly close enough. A sharp police whistle blew, followed by a voice from a loud megaphone. "You must disburse! *C'est votre avertissement finale. Retournez maintenant ou vous serez détenu!* This is your last warning. Return to your homes or you will be detained!"

A scuffle broke out. Angry screams. A police officer shouted, "Holster your weapon!"

"He's got a gun," someone from the crowd cried out, "get down!"

Shots rang out. One. Two. Ten. So many and so fast. Yvonne watched, horrified, as two members of the crowd fell to the gutter.

The rest turned and ran. More shots. More people on the ground. Pandemonium.

Gérard flinched and covered his eyes with his hands. Yvonne shielded him with her arms and body, pulling him into her and turning her back to the crowd. She had to get Gérard out of there. She placed a hand on his shoulder to guide him away. Then she felt something warm.

Blood. His? No, not his. *Thank God!*

But—wait—it couldn't be. Yet it was. Hers. Yvonne watched the deep red blood run down from her shoulder over her chest. She felt a burning pain, and swayed. She could not remain on her feet. Still holding Gérard, she slipped to the ground, woozy, confused, afraid.

She concentrated on the face of her son. "Gérard, get to the market," she yelled. Even to her own ears it sounded more like a whisper.

Gérard turned, took in the horror, and turned back to her. Bent down to her. *"Maman,"* he cried.

"Non, Gérard, écoute...please...you must...*écoute maman.* Go to Tante Celeste and Oncle Henri... NOW! *Maintenant!"* Yvonne gathered her face's features into what she hoped was an approximation of calm assurance. *"Maman...maman...*is fine, Gérard. Please, go. *Vite.* I'll be right there. Go!"

Gérard was a good boy. He listened to his mother. Tears running, still calling for his dear *Maman,* he turned and ran.

Yvonne watched as he made his way down the street, weaving in and out of bodies twice his size and more. He was almost there. Thirty...20 meters away. *Go, mon petit, go.* Why was her head so heavy? She lay it down. He would be there by now. He would be safe. Rivulets of blood were pooling beneath her quickly. She closed her eyes to rest. Her son was safe. That was all that mattered.

• • •

Gérard was almost at the market. The full force of the mob was bearing down on him. "*Maman*!" he screamed, terrified, but he couldn't hear her answer. Now there were people running everywhere, pushing him out of the way, shoving him aside. Where was the market? He couldn't see the market!

A man spotted the boy. They locked eyes, the man's determined and hard, Gérard's wide with fear. The man grabbed Gérard and scooped him up just as he was about to be trampled. The next thing Gérard knew he was being carried with the mob down the street.

"Maman!" he cried out once again, but he had lost his sense of direction. She was nowhere in sight. So many people. Gérard was carried for blocks, kilometer after kilometer, passed from man to man through the crowd as it surged onward. Pursued. By whom, he didn't know.

Then he was roughly shoved into a car and they were speeding away from the city—away from his home. Gérard and others. All men. All big. They spoke a language he didn't understand, but he knew they were angry from their voices. He'd heard voices like that on the television. He cried. He wanted his *maman*. Where was his *maman*? She'd always told him to be brave, but he couldn't be. Not now. The men looked at him pityingly, but had no time for him, couldn't understand him.

Suddenly they came to a stop. A police officer demanded they get out of the car, his gun drawn and squared. Gérard had never seen a real gun, only ones on the cowboy shows on television, but he knew this was a real one because his rescuers did as they were told and Gérard let himself be led from the vehicle. Gérard heard his mother's voice. *Do as you're told, son, and all will be well.* They were at a bridge. The police took away his rescuers, who did not defend themselves. "Little boy," one officer said kindly. "Are you hurt? What did these men do to you? Did they kidnap you?"

Gérard was not entirely sure what that meant, but shook his head no anyway.

"Come with me," the officer said, and took Gérard by the hand to a police car.

Gérard watched from the backseat as his new friends were directed to the river bank, guns pointed at their backs. He squirmed on to his knees to see more clearly. What were they doing to them? To all the people lined up alongside them? Gérard watched with wide eyes as one by one his rescuers were dragged, fighting now, screaming, into the Seine and then held under the water. For a long time. Held down until they stopped fighting.

Gérard felt sick at first, then curiosity got the better of him. He opened the car door, walked closer to the officer who'd spoken to him, and took his hand. The officer flinched and shook free. "Get back in the car, boy," he said, "this is no place for you."

Gérard didn't move, however, and the officer let him be. He stood silently for what seemed like days. All those people who had been on the riverbank were now in the water and floating downriver with the strong current. *"Mais, pourquoi?"* he asked. "Why? Were they bad men?"

"Don't ask stupid questions," the officer finally said. "Get back in the car—now. Before I have to put you there myself."

• • •

Gérard Finck spent the rest of that day in the police station. It was almost dusk when his father finally arrived to bring him home. He'd never seen his father cry before. It made Gérard very uncomfortable, and he squeezed his father's hand tighter. He wanted *Maman*. Where was *Maman*?

"If you want to take your son home, you need to sign here and show identification," Officer Bernard stated. He seemed to be the less experienced of the two officers, constantly glancing at his partner, Officer Martin, to confirm he was correct in his actions.

"But...I don't have it with me," his father said. His face was raw with emotion. Pain. Sorrow. Despair. "I came here as soon as I heard what happened."

"Papa," Gérard said, "I want *Maman*."

"I know, *mon fils*, I know. Look," he said to the policemen, "I've filled out all your forms. I've answered all your questions. Please, just let me take my boy home."

"Alors, nous avons besoin le documents," said Martin. "It is policy. We cannot release a child without identification."

"Mais...But my wife...she is gone! Because you people are acting like, like…."

"Papa, qu'est-ce que tu dis? Maman est partie?" Gérard asked.

"Not now, Gérard, not now. I'm speaking to the officers." Thomas turned back to the men. "My son has been severely traumatized. What he saw in the Seine...no child should see such atrocities. I'm taking him home. If you have a problem with that, you will have to arrest me!"

Martin saw his young partner reach for his weapon, but put a hand on his arm before it could be drawn. "*Monsieur*, we apologize for seeming insensitive, we know this has been a difficult day. But we do have our procedures and protocols that require following. You and your son do not have the same surname, and you do not have any identification. Please try to understand this from our point of view."

The officer's English was very good, even Gérard could hear that. Papa also spoke English very well. He was always trying to teach *Maman* new words. "What do you want me to do, then?" Thomas said. "He still holds his mother's name. But I am his father."

Officer Martin sighed. "Please sign our forms and provide us with several ways to reach you in case we need to speak with you again," he said. "You are fortunate that we are allowing you to take the boy with you."

Gérard's father took his hand and moved to the door. Officer Martin opened it to let them pass. "We are very sorry for your loss, *Monsieur*...Roche." He gave Gérard's father a strange look.

Gérard and his father left quickly.

• • •

Officer Martin did not get a chance to look over the forms until later that day. When he did, he began to perspire. The boy's father—*mais non,* it couldn't be—but it looked like the boy's father was, indeed, not just any Roche. He was Thomas Roche.

The confirmation almost sent Officer Martin to his knees.

17

November, 1959—Atherton, California

McCoy had been gone for a little over an hour and Warren still couldn't rest, couldn't sit still. He tried closing his eyes to conjure the images of the fight, but it was nothing more than a blur. That prick Lance had won even while losing. Some people were just allowed to be douchebags.

Don't worry, this will all blow over. McCoy will handle it, Peter said.

Warren didn't respond. Nor had he responded the previous dozen times Peter had interjected with some wise crack or pearl of wisdom. Warren had never been so mad at his friend before. But then again, his "friend" had never done this to him, to them, before.

At some point after 2 AM, Warren took his socks off and balled them up. He passed the time by throwing them against the concrete wall as hard as he could so they'd bounce back to him. A pathetic, mind-numbing distraction that lasted until his jailer returned. "Nichols," he barked, "charges have been dropped. You're free to go." He toggled a lever and the steel doors opened, releasing a shocked Warren from his own personal hell—at least for the moment. "Follow me to get your belongings."

I told you so, Peter said in a sing-song.

He was right, much as Warren hated to admit it. McCoy might actually earn those fat paychecks. Still, it was surprising that the charges had been dropped completely. He followed Officer Johnson through a narrow hallway and around a corner to a small window in a vacant room. He sat down on the bench to put his socks back on while he waited for his shoes and other confiscated personal belongings.

After an interminable wait, a second officer appeared and beckoned for Warren to step forward. He handed Warren a form to sign detailing each item being returned. "One pair of shoes, one watch, one belt, one wallet containing $129, one gold chain."

Warren retrieved his things.

Make sure everything's there, Peter said. *Can't trust cops, you know.*

Warren rolled his eyes but did as Peter suggested. Everything seemed to be there. Including the business card Mr. Black had given him; the black one with the flaming blue circle on it, which was no longer tucked away in his wallet. Warren paused.

This is it. Peter said. *The universe is giving us a sign. Now is the time to reach out and see what Mr. Black has to offer.*

"Through there," Officer Williams said, and pointed to the door that led out of the police station.

Warren shoved the card back in his wallet. Apparently, the cops were in a hurry to get rid of him. He put his wallet in his pocket and stepped outside and took a breath of fresh air.

"Need a ride?" said a voice to his right.

18

October, 1961—Paris, France

Something did not feel right. Thomas felt it in the way Officer Martin had looked at him, said his name. After years of running. Covering his tracks. Looking over his shoulder. Staying away from Yvonne and Gérard long enough to make certain they would never be targets. After all these years, it seemed he'd been discovered. And by a lowly cop. Why the cop hadn't pursued Thomas was an interesting question. Was it possible he'd been given a reprieve after Yvonne's death? Because he had his son with him? No. No one who was part of the Circle offered reprieves. It wasn't done. Ever.

On the walk home that day, he kept looking around fearing they were being followed, but there were so few people on the streets a tail would have been easy to spot. He held tight to Gérard's hand and led him back to the apartment where he would soon have to share the horrible news of the boy's beloved *Maman's* death. Tell him that Yvonne would not be coming home.

Was there something he might have done differently? Was he to blame for his wife's death as he was for so many others? If it were not for him, would she still be alive?

Unanswerable questions, perhaps, but his guilt ran deep on all counts. It didn't really matter who might claim responsibility for what they were now calling the Paris Massacre, that it was men like Charles deGaulle and Maurice Papon who had the blood on their hands. Somehow, he knew that if things were different, she'd still be alive.

Unfortunately, there was no time to mourn the loss of his beloved wife, the mother of their son. No time to plan a funeral service. No time to remember what life was like only a matter of hours ago, before the earth had gone from a place of beauty to a pile of nothing but ash. He'd give anything to relive the day, do it over differently. After years of living the Circle life, he'd gone soft. He'd let his guard down.

Officer Martin was a very real threat. A Watcher, most likely. If he were a hunter like Spade, they would probably have had a very different conversation. But Watchers were always looking to climb the ladder, weren't they? This Martin guy would be thinking about the reward, and/or promotion, coming to him for turning Mr. Spade, "the one who got away," to the current Mr. Black of the Paris Chapter.

Attack was imminent. Simply a matter of when and by whom. Adrenaline was pumping through his body in a way it hadn't since he'd left the Circle. How he'd missed it, the thrill of the chase. He'd stifled it, but it was still there, and now that it had been activated, there would be no quenching it until it did what it had to do.

"Papa?" said Gérard, *"J'ai faim."*

"*Oui, mon fils*. I know you are hungry. Come, we will get you something nice to eat."

First things first. Number one: Formulate a plan to keep his son safe.

Then another one to do a disappearing act of his own.

• • •

The Circle, Paris Chapter

"*Trois Doigts.*"

"I need to speak with *Monsieur Noir*. Right away."

"And who is speaking?"

"Officer Martin. *C'est urgént!*"

The safehouse was known as such only to the select members of the Circle, but this included the barkeep, who viewed himself as its gatekeeper.

"Rafi," he said to the man cleaning glasses behind the bar, "keep an eye out for me."

Rafi nodded, and the bartender went to deliver his message. Having a successful bar in central Paris was a coup in itself. But as the Circle's chosen "safehouse," success came with a level of security and the promise of endless business previously unimagined. And since Alain's father had willed him the *Trois Doigts* 15 years ago, business had never been better. He often wondered if his parents would have approved of his partnership with the Circle, but always came to the same conclusion. Who cared?

As proprietor, Alain had certain responsibilities and expectations. Knowing when to disturb Monsieur Noir was the most important. Behind the bar was a list of names of people permitted to speak with Noir, and Officer Martin was on that list. Along with several other Martins, Bernards, and Dubois. Basically, those with the right surnames and the right phone number.

In the far corner sat a heavyset man wearing a black turtleneck under an impeccable Brioni suit. His thinning gray hair matched eyes set back into his face behind spectacles. A day-old scruff almost hid the inch-long scar running perpendicular to his jawline on the left. *Le Parisien* was open to the financial section. A plate of brie and a small baguette sat next to his usual glass of Cheval Blanc, 1947.

No one liked to interrupt Monsieur Noir when he was reading the financials. The barman took a breath and stepped forward. "Monsieur Noir, *je suis desole,* sorry to disturb you, but there is an urgent call. From Officer Martin."

Noir slowly put down the newspaper and removed his reading glasses. "And?"

Alain blanched. "*Alors, Monsieur,* he said it was urgent. *C'est tout.* That is all."

Noir went still.

Alain waited.

"Well, then? I suppose you had better bring me the phone, hadn't you?"

"*Oui, monsieur.* Right away, *monsieur. Un moment, s'il vous plaît.*"

Alain quickly returned with a phone.

"What now?" Noir said into the receiver. "I do not like to be disturbed. Is this not something you can handle on your own?"

"*Non, Monsieur Noir.* I do not believe so. You asked...the Chapter wanted to know...."

"Spit it out, Martin, I haven't got all day."

"*Oui, Monsieur, oui.* But it seems we have located Mr. Spade. *L'American.*"

There was a long moment of silence.

"...*Monsieur*? Are you still there? I said that—"

"I heard what you said," Noir snapped. His mind raced with the news. Was it possible? Mr. Spade! What a coup that would be, to bring about the demise of the American who had killed the three famous musicians. The idea that he had been right here in Paris—well, the potential rewards were... *incroyable.*

The manhunt had turned up nothing for two years. And on Paris' darkest day since the Nazi occupation, Mr. Spade had chosen to reveal himself? Why? How? "Explain yourself," he said.

"His wife, *monsieur. Elle est morte.* Killed during the riot. Apparently he has a son. We found him wandering the streets...by the Seine. We didn't know who he was. We called his father to pick the boy up at the station. I saw him with my own eyes. He signed the paperwork. To take the boy home...."

"Interesting," said Noir, keeping his exhilaration to himself. "Bring me the details. Now," he reiterated, and hung up the phone.

Not since the creation of the Circle had anyone ever escaped its clutches. Escaped death at the Circle's hands. *His* chapter, not London, Los Angeles, or Moscow, not even New York, could be the one that brought down the man that had done the impossible. At least until now. He tried not to picture himself being promoted to the Council as he patiently waited for the intel that had eluded the Circle for far too long.

19

November, 1959—Atherton, California

Warren snuck a glance at the well-preserved, silent man sipping Scotch, or maybe bourbon, on the seat of the Cadillac Fleetwood Limousine across from him. Peter was practically frothing at the mouth at the possibility of the unknown. Warren's palms were sweating.

When he finally spoke, the sound of the man's voice startled him. "And your stay in the Atherton jail?" he said. "I assume they treated you well."

"Um, sure, I guess. I mean, I've had better," Warren said. Who *was* this guy, anyway?

The man laughed. "I'm sure you have, young man. I'm sure you have."

Warren waited while the man sipped his drink.

Well, what's he waiting for? said Peter. *Why is he keeping us waiting?* Peter was not known for his patience of late. Well... ever.

"I imagine you are curious as to why I am here," said the man.

"You might say that," said Warren.

The man nodded. "All in good time," he said. "Let's start with this. I was called when Officer Johnson noted my card in your wallet."

"The cop? But, why—?"

"Mr. Nichols. Please. Allow me to finish."

Warren blanched. The man's tone brooked no argument.

"Thank you. I will tell you this, Mr. Nichols. You were fortunate. Extremely fortunate. The timing could not have been more synchronistic. Because, quite simply, that card saved your life."

Warren opened his mouth again to speak, but the man went on.

"When the Circle identifies a young man such as yourself as worthy, the watching process begins. This time it began when you were shipped back to Atherton for your parents' funeral. My condolences again, by the way."

Warren was shocked. "The watching process? I was being watched? By whom? Why?"

Peter sneered at Warren's use of good grammar. He wanted to *get to the good stuff*. Warren tried to ignore him.

"I offered you answers when we met at the funeral, did I not?" said the man, ignoring the question.

"Well, yes. To a question I'd never asked. Not out loud, at least. So how did you—why would you—?"

"It's my business to know, Mr. Nichols. To know and to act. As you know, my name is Mr. Black. While it is not my legal surname, it is a title, one I have earned over decades of work and application to my craft. I am the oldest member of the San Francisco chapter of an organization called the Circle." He paused for the information to land. "The Circle is comprised of like-minded individuals, those who have had, shall we say, similar thoughts, similar...urges. Unlike most people, however, we have found a way to live in harmony with such thoughts and urges. We make a choice to allow them to flourish. Rather than suppress them, we embrace them, and in doing so, live a life of true salvation."

*Are you getting this, man?*Peter yelped in his ear. *This is what we've been waiting for!*

Warren wasn't convinced. Was this guy for real? Was he saying what Warren thought he was saying? That these guys in this "Circle" did whatever they wanted? That it might include...*killing*? He must have heard wrong.

"Look," Warren said. "I'm not sure where you're going with all this, but thoughts like that—they're not normal." Immediately, Vivian came into his head, and he felt the flush of shame. "I want to be normal. To live a normal life."

No, that's not what we want! We want to be let go...free! Peter objected loudly.

"Do you," said Mr. Black. "Is that what you really want? Normalcy? Complacency? A stifling, unfulfilling life?" Black waited a long beat. "I am offering you something different here, Mr. Nichols. A one-of-a-kind opportunity to be who you really are. Do you understand the scope of that offer?"

Warren didn't know what to say, but Black didn't give him a chance anyway. "Answer me this, Mr. Nichols. How did it feel when you held that knife in your hands, when you took that step to sink it deep into Morgan Brown's abdomen?"

The truth? Warren didn't know. In every fight he'd been in, Warren knew he never felt as alive as he did in those moments. But the fight that got him arrested, of that he had no memory. That was Peter. Warren had let go and let Peter take control before, during, and after his attacks on Morgan and Lance. Peter spoke for Warren before he could stop him now, too. "Like stepping up to the plate and not getting to swing the bat because a runner got caught stealing."

Warren knew it wasn't right to feel that way. But Peter swelled with the potential. And the shame Warren felt was oddly receding, moment by moment. With every word this Mr. Black said.

"The Circle, Mr. Nichols, will always let you swing the bat."

20

October, 1961—Paris, France

Gérard was disturbingly quiet. He knew something had happened to his *Maman,* Thomas was certain. He sat Gérard down at the kitchen table and put a coloring book and some crayons within his reach, but the boy did not move toward them. Thomas moved about the small room with rapid, decisive movements. For a moment Thomas thought he might collapse from the pain. How was it possible that she would never come home again? Even for someone like him, a killer, a killer who knew the nature of death more than most ever would, this new reality threatened to bring him to his knees.

Gérard's wide eyes followed every move he made.

Finally, Thomas sat down and took Gérard's hands in his own. "My son," he said, "I have something I must do. *Oui?*"

Gérard nodded with uncertainty, watching as his father ran to the bedroom and opened the big roll-top desk, the one he was forbidden to open. *"Papa,"* he began, but went quiet when Thomas picked up the phone. He spoke with someone about an airplane, about something called a "trust." Then he made another call to *Oncle Henri* and said the name Foster. Gérard did not know anyone named Foster, but maybe they were going to go up in an airplane. Gérard had always wanted to fly in an airplane. Would *Maman* go with them?

Finally, his father finished with his phone calls and sat down next to Gérard. "Gérard, *mon fils,* I need you to be a good boy for a little while," he said. "I have to go out. You will stay with Nicholas and Rina next door...while I am away." Thank God for neighbors like Nick and Rina, who would take Gérard without question.

"Where are you going?" asked Gérard. *"Ou est Maman?* I don't want to go *chez Rina.* I want to stay with you." He began to cry.

How could a heart break twice, Thomas wondered. First for his wife, now for his son. "And I want to be with you, *mon fils,* all the time. But that's why I have to go. I have to take care of some business. When that is finished, we will never have to be apart again. *Comprends-tu?"*

Gérard nodded, but he did not understand. Why would Papa not tell him where *Maman* was? Why was he leaving again? Without Gérard?

A picture of the bodies floating in the Seine suddenly returned unbidden. Shaken, he ran to his father and clung to his leg. Something was wrong. Very wrong. He wanted the comfort of his father, the comfort of someone who loved him. He wanted to talk about what he'd seen on the Seine. Maybe not today, but someday. But his father was in a hurry. Then Papa gave him a final kiss on the forehead and Gerard was left to watch as he walked away down the corridor.

• • •

One: Keep Gérard safe. Check.

Two: Secure Gérard's future. Check.

Three: Stay alive.

Thomas was a little sketchy on just how he was supposed to do that. First he needed a weapon. Stupidly, he had gotten rid of his revolver when Gérard became old enough that his curiosity seemed to outweigh the risks. Again, stupid. He ran back into the apartment and took quick stock of the possibilities, grabbing the meat cleaver and shoving it into his belt. It would have to do, and felt oddly familiar. He was about to find out if what they said about riding a bike was really true.

Finally, he went to meet Henri, who had reluctantly agreed to violate curfew, in the alley behind the market. It was a dangerous move, but a necessary one.

He took back streets on his way to elude detection, but also to bypass the spot where Yvonne's body—his beloved wife Yvonne—had died. If he saw even a drop of her spilled blood he didn't know if he'd be able to take another step.

As he rounded the final corner, he smelled the smoke from Henri's lit Galois. He would miss that smell. Henri was a heavy smoker, had been since the age of 10. Heavyset and out of shape, Henri had the disposition of a saint.

It was proof of Henri's trust that he never asked why, never asked Thomas to reveal his secrets, even as they discussed one last time what needed to be done, knowing it might be the last time they'd ever lay eyes on each other again. "Thomas," said Henri, his eyes red and moist. "I am so sorry." Henri enveloped Thomas in a warm embrace.

Thomas pulled away and nodded.

Henri continued, "Celeste found this where...where Yvonne...when she went to put flowers where Yvonne...fell." He placed a glittering strand in Thomas' palm.

Yvonne's anklet. Her wedding present from him. Gold, linked with five small sapphires. He closed his hand around it and wiped the tears with his sleeve. *No. Not yet.* There was no time to grieve now. That would have to wait for another day.

If he survived.

• • •

Mr. Blacks—or *Monsieur Noirs,* in this case—didn't hunt. That was the Circle's mandate. But the man with the cigarette hiding in the recesses of the building across the street cared nothing for protocol anymore. He'd done his time. He deserved this.

He'd watched Spade leave his apartment without the child. That made his job easier. No one wants to kill a child. Not that he would hesitate if he thought for one moment that it would protect the integrity of the Circle...or his own interests.

Most of the hunters used the words "adrenaline" and "exaltation" to describe the way they felt while in pursuit. In this, Monsieur Noir was no different. Once upon a time he'd been Monsieur Couteau and at the top of his game, over three years ago now. An up-close-and-personal kill wasn't necessarily in the cards anymore given his dwindling abilities. Years of French cuisine, wine, and women have clearly caught up with him. Yet there was no hesitation on Noir's part that he was up for the task at hand. After all, he'd had practically a lifetime of practice.

The wall was hard against his back and the street quiet. Curfews tended to have that effect on things, whatever the politics of the day. The Circle, on the other hand, eschewed politics other than its direct link to financial gain.

As Noir followed Thomas Roche, he thought about the promotion he was sure to receive when Mr. Spade was dead. A position on the Council. This was one opportunity he would not pass up. Nor would he forgive Spade's disregard for the

Circle's tenet that one did not kill civilians. Civilian death meant police investigation, which meant potential connection to the Circle. There were simply too many police officers in the world to control all of them.

When Spade turned up the alley behind the market, he thought he might have his chance until he saw the two men embrace. Well, no matter. Pursuit was what made the kill so pleasurable.

21

November, 1959—Atherton, California

Warren moved through the crisp morning air up the steps to his front door. The foyer light was still on. The card in his hand felt like a lit fuse. Mr. Black's offer to join the Circle was going around and around in his head like a, well, a circle. Apparently, "they" had "identified" Warren based on his lineage alone, but had continued to follow him as his reputation for violence and malfeasance manifested and increased.

Peter's reputation.

Apparently, the event that kicked off the Circle's "watch" was the first deal Orville McCoy had made on his family's behest several years earlier.

Their continuing conversation had led to many questions, the answers to which seemed completely unfathomable, yet predictably *right*. And daunting. "We kept tabs on you, of course," Mr. Black had told Warren. "The Associate Dean of Stapleton Academy is a Watcher for our New England chapter—who else better to serve the Circle's highest purpose?" Warren's mind spun with the implications. "You adjusted well to your isolation, built up your strength, using your brain to rise to the forefront. Recruits are not normally considered until later in life, so you should feel honored we broke protocol to deliver this message personally."

Warren, fascinated, took Peter's advice and gave him the floor. He was too tired to fight him. "So, to sum this up," Peter said, "you're saying what it takes to be a member is to be smart, strong, and interested in the pursuit of my soul's purpose."

Mr. Black actually smiled. "I like the way you think, son. Your get-out-of-jail-free card, Mr. Nichols? That was the easy part. Charges dropped, record expunged.... No one will ever admit that you spent time in a cell. That part was free of charge."

"What does that mean?"

"That there are many coveted benefits to your membership in the Circle, as well as a number of conditions."

Figures, Peter told Warren. Then to Black, "How much is it gonna cost me, then, this membership of yours?"

"Cost you?" said Black. "Why, nothing, Mr. Nichols. Not financially, that is. You will be privy to participate in the unlimited funds accessible by all members of the Circle. Fortunes that have been donated by men—and a few women—around the world. It is that financial support that allows us to move freely about the world, and do what we do."

"Donated? Are you saying that you expect *me* to give *you* the millions coming to me from my parents' estate? The one I've been waiting for until today? In return for this one favor?"

"That one favor freed you, Mr. Nichols. For life. I would

think about that before disparaging the offer further." Black paused. "But again, that favor was free of charge," he said. "You must see that any money you surrender to the Circle will pale in comparison to the vast sums that will become instantly available to you. Your current net worth, north of $200 million, will simply be added to the communal pool of all Circle members' monies worldwide. *Tens of billions* of dollars, Mr. Nichols. To use as you wish, whenever you wish. Without limitation or oversight. You see, it's not about taking money *from* you; it's about securing our way of life. By accepting membership, you agree that the Circle's way of life is worth protecting, and more important than your own."

Warren resurfaced, the words resounding in his head. *More important than my own life? How is that possible?* Sure, there was the fact that he'd never have to worry about money again, no company or board full of old suits telling him what to do, or even any investing decisions to make. The freedom to do whatever he wanted. To be whatever Peter needed to be without restraint. But there had to be a catch. There was always a catch.

The catch came in the form of the Circle's rules. First, that no "innocent" people would die. Which begged the question, if you were allowed—encouraged? invited? expected?—to kill without constraint, that kind of meant people died, right? The whole thing was inconceivable. Probably a hoax.

But maybe not, said Peter.

Mr. Black had sipped his drink in silence until Warren came to the obvious conclusion. "You mean, you kill...each other?" he asked. "On purpose? And you get to do it whenever you want?"

Mr. Black smiled again. Warren was beginning to learn that it was a smile that never reached his eyes.

"We prefer the term *hunt,* Mr. Nichols," he said. "Membership gives you the right to hunt and kill—but only fellow members. That rule is sacrosanct, you understand? You will hunt a member, while another member is hunting you, and so forth. It is a way of life. It is not a game. And, once you agree to join, there is no escape. There are no options, and no way out. *Ever.*"

When Warren took a moment to digest this information, Peter moved in. "So, are you saying you'll have to kill me if I say no?"

"Heavens no, Mr. Nichols," Mr. Black chuckled. "First, you're not a member yet, so that would be against the rules. Second, I'm one of many, dozens, in fact, of Mr. Blacks around the world. Mr. Blacks who have all survived to the age of 60 and who are rewarded by no longer hunting, or being hunted."

"So, let me get this straight. You want me to become a killer for the next 42 years?"

"*If* you live that long," Mr. Black said bluntly.

By that time, the Limousine had pulled into the Nichols' estate and Mr. Black had turned to Warren, pressed a card into his hand, and told him, "This is goodbye, Mr. Nichols. For now. You should take as long as you need to make your decision. Do not speak of this to anyone. The Circle will know if you do, and you should know it comes at a risk."

Warren felt the lump in his throat double in diameter. The chauffeur opened the door and Warren got out of the car. Before he could say anything else, it was pulling away and passing through the gates. He looked down at the card, turning it to the light. There, in the corner, in some kind of reflective ink, was nothing more than a symbol: π. Warren looked at it and returned it to his pocket. "What the hell have you gotten me into?" he said out loud.

Everything we've ever wanted, said Peter.

"Maybe everything *you've* ever wanted," Warren corrected. "Let's leave it at that."

• • •

"I'm surprised to see you home so soon."

Vivian. Warren felt unprepared for what was surely to come.

"Well? You don't have anything to say to me, Warren? My mother and I go out for ice cream with you and end up watching you turn into a monster? I have never been so afraid for you—and *of you*—in my entire life."

She said afraid of you, Peter said, seeing a chink in the armor of Warren's feelings for Vivian when Warren immediately went still. "Hey, that's not fair," he said. "You heard what they said about you. You saw Lance pull a knife. What was I supposed to do? Let them kill me? Let them get away with what they said about the person I...care about...more than anyone in the world?"

Vivian's eyes narrowed, but she was not placated. "Warren, I understand that you were upset. That you have some kind of history with those idiots. But nothing is so terrible that it should make you lose it like that. And look where it got you. All the way to jail.

"Hey, how did you get out, anyway? They're in the hospital! Both of them. Was it McCoy?" She looked at him. "Of course it was. He's always been able to get you out of everything, right? How did he do it this time?"

Here we go with the damn questions, Peter moaned.

"They dropped the charges," said Warren. "It was taken care of, let's leave it at that. Like it never happened."

"Like it never happened? I was there, Warren. I saw what happened. How soon do you think I'll be able to forget what I saw? What I saw you do? Is that all it takes to make things go away? Money?"

"That's not fair," Warren said again. "I don't know what happened. The charges were dropped, I don't know why.

Maybe they talked to other witnesses. Maybe Jeff confessed to starting things up with the others. Why does it matter *why* the charges were dropped as long as they were?"

"It matters to me," said Vivian. "That's why. And it doesn't change the facts."

There was a tightening in Warren's chest. "And just what facts are those?"

Here it comes, Peter said. *Watch for it....*

"The fact that you lost control."

See?

"I didn't lose contr—"

"Is this going to happen every time we go out? Every time someone looks at us sideways? Every time I want to kiss you in public?" She took a breath. "Look, I love you for defending my honor like that, but I don't need you to go walking into a knife because some jackass called me a name. You're worth more to me alive than you ever would be dead. And you need to understand that with 100% certainty."

"I do," said Warren. When he was young he'd often thought of "introducing" his two best friends, but Peter always said it would be a mistake. But sometimes he regretted that keeping Peter out of the picture so completely had complicated matters. If Vivian knew—well, now was not the time. He alone had to deal with the consequences of Peter's actions. And this fight with Vivian was one of those consequences. "Trust me, I do," he said, pleading with her with his eyes. For a minute he thought he saw her shoulders move down a notch, but then he ruined it. "Those guys just, well, they always get to me."

"Those guys," said Vivian, "or anybody who says the wrong thing?"

Warren did not answer.

"We all know why you got sent to Maine," Vivian said. "I am under no illusion about who you are and what you've done. I thought it was all in the past. But maybe you need to figure this all out before we go any further. Maybe you should get some help. I need to feel safe around you, or else you and I—this—can't work."

"No. No, no, no, don't say that to me," Warren said, hurt and angry. This was so not where this conversation was supposed to go. "I did all of this for you. I got into this mess fighting for you. Don't tell me that it was all for nothing." He took a deep breath. "That guy you saw, the Warren you're afraid of, I can keep him—I mean, it—under control."

It? chided Peter. *We'll see about that.*

Shut up!

"I want to believe you, Warren. But believing isn't enough. Get the help you need, get your mind right and I will be here waiting. I've waited this long, I can wait a little longer."

Warren saw the sincerity in her eyes, but also the fear and the doubt. His life was crashing down before it ever had a chance to get off the ground. "I don't need help. I need *you*. My parents sent me to more shrinks than you know. They've never done a damn thing for me. Talk, talk, talk, that's all it ever is. Please, Viv. Please don't be like all the rest of them. Don't tell me I need to go somewhere else, to some doctor who doesn't give a damn about me. I don't think I could take it. All I need is right here, right in front of me. Don't be the one that sends me away again, not you. Because if you do...I won't come back."

Good for you, said Peter. *That's setting her straight.*

Warren regretted the words as they left his mouth.

Vivian's eyes said that she desperately wanted to be the answer to Warren's problems. To be his savior, his champion. But her body language said something else entirely, that anything she could do would only be a Band-Aid on a much bigger issue.

See? said Peter. *She's just like everyone else. Just like your parents, she wants someone else to deal with you. Well, I'm still here and I'll never send you away.*

Warren considered Peter's words carefully. While they weren't entirely accurate, there was some truth to them. Peter had stuck around this long, hadn't he? Could it be that he'd never leave? And, if that was true, if Peter was what scared Vivian, the only way to keep her safe was to keep her as far away from him as possible.

"I can't be the help you need, Warren," Vivian said sadly. "I will stand by you while you get it, but that's all I can do. The rest is up to you."

Warren swallowed the lump in his throat. "Well, then, I guess we're done here," he said.

Vivian went pale at the harsh coldness in Warren's voice. Her bottom lip quivered as she held back tears. Yet she did not say a word as he turned to go.

In his room, tears running down his cheeks, Warren reached for the black card in his pocket.

Finally, said Peter. *It's just you and me now, buddy. Time to let loose and let the good times roll.*

• • •

In the morning Stacy Chambers rose early after a sleepless night. She was no eavesdropper, but from the sound of it, things hadn't gone well between Viv and Warren. She was surprised by his arrival home and it was hard not to barge in and demand answers to her questions, but this was between them. Vivian was a mature young woman who could handle things on her own. It's just that there were two warring factions in her: one that wanted to kill Warren herself for behaving so despicably, so...horribly, and one that wanted to protect him the way she had when he was so young and defenseless.

She sighed, shrugged on her robe, and went out to get the morning paper. There was an envelope wedged under it. Oh, no, she thought. Sure enough, inside were the deed for the house, the check he'd written yesterday, and a note.

Stacy and Vivian,

It's clear that you don't feel comfortable around me anymore. I'd be lying if I said I understood, but I respect your feelings enough to know it's best for me not to stay. I want you to keep the house, and the money. It's yours. You've earned it. Vivian suggested I seek help. I'm taking her advice.

Thank you for giving me some sense of family, even if it was for just a little while.

– Warren

Stacy let the papers fall to the ground. She felt as if she'd lost her second child, her son. When Vivian found her and read the note, she shook her head and held her mother's hand. Warren Nichols was gone again.

22

October, 1961—Paris, France

On another day Thomas might have noticed how clean the market was, how empty it felt, their footfalls the only sounds disturbing the unnatural quiet as Henri led Thomas to the back office. When the door closed Thomas took two envelopes from his pocket.

"I need you to mail this envelope for me, Henri. To my attorney. Tomorrow. I know it's heavy. I will give you the postage." Henri waved him off. "And put this other one in your safe. It's for Gérard."

"For Gérard?" said Henri. "What do you mean? Why can't you give it to him yourself?"

"I don't have time to explain, Henri, *je suis desolé*. I'm sorry." He lowered his voice. "But there's a chance I won't make it through the night."

"Through the—*mais, pourquoi?* Are you ill? Do you need to see the doctor? I—"

"No, no, Henri, it's nothing like that. It's just that—I'm sorry. Like I said, I can't explain now. But I'm asking you to keep this letter for him until he's old enough to read it for himself. It explains why I am doing what I must do, along with all the financial resources at my disposal—all that is rightfully his when I'm gone."

"Gone? Where are you going? What are you saying? This is crazy! Are you in danger? If you are, we can help. Tell me how, Thomas."

"Henri, you are my best friend, but I can't put you and Celeste and Charles at risk, and the less you know the better."

"We can go to the police together, then, Thomas. They will have to—"

"*Non, Henri! Promets moi!* Promise me that you will not go to the police. No matter what you hear about me in the next few days. Do you understand? No police!"

Henri sagged, relenting against his better judgment. "What do I tell Celeste? She knows you were coming to the store."

"As little as possible," said Thomas.

Henri looked at Thomas when there was a shuffling in the alley. *Trash?* mouthed Thomas. Henri shook his head. *"Pas aujourd'hui,"* he whispered. "Not today." More shuffling sounds, then a few muffled words. A dog barked.

"I've been here much too long," Thomas whispered. "I have to go. I'll leave through the other door. I won't endanger you any further. Please, take care of these things immediately so they are not seen by anyone else."

Henri stood motionless until Thomas was gone and then shook his head and went to do what he'd been bidden.

• • •

Thomas' strides were long and sure as he ran from the market feeling the pavement beneath his feet, the wind in his face, his heart pumping. Faster and faster. They were close, too close. The Circle was everywhere. That he'd lasted this long was a miracle. Flashes of memories from his tenure as a member came rushing back with every step, as if he'd never left. Memories he hadn't allowed himself to think about in a long time. It was crazy to think that all those years he'd gone along with the idea of forced recruitment, inducting people against their will. Because here he was in a similar position, yet without a safe house, without sanctuary, without funds. He was out-gunned, and would be hunted until the day came when the Circle claimed what was rightfully theirs.

23

April, 1960—Washington, D.C.

Warren requested to be stationed on the east coast upon his initiation, as far from his former family as possible. Other than that, he didn't care where he was. He ended up in D.C. Without the chains of the external world, Peter had become stronger, had more of a say in Warren's actions, even acted as his leader in times of stress and uncertainty.

His continuous presence assured Warren that this was what they were meant to do. Peter was his oldest friend. His only friend. Just like old times. Only now there was no reason to pretend. It was as if two minds had merged into one body. Warren was already seeing himself as a plural version of himself, as "we" and "us" instead of "I" and "me." There were no more conversations, only decisions. No more discussions, only actions. The proof was in the mirror as well, in the musculature he'd been building, sculpted by a steady diet of gym workouts. Fueled by hate.

The Circle was the family they always wanted. The Circle understood them. Embraced them. Never judged them or their thirst for more. When they dove in, they did it with both feet—and planned never to look back.

Their first mark was a guy called Mr. Blunt, apparently named for the way he bludgeoned people to death with a blunt object. The Circle's naming procedures had them feeling like they were in a board game. Yet, late into the night they found themselves considering the options for their first kill and the name they would be assigned. Their own signature. They loved everything about the Circle. The rituals. The rules. The freedom. A never-ending test of skill and prowess and power.

Mr. Blunt lived in a fairly standard townhouse by D.C. standards where he spent his evenings. Despite regular visits to his many mistresses, he unfailingly returned home. It was where he let his guard down just enough to catch up on his much needed rest. Every member, from the most skilled to the most bumbling neophyte, needed sleep. And it was in Mr. Blunt's home, where they decided they would strike.

Late in the evening, they were watching Blunt's townhouse from the rooftop across the street. They waited and waited, excitement and apprehension nipping at each other's heels within their mind. An hour passed. Then another. Finally, sometime after midnight, Mr. Blunt returned home, stumbling only slightly from drink when he went to insert his key in the door.

Pathetic, right? Let your guard down like that and you deserve to be offed.

Blunt turned on the lights and moved from the front room to the back and then back again. From his wet hair and robe, visible through binoculars, he'd apparently showered. Again revealing his obvious lack of skill. Coupled with a big ego, not taking the time to set your traps against intruders was what would take him down. When the last light went out, it was as if the world had shut down to join them in wait.

They waited another hour until they could wait no longer. It was after 2 AM, but other than recognizing the need for careful movement, the effects of the lovely spring night went unnoticed. Suddenly, Warren resurfaced. Blood was pumping through his body and his hands were shaking.

I can't do this, he told Peter. *This is a mistake.*

A mistake? scorned Peter. *You're crazy. This is the best we've ever felt. What you feel is nothing but the rush, like jumping out of an airplane before the parachute opens.*

Warren took a breath. Peter was right. Fear was only residue from his past and had no business in their life anymore.

They reached the building. Warren put his hands on the wall in front of him and willed them to still, for his pulse to slow to normal. With Peter at the helm, Warren felt like both the captain and the passenger in his own mind. A conscious, conscientious, yet willing, observer to his own deeds.

They eased the window open and silently entered the lower room. From their days of surveillance, they knew there was no over-the-top security system. Any equipment like that would have been easily visible given the bulky nature of the technology of the day. Thus, they only had to be mindful of the trip wire set up a few feet away from the window, which they easily avoided without a sound or disturbance. They made their way through the living room and to the stairs. They knew to avoid the fourth step for another trip wire before continuing to the second level, but that was as much detail, as far as they'd been able to see from their perch across the street. Fortunately, the carpeted stairs absorbed their footfalls.

The second floor had been renovated at some point and was now an open kitchen with a huge center island, matching appliances, a sitting area, and a long bar along one wall. It was the third floor, uncharted territory, where Blunt slept. They had done their homework to research the most recent blueprints of the building they could find, but Blunt was not without resources and aside from the living space downstairs, things were not where the plans had shown. Carefully they ascended the steps from the second to the third floor, surprised at the lack of booby traps set. For a moment, they stopped. *What if we've tripped a silent alarm?* Warren said.

No way, said Peter. *You think he'd engage a security company when the Circle is involved?*

Good point, said Warren, and took the last two steps in one. They were struck in the shoulder with something hard as they rounded the landing. Pain shot down through their arm as they tumbled backwards down the stairs, making contact with each one with a painful thud until they came to a stop on the second floor landing.

They struggled to the surface to see Blunt already halfway down the stairs swinging a heavy object. *Get up,* screamed Peter. *If we don't, we're dead!*

They regained their footing just as Blunt swung at their head, managing to deflect the blow, absorbing some of its force with their hands. Still it hurt like hell and they were still dizzy from the fall. But Blunt was also off balance from the swing. This was their chance.

They struck Blunt with an open palm to the throat causing him to gasp and choke. Then in the kneecap with what had turned out to be Blunt's instrument of destruction, a two-inch thick section of pipe, which had fallen just within their reach. Blunt fell to the floor gasping. Before he had a chance to catch his breath, they raised the pipe and struck him again on the other knee and then the right shoulder blade.

Blunt grimaced and reared back from the blows. He was weakening.

It's time, Peter said. *Finish him off.*

Warren nodded. They wrapped their right arm around Blunt's left, locking it in place, then clasped their left hand around Blunt's trachea and squeezed. Blunt feigned with his right arm to land a blow, but it was a lame attempt and easily parried.

Squeeze harder, said Peter. Then, as though he couldn't bear to be on the sidelines, *Let me do it!*

Warren relented and looked on as Peter released Blunt's other arm and encircled his throat with both hands. Blunt was gasping for air, spitting and drooling. This is what it feels like, thought Warren with wonder, as the veins and muscles in Blunt's neck tensed beneath his hands. *This is what it feels like to let go.*

Peter squeezed. Warren squeezed. Kept squeezing. Harder and harder, until all color and life had been drained from Blunt's body.

Peter released his grip and Blunt dropped to the floor with a satisfying *thud*. Warren looked at his watch. Six minutes and 19 seconds to kill a man with our bare hands. Not bad.

"You did it," Warren said, back in control of his hands, which were still shaking from the adrenaline. "I can't believe you did it."

We did it, said Peter. *You and me. Together.*

24

October, 1961 – Paris, France

From his vantage point in the alley Monsieur Noir could barely see the back door to the marketplace. He knew his target was inside and thus had precious few moments to get into position before the opportunity slipped away. Of course if the moment wasn't perfect he would abort. There were other days, other venues. He could always go back to the apartment building and ambush him there. Not the preferred option, though, not with the child.

At Noir's age he should have come up with a better plan, too, he realized. His worsening arthritic limbs had given him reason to pause, embarrassingly so, and only with the aid of a couple of accommodating trash cans had he been able to select his perch atop a garbage dumpster in the dark corner of the alley. The younger and more agile Noir would have had no trouble scaling the pipes that framed the building.

His pistol was securely tucked into his waistband. He attributed his enviable marksmanship to his time serving in the second World War. He reminisced about his experience there for a quick moment. Friends and neighbors' unable, then forced, to choose sides. Of course, why anyone would choose to side with the Nazis was despicable. But his country, neutral at first, then torn, had been thrust into the savages of the war with no clear direction.

For him it was general infantry, never a hesitation. The German forces under Hitler's command needed to be stopped. They threatened the world on so many fronts, not the least of which were the reports of mass genocide. His own marksmanship had quickly earned him respect and honor, and a valuable place in the Belgian army.

Noir struggled to keep his balance as he reached the second floor; holding onto a large chimney pipe. The garbage truck at the front of the alley would have been a far better option—if only it had stayed put. When its next pickup was down the alley, however, he'd had to find a way to scale the building or be discovered. Clinging to the pipe with both hands he swung his legs up to the next window sill and hoisted himself up to a squatting position. He stopped there, confident that he was now invisible to the trash compactor's headlights.

Two men got out of the truck chatting. "*Merde.* It's not right, making runs during curfew. This lousy job...."

"Yeah. You'd think with a national emergency and all we'd at least get some day shifts."

In another moment they'd moved to the very dumpster on which Noir had just been standing. One on either end they turned the dumpster 180 degrees to lift it and dump its contents into the truck.

This was his chance. When the driver activated the loud machinery and the cacophony filled the alley, Noir climbed another two stories higher. *Only one more before the roof. Don't think about. Just do it!* The dumpster landed back on the concrete with a screech of metal. The men were still bemoaning their fate loudly over the truck's machinations. All the cover Noir needed. Apparently, the thrill of the hunt still burned within, for his arms did as they were told and hoisted him up and over.

Other than the dog behind the top floor window his movements were completely undetected. He froze. Dogs bark; it's what they do. But this one simply cocked its head and peered out of one eye for a moment, then went back to sleep. Releasing a breath, Noir moved on into position.

He maneuvered across the rooftop until he was directly above the entryway for the market. He was prepared to wait all night, and was pleasantly surprised when he didn't have to wait long. The door below swung open and a man, a man who had to be Spade, raced across the street. Now that's a shot I can make, he thought. Noir reached for the pistol and took aim. He took a deep breath followed by a slow exhale. Then he pulled the trigger.

25

November, 1963—Dallas, Texas

It had been three years since the Circle's members unanimously bestowed the name Mr. Vice, short for Vice-Grip, on Warren Nichols. For Peter it was the final nail in the coffin of his old life as Warren's "friend," a sign that he was in charge. Being Mr. Vice emboldened him to shed himself of Warren completely. There was no "we" anymore. No "us." Just the powerful singular that came with being a man, a hunter, and a millionaire. *Free at last.* In those three years Mr. Vice had opened dozens of blue envelopes. But the one he opened in September of 1963 would come to define him more than any other. Staring back at him was none other than the infamous Mr. Crash.

Just looking at the picture of the attractive middle-aged man before him, Mr. Vice knew this one would take time and patience. More than the others. The Circle was not without its sense of humor. Assigning a target as difficult as Mr. Crash to a young, though formidable, member was clearly intended to mollify him after his years of mowing down members like bowling pins. Mr. Vice sensed he owed them a debt of gratitude. Slowing down was exactly what he needed to do if he wanted to live as long as he planned.

Mr. Crash had become a legend in his own right because he did not hide in the shadows. Quite the opposite: a stunning, very public life. All in plain sight. Mr. Crash may have been his name in the Circle, but he was a public servant, an elected official. Many Circle members were considered pinnacles of success by society's standards given their supposed financial prowess, though only in rare instances was it ever obvious where the funds came from. But this was a stroke of brilliance. With one election win over a decade prior, Mr. Crash had become front page news, a member of Congress, with a career that appeared to have no limits. Not to mention almost round the clock monitoring from law enforcement and paparazzi alike. He was almost untouchable.

Almost.

Every man had a weakness. A soft spot. A vulnerability. And Mr. Vice would find it, as he always had before.

As its name implied, the Circle's "safehouse" was a place of safety from fellow hunters. On the other hand, one could tend to forget one was surrounded by hunters for whom you might be prey when one was drinking the finest bourbon, smoking the finest Ramón Allones cigars, and experiencing the feel of a beautiful young woman's bottom on your knee. And forgetting, even for a minute, could lead to loose lips.

Which was how Mr. Vice had stumbled across Mr. Crash's "secret" tunnel built beneath the streets to travel from the safehouse to his home over a block away. Convenient—for Crash and his mistresses alike. The high-class hookers the Circle employed survived by knowing their place. Being where they were supposed to be when they were supposed to be there and speaking only when spoken to. It was just happenstance that one such woman had broken her stiletto heel on her way into the secret passage as Mr. Vice had rounded the corner to get to the men's room. Both of them had frozen, looking at each other, him with a glint in his eye, her with panic. Then she'd snatched up her heel and hightailed it through the doorway. Before Mr. Vice could take even a step, the door had slid closed and she was gone.

It was a coup to have the information. But how do you kill a man that everyone is watching?

• • •

Months of planning. Over a million dollars in various bribes. Bumps in the road along the way. Lots of them. Spend months planning one job, you have to do it around the fact that you're being hunted as well. In the months of planning for Mr. Crash, he'd killed two members that were tasked with hunting him down. He was annoyed by the inconvenient detour in his quest, but didn't forget to savor the way each of them gasped for air under his grip.

The day was fast approaching. Mr. Vice's relationship with Crash's secretary had paid off in spades. He always knew when Crash was headed out of town. In this case, however, his trip from D.C. to Dallas would be the last for quite a while. Vice had to follow or risk losing his target to another chapter.

His plan, executed perfectly, would be studied by Circle members for generations to come for its genius. Securing the locations of his target, for example, through his public itineraries and...other means. His plant inside the politician's close circle had the means to access even Crash's more "private" trips. This time he'd paid his plant, a close advisor to Crash, to make last-minute changes to his plan due to "security concerns."

Well-placed bribes ensured Mr. Crash's vehicle was a Lincoln Continental Limousine with a convertible top. Mr. Crash's motorcade route was confirmed. Mr. Vice had taken his time deciding the best spot for the take down, the 6th floor of a building that would provide him the best shot with his rifle. It was a tight window of time, but he would have 30 to 40 seconds of an unobscured line of sight. More than enough time to fire a miracle shot.

• • •

Just before 12:30 the motorcade turned the corner of Dealey Plaza. Mr. Vice took aim through the scope of his rifle. He was sweating, tiny beads just over his eyebrows. He hated the sensation, hated that he'd let the moment get to him, all because of the thousands of people lining the streets. He tried not to think of Mr. Spade, and the consequences if he were to miss, as he wiped his brow with the sleeve of his shirt.

Then, there he was. Mr. Crash. Waving at people with that stupid grin on his face. Vice took one more careful look through the scope and waited for the crosshairs to settle just right.

There was a stillness. The gravity of what he was doing slowed reality down to a crawl. Regardless of the ramifications, Circle business trumped all else. One hunter was the same as another. Ripe for the kill. He pulled the trigger. Not once, not twice, but three times in rapid succession, and it was done.

Pandemonium ensued. Tens of thousands of people flooded the streets as the vehicle carrying Mr. Crash—President John. F. Kennedy—raced up Stemmons Freeway, assumingly toward Parkland Memorial Hospital. Mr. Vice left his post, leaving everything behind, rifle and all. He didn't need it; he wasn't going to use it again. The book depository employee entered just as Vice was going out the door. They said nothing to each other. Watchers came from all elements of society, but this one had the distinct good fortune of being a part of history the world would never forget. He offered a silent nod that could have been congratulations, or appreciation, or even boredom. Vice would never know. He didn't care.

He had more important things to think about. Like blending into the chaos, mimicking the crowds of shocked citizens who'd witnessed the assassination of the President of the United States. It was the Watcher's problem now. That's what they were compensated to do, and did so well. The scene was in capable hands.

A smile crept across Mr. Vice's face as he realized the importance of this kill. Yes, his target was dead and yes, he got a month-long furlough. But it was bigger than that. It stated, in no uncertain terms, that the level of the stakes made no difference. The Circle endures. The Circle always wins.

There were toasts made in Mr. Vice's honor in every Circle safehouse from Dallas to Denmark. *The sonofabitch did it. Unbelievable.* With three pulls of a trigger he became an instant legend. The assassination of President John F. Kennedy and a country in mourning was in all the headlines, but for the members of the Circle, the death of Mr. Crash only meant that another major player was off their ever-evolving chessboard.

October, 1961—Paris, France

Pain. Instant. Unforgiving.

Thomas reached for his left shoulder and his hand returned covered in blood. He stumbled forward, unsuccessfully attempting to maintain his footing, and crashing down to the street, his body scraping along the pavement as he fell.

He tried to trace the trajectory of the bullet but when he looked to the rooftops he saw nothing. No time to look for the shooter. He had to get to cover. Over there. Behind the steps. Then another troubling thought. Had Henri followed him outside? Was he safe?

Thomas staggered to his feet to make a beeline for a set of concrete stairs leading up to an apartment building just before another bullet tore through his right thigh. He collapsed in a heap. The pain was intense and his fight-or-flight instincts were at war with each other. He couldn't fight what he couldn't see. It had to be coming from the roof above the market. How the hell had they found him so fast—in mere hours? Breathing heavily, shoulders slumped, he lay on the ground. So stupid, he thought. As if the Circle weren't everywhere.

He attempted to put weight on his right leg but he could barely hold himself up for a few seconds before the pain receptors took over and he collapsed again. He crawled for cover. Surely the neighbors would be calling the police soon. But then another painful reminder surfaced. Curfew. The riots were still active in other parts of the city. Gunshots had become so commonplace that the police would likely pay them no more mind than any of the other sounds in the city. Not that the police were to be trusted either.

Thomas hadn't quite made it to cover and was attempting to curl his right foot into his body when a third shot sounded. Again he looked to the rooftops. Still nothing. His assailant was as invisible in the night sky as a winged bat. And here he was trapped behind a set of stairs with no weapon. He peered his head around trying to get even the slightest view of a figure on a roof, but spotted only chimneys. Then his body went into shock. He closed his eyes.

• • •

Thomas regained consciousness with a start. He had no idea how long he'd been out. Seconds? Minutes? He could barely move. He lifted an arm slowly to see if he could, fully expecting it to be shot off. But no shots came. Maybe he could flee from his current position, make it somewhere less out in the open. But where would he go? He looked down. The sidewalk was covered in blood. His blood. The same way Yvonne's blood had spilled what felt like a lifetime ago. So ironic. From his position in the street he could actually see where she had passed, maybe 50 meters away. He was trapped. He knew that. He'd never make it off this street corner alive. His hunter wouldn't allow it. It was over. He had failed. Yet in failure he had found success. The lawyer and Henri would take care of Gérard. His son's future was secure.

Anyone can crawl 50 meters. Do it. His left leg still functioned and his right arm as well. Surely he could make it 50 damn meters. Wherever his assassin was hiding, he had apparently cleared out from his first position and was seeking, or had sought, a more suitable one. If it were he, Thomas would choose up close and personal when the final shot was delivered. Make absolutely certain that his target was gone.

Dragging and crawling, he made it halfway there before he heard footsteps behind him. Slow. Measured. His would-be killer. Who else would remain so unphased by the sight of a man bleeding to death and crawling across the sidewalk?

"*Monsieur* Spade, I presume," the man said.

Thomas didn't waste energy turning around. *Twenty meters to go.*

"*Monsieur* Spade, you have been a bad boy," said the voice. "You broke the rules. People who break the rules must be punished."

Fifteen meters. Then Thomas remembered the cleaver still in his belt and stopped. With his good arm he rolled himself over. The face he saw before him was not what he was expecting. It was old and sagging. Not a face eligible for the hunt. And yet, here he was. As he stared up at his attacker, Thomas inched back farther and farther. His left arm lay useless in his lap and his right leg dragged on. He stopped again, shifting his torso to his right side with his right arm lodged slightly behind him.

He felt the grip of the cleaver with his fingers, and waited. He would have only one shot and it would have to be perfect.

"*Monsieur* Spade. You didn't think you could escape the Circle, did you?" the man said, shaking his head sadly, as if he felt badly for Thomas' lapse in judgment.

"No, of course not," Thomas said, hoping to buy himself some time. "It was an accident. You must understand. How could I—I didn't know they were going to be on that plane. I had no idea. Otherwise I would never have—" His confession was genuine. And saying the words out loud, even in those circumstances, after so long, felt cathartic. But would it be enough for the Circle's absolution?

"This is none of my concern," the man with the gun said dispassionately. "There are rules, and you were sloppy."

He was right, of course. For years Thomas had been running for his life, but had never really confronted his responsibility for the three civilian deaths. Had he been more prepared he wouldn't have been so careless. It wouldn't have cost the lives of innocent men. And he wouldn't be lying on the ground in the middle of Paris, staring down the barrel of the gun that would take his life.

Thomas fought the pain in his shoulder and raised his left hand to the old man, pleading his case one more time for Gérard's sake. "Please. Talk to them. I'll do anything."

"You know just as well as I that nothing can be done," the man said. "No one breaks the rules without consequence. The Circle does not allow it." He cocked his pistol and took aim. "You should consider yourself lucky we don't wish to take the boy as well."

Thomas couldn't bear the thought that his impetuous mistake could cause the death of his own son. He gripped the cleaver tighter in his fingers. "At least tell me your name," he said, distracting himself from the thought. "Let me know the name of the man that bested me." His killer smiled a crooked smile and lowered his weapon ever so slightly. "Couteau," he said, "at your service. I was known as *Monsieur Couteau*."

"Ah," said Thomas, as if he cared. "Mr. Knife. So...why the gun, then? Not so good with a knife anymore, eh, old man?"

The smiling mask slipped from Monsieur Couteau's smile.

Thomas saw his chance. He withdrew and sent the cleaver flying the short distance into Couteau's chest. Couteau's gun went off, the bullet grazing Thomas' ear and lodging into the concrete behind him. As Couteau went down he pulled the trigger again. This time the bullet found its way to the pavement at Thomas' feet and Couteau went down.

Thomas felt an inappropriate laugh bubbling to the surface. This man, Couteau, one of the oldest hunters, had fumbled due to a bruised ego and now his prey would live to see another day.

Thomas staggered to his feet and held his left arm with his right against his chest. He looked down at the man at his feet, covered with blood, eyes caught in a moment of surprise. Thomas leaned over to separate the man from the gun as he thought about his new life with Gérard. How he would protect his son the way a good father should.

It was as he bent down that he saw the twitch in Couteau's finger. Then felt the searing heat of the next bullet. But only for a split second. Because when the bullet tore through the back of his skull, Thomas Roche was no more.

Part II

October, 1974—Paris, France

At the time Gérard nearly strangled Foster Dad #6 with a vacuum cleaner cord, he was still considered a juvenile. While in "detention," a.k.a. jail for younger delinquents, he had lots of time to think. Years of psychoanalysis focusing on his "dire circumstances" as a youth—left with neighbors after the death of his mother and abandoned by his father or his later, "distressingly violent" inclinations since—had offered no particular enlightenment from anyone's perspective. His only goal while in detention was to bide his time until his release on his 18th birthday, and enhance his unique skill set while he was there.

Not that he had anywhere else to go. Even Celeste and Henri were long gone from his life. They'd tried to gain custody, sure, but the endless bureaucratic process had won out in the end, and after years in foster care, Gerard had given up all efforts to stay connected. He hadn't seen them in forever, but who needed them anyway?

As early as age seven he was showing signs of sociopathic behavior. Foster Mother #2 had caught him with his hands wrapped tightly around a parakeet. Fell out of the cage, he told her. He was just putting it back. She knew better. He was gone by week's end.

At 10 he drowned a cat. Besides clawing up his coveted Beatles poster, the cat's name pissed him off. Pierre, or Pepe, or something like that. He'd sliced it up the middle and left it in the woods for the birds and animals to dispose of. His mistake was keeping the collar. Foster Mother #4 found it hidden in a drawer putting away laundry, the snoop.

In the next "home," there were no pets. The dogs next door never stopped barking, though, and had to be dealt with. Interesting to study how effortlessly animals devour their own. That was Foster Family #5.

Gerard spent his time alone reliving those moments. It served Foster Dad #6 right for looking through Gerard's notebooks like that. Right on the front they said, "PRIVET." What did he think would happen once he knew what was going on inside Gerard's head—and what Gerard was doing when no one was looking. The state foolishly felt it could rehabilitate him. The state obviously didn't know what he had become.

They never would.

The lawyer showed up on his 18th birthday, just before he was about to be discharged. Out of the blue. Twenty months of his life wasted in that place and all of a sudden some lawyer guy wanted to talk.

"Tell him to get lost," he told the guard.

"Shut up," said the guard, and shoved him into one of

the stifling rooms where the outside world met the inside one. Once the lawyer saw Gerard wasn't listening, he pushed an envelope into his hands, then sat back and waited. When Gerard refused to look at it, hearing only "your father" and "many years ago," the lawyer sighed, called for the guard, and left before Gérard could tell him to stick it up his ass.

When he was alone, though, curiosity got the better of him. But if this was from his father, why hadn't he seen it before? Why had he been made to wait?

The envelope was yellowed and the glue cracked. The handwriting barely legible and unrecognizable. He opened it and unfolded several thin sheets of paper.

No money. Big shocker there.

Why bother reading on? And yet....

Gerard thought about tossing the pages in the trash, but again he couldn't. The pull was too strong. Opening them, the first words he saw other than his own name, spelled with an accent in the French way, were *killed* and *hunted.* That's when he decided he'd start at the beginning.

As he read, he wasn't sure if he should be fascinated or insulted that someone should think him so dull-witted that he'd believe the bullshit on the page. Because apparently, if it were anything but BS, his father was not only alive, but a multi-millionaire. A member of an elite organization known as the Circle. A hunter and killer of men. Gerard's heart beat faster and faster. *His* father? That mild-mannered American who'd become a memory so vague as to be nearly unreal? A man who had "accidentally killed" three innocent men—musicians—back in '59 and had been on the run ever since?

Gerard read on and on, nausea deep in his belly. He was supposed to believe that his life was in danger and this...this killer, his father, had been fighting to keep Gérard alive all these years? For a brief moment hope bloomed that his father was coming to get Gerard, to bring him back into the fold.

That hope died at the next sentence Gerard read. *If you are reading this letter, you will know that the Circle has been successful in tracking me down and killing me. I am sorry, my son. I am sorry I could never be a true father to you. I am sorry...for everything. But, please, if you have even a sliver of belief that what I am telling you is true, find Celeste and Henri from the old corner store in Paris. Find them. They have something to give you. It is all there is left of the life I left behind after your mother died. It will never be enough, but it is all I have to offer.*

Gerard shoved the letter back in its envelope and stashed it in his duffel bag. Truth or lies, it was time for a trip to gay Paris.

28

June, 1975 — Washington, D.C.

By his own count, Mr. Vice had killed 51 people. Mostly prey, with an occasional unfortunate hunter in the mix. He didn't keep trophies like some of the men in his chapter. Like Mr. Rings who took--what else?--rings from the fingers of his vanquished foes. Vice found that quiet reservation played more to his mystique than that kind of obvious redundancy or boisterous braggadocio. Mr. Heel, for example. Named for crushing his first victim to death with the heel of his boot, if you could believe it. Where was the mystique in that? The creativity? Mr. Heel had made an art form of forcing all within earshot to relive the experience with him, too, as if it were something to celebrate. Vice played along, as did the others—at least, Vice *thought* they were just playing along—but the conversation in his head stood in stark contrast.

Vice did relish the frequent opportunity to size up his fellow members. To learn how to exploit Mr. Heel or Mr. Ring, for example, should he ever find himself pitted against one of them. Cordiality was key in the safe house. Most members eventually let their guards down, lulled by the companionship of the like-minded. Not Vice. Which is why he'd seen almost an entire changeover to the D.C. chapter since his arrival.

Vice was enjoying his time off. He had nine days remaining on a holiday after the successful termination of Mr. Sleep. Why Sleep had earned that name Vice wasn't sure. It was interesting that no one had ever mentioned it, and annoying, given his love of details, but in the end dead was dead.

Vice had taken to keeping a journal of his kills, perfecting his coded entries over time. 675 Sleep, 1, 1, 3, 2, 22. Shorthand for the fact that in June of 1975 he'd killed Mr. Sleep, his target (1), via strangulation (1), at a neutral location (3), the rank of Mr. Sleep's effort in their fight (2), 22 days after receiving his blue envelope.

On this day, Vice was leafing through his Book of Kills as he sat on a bench overlooking the Reflecting Pool by the Lincoln Memorial. The humidity wasn't nearly at its mid-summer peak, so while it was hot, it hadn't reached the impossible-to-breathe stage yet. Bold pigeons used to generous tourists ventured near looking for crumbs. Vice shooed them away with his foot. Couples, families, tour groups milling about. Typical day in the nation's capital.

He liked to jump around the book, but he always started with the first page. The same smile always crossed his lips when he turned to the page of his Blunt kill, but he didn't need to read it to remember it. *1259, Blunt, 1, 1, 3, 5, 27.* The carpet under his feet. Blunt's breath as he grappled for a molecule of oxygen.

He flipped forward several pages. *461, Spike, 2, 2, 1, 6, 0*.* Mr. Spike was not one of his targets, but Vice's hunter (2). Vice did not strangle, but stabbed him (2). Vice had been in his own home (1). Spike, the aggressor, had put up one hell of a fight (6) and finally, (0) because Vice hadn't known his attacker's identity. And don't forget the *, a reminder that he himself had been unnecessarily "sloppy and careless." Always good to keep notes for improvement.

Forward a few more pages to his Crash killing: *1163, Crash, 1, 3, 3, 0, 82.* Of course, Mr. Crash was his target (1), killed at a neutral location (3), shot (3) and put up no fight (0). Eighty-two days from assignment to assassination, Vice's planning had been his longest and most meticulous. He looked up at Lincoln's statue. What were the chances the Circle had killed this president, or any president, for that matter. An interesting, if meaningless idea. A loud voice behind him brought him to his feet, his instincts kicking in. He was on furlough, his reason told him, but he had survived this long by remaining vigilant. The voice belonged to a woman. It sounded as if she were yelling, "Moron, moron." Could that be right?

His fist curled as the woman came closer.

That's when he saw her face, and knew things were about to get complicated.

"Warren," she was saying over and over again. "Warren, is that really you?"

29

1974—Paris, France

Gérard's first stop was a long overdue visit to his old friend Officer Martin, who had risen to the rank of Lieutenant. Martin was currently tied to a chair in his own living room after a pathetically short interrogation during which he'd copped to the reality of the Circle. And to Gérard's true identity. Funny how seeing this man brought back some vague memories from a time Gérard had eliminated from his conscious mind.

Gérard looked at the weak old man, savoring each bead of sweat cascading down his sagging, bloody face. Each muffled grunt coming through the rag and duct tape. Each twist of his wrists as he struggled to free himself from the ropes that bound him to the chair when Gérard attached the set of jumper cables to the car battery. The sight of a single drop of snot mixed with blood trickling out of his captive's nose both repelled and attracted him. The man was nothing but a pussy.

Gérard swore he could hear Martin's heart beating faster and faster; could feel Martin's breath shortening; could sense every neuron in Martin's brain firing at once, thinking, scheming how to escape the inevitable torture, praying for help to come bursting through the door like some movie.

He crouched down in front of Lieutenant Martin and stared into his eyes. At the coldness of the empty stare boring a hole into his soul, Martin groaned. Without a word, Gérard clasped each end of the jumper cables to Martin's right big toe. Then the left.

Martin gyrated and convulsed for only a half a minute, but to Gérard, looking on with wicked delight, it seemed like hours, as if the scene were playing out in slow motion. This was the man who'd stolen his father from him. The man who'd stolen his life. When Gérard removed the cables Martin had just enough breath to catch. Gérard watched him, interested, curious. He took a long, considered sip from the glass of wine that remained on the table, still set for the dinner Martin had prepared for himself. Gérard knew Martin would not last long, so this next move would be his last.

He stepped behind Martin's chair, tipped it backwards onto its rear legs, and dragged it into the bathroom. He turned it around and tipped the chair forward so Martin's head was face down in his bathtub, smeared against the porcelain. Then he plugged the drain and turned on the water.

Martin's lack of physical freedom made movement of any kind difficult. As the water filled the tub, his only hope, impossible as it was, was to keep his nose above water. Soon, his face was submerged below the surface. Martin took a last desperate breath. Gérard held his own. In another moment a few bubbles were the only sign of ongoing life.

Gérard's erection was immediate, just like the ones he had when he was younger, but now attached to something real, concrete, and meaningful. The repressed feelings he'd had for the past 13 years burst through with a renewed sense of knowing.

Get a grip, he told himself. It's information you need right now, not sexual release. He lifted Lieutenant Martin, sputtering and red-eyed, out of the water and removed his gag. Water and air spewed from his lungs as he attempted to suck in mouthfuls of oxygen.

Gérard sat on the edge of the tub. He took Martin's head by the hair and tilted it back. *"Alors...le Cercle,"* he said. "I want to hear everything. *Maintenant."*

Martin defiantly shook his head.

Back into the water he went. Bored with the game, Gérard's hand went to his pants. Martin continued to struggle for the short time it took for Gérard to climax. Who knew watching someone die by your own hand would be so gratifying.

• • •

Eventually, inevitably, Martin had given Gérard what he needed. Fear of recrimination from *le Cercle* couldn't quite compare to the fear of what Gérard promised to do to his family if he did not get the answers he sought.

Pathetic, the love for family some people had. Weakened the ability to do what needed to be done. Which is what made Gérard so invincible. He had no one, cared for no one, was beholden to no one. The mere mention of Martin's daughter and grandson was all it took.

The man who killed his father, *Monsieur Noir*, was already dead, after suffering a meat cleaver to the chest in a battle with Gérard's father. Gérard felt an odd sense of pride. His father had not gone quietly into the night. He'd fought back and killed his aggressor. Martin was also kind enough to reveal his own status as an *"observateur"*—or a "watcher"—and *le Cercle*'s safehouse address in Paris before his last plunge into the bathtub water where his lifeless body became a husk. Nothing but an empty shell. Fascinating how quickly a life could be snuffed out.

Gérard felt his appetite had been whetted for something he'd unwittingly been waiting for his whole life. The scene on the Seine when he watched all those people die. That's when it started. Or was it after the death of his mother? He shrugged. Regardless, he'd been baptized in a river of death to a symphony of screams that had become both his solace and his nemesis. Neither of which he could, or would, live without.

• • •

Gérard used Lieutenant Martin's bath towel to dry his face and hands. He looked down at the red cloudy water that enveloped Martin's body in the tub below. For the first time, his purpose and his path were clear. The French had stolen his mother and the Circle had taken his father, and he would not rest until he had rectified the travesties inflicted on him. The list was lengthy, but with Martin in a puddle of bloody water at his feet, he was off to a good start. He may not be able to wreak vengeance on the French, but the Circle? They would pay. What they held dearest—their rules, their order, their sacred values—all were destined for a fall.

But first a visit to Aunt Celeste and Uncle Henri to see what dear old Dad had to say.

June, 1975 — Washington, D.C.

Like being forced into a time machine, Warren emerged from the shadow of Mr. Vice as he took in the vision of his first — his only — love.

Warren Nichols was barely a man when he'd left California. Now in his mid-30s, he was a passenger, a witness, to his own life. A life he never thought possible, or even plausible. He was aware of Mr. Vice's activities through the years, of course, but was incapable of stopping him. He was much too powerful.

God, she was beautiful. He'd always loved her curls and felt slightly cheated by her straightened hair. But her eyes were the same, just as what was behind them. The softness, the compassion. Was that a tear in her eye...or just a reflection from the water at their feet? She was wearing light blue medical scrubs and a white coat. Her badge had flipped around, so...doctor or nurse? Could her wish to be a doctor have come true? He knew he was staring, but it was all he could do. They looked at each other. Finally, he made the first overture. "Vivian? Is it really you? I—"

"You sonofabitch!" she said at the same time.

Warren was shaken by how much it hurt him to hear her say that. Sure, he deserved it. But prepared for it? He'd been cultivating veins of ice for a long time. Having any kind of a true emotional response felt unfamiliar. Uncomfortable. Unacceptable. "Vivian. I—"

"Sixteen years," Vivian said, keeping her distance. "No contact. No calls. No letters. Nothing. We thought you were dead, Warren. *Dead.* Do you hear me? How could you do that to us?"

"You don't understand, Vivian," Warren said coolly. "But it would not have been fair—to either of us."

"Really?" said Vivian, just as coolly. "And you decided that for the both of us? And exactly what gave you that right?"

The right? What, you mean the right to stay alive? The right to be who I really am? The right to get away before it was too late?

The voice inside, Peter's voice, was strong and angry, as always. Vivian wasn't wrong, but how did that even matter anymore? Water under the bridge. Besides, if Vivian was afraid of Warren back in California, it was absurd to think about how she'd feel knowing that hunting and killing was all he did. What he lived for.

"You're right, I'm sorry," he managed to say smoothly. He'd learned charm over the years, too, and it was paying off. There was nothing more disarming than the phrase *You're right,* even if you didn't mean it.

"Sorry?" Vivian looked at him and shook her head.

"You look great," he said. This time, he did mean it.

Vivian looked unconvinced. Not surprising since she'd known him better than anyone else in the world.

Then. Not now. She doesn't know you anymore.

Yes, she does. Look at her. She's always been able to see into my very soul. Even now.

You mean the soul of Warren Nichols? That soul died eons ago.

She was waiting for him to say something. He could tell she was about to leave. He, Warren, didn't want her to. Not that there was a chance in hell she might still be able to see the man he used to be. To see that he still had enough of a soul to be the man she'd known in a whole other lifetime.

"Look," he started, and then suddenly, she was in his arms.

"I hate you," she said, crying, her fists pummeling his chest. "You hear me? I hate you."

Mr. Vice felt his spine tighten, repelled by the intimacy, the unexpected, inconceivable connection.

Warren felt his spine melt in her arms.

Her hair still smelled like lavender. He breathed it in, with each inspiration dispelling the voice in his head that told him he was crazy. That the Circle owned him. That he was a dead man. But he was helpless to resist. Vivian's magnetism was too great. Her power over him, too strong. His will, too weak.

"So you're a doctor now?" he said, holding her hands still.

She nodded without backing away. "George Washington University Hospital. They were the only ones that offered me a chance. You know, what with my—" She didn't need to state the obvious. "So I took it. I haven't looked back."

"And how is Miss Stacy these days? Is she out here with you?"

Vivian nodded again. "We used some of the money you gave us to buy a place. In Maryland. Not too far. A little land.

Quiet...."

She wiped the tears from her eyes, brushed a few strands of hair away from her eyes, and tucked them behind her ear. Warren's heart sank. There was a ring on her finger. On her left hand.

Vivian saw him looking at it and blushed deeply.

"Who's the lucky guy?" he said.

Vivian slipped her hand into her coat pocket. "Gary," she said, "my husband."

Warren said nothing for a moment as Mr. Vice chimed in once again. *See? What did I tell you? No one can be trusted. Ever. This chick is as unreliable and insincere as the rest of them.*

"Congratulations, I bet he's a great guy," Warren said in a voice not quite his own. It's a good thing, he told himself. Married means nothing can ever happen. Married means I'll never have to see her again. Married means safety. For both of us.

They moved together to the bench Warren had occupied earlier and sat down far enough apart to look at each other.

"We're separated right now," said Vivian. "We, um, have some things to work out. He says I work too much. I say he sleeps around too much. It's...complicated."

Warren felt pity and rage in the pit of his stomach. He checked it. Pity was an emotion that could quickly turn into empathy if it wasn't stopped soon enough. And Vice had no room for empathy in his life. It didn't matter if she was separated. It wasn't his place to get involved. To worry about her. To want to beat the guy who hurt her into a pulp.

This train of thought would get him nowhere other than dreaming up ways to protect and support her. Her life at the hospital couldn't be easy either. Under the microscope to prove herself all the time....

"Warren?" said Vivian.

Warren came to. "Yeah. Sorry. It's just that...well, the guy's an idiot if he can't see what he has in you."

Vivian smiled a small smile. "We'll see," she said. "We're trying counseling—at my insistence—but you know how men are...." She laughed weakly. "Anyway, in the meantime, I'm staying with Mom while it gets sorted out. *If* it gets sorted out."

"That bad, huh?" said Warren, out of his depth.

Vivian shrugged, then slowly got up to leave. "I have to get back to work," she said. "It was...nice to see you, Warren."

"Nice to see you, too, Vivian," he said, and watched her go.

1974—Paris, France

The smell of the freshly baked baguettes, the stickiness of the floors, the joy on the faces of the patrons were foreign to Gérard, yet his connection to the tiny market on the corner of Rue Poissonnière was visceral. As if he'd been there only yesterday, not over a decade ago.

With Lieutenant Martin dispensed, he'd need to secure a place to live. Money. A job at the market? The pay would hardly be enough, but proximity to this supposed "family" was key. He grabbed an apple from the stand and took a bite. The cashier, an older man with tired eyes, looked at him warily. Gérard took a large bite of his apple and the man scowled. As if Gérard planned to steal the fruit from under the guy's nose. Not that Gérard minded being thought of as a criminal, just not a stupid criminal.

"Combien?" he asked.

"Vingt centime."

Gérard tossed the man a franc and stepped away to pick up a few more apples. He tossed a couple in the air and caught them just to irritate the guy. *"Je cherce Celeste or Henri,"* he said.

The man looked up, surprised. *"Eh? Celeste et Heri?* What business you have with Celeste and Henri?"

Gérard reached into his back pocket. In a flash the old man had a bat in his hands. "I don't want any trouble," he said. "Keep the apples. Just leave."

Gérard almost smiled at the idea of an old man with a bat stopping him. "Calm down, calm down, old man. I'm not going to hurt you." He removed the letter from his back pocket. "It seems they are, that we are...family."

At the commotion, a young man barreled up the aisle. *"Grandpapa, qu'est-ce que tu fait?* He turned to Gérard and asked "Can I help you with something, *monsieur*?"

The kid was in decent shape. Glasses, but not those thick coke bottle kinds. Dark brown, almost black, hair, about six feet and broad like a footballer. Gérard considered smashing his nose, but it would not serve his purpose. He smiled.

"Grandpapa," said the kid again, "put down the bat."

Slowly the man did what he was told. Unwillingly.

"He said he's here to see your parents," said the old man.

Gérard nodded.

"You know them...my parents?" the kid said. "They are retired now, you know. On the Côte d'Azur. May I help you with something?"

"Well, Charles," said Gérard, referring to the tag on the kid's shirt, "You probably don't remember me. But my parents were Yvonne and Thomas. You sat for me sometimes when my parents were out, at least that's what I was told. My name is Gérard."

At the names of his parents, the old man stumbled back a step and covered his mouth. "Gérard...." he whispered. *"C'est tu?"*

"Non! Ce n'est pas possible," the kid said. "Is it true? Is it really you?" He stepped forward to shake Gérard's hand and kiss him on both cheeks. Gérard tried not to show his distaste.

The old man spoke. "But...we have not seen you since... *depuis que tu as six ans*. Six! After your mother – and then your father had to – *Ce qui vous est arrivé?* Where have you been for so many years?"

I was five, Gérard thought, but didn't correct the old man. What would be the point? "What difference does it make?" he said. "I'm 18 now and don't have time for reminiscing."

Charles stepped back immediately as if he'd been slapped. "Did you know that my parents begged the government to bring you back home to live with us? That they would not let us keep you? Did you know how they suffered knowing you were gone?" He looked at Gérard. "But it seems you are not interested in conversation. So, *alors*, what *are* you here for?"

Was Charles to be believed? Either way, he was right. Gérard was not here for tea and conversation. "Apparently my father left something here for me. At least that's what this letter says."

Charles had gone cold. "Sure, I know all about it. Whatever it is." He turned toward the door at the back of the store. "Follow me."

Charles led Gérard into the employees' area. Behind a swinging door a large collection of boxes and crates were stacked one on top of another in a precarious pyramid. A walk-in refrigerator held dairy products and there was a humming freezer that housed ice cream and other unrecognizable products. The market had done well for itself, it seemed. Finally, they reached the office. Charles waved him in and sat down behind the big desk covered with papers, receipts, invoices.

"When my parents gave me control of *le marché* there were many rules and plenty of, *conseils non sollicités*. Unsolicited advice. Good advice, however. How to spot a phony bill. Who not to trust with a cheque. The names of the best produce and dairy sources...you know...."

Gérard didn't know, but shrugged.

Charles got up again when he saw Gérard was not planning to take the proffered seat opposite him, and went directly to a section of the floor piled high with file folders and the like. Kid might know his business, but he wasn't much in the organization department.

Charles was still talking as he set aside the files and pulled back the threadbare rug underneath to reveal a safe. Gérard held his breath as Charles turned the dial to the correct combination and then pulled up the safe's door with a screech. "So you see," he was saying, "before they left, they also gave me instructions about this." He held up an envelope.

It was all Gérard could do to keep from snatching it out of the idiot's hands.

Finally, Charles rose from the floor and handed over the envelope that matched the one in Gérard's pocket. "Of course I've always wondered what was in it that was so important," said Charles hopefully.

And you will keep wondering, thought Gérard.

• • •

Later, in his hotel room, Gérard removed the envelope from his pocket and considered its contents. He'd left the market with hardly a word to the old man or the kid, who'd watched him leave with disappointment and puzzlement in their eyes. As soon as Gérard was out the door, they were out of his mind.

The note inside was simple, only a few lines. *Gérard, if you have this, that means you believed me. Ever since you were born I've been taking money from the Circle. When I was forced to run, I took as much as I could. It's all for you my son. Go live your life. I love you and I'm sorry.*

There was something else behind the note. It was small, about 10 cm. wide and thick, like cardboard. A bank book, from a bank in Zurich. When Gérard opened it and saw the amount in the account he rubbed his eyes and looked again. It wasn't possible. *There's no way....* But, apparently, there was. At the time of the last deposit, in October, 1961, the account had over 47 million U.S. dollars that had gained at least 8% annually. Over 13 years! More money than Gérard could ever need, could ever imagine. He could only speculate the amount today. He'd need a calculator...and a math tutor.

32

June, 1975—Washington, D.C.

Warren lay awake staring at the ceiling, thinking over the last few days. He'd never ever believed in fate, but perhaps he should reassess. Otherwise, how could this have happened?

The woman beside him stirred with a sigh and Warren gently placed a hand on the smooth skin of her hip. The sheet had slid down and the curve of her still stunned him every time his eyes fell upon it.

The day Vivian spotted him in the park, Warren was so far from, well, being Warren, that he'd almost been forgotten entirely. His life as Mr. Vice was as set as a sword in a stone. Which is why he was at a loss to say just how that sword had been removed. He was no King Arthur, but somehow a miracle had occurred.

He had let Vivian go that day. Painfully. He had watched her turn and step back up to the walking path and away from him. Back to her carefully constructed life at the hospital as a doctor. Back to her less than satisfying life as a wife.

He didn't know why he did it, but he found himself following her back to the hospital, as if guided by an invisible path of breadcrumbs. He left his phone number for her at the receiving desk. He'd almost given up when, a few days later, she'd called him. "I need to see you," she said. No preamble. No theatrics. His heart leapt.

• • •

"He's the attending on the pediatrics floor," she'd told him when they met for coffee near the hospital but far enough to avoid nosy eyes. "My husband. I'm E.R. so we…our shifts rarely coincide. They haven't for a long time. One day—it sounds so trite when I say it—but one day I got a call to cover someone and ended up on his floor…where I found him in the on-call room with not just one, but two nurses. Not that I was surprised," she said, "we hadn't, well, you know, in months."

Warren probably had no right to judge, but any asshole who cheated on Vivian had to be a complete dick. Being so brazen made him arrogant as well.

"I was supposed to be home, right? I should never have seen it. I guess it might have carried on like that for years. An endless, meaningless, marriage."

"I'm really sorry Vivian." Warren told her.

"It's my own fault," she said, holding up her hand when he went to argue. "I didn't fight for it. I knew we were growing apart, and I let it happen. But that's why we're…we're going to counseling. See what happens."

Counseling? That's what she's here to tell me? They're going to f – ing counseling?

Warren put down his coffee mug and waited. It was a skill he'd picked up and cultivated in the Circle. Wait long enough and people will tell you just about anything to avoid the silence. But his blood was seething. He'd like to introduce this Gary guy to Mr. Vice. Personally.

The waitress poured Vivian another cup of coffee and she added some cream. "But…who am I kidding? The counselor is a man. And everyone knows men have *needs,* right?"

Warren continued to wait. Vivian's bitterness was cutting.

"It's not like we'll ever be happy anyway, no matter what I 'forgive and forget.'"

Finally, Warren felt the need to speak up. "Why don't you leave him, then? Why keep putting yourself through this if you know it's over?"

Vivian took a sip of the lukewarm coffee and grimaced. "It's just that, well, we work together. It's not like he's going away. And I guess I was raised to…I just need to be able to say that in the end I did all I could. Even if I did get those skanky nurses fired," she added halfheartedly.

Warren's smile was also lackluster. It wasn't the time for jokes. Then it hit him. The only reason she hadn't left him. "So, um, you have kids with this guy?"

"No," she said. "No kids—no time. Same old story. We were going to wait until we were both established so it wouldn't be as hard to take time off when we needed it. We were waiting on me, actually. But, as Gary said, I work too much."

Another joke?

Vivian looked up. "I'm sorry, Warren. I didn't mean to dump this on you. It's okay. I'll be fine. And I want to hear about you, about where you've been since…since…." She didn't have to finish.

"I went into lobbying," said Warren, pulling out his usual cover story. Lobbyists and D.C. went together. "Well, I guess it's more like I hire lobbyists, I don't need the money, so I pull the strings." he said. "Ever heard of the Privacy Act? The Fairness Doctrine?"

Vivian shook her head no.

No one ever had. So few people read the newspapers anymore. "Well, they exist because of us," he said. Not a word of it true, but it sounded good and, as expected, Vivian moved on. Lobbyists were only interesting to other lobbyists—and people who needed them.

"What about you, then, Warren," she said, not looking at him. "Married? Kids?"

"No," he said. He waited until she looked up. "I let the right girl slip away and no one else could ever hold a candle to her."

Vivian blushed and looked away. "You didn't have to leave Warren. You chose to go."

"I did choose to leave. But I also had to go. You were right. I needed help. It would have been wrong of me to put that on you."

"But…why did you walk away like that? Why didn't we ever hear from you?"

"I was young and angry, and…." Warren said.

"And stupid," said Vivian.

"Yeah. And stupid," Warren agreed. "But I got the help I needed. I'm good now. But there were too many years in between. And I…I thought it was too late."

Vivian reached out and touched his cheek. "Warren, that's crazy. It's never too late. We missed you. We love you. We're your family."

• • •

They'd ended up at Warren's place that night. Not right away, of course, but eventually there was dinner and wine, and then dessert and brandy. Vivian was hesitant, and Warren insisted he'd keep his distance. And he had.

The next time was different. Gary the creep was away at a conference and Vivian had done the unthinkable and switched shifts with another doctor. It meant she would have to work on Christmas, but she told him she didn't care. She'd led Warren to her home in Bethesda, a traditional colonial on a large, landscaped lot overlooking the Potomac River. Floor-to-ceiling windows let in the natural light and much of the wall space was hung with colorful artwork. It looked expensive and she wore it well.

Warren had paid the taxi driver with a $100 bill and asked him to wait, not wanting to make any assumptions and screw things up. But as he walked Vivian to her front door, she leaned against him, as if no time had passed. He knew if she'd let him, he would not be able to keep away from her. Marriage or no marriage. He waved the taxi driver away.

In the house Vivian poured them wine and turned on the gas fireplace. The lights were dim, inviting. She sat on the sofa and looked up at Warren. Waiting.

Warren was helpless to turn away. He set down his glass and kneeled at her feet. "Vivian," he said, and kissed her.

She kissed him back.

"Are you sure," he asked.

"I'm sure."

"But—"

"No buts, Warren. Never again."

Warren had actually been concerned about more than Vivian knew. Scars covered far too much of his body. As muscular as he was, when she saw his healed wounds she'd never be able to refrain from asking how and why.

But she surprised him once again, covering each scar with soft loving kisses and big eyes. Never saying a word.

And now, here Warren lay. In bed next to the most beautiful woman he'd ever known. As he turned to her to make love with her again, Mr. Vice was no more than a vague irritant lodged somewhere in the recesses of another life and time.

Which is when he realized he had a problem.

A serious problem.

The Circle.

• • •

For weeks it had been eating at him. How to leave the Circle. To leave Mr. Vice behind. They had served their purpose, it was true, and he'd become a killer of men (and the occasional woman). But there was no more room in his life for killing. Not since the moment he'd seen Vivian again.

It was as if the world had cracked open and everything that was dark had filled with light. And he could not let it go. He would not let it go.

The question was how. Warren knew the consequences for abandonment: Execution. No disciplinary action. No warning. Just death.

The epic saga of Mr. Spade was legendary in the Circle. Fleeing to France hadn't kept him from the Circle's far-reaching clutches. And who knew if there had been any others in the distant past. If anyone had ever escaped, would members know about it or be sworn to secrecy? Warren didn't know. All he knew was there had to be a way. Because he would not be forced apart from Vivian for a third time. There were still eight days left to his—to Mr. Vice's— latest month-long furlough. Plenty of time to handle the necessary reconnaissance.

If only he knew what he was looking for and how to begin.

The turn of the door knob roused him from his thoughts. His first instinct was to reach for a weapon. He swept his eyes over the room and then picked up the lamp next to him on the night table. Not much of a weapon, but you work with what you have.

The door opened. How had they found him? He was still on furlough. This was unprecedented. And what about Vivian? Would the killer take her out, too?

Sweat beaded on Warren's brow. *And who are we now, buddy-boy, a voice said in his head. Warren the wimp or Vice the Vicious?*

Shut up, Warren screamed silently.

The door opened wider.

"Vivian? Are you still asleep? I've never known you to sleep so late, not even on weekends. I brought you up some breakfast, honey. I made some nice blueberry muffins and—Aagh! Omigod!"

The woman who'd entered the room dropped the tray she was holding on the floor. Vivian, woken from sated slumber, bolted upright.

"Mom!" she said. "I—I—"

"Vivian! There is a man in your bed! And he's holding a lamp! What's going on? Are you okay? Where's Gary? Should I call the police?"

As if that would do any good, Warren thought with a silent chuckle.

"Miss Stacy?"

"What? Who? How do you know me? What are you doing here? Vivian?"

"It's Warren, Mom. *Warren.* He's back."

Miss Stacy had aged to perfection. The good life had agreed with her. No more cleaning up after others. No more maid.

She stared at him. Then sat on the bed. Tears filled her eyes. "Warren? Is it really you?"

"It is, Miss Stacy. It's really me."

"But how—when—?"

"Mom," said Vivian, "why don't you let us get dressed and then we'll join you downstairs for a more...civil conversation."

Miss Stacy—Warren could no more call her by any other name than he could stop loving Vivian—picked up the tray and a couple of dishes without comment, and left the room.

Vivian looked at Warren and sighed. "Well, it's not the way I would have chosen to share the news, but it sure was effective," she said, and got up to make herself presentable.

• • •

They spent the majority of the morning reminiscing and catching up with Miss Stacy. For Warren, it was surreal. One day he's living life as Mr. Vice and the next he's eating cereal, toast, and bacon with his favorite people in the world. People he thought he'd never see again. And as luck would have it, Vivian had a couple of days away from the hospital, and Miss Stacy, well, she was free to do as she liked these days, choosing to spend her time volunteering at local charitable organizations.

How he'd missed the simple things. The last time he'd had a vaguely carefree morning was during one of Mr. Vice's furloughs in Madrid, with a beautiful young woman named Carmen. She spoke just enough English, and he, just enough Spanish, for them to talk and laugh and fulfill each other's needs. But nothing could compare to this. The lack of pretense, the ease. Wait. *Lack of pretense?* His whole life was a pretense. A sham. Feeling so "at home" was making him delusional. Making him think he could actually have such a life. One where people cared about him—about *him*. He felt like a ping pong ball moving back and forth from euphoric to stricken.

When he left after breakfast, giving himself enough time to shower and say his good-byes, he could barely meet Vivian's eyes for fear of spilling his guts. He'd noted her wedding ring was no longer on her hand this morning, an act that said everything she didn't have to. Wrapped in her arms, her warm body so supple and soft and yielding, his willpower was deteriorating in equal measure to his increasing desire to know her, and to be known. *Really known.*

33

1976—Zurich, Switzerland

With all of Gérard's money annoyingly tied up in one little bank booklet, he had no choice but to find both employment and living arrangements in Paris. As soon as he realized his circumstances, he'd quickly changed his tune toward Charles. Burning that bridge would do much more harm than good, and what he could offer was invaluable. And it hadn't taken much, pathetically naive as he seemed to be about the ways of the world. The rental apartment upstairs had been vacated recently, too, and was there for the taking in return for stocking shelves and handling basic janitorial work. Totally beneath Gérard, of course, but again, circumstances must. He'd do what he had to do and keep his disdain for the job—and these store owners—hidden.

After a while, Gérard surprised himself by enjoying the company of the crusty old man, Charles' grandfather, Jacques. Feisty, short-tempered, and ill-mannered, he was easier to be around than anyone else. Gérard figured he either saw right through Gérard's act or didn't care a whit one way or another. Which suited Gérard just fine.

Gérard learned that Jacques fought the Nazi's at Dunkirk. After the battle, Jacques was captured and sent to Germany where he spent the better part of two years working in the mines, taking the place of German men who'd been sent away fighting. It was there that Jacques said he decided he would never be pushed around again. There was no way to miss Jacques' hatred and disgust for his fellow soldiers, those that allowed themselves to be befriended by the Germans.

"We work right next to them," Jacques said. "Shoulder à shoulder *avec l'ennemi, tu comprends?* Cowards! All of them. Drinking with them." He slammed his fist on the table. *"Une disgrâce, tu comprends, absolument une disgrâce."*

Not that it was odd for camaraderie to blossom between POWs and German citizens. Not all citizens were Nazis. It was Gérard's impression, in fact, that many, more than expected, were against the war and merely wanted to get on with their lives. A natural inclination, no? To go back to the way things were? Not that it was true for Gérard. He would never go back. Jacques may never look at a German and see anything but a Nazi again, but Gérard would never see any human as more than fodder for his own advancement.

Certainly it was a staunch approach similar to Gérard's single-minded quest for revenge. His enemy? The Circle. Along with every member ever to have joined its ranks.

When Jacques died in 1975, Gérard would feel more than he'd felt for another human being since childhood based on their bond of hatred.

As for Charles...well, Charles was easy, too. Easy to please. Easy to deceive. Easy to manipulate. It was a perfect relationship. Given his need to return the market to order and manage its day-to-day happenings, he began to see Gérard as the long lost brother returned to his rightful place and family. Why bother to dissuade him?

Still, the demands of the drudgery kept Gérard seething inside. As soon as he had the money, after two endless years saving his francs and *avec la famille,* it was time to move on. He bought a well-used Citroen GS Pallas, acquired a passport, and said *adieu* to Charles forever.

It was only six hours to Zurich and his meal ticket awaited.

• • •

Morning at the local hotel in Zurich came fast. First stop the Swiss National Bank of Zurich. Pulling up in a taxi, he'd expected something more imposing than the simple stone building. Only four stories high with archways at each entry point. Gérard carried himself with a swagger that came naturally, and his suit, the one he was wearing that had cost a month's savings, gave him the confidence to glide into the bank as would any wealthy financial patron. The vaulted ceilings and smooth marble floors lent an air of civility, but otherwise it was not particularly lavish. If he expected something out of a James Bond movie, he was sorely disappointed.

Bank tellers, about 10 of them, stood behind a long black onyx kiosk, each station equipped with a small segment of metal bars separating them from the public for safety. Illusion only. If someone really wanted to rob the place, one leap over the counter with a gun would do it.

Gérard purposefully sought out a female teller. One not too young, not too old. Someone who'd appreciate the attention of an attractive young man. She greeted him with a smile.

"Willkommen," she said when he arrived at the kiosk, *"wie kann ich Ihnen heute helfen?"*

German. Should have known. Gérard shrugged and smiled lopsidedly.

"Ah," said the woman. *"Benvenuto, come posso aiutarti oggi?"*

Now Italian. Had to give the woman credit, though. She was trying.

"Francais?" he said this time, charmingly hopeful.

"Ah, oui, monsieur," said the woman with a smile. *"Bienvenue. Comment puis-je vous aider aujourd'hui?"*

A bank teller who spoke three languages. Not bad. Gérard quickly passed over the bank book left him by his father and asked for a current balance. Then he held his breath.

The teller took the outdated bank book and ran her hands over it. "I haven't seen a book like this in a very long time," she said. "It must be very old.... Yes, it says here the last entry was 13 years ago—quite substantial."

Substantial? I should say so. Gérard's patience was wearing thin. He wanted to grab the woman by the throat and shake the money loose from her body.

"Oui," he said. "And I would like to make a substantial withdrawal."

The woman nodded, and then gestured toward a lounge area with high backed leather seats, offering coffee and pastries. "Please, why don't you have a seat over there in the lounge? If you bear with me a moment I will come get you when it is all sorted."

"I think I'll stay here," Gérard said, still smiling. There was no way he was going to let that book out of his sight. The teller flushed, but all she said was, "As you wish, *monsieur,*" and retreated into the offices behind her, likely to receive the stamp of approval from a higher authority. Gérard saw the teller show the bank book to the manager through the blinds of the office. When the manager snatched it from her hands, the teller stood back. The encounter seemed tense. Gérard's hand was nervously tapping the counter. He made himself stop. *Cool. Stay cool. You're suave. You have this. It's your money.*

Gérard felt the manager's eyes on his, a stare he met with considerable difficulty.

In a moment the manager was at his side holding the bank book. "Please," he said in flawless French, "if you will, sir...come with me."

Gérard followed the man back to the office, keeping his eye on the bank book. He was not looking for trouble, but he would not be pressured to wait for the money that was rightfully his.

The manager, a Benjamin Baumann, offered Gérard a seat before closing the office door, adjusting the blinds, and retaking his own seat behind his desk.

"No problem, I hope, Herr Baumann," Gérard said mildly as if he went to banks in Zurich every day and took out vast sums of money.

"Not at all, *Monsieur....*?"

"Finck," said Gérard. "Gérard Finck." He reached for his passport and flipped it open to hand to the manager.

The manager took his time scrutinizing Gérard's identification. Finally, he handed it back to Gérard. *"Monsieur Finck,"* he said, "it is our pleasure to assist you today."

Gérard recognized it right away. Respect. The manager's voice was dripping with it. Money and respect go hand-in-hand. His heart rate kicked up a notch.

"In the past 13 years," Baumann went on, "this account has grown substantially."

Get to it, already, man. How long was Gérard going to have to wait until this guy got to the bottom line? He tapped his nails on the desk and swung his knee to convey his impatience. Rich men don't wait.

"At 8.25% interest" – here the banker choked a bit as if the high interest rate was an affront to his health – "your account has increased to a total of $154,353,482.82."

No. It couldn't be. He must have heard the number wrong.

The banker handed him a slip of paper with the numbers written on it. Gérard had not heard wrong. It was all his – and he had done nothing for them other than deserve them for living the life he'd been forced to live.

Gérard smiled and picked up a pen.

34

June, 1975 — Washington, D.C.

If you didn't take into account Mr. Vice's penthouse apartment at the Ritz Carlton in Georgetown, you might be fooled into thinking he was simply a well-dressed man with a high-paying job in politics or finance. While tempting to flaunt one's inexhaustible supply of funds, Mr. Vice preferred to stay slightly more under the radar. If renting one of the most prestigious apartments in one of the most prestigious hotels in one of the most prestigious locations in D.C. could be considered under the radar.

It wasn't the space he coveted, the four large bedrooms and three baths, nor even the stupendous view of the D.C. skyline, although it was not without its appeal, but all the other perks. The fact that no one questioned his odd hours, the staff at his beck and call, and, most important, the highly inaccessible domain. Penetration of the penthouse from the floor below was virtually impossible. Only one way onto the floor without an elevator key and that was up the one set of stairs on the opposite end of the hallway from his door. And that stairwell led to a door that triggered a fire alarm when opened. It was as close to impervious as money could buy.

Warren Nichols felt like an interloper in Mr. Vice's apartment. Ironic, since in Warren's mind it was Mr. Vice who was the interloper now. The more he thought about it, the more he realized that Peter/Mr. Vice was an evil Jiminy Cricket guiding him into the darkness.

But how could he overlook how much he'd needed Peter when he was a boy? How much their partnership had saved him from the rampant parental neglect and loneliness? Peter's subtle manipulations had only encouraged Warren to violence, starting with simple altercations, fighting over toys in school, events easily chalked up to "boys being boys." Warren had gone willingly. To a place he felt in control. Where he *mattered*. By the time he'd met up with the idiots at the ice cream shop the only thing keeping him from releasing every ounce of anger and resentment he harbored to beat them to a pulp was the fact that he'd had an audience. And by the time the Circle had made him the offer of a lifetime, there was nothing to keep him from accepting it.

Peter and Warren had become equal partners in D.C. The workouts, the training, studying up on potential targets. Peter was in his element. Once he'd hunted and killed Mr. Blunt, giving birth to Mr. Vice, he had almost forgotten Warren ever existed.

Until Vivian.

Because one look at Vivian was all it took for Warren to resurface through the murky waters of disillusionment, ancient history, and power struggles. And with only eight days, seven and a half to be accurate, on the clock, Warren would have to think fast to find a way out of the very organization that he'd viewed as his savior.

Since he'd been with Vivian and Miss Stacy something interesting was happening. Warren had been able to think more clearly as himself, Peter—and Mr. Vice—taking a backseat. Warren was a little nervous about their apparent lack of interest in these new developments, but was unwilling to ask any questions. As he saw it, there was one answer and only one answer, which meant Warren had to make it good. Alive and in hiding was not an option, as proven by the infamous Mr. Spade.

Mr. Vice would need to die.

• • •

The conundrum was clear. Asking help from the part of you you're attempting to kill off is more challenging than you might think. Not only did Warren need to fake Mr. Vice's assassination, but his own. Wipe them all—Warren Nichols/Peter/Mr. Vice—from the face of the earth.

From his years in the shadows, however, Warren had taken note of Vice's meticulous methods of preparation to ensure success. Like painting a wall or fixing a window, it was all about the prep. So Warren spent his remaining "free" hours studying the members most likely to open the door for a manageably believable, yet entirely false, death.

Members who cherished the up-close-and-personal approach were out. Without blood on their fingers and body parts as trophies they were rarely satisfied. Those who killed from afar, snipers with long-range weaponry, were also not an option. That left those who employed poisons and chemical reactions. Two Circle members came to mind. Mr. Freeze and Mr. Venom. If "Antifreeze" Freeze or "The Snake" Venom were to target him, Warren would conceivably have the best chance at staging his own demise.

At dying...and staying dead.

Convincing Mr. Vice to aid in his own fall would likely be problematic, but Warren would not be dissuaded. He had to try. For Vivian. "Peter," he said aloud. "I need to talk to you. I need your help."

Peter hasn't existed in years, said Mr. Vice. *You know that.*

"Yes, of course, you're right," said Warren. "But, regardless, I need to know when Freeze or Venom is coming for me—for us. And for that I need your help."

Oh, so now you need my help again, said Vice. *I might be offended if I cared.*

"Fine," said Warren, "I get it. You like to be in charge, but—"

I AM in charge! roared Vice. *And have been for years. What are you playing at here?*

"I'm not playing at anything," said Warren. "I'm tired. I just think it's time to let Warren go.... Altogether."

Silence.

"Vice? Are you there?"

I'm here. But I ask you again, what are you playing at? Why now?

"Like I said, it's time. I'm ready to go the distance. For that, Warren Nichols needs to disappear forever."

You're not attempting to steal my kills, little Warren Nichols, are you? said Vice.

Warren forced a laugh. "Steal them," he said, "as if. If I disappear, there's nothing to steal."

Vice laughed now. *Point taken,* he said. *Warren's finally ready to put on his big boy pants. Tell me, what do you have in mind?*

"There's something I want to try," said Warren, treading carefully, keeping his ego in check. One slip-up with Vice and the game could be over before it had started.

More silence. Warren held his breath.

Then, *Closet. Lever under lowest shelf.*

Warren let the air out of his lungs slowly and walked to the closet. He found the lever just where Vice had said it would be. He pressed the button. A sliding panel rose up to reveal a space large enough for a cache of weapons, cash, and paperwork. Warren was only interested in the two large envelopes, one manila, the other sky blue. The first thick with papers and showing wear and tear at the corners, the second thinner and seemingly less handled. He remembered the blue one, which still had his name on it in thick block letters: "NICHOLS." He opened it and saw the information about Mr. Sleep, Vice's last target. *That one holds every target we have ever had,* Vice said.

At Vice's use of the word "we" Warren started to feel hopeful.

Our most recent target? Mr. Sleep. At the top. Our next target will be added to the top of the list in...exactly seven days, nine hours, and 54 minutes.

For a minute Warren felt something akin to what he imagined it was like diving deep in the ocean. A sense of floating, a lack of gravity keeping him grounded. Obviously, Vice had been keeping these meticulous records for years. Yet that would also mean that Warren himself was a part of that undertaking.

Warren felt ill. He pulled himself together. Vice could smell fear like decaying fish. "What about this one," asked Warren, holding up the much thinner manila envelope.

That one is a list of every member ever assigned to kill us.

Warren froze when he slid out the papers filled with names. Page after page of names. All the hunters who had come after Vice. Him. Them. He put his head in his hands. All these years. So many killings. So much survival.

Look who's on top, said Vice.

"Mr. Venom."

Right. Indeed, said Vice. *He's been after us for months. Waiting out this furlough has been killing him. Ha-ha, little joke there. Anyway, the details are all in there. Poisonous snake in the bed of his first victim. Easy kill, but boring, I suppose. Since then he's graduated from snake venom to poison of various varieties. Even blow darts at a distance. Deadly as they come, this Mr. Venom. Good at surprise.*

This was not good news.

"Current poison of choice?" asked Warren, hoping to narrow down the playing field.

He's back to snakes. Australian snakes. As it says in the packet, Vice added, annoyed. *There is a list. I assume you can read. So read it. I hope you won't need me to guide you every step of the way.*

Warren shook his head. "Of course not," he said as convincingly as he could, and pulled out the list. On it was a comprehensive guide of various snakes, their venom, and their potencies. Some of them existed on the Inland Taipan of Australia and were said to be the most toxic of any reptile in the world. One bite contained enough deadly venom to kill more than 100 people. *Nice thought.*

Next on the list was the Australian Brown Snake. More good news. 0.00007 ounces of venom from one of these babies was more than enough to kill a human. Then came the Malayan Krait of Indonesia, along with the Taipan and the Tiger Snake, also of Australia. The Tiger snake was very aggressive, killing more people in Australia than any other snake on the continent.

"He'd be daft not to go with the Tiger snake," said Warren. "I would."

My thoughts exactly, Mr. Vice agreed.

"Although the Inland Taipan or the Australian brown would be the best choices, importing such a deadly animal into the United States would be a risk I wouldn't want to take. Customs undergoes plenty of scrutiny these days and the

Circle doesn't like scrutiny. From what little I know," Warren added quickly.

The Circle controls a lot, but you're right, international customs are tricky. All in due time.

"The Malayan Krait is out, too. We're not exactly on great trade terms with that region of the world right now and imports are under an intense microscope. Besides, you said he uses Australian snakes, so that doesn't fit the bill."

Very good, said Vice. *You're learning quickly.*

I should be, Warren thought. Since we seem to have the same brain. He chose to leave that unspoken. Instead, he said, "Which leaves the Taipan and the Tiger snake. I don't risk the Taipan because someone over in customs might confuse it with the Inland Taipan and hold up delivery. Once again leaving the Tiger snake as the logical choice."

Well, well, well. Detective Warren on the case, Vice applauded loftily. *I have deduced the same. Here's the real question, though. You want to get your hands dirty? Slaughter Venom?*

Warren gulped, but nodded.

Then you have to know when he'll strike and what you'll do to prevent it.

Warren mulled over that last statement of Vice's. How would Warren know when the killer would strike? Wasn't that impossible to predict? And if he couldn't predict it, then how could he prevent it? There was only one alternative that he could see.

"That's where you come in," he said to Vice. "We need to make him think we slipped him a detail about where we'll be and what we're doing."

Ah, said Vice. *Subterfuge. The name of the game. Make him think he has the upper hand. Any ideas?*

Warren thought. "A celebration," he said. "Something he won't be able to pass up. Killing a man in a public place, leaving no trace...most members would jump at the chance."

Go on....

"The anniversary of my parents' death," Warren said, "it's just passed. We always go for a celebratory meal around this time of year. We'll let it slip. The restaurant. The time. All we'll have to do is sit back and wait for him to strike."

As much as I admire your willingness to get your feet wet here, Vice said dripping sarcasm, *that's the most lamentable excuse for an idea I've ever heard. What's to keep him from poisoning your food before it ever gets to you?*

"Nothing."

Silence.

I think we're done here.

"Hear me out," said Warren. "Venom has to think he was successful before he leaves the restaurant. All I have to do is have a syringe of antivenom with me. Shouldn't be all that hard to procure with our resources. Look. It says when Tiger snake venom is injected the victim experiences a rubbery taste in the mouth. Sounds like a pretty clear indicator to me. I taste rubber, I inject my thigh. Easy. Of course then I'll fall over into my soup or fish or dessert and wait until he shows up to admire his handiwork. When he does, I'll finish him off."

Do you really think you're ready to handle that? You're just a baby. You'll end up dead. We'll *end up dead. Hard pass. I should never have entered into this conversation.*

"Wait," said Warren. "It's nothing you didn't prepare me for back in California."

No answer.

"Hey, are you listening? I can do this."

But Vice was gone.

• • •

Tell me how you're going to kill him.

"You're back," Warren said. *Thank god.* "You had me worried there for a minute. I've always been good with a knife, you know. And I've always been a sucker for blood."

Sure, said Vice, *but this is the real thing. If you chicken out, if you aren't willing to go the distance, you'll get us both killed.*

"I can do this," Warren said, not wanting to lay it on too thick, but sensing it was time to make it stick. "I need to do this. For us. For us to be stronger."

This doesn't have anything to do with Vivian does it?

Warren was blindsided by the question.

What? You think I don't know what you do? You think I forgot that we saw her, how it felt to – "

"No! Of course not!" Warren did not want to think about Vice watching while he and Vivian had...while they'd done what they'd done. He had to think fast. "If this was about Vivian, why would I be so hyped to off someone myself? We both know that night with Vivian was a mistake...nothing but a quick screw." His stomach curled as he said it. "The Circle is the place for us. That's our home. It was the right decision years ago and it hasn't changed. So don't you think it's about time I get off my ass and start enjoying the life you created for us?"

Time to bring out the big gun. Go for the ego.

"And with our two minds working as one, I can see Mr. Black in our future. Can't you?"

An agonizing silence prevailed during which time Warren had plenty of opportunity to realize just how crazy he was to think he could suppress his true thoughts and intentions from Mr. Vice, from Peter...from his own mind.

Then, *Okay, Warren Nichols,* Vice said. *You have a deal. I'll start planting the seeds at the safe house.*

"Just promise me you'll let me handle the kill on my own," said Warren. "The only way it'll feel like *my* kill is if I know you're not there. I don't want your hand on the knife this time. Just mine."

There was another silence as Vice took his time answering. *I suppose I can agree to that. But this had better be the last time we ever hear the name Warren Nichols again. When Venom is dead, Warren Nichols will have ceased to exist. Forever. Are we clear?*

Oh, we're clear on that alright, thought Warren. A lot clearer than you think.

35

1976—Zurich, Switzerland

Benjamin Baumann politely sat back to provide Gérard the appropriate space and time to process the information he had just received. It wasn't every day that even he, the manager of the bank, saw a bank book accrue so much interest without notice on the holder's part. Without inquiry of any kind. Unusual at best.

Gérard accepted a glass of water from the manager's assistant and downed it. He hated that he had to ask, that it put him in a vulnerable position, but felt he had no choice. "So...what now?"

"My advice, *monsieur,* would be to leave it alone. Take out small sums as needed," Baumann said. "This interest rate—well, let's just say that it is extremely good, is it not? I suggest you let the account accrue over time."

Yeah, and in the meantime, your bank keeps all my money to "accrue over time." I don't think so. "Hmm," said Gérard, pretending to consider it. "Then again, on the other hand, I could not possibly spend so much in a thousand lifetimes. Why grow it when I'd much rather spend it."

The bank manager blanched. "With all due respect, Mr. Finck, perhaps this will help you make a decision. If you leave your money and allow it to accrue, by this time next year you will have earned an additional...*11 million dollars.*" Baumann handed Gérard the calculator to prove his calculations were accurate, then took it back and typed a series of numbers in again. "In another five years you stand to earn an extra *65 million dollars.*"

Gérard's head spun from the numbers. Numbers far greater than any he ever imagined in his life. He willed his heart to slow and spoke quietly. "Five years...hmm, yes, I see." Baumann looked hopeful. "But...no." Baumann's face fell. "I want access now. Full access."

"But—but—I really would advise against removing anything more than a few mil—" Baumann stumbled.

"I am not asking," said Gérard, becoming tired of the game. "I would like to know how you will accommodate my request."

Baumann cleared his throat and felt ill. Alas, even when the customer was an idiot, he was always right, although the higher-ups would certainly have his head on a platter when they got word that so much money had left the bank. He stood. "Yes, sir. I understand, sir. I will direct you to our credit department." He pressed a buzzer. "Miss Zutter will arrange for you to withdraw the funds you want by way of cashiers cheques."

• • •

Through the bank's labyrinth Gérard followed Baumann into the central offices of the Swiss National Bank. Up two flights of stairs to the third floor with its elaborate and intricate artwork and moldings. Large marble tiles, each one subtly different from the next, were set into the floor like enormous granite snowflakes. The doors of the office easily stretched 10 feet high.

When they arrived at the far office in the corner Baumann knocked three times quickly in succession. The large oak door creaked as it opened. Inside the office, alone, was a middle-aged woman with wavy brown hair, a white sweater casually knotted about her shoulders, and slim glasses resting on the bridge of her nose. They seemed to have interrupted her lunch hour, which offered an unappetizing odor of sauerkraut.

"Oh," said Baumann, "Jeneane, I'm sorry to bother you on your lunch, but this is Mr. Finck. He is a new customer with an old account."

Miss Zutter swallowed hastily and set aside her food.

"Please see to it that he gets the access and guidance that he needs."

"Yes, sir."

"Good." He turned to Gérard. "I leave you in Miss Zutter's capable hands, then, Mr. Finck."

The heavy door swung slowly closed behind him.

"Je suis desole," Gérard said with a gesture to the woman's lunch. Fortunately, she took the hint and tucked it away in her desk, although the smell lingered and churned in Gérard's stomach.

"It is no trouble Mr…Finck, is it?"

Her French accent was abominable, but understandable. Gérard nodded.

"Please, sit down," she said. "How can I help you?"

Gérard had had plenty of time to work out his storyline in advance. The abbreviated version conveniently eliminated his father's membership in and murder by the Circle. All he required was a believable minimum. "My father left this for me before he passed," he said sadly, holding up his bank book. "I had no idea...none at all...that there was so much money involved." He looked down, hoping the astute Miss Zutter would take his reticence for grief. "But you see, dear Miss Zutter, my father was...not well....and there are now funeral expenses and debts to pay…."

He let it hang, waiting out the uncomfortable silence.

"I can assure you, Mr. Finck, I will help you in any way I can. And I am sorry for your loss."

Gérard inclined his head slightly in acknowledgment.

"Still, Mr. Finck, you must know that financial advisors, those of us in the banking industry, feel it is their duty to advise against frivolous spending."

"And with all due respect ma'am," Gérard said, hardening his voice slightly, "it is not your money, nor your business."

Miss Zutter gave him a long look, nodded once, and stood up quickly. "Let's go over here, then, and sort this out together, shall we, Mr. Finck?"

A moment later she had polished her glasses and was studying Gérard's bank book. She flipped forward, then back to the beginning pages, scrutinizing it like a detective. Her eyes widened. Her hands stilled. A bead of sweat formed at her brow. Something was going on, something Gérard did not at all understand.

"Miss Zutter?" said Gérard. "Are you feeling unwell? Is there something wrong?"

Surely it couldn't have to do with the account. People like her dealt with large accounts every day. He reached for the bottle of Coca-Cola she'd sat next to her on the desk.

She waved him off. "No, no. It's just that…."

"Yes?"

"Well, I probably should not say anything, but…."

Annoyed, Gérard snapped, "Tell me, already. I'm losing patience here."

She nodded. "I apologize," she said. "It's simply that, you see, I have been waiting for this opportunity for a long time."

"Opportunity?" repeated Gérard, perplexed.

"Yes," said Miss Zutter, "because I know this account."

"What do you mean, you know it?"

"These dates. These amounts," Miss Zutter said, pointing to details of each deposit. "I've been monitoring this account since before you were born, Mr. Finck. I simply cannot believe you are here. Sitting here, in front of me right now."

"Okay, that's enough," said Gérard, who disliked being in the dark as much as he disliked stodgy old women. "Either tell me what's going on or find me someone else to get me what I need."

"Please," said Miss Zutter, "just let me explain. It was Mr. Spade who set up this account."

"That is absolutely not true," said Gérard, shaking with rage. "My father, Thomas Roche, opened this account. I have the letter to prove it."

"Then," said Miss Zutter, removing her glasses and sighing, "then I suppose Mr. Spade must be your father."

36

June, 1975—Washington, D.C.

Nurses and patients and doctors scrambled about on the ground floor of George Washington University Hospital attending to more patients than they could handle, as usual. Vivian reading the chart in her hands, walked down the hall in sneakers that weren't as comfortable as they used to be. Shopping had never been a priority and with her responsibilities came less time to take care of personal business. She sighed. If she didn't get a new pair soon she'd probably trip and break her leg, end up in her own E.R.

She pulled aside the curtain where a young man in his 20s with a short military-style crew cut lay with a severe laceration across his bicep. The blood had slowed considerably, but he probably had lost a lot of it before arriving in Emergency, and was looking light-headed. No one wanted patients fainting on their watch from lack of blood.

"Mr.…Benson, not doing so well today, I take it."

He shook his head, which began to droop. "...Don't feel so… good."

Vivian turned to the nurse. "What do we know?"

"Bar fight. Some goon slashed him open with a beer bottle."

Alcohol. Possible drug use. Loss of blood. Terrific. She turned to her patient. "Mr. Benson, I'm going to set you up with an IV. We may have to get you some blood. Do you know your blood type?"

"Um...regular…?" he managed.

"Regular." Of course. Vivian sighed. She turned to the nurse again. "Alex, two pints O-Neg right away. And a suture kit. We've got to close this wound up. And get the officer who brought him in here, they're gonna want to get his statement."

• • •

After she'd attended to Mr. Benson, delivered the necessary care, and made her report, Vivian pulled away the curtain and moved along to the next patient in line. In the E.R. there was always a next patient. "Dr. Chambers to Receiving, Dr. Chambers to Receiving." She sighed again at the call overhead. Normally, she approached every day, every call, every patient, with a renewed vigor. These days, all she wanted to do was sit in a corner and read a trashy novel. What could they possibly want with her in Receiving?

After an abrupt about-face and a quick pace down one long hallway, a left down another, then a right at the end of that one, she finally arrived at Receiving. "This had better be good," she said to the attendant at the desk.

"Good enough to warrant a trip down to reception, I should think," said the attendant. Looks like someone decided to apologize." A tall vase filled to capacity with long stem roses sat on the counter.

"What is this?" Vivian asked. "For me?"

The attendant nodded. "From Dr. Thompson, I'll bet," she said.

A nurse came up to the desk. "If those are from who I think they are, he can cram them up his ass, thorns first," she said. Then she spotted Vivian behind the flowers. "Oh, Dr. Chambers," she stuttered. "I didn't see you there. I'm sorry...I didn't mean to...."

"Enough," snapped Vivian. She would not give them the satisfaction of seeing her melt down in public. *If that bastard thinks a bunch of flowers can make up for what he did then he's got another*– She ripped open the card, read it...and almost fainted herself. For so long, she'd waited to hear words like this. Instead, all she'd gotten were empty apologies, vacant pretenses of affection with nothing to back them up. She had forgotten that words could also fill her heart with hope. Aware of the hospital staff looking on, waiting for her to drop a crumb, she quietly put the card in her pocket. "I don't have time for this right now. I'll pick up the flowers on the way out."

Back in her office, though, after three more patients, she read the card over and over again, making sure each word was exactly how she'd read it the first time.

Vivian -

I can't make up for the past, but I know I'll love you for my whole future. You are my everything.

—Warren

In the safety of privacy, the tears that had threatened to fall earlier welled up again. She forced them back. There was no slack for women doctors, who were subject to standards no man would ever have to reach. Let them think the flowers were from her husband. She was still married, at least legally, and couldn't bear a scandal. Another one, that is.

• • •

The girl, a nine-year-old, had apparently fallen down the stairs. Olivia. A real trooper. Few tears, and more concerned about the state of her French braid and whether her injury would keep her from skateboarding than her pain level. Vivian wished all her patients had such backbone. Still, the shoulder was a relatively easy fix, where the lump on her head meant she'd need to be admitted for observation. Which meant the 6th floor, 6 West, Pediatrics. Stomping grounds of her least favorite person in the world right now. How would it feel to see him now? To see the husband she'd thought she'd loved—until Warren showed up to show her she had something else worth fighting for.

Ordinarily she'd cringe at such a thought, but the events of a few days ago had given her a new perspective, a new light at the end of what was once a very dark tunnel. Her marriage was over the second she'd seen Warren sitting on the bench at the Lincoln Memorial. She took a deep breath. Dr. Gary Thompson was a colleague. A professional. She would act accordingly.

Stepping onto the 6th floor was always an experience, where the atmosphere was a curious mix of optimism, hope, and desperation. Colorful walls attempted to make up for what was really going on: the caring of sick children. Children requiring a whole different set of skills and attention. This unit was done up in an aquarium theme. Bright blue paint with undersea life murals. Fish, octopus, turtles, whales, dolphins, crabs, seahorses, starfish, even air bubbles, seaweed, and a sandy ocean floor textured for a sensory experience.

Vivian loved it up here, though, because you could always find a reason to smile. Well, unless your child was here for treatment for something serious. Then this place was hell on earth. Sometimes she was glad she'd never had children. What if something happened to them? She wouldn't be able to survive.

As little as Vivian thought of her husband's personal values and actions, there was no denying he was good at his job. Probably why he appealed to the nurses—female *and* male—not that he'd shown any tendency in that direction, at least that she knew about. Handsome, loves kids, enough charm to charm the skin off a snake. No wonder the guy walked on water.

And there he was.

He nodded in her direction. Not *at* her. At a spot on the wall behind her. Fine, no attempt at small talk, then. Worked for her.

"This is Olivia," she said, moving to the child's bedside. "Olivia, this is Dr. Thompson. Olivia is nine years old, isn't that right, Olivia?"

"Nine and a quarter," Olivia answered bravely.

Dr. Thompson introduced himself and shook hands with Olivia's parents, but still did not meet Vivian's eyes.

"Olivia seems to have had a nasty fall, Doctor. We fixed up her shoulder already, though, didn't we? And I've got to tell you, this girl is a real trooper."

Olivia offered up a small smile.

"It's just this little bump on the old noggin that needs a look."

"It's nice to meet you, Olivia," Gary said, extending his hand for a high five. When Olivia gently struck it, he recoiled as if in pain. "Ow," he said, shaking it off. "Did you have to set her shoulder so well, Dr. Chambers? I think she's reached

Super Girl status now." Olivia managed a giggle and her parents smiled.

Gary pointed to a room at the end of a hall. "These nurses are going to take you to that room over there, Olivia, okay? I'll be right in."

He turned to Vivian. Finally. Ordinarily, Vivian was a sucker for the routine of welcoming a new patient to the pediatrics unit. The playful banter was a welcome break from the norm. Plus Gary's insistence that he personally greet each new patient to the floor was something she admired about his work ethic and his desire to keep the unit as comfortable and as friendly as possible.

Today, the banter felt forced. This was someone she'd thought she knew, yet learned she didn't. She dropped the smile that she'd conjured up for the patient and her family. "Hematoma over the right eye. Initial tests came back negative, but her balance was off with the heel-to-toe test, so she's all yours now. Also, Mom stated this was a fall down some stairs, but…." She sighed.

Gary's eyes darkened. "We'll look into it," he said.

No one took potential child abuse lightly.

She nodded. "See you later, then," she said, and turned toward the elevator.

"Hey...V?"

Vivian turned halfway at Gary's call, but stood her ground. He followed her out into the hallway.

"Any idea why people are saying I choose one heck of a way to say I'm sorry?"

He'd heard about the massive bouquet, then. *Word travels fast in a hospital.* Most days it felt like nothing more than a glorified high school with the way the rumor mill churned. This was not on the agenda right now, though. Or, possibly, ever. Her business may be everyone else's in their eyes, but she did not have to buy into that game. Not even with her so-called partner.

"The flowers?" she said, waving it away. "From a friend I ran into the other day. Guess they wanted to say thanks."

"*They,*" Gary pressed, "or *he*?"

Vivian went cold. "I'd say that's none of your business," she said.

"*He,* then," Gary hissed. "You're *dating*?"

"As I said, that's none of your business. We're separated. And it's not as if you have a moral high ground to stand on, remember?"

"Separated doesn't mean divorced," Gary fired back. "If I cheated, so did you."

Besides the fact that Gary had a new patient waiting for him to attend to, this conversation was headed downhill fast. *Stay calm. You are a doctor. You are a woman. If you explode, it'll be all over the front pages tomorrow. You could lose your job. The job you love.*

"Don't you dare compare yourself to me," she hissed in a whisper. "You cheated on me. You cheated on us. Here at the hospital and at home—in our bed. You don't cheat on someone you love...Unless, of course, you don't love them. Right, Gary?"

Gary blanched. "Love has nothing to do with the fact that you're fucking someone else," he said. "You're nothing but a whore. I should have listened when everyone told me marrying you was a mistake."

Vivian felt her hand fist. This conversation was unbelievable. Unconscionable. Unreal. Like talking with a petulant teenager. "You can't cheat on someone you don't love. *You* taught me that. Goodbye, Gary," she said. She had to get out of there before she did something she'd regret. People were already staring. She made a move toward the elevator.

"Hey, wait just a minute," said Gary, yanking on her arm. "We're not done here."

That did it. "Oh, we're done, alright," she said, and swung around to connect her fist with his eye. "Hematoma on 6 West," she said to the shocked staff in the hall as the elevator doors opened, "and it's a doozy."

37

1976—Zurich, Switzerland

"What are you saying?" demanded Gérard. "Who are you? And what is this Circle, anyway? Why would my father's money belong to them? He left it to me!"

"If you give me a moment, I will explain everything," said Miss Zutter, getting up, checking that the door was fully closed, then locking it. Immediately, Gérard felt claustrophobic. Was the woman crazy? What was she planning to do to him?

"Mr. Finck," she said, turning to him before he could speak. "There is no easy way to say this. My name is really Jeneane Earnest. You have heard of Coco Chanel, I assume."

This was getting more bizarre by the minute. Of course he'd heard of Chanel. Not that he'd ever gotten close enough to catch a whiff of the perfume.

"Well, the truth is," she went on, "Coco Chanel was... my mother. My father was Pierre Wertheimer. " At Gérard's expression, Miss Zutter smiled sadly. "Hard to believe, I know," she said. "Yet it's true. I was their dirty little secret. The result of an illicit affair. One that went on for years, apparently."

"No offense," said Gérard coldly. "But what does this have to do with me and my right to the funds my father left me?"

"Please," she said. "Sit down. It's a story worth telling. One that will bring to light what you want to know."

Gérard, wary yet curious, finally nodded and sat back down.

"You see," said Miss Zutter, "I'm the woman your father trusted to start this account for you. I thought he was crazy to do it, but in the end I supported him."

"All I know," said Gérard, "is that this thing called the Circle killed my father. And isn't blameless in my mother's death, either. If you are a part of the Circle, that makes you an accomplice, as far as I'm concerned." He pushed his chair back to stand again. He'd get someone else to help him. He was done here.

"Calm down," she said, "please. I beg of you. I will explain everything."

Once again, Gérard returned to his seat unwillingly, thinking it was probably better to hear the woman out since she obviously had information about the Circle that could help him. Plus, if his father had trusted her with his money, it was possible she was worth listening to.

"As I said," she went on, "I supported *him*—your father, that is. I would hardly say that classifies me as part of the Circle. My mother and her lover—well, let's just say their partnership had begun long before their affair. My father was married. With sons of his own. My mother kept the affair secret and never married. Ultimately, when she emerged from what she called her 'sabbatical' with a new fashion line, it came with her new lover, the Duke of Westminster."

She shrugged. "They had no use for me and it was off to the orphanage I went. I was still a baby. And so it was many years before my father came to me—found me—when I was almost 18 and would be freed from the confines of hell."

Gérard nodded. This was something he knew about. First hand.

"The only mothers I knew were Sister Margaret Mary and Sister Catherine, one more cruel than the other. To hear my father tell it, it had been—*I* had been—an 'inconvenient situation.' Not a particularly helpful way to think about yourself, eh, Gérard?" She didn't wait for a response. "But, honestly, I'm glad he was the one that found me and not my so-called mother." Her voice became strident, her accent heavier. "That horrible woman turned out to be a Nazi agent. A treasonous traitor to France."

Gérard had heard tales of Chanel's dealings with the Nazis during the occupation from Jacques. How she had come to seize control of the Wertheimer properties, claiming ownership after, as she had reported, they had been "abandoned" by their Jewish owners.

"Still," began Gérard, "what does this have to do with me—with my father? I'm tired of all this storytelling."

"Please, be patient," said Zutter. "I am getting there, I promise. As time went on, I became my father's confidant. At first I was surprised by his lack of concern about Coco's traitorous actions, her takeover of his assets. But soon I discovered why. My father, Pierre Wertheimer, was one of the founding members of the organization called the Circle. In fact, he was there for their very first meeting, which took place at William Randolph Hearst's estate."

Everyone knew about Hearst and his infamous wealth and properties. Gérard's ears perked up.

"There were nine initial members of this Circle, including Hearst and my father. It was Hearst's idea to make blood pacts, to pool fortunes. To agree to, adhere to, and embrace a life of hunting, chasing, and killing. *Killing*, Mr. Finck. The hunting and killing of other men."

She gave Gérard a chance to take this in, stepping to the sidebar to fill a glass of water and bring it to the table for him. Gérard drank greedily. Could what Zutter was saying be real?

Zutter filled his glass again before speaking. "In 1929, Mr. Frank Baumgartner was the first of the original nine members to go, the first to die at the hands of a fellow Circle member."

"It's a great story," Gérard agreed, "but once again, what does it really have to do with me now? Or why I should trust you." He looked pointedly at the locked door. "If what you're saying is true, you could be about to kill *me* right now."

Zutter laughed without humor. "If that were true, Mr. Finck, you'd already be dead. And why would I bother to spend all this time sharing such things?"

It was a good question.

"And the truth is, I tried. To join, that is. I wanted to join the Circle more than anything. I pleaded with Father to let me join. Compared to living life as the illegitimate daughter of a traitor and a defeated millionaire? No contest. But he wouldn't allow it. It was 1945, don't forget, and women were expressly forbidden from entry, at least in the hunting capacity. That's why he set me up here. At the bank. Overseeing the Circle's finances. Keeping all the Watchers in line."

"Watchers? What are Watchers?"

"You've got a lot to learn," Zutter said. "Considering the circumstances, I suggest you try to be a bit more patient."

Stung, Gérard bit his tongue. Zutter's steely spine had begun to reveal itself.

"Needless to say, this new position didn't satisfy my needs. I'm like you, Gérard. May I call you Gérard?" Gérard nodded warily. She went on. "Like the rest of the Circle members. I want to be a killer of prey, prey that is worthy of my skills. Not of a bunch of pathetic Watchers—those who do as their name suggests: watch and clean up after the act. I want to be hunted, too, to experience the thrill of vanquishing an enemy who thought he could get the better of me.

"My father—the Circle—robbed me of that, Gérard. Which is why I am going to help you."

From a shrinking violet in spectacles, Miss Zutter had transformed into a hardened, if middle-aged sociopath. Gérard was fascinated. He chose to wait for more to be revealed.

"Good for you, Gérard. I see you are already improving your skill of patience. I knew as soon as I met you that you would be the one. That you would appreciate what I have to offer. You see, I know everything there is to know about the Circle. Their strongest branches. Most dangerous members. I know...it all."

"But the Circle destroyed my father," said Gérard at last. "I—"

"You may hate the Circle and you may despise their rules, which caused your father's death—and kept me from achieving my own objectives—but you, dear Gérard, are fortunate. Extremely fortunate that you have not been removed, taken out as collateral damage. Hunted down the way Mr. Spade was. That is a very unusual situation in which to find oneself. And an opportunity to make things right. To seek revenge."

Gérard thought about it. "But I'm looking for more than just revenge. I want to bring it down. The Circle. The whole organization."

"Then you need me more than you know," said Zutter, "because I know the tricks of the trade. I can teach you to survive."

"I am already a survivor," Gérard said, insulted.

"Not the kind that survives the Circle, you're not," Zutter said. "You may be like me, you may have the need to kill deep inside you, but that isn't enough to make you a survivor of hunters. To keep you alive."

"Speak for yourself," Gérard said. "I got this far, didn't I?" The conversation was becoming tiresome and he had more important things to do than listen to a history lesson, as informative as it had been. He rose from his seat.

"Mr. Finck," said Zutter, reverting to the formal and handing him a business card with an address scribbled on the back. "Meet me here tonight, 1:00 AM sharp. I assure you, you won't regret it."

Gérard pocketed the card. "Maybe I'll be there, maybe I won't. But I'll be back tomorrow, *Jeneane,* and I want my money."

• • •

The address, he learned, was nowhere special, just an overpass by Lake Zurich. What surprised Gérard was that he'd taken the bait of a woman he hardly knew, who had told him an unbelievable yet amazingly probable story that would explain his life. A life so similar to her own. After a barely decent yet cheap dinner near his hotel he'd retreated to his room where he'd attempted to shut out the voice telling him to take the business card out of his pocket. By midnight it was clear he would no more be able to ignore it than he was to ignore his need for vengeance.

Would Zutter try to convince him to join forces with her? Was that what this was all about? Or was it some kind of a trap?

He parked the Citroen and looked out at the calm water, thinking about his recent tête-à-tête with Lieutenant Martin and further back to his childhood as he stood on the riverbank of the Seine watching the carnage as it happened. He picked up a rock at his feet and hurled it as hard as he could into the water where it landed with a splash. He watched the water ripple outwards. They said that things in life had that kind of effect. If that was true, his childhood had led him to this very spot for a reason.

Gérard returned to his car and continued to wait until his impatience surfaced and he turned the key in the ignition to leave. No one made Gérard Finck wait. No one.

Then he saw approaching lights in his rear view mirror. The car pulled alongside, rolled to a silent stop, flashed its lights once, and then turned off. The door opened and Jeneane, dressed in black, emerged. She came around to the passenger side of Gérard's rusted-out vehicle and climbed in, recoiling only slightly at the smell. Gérard had eaten many meals lately in this car. "Why the hell am I out here?" he said without preamble.

"Good evening to you, too," said Jeneane. "Let's get right to it, then. You say you're ready to take on the Circle," she said. "I think you need my help."

"You already said that. Tell me more."

"You don't want my help. You think you can handle this alone."

"That's right. I do."

"Well, you are certainly welcome to try that approach, Mr. Finck, but before you do you should know that members of the Circle won't be as easy to kill as Lieutenant Martin."

Gérard's eyes went wide. She knew about that? How? No one knew. "I don't know what you're talking about."

"Really, Mr. Finck. You think this is something the Circle would not notice? That *I* would not notice? The Circle put me in charge of their finances, and that gives me access to everything. Do you think for one second that you can kill a Watcher without anyone noticing? Without *my* knowing about it?" She shook her head.

Gérard felt cornered, a feeling he detested. "What are you going to do?"

"Do?" she asked. "*I'm* not going to do anything." She paused, then looked casually at the side view mirror toward her BMW. "*We* are going to do something. Yes?"

She was waiting for a response. Finally, Gérard nodded.

"*Gut*. Then you will follow me."

She got out of Gérard's car and back into hers. Gérard followed her closely as the BMW drove slowly, yet consistently, around Zurich before stopping at a beach area by the lake. The BMW parked and Gérard parked next to it. He felt jumpy, defenseless. He felt for the knife in his pocket to remind himself he was armed. Jeneane emerged from her car and gestured for Gérard to do the same. She waited a beat, and then beckoned for him to join her at the BMW's rear.

"You say you're prepared to take on the Circle," she said. "May I ask how? With a single kill under your belt? A kill so poorly executed that any hunter worth his salt would hardly abide?"

Gérard bristled at the criticism.

Jeneane went on. "You must understand, Mr. Finck." Apparently, their return to the more formal form of address was the way it was going to be.

"These are men *who hunt*. That is nearly *all* they do. Day in and day out. They take joy in killing each other. Yet during those times when they are not hunting, you would not suspect them of such acts. They are civilized. Dignified. Have friends in important places. Politicians, business magnates. They are people of influence. Respected. They are friends only to the point that they must hunt and kill that friend, at which point they do not hesitate."

She opened the BMW's trunk. Gérard shrank away when he saw what lay within.

"This is Mr. Schmid, Mr. Finck," said Jeneane. The man, bound and gagged and bleeding onto the plastic tarp set down to cover the car's upholstery, gazed at them with wide desperate eyes. "Mr. Schmid *was* a Watcher of the Circle."

Schmid whimpered behind the gag in his mouth, obviously hoping for a miracle.

"Mr. Schmid would like to live. But he also knows the rules of the Circle. The rules of the Watchers. Don't you, Mr. Schmid?"

Schmid scooted back a few inches in the trunk, but the light had gone out of his eyes.

"And he knows that when a Watcher is identified by a member, his services are no longer needed." She withdrew a long bladed knife. "And who do you think takes care of these things, Mr. Finck?"

Jeneane's arm raised up and then came down in a whoosh to stab Schmid in the abdomen. "I do," she said. "I've been taking care of this chapter's messes for over a decade. Since my father died. You see, someone has to do the dirty work, Mr. Finck." She handed the knife to Gérard. "It may as well be us."

Gérard held the knife for a long moment, looking down at the man whose life was oozing out of him. It was sticky in Gérard's hands. "No," he said.

"No?" said Jeneane, surprised.

"No," Gérard repeated. "I want to do this my way."

Jeneane smiled.

• • •

It wasn't a long walk to the water, yet made uncomfortable by Schmid's lack of cooperation. The wound in his abdomen was deep, his legs unable to keep him upright. Gérard was forced to drag him along the sand to the water's edge. Like dropping a stone into the water, thought Gérard. Who knew how far the ripples would travel?

Schmid was without resistance as Gérard plunged his face into the water. He held it there until the form in his hands was nothing but dead weight, and watched as the water settled after its disruption. After a moment, the ripples dissipated into nothing more than vague black lines easing into darkness.

Gérard turned to Jeneane. She was much younger than he'd originally thought. Without her glasses, severe clothing, and hair pinned up, she was in fact, not unappealing. He dragged Schmid by the leg up the beach just enough so he wouldn't float away, then stepped back toward Jeneane. When she didn't move away, he moved in to kiss her.

And choked when she struck him in the throat with her open palm. Gagging, he stumbled back.

"Lesson number one," she said. "Never let your guard down." She looked downward pointedly. "Killing is exciting, no, Mr. Finck? But I would suggest you get your...urges... under control."

Gérard couldn't answer as he was still gasping for air, but managed a nod. At least his arousal had fled along with his breath.

"And that is all well and good, Mr. Finck, but not with me. There will be no room for that in this relationship if it is to be fruitful for both of us. And in the Circle. A kill is only that: a kill. Our needs, whatever they are, outside the killing, are to be met elsewhere. Is that understood?"

Gérard nodded, finally able to breathe again.

"After a kill, Watchers are dispersed to sanitize the site. It is not in your best interests—or anyone else's—to linger, to...

accommodate those needs. Furthermore, you will need to do exactly as I say. There will be no argument. Ever. If you want to infiltrate the most secretive society in the world, you'll need to act the part. Given the amount of work we will have to do to achieve that result, time will be involved. You will need to exercise patience. Can you do that, Mr. Finck?"

He wanted to hit her. He wanted to beat her to a pulp. He wanted to jump her bones. But instead he only nodded.

"And from now on, you will only refer to me as Miss Zutter and I will address you as Mr. Finck. Is that understood?"

Gérard nodded again.

She led him back to Mr. Schmid's lifeless body and showed him how to puncture the lungs so any remaining air would be expunged, allowing the body to sink to the bottom of the lake.

"Ordinarily, the Watchers take care of all kills, but this is not our situation. Outside the protective umbrella of the Circle, we will have to cover our own tracks. Your particular propensity for drowning creates an opportunity as well. If you know how to exploit it. In this case, however, the police won't be looking for him. And if the body turns up, information about it will come to me. I can make it go away."

She gave Gérard a long look. "By the time I'm through with you, Mr. Finck," she said, "you will be unstoppable. *We* will be unstoppable."

Together, they pushed the body out into the water and watched as he slowly drifted away and then submerged into the darkness.

38

June, 1975 — Washington, D.C.

Vivian was curled up in her favorite chair, the plush shabby chic one by the fireplace in her mothers' house in Bethesda. She was reading a book, or pretending to, anyway. Nothing memorable, some Barbra Cartland novel her mother had handed her to distract her. It wasn't working. Instead she was reliving the scene with Gary at the hospital over and over. And on 6 West! Where there were children! Families! Each time felt like the shock of a cattle prod. There was no excuse for his behavior. She sighed. Not that hers was any better. Decking your own husband, another doctor, no matter how much of a jerk he was, in your workplace, was not something she'd be proud to add to her resume. She flexed her hand, still sore from the punch, and smiled. She might regret her actions, but wasn't sure she'd take it back either.

On the coffee table in front of her was the vase of long-stem roses Warren had sent her, 17 of them. Why 17, she wondered.

The knock at the door startled her even though she was expecting Warren's arrival. They were going to see each other for the first time since he'd spent the night. She was excited. Nervous. Floating with anxiety and anticipation. Like a teenager she leapt to her feet. "Coming," she called.

She smoothed out her dress, a stunning new one, an indulgence in silver, with a beguiling scoop neck and padded shoulders. The skirt flared out just skimming her knees to showcase her long beautiful legs. Gary had always said they were her best asset, but in a way that made her feel it was her only one. In this dress, she felt beautiful all over, and knew her skin tone against the sparkling silver was luminous. She hadn't felt this lovely, or this loved, in a long time. She opened the door with a beaming smile, which fell quickly at the sight of a man in a uniform.

"Vivian Chambers?"

"Yes...?"

"Certified letter here for a Dr. Vivian Chambers." The man took out an envelope from the satchel she hadn't noticed on his shoulder.

"Yes, that's me," She said cautiously.

"Sign here, please." The man, expressionless, offered her a clipboard and pen. Vivian signed her name, a quick doctor's scrawl. The man tipped his cap. "Have a nice evening ma'am," he said, and left.

The hospital's letterhead on the upper left corner was all she needed to see. *Didn't take them long, did it?* There were sure to be repercussions for punching the head of Pediatrics. She just figured they'd wait until she was back at work. She opened the letter and read, disbelief clouding her features.

Dr. Chambers,

As you know, George Washington University Hospital has a zero-tolerance policy with regards to violence in the workplace. Your actions were found to be too emotionally charged and in stark contrast with the professional work environment we strive for here. Therefore, in light of your altercation with Dr. Gary Thompson two days ago, the board has unanimously voted to terminate your position with this institution. We thank you for your years of dedicated service and wish you luck as you continue your career.

This decision is not subject to appeal.

Regards,
Philip Locke
Board President

Gary. That sonofabitch! This was his doing. A reprimand would have been justified. But...termination? She'd be finished as a doctor if word got out. This never would have happened if she were a man. She picked up the closest object to her, a small yet costly piece of ceramic sculpture, and hurled it against the wall where it shattered in bits.

"Viv, is that you? Are you okay?" Stacy stepped into the foyer and took in the broken artwork. "Vivian…?"

Suddenly, all Vivian's rage left. She walked into her mother's arms. "They won, Mom. Gary won." One mistake by a woman and this is what happened. The all-white, all-male board of directors saw her as a threat. More like a threat to their manhood. More offensive than all the shame Gary had brought on by his actions. Actions he'd flaunted for those same white men who wished they had the same prowess over women. Everything she'd worked for. Everything she'd tried to avoid. Gone. Wiped away with one action and a few strokes of a pen. She handed the letter to her mother who read it slowly.

"But, Vivian, I don't understand…."

"What's not to understand, Mom? It's simple. I'm finished."

"But there must be something you can do," said Stacy. "You're a great doctor. You've worked so hard all these years…they can't just…."

"Apparently they can," said Vivian. "But you know what, Mom? You're right. I will not take this lying down." She reached for her handbag and keys and slipped on her heels. "The bastard is not going to get away with this."

"Where are you going?"

"I'm going to do what I should have done a long time ago. Take care of business."

Vivian opened the door and smacked right up against a hard surface. "Warren!"

"Vivian. Is everything okay?"

"No. Everything is not okay. I'm sorry, Warren, but there's something I need to take care of."

Before Warren had a chance to press on, Stacy was handing him a letter. "What's this?"

"Read it," said Stacy.

"That bastard Gary got me fired," said Vivian.

"Fired?" said Warren. "But how...why…?" He read the letter. "I see," he said slowly.

"I'm sorry," said Vivian, "but I have to go. Like I said, there's something I have to do." She went to brush past him.

"Wait," Warren said. "Let's talk about this."

"What's there to talk about? He got me fired."

"I can see that...I guess. But why?"

Vivian deflated a little. "Isn't it obvious? I punched him. In the face."

Warren actually smiled before quickly recovering. "Oh," he said. "Well, I guess that'd do it."

"Yeah. But he's not gonna get away with it. I'm gonna kick that idiot's ass from here to—"

"Hang on, then," said Warren. "I'll drive."

• • •

Traffic into D.C. was always bad, but Friday nights were generally heavier and the ride to the Thompson-Chambers household, located not far from the hospital in a respectable condo, was a long one.

"So," Warren began, "Do you have a plan? What are you going to do, break the door down?"

"No need to be uncivilized," Vivian said. "I'll ring the bell. *Then* I'll knock him out."

"I like that plan," Warren said. "But what if he's expecting you? He must have known that letter was arriving today. Who says he'll even be home?"

"He's home, alright," Vivian said. "When I'm not around he's busy diddling nurses in what was once our bed."

"Diddling?" asked Warren.

"Yes, diddling," said Vivian. "It's better than all the other words that come to mind." A thought hit her. "Oh wait, they're former nurses now. You think he got me fired because I got them fired?"

"Maybe," Warren said, "But it's probably more because he got punched by his wife, a doctor, on the ward where he worked in front of a bunch of people. Man, to have been a fly on the wall for that."

"It was pretty sweet," Vivian said, flexing her bruised hand again. "You know what I said—well, yelled, actually—after I hit him?"

"What?"

"*Hematoma on 6 West!* And then I walked away."

She was laughing, so that was good.

"A hematoma is a really bad bruise," she offered.

"Yeah, I kind of knew that," said Warren. "I'm proud of you, Viv. I guess you could say that punching him was in the heat of the moment. But I don't know, going to his house? That might only make things worse."

Vivian straightened.

Warren tried to keep his eyes on the road. "I remember a long time ago you once told me that just because someone called you a name or hurt you didn't make it right to fight back, at least like this."

Vivian was quiet. For so long that Warren was afraid he'd crossed a line. This was her life, after all. Her career. Her marriage.

Finally, Vivian turned to him and let out a frustrated moan. "You're right," said. "As much as I hate it, attacking Gary is not going to make things any better."

More quiet.

"But I'm sorry," she said.

"Why? Sorry for what?"

"For how things ended all those years ago. I said some things that weren't fair. I wasn't fair."

Warren pulled the car onto the shoulder. He wasn't prepared for the apology. He'd pushed the ugliness of that night so far back into his subconscious he'd doubted even Mr. Vice could find it. "Thank you," he said. "That means a lot to me. But you were right. I spent a lot of time in...my support group," he said carefully, "dealing with that night. And everything that led up to it."

Vivian leaned over the center console of the car, and kissed him. The taste of her lips on his was still the best flavor in the world. "Thank you for stopping me from doing something stupid," she said.

"My pleasure," he said. "Now how about we go back to your place and order a pizza? Just don't change that dress. I haven't had the chance to tell you just how ravishing you are in it."

She smiled and kissed him again. "Well, I still have to deal with being unemployed, but I guess that can wait. Hey, why 17?"

"Seventeen?"

"Roses. You sent me 17 roses."

"Easy," said Warren. "One for every year we lost by not being together."

Vivian was touched. "But wait. It was only 16 years."

"Well, there are really only 16 blossoms. The one in the middle is silk. That one is for our future. Because our future is forever...because silk never dies." He wanted to tell her about his plans for this future he'd mapped out. How they'd move to a small town somewhere, where Vivian could have her own practice, start fresh, but it was probably too soon for all that.

Vivian took his hand. "Warren," she said. "It's time to turn the car around. We have some serious catching up to do."

39

1978—Zurich, Switzerland

In the two years since meeting Miss Zutter, Gérard had applied himself to learning everything he could under her tutelage. He'd become far more organized. Calculating. He'd learned how to tamp down his impulses, like the one that had led him to Lieutenant Martin's back then and resulted in his messy demise. Gone was the carelessness. Gone was the arousal, at least in the moment. He had developed a capacity for compartmentalization that was truly commendable. As mentors go, Miss Zutter knew she had proven equally worthy.

He'd been living in her home, where he studied and practiced new tools and techniques, and watched as his money collected more interest by the day. Miss Zutter's idea. The more money a member brings into the Circle, the more the member tends to be underestimated. Like getting into a prestigious job after marrying the boss' daughter. "If they think you're nothing more than a bank, they'll assume you're lacking the skills to do the job," she told him. "Everyone wants to be assigned to kill the new guy." Gérard's finances and assumed lack of skill would mask his current level of expertise and give him the upper hand on his first assignment.

Miss Zutter was very well versed in what she called "the human condition." She had begun teaching him to read facial expressions. Body language. Subtle, seemingly insignificant motions or ticks. Gérard was getting the hang of it quickly. She took him to local bars and restaurants and encouraged him to start testing his skills on various female patrons of all ages and walks of life. She was especially pleased when his success led him to bedding one of them; she'd picked them out and his success was proof of her own.

Not that it was easy. Gérard Finck was unpolished. Unsophisticated. Uncouth. In the beginning, it was crash-and-burn. But Jeneane Earnest was not a quitter. She felt like Pygmaleon of Greek mythology. Like Henry Higgins coaching Eliza Doolittle. Coaching Gérard on how to speak purposefully, yet casually. Being attentive and active with his listening. All tactics for extracting information. Combining these skills with his quickly growing ability to read body language was transforming him into a master of the conversational arts. In reality, it hadn't taken all that long. Gérard was a natural charmer with the ladies and good looking, like an unpaid gigolo. The women loved him.

It would be easy for Jeneane to settle for a physical relationship with her student. Very easy. But it would also be dangerous. Their liaison was platonic and she intended to keep it that way. His age did not matter, only that she grew his skill set. There was no time for petty emotions, particularly jealousy....or even lust.

• • •

Gérard was feeling antsy. He'd accompanied Miss Zutter on several of her clean-up missions, of which there were far more than he'd expected there to be, but there had been no other kills he'd attended to personally. Watchers, it seemed, were relatively dispensable; in just two years, five had to be eliminated due to lack of preparation, poor results, or just plain ignorance. The work took them all across Europe; Italy, Austria, Germany, and two in Belgium. The Circle was meant to run smoothly, and sloppiness was not tolerated.

It did not escape Gérard that he was becoming a walking contradiction. That his goal of infiltrating the Circle meant preparing by mentoring under the one woman capable of bringing them down without him. If Miss Zutter were somehow kept from doing her job so effectively, taking out undeserving Watchers, their inadequacy would soon compromise the success of the whole organization.

Gérard pondered that fact often. And was doing so while seated at a high bar table sipping a rum and coke when Miss Zutter snapped her fingers in his face.

"Are you listening to me?" she said.

Gérard did not like the fact that this woman could, literally, snap her fingers and expect him to do her bidding. For a moment his hand tightened around the heavy glass in his hand and he pictured bringing it down upon her head, over and over, until her days of humiliating him were over. But when his senses returned, he felt just like a little boy called out in school to answer a question he wasn't expected to have the answer to. This attempt to embarrass him, however, did not yield similar results.

"Of course, Miss Zutter," he said. He had mastered the art of listening without looking. Fine tuning his ears, homing in on conversations he had no part in, revealing nothing. He repeated Miss Zutter last sentences verbatim. "There is another Watcher that requires our services. We are going back to France."

Miss Zutter sat back. "Well, at least I have taught you well, Mr. Finck," she said. She clinked her glass of Merlot with his glass and took a slow sip. "We leave first thing in the morning. In the meantime," she said, scouring the crowd. "That one. Tall brunette, black dress, end of the bar."

"No surprise."

She raised her eyebrows.

"She's with three friends. You're challenging me."

"Indeed I am." She looked at her watch. "You have 90 minutes, starting now."

Gérard sputtered. "Not enough time. It's too early. They just got here."

"Ninety minutes," Miss Zutter said. "No excuses. Let's see what you're made of."

Gérard looked at his own watch: 8:38. He let out a long sigh, put on his game face, and made his way over to the bar. Through the sea of patrons, drunk on the way to rowdy, Gérard pushed his way through to place his order between the brunette and one of her friends and made sure they and the bartender saw the hundred franc note he was waving in the air. "Rum and coke," he yelled over the din. He locked eyes with the tall brunette. "And a round for whatever these lovely ladies are drinking." The bartender nodded and the money disappeared in a flash.

Gérard turned to the women, his killer smile in place. "So, having a good time tonight?" he said, studying each in turn.

There were four of them. The tall brunette, clearly the alpha, sipped from a highball glass garnished with a lime through the drink stirrer. Miss Zutter wouldn't have it any other way. The blonde to leggy brunette's right in a dress with more cleavage than material was already looking to her friend for guidance on how to proceed.

The other two, another blonde who looked half in the bag and a dark-haired waspy type who probably ate men alive, leaned against the bar to see what would happen.

There was a long pause as the brunette made her decision. "Why, thank you, sir," she said. "That's very kind of you."

And that was it. He was in. "Friday night, huh," he said.

She raised her glass. "Can't come fast enough," she said.

The drinks arrived. Gérard raised his glass. "Here's to the weekend, then," he said, and smiled at the brunette. "Charles is the name." A common one, easy to remember, thanks to his pal at the market, and just as easy to forget.

"Aria," she said.

"So, what brings you ladies out tonight?"

"Oh, you know," said the blonde, slurring her words a bit, "jush a few friendsh out for a drink."

"You'll have to forgive my friend here," said Aria. "It's been a long week."

"I hear that," Gérard said. "I'm not from around here. Just looking to make new friends." He kept his eyes on Aria, but took in everything, from the blonde with the cleavage's mojito to the other brunette's dirty martini.

"Bartender," he called. "Keep the tab going. Whatever these lovely ladies want. I'm buying."

They were his.

• • •

It was 3:40 a.m. when Gérard slid out of the king-sized bed to dress. They were leaving for France in the morning—this morning—and he had to pack. He hadn't made the deadline, but he'd ended up with the mark, Aria, *and* her friend, so that might count for something. Still, the failure, his accomplishment late by eight minutes, annoyed him. Worse, it could well annoy Miss Zutter.

40

June, 1975—Washington, D.C.

Warren was commemorating the death of his parents at the Old Ebbitt Grill, the oldest restaurant in the D.C. area. Mr. Vice had made sure Mr. Venom was aware. Vice chose the location not as much for its history, but its blatant disregard for modernization. Secluded booths in the rear of the restaurant for those whose affairs required the avoidance of prying eyes. Easily disregarded as urban legend, there were as many as seven different private booths in the rear of the Old Ebbitt Grill. The one farthest to the rear, where Warren was currently sitting, armed with antivenom in a syringe in his pocket, was said to have been frequented often by president Andrew Johnson.

You ready for this?

I'm ready, Warren said to Vice. *Now leave me alone. One of us is honoring his late parents here.*

Sure. And pigs fly.

Fine. We both know honor isn't part of this equation. But I'm busy. You still need to leave.

I'm going, I'm going. But remember, if something – anything – goes south, you abort. Understood? I will not have everything I've worked for destroyed. Is that 100% clear?

Of course it's clear. My life is on the line here, too," Warren said, in case you've forgotten.

Our life, Vice reminded him. *We're in this together.*

Warren nodded.

Good luck, then. See you on the other side, Vice said with a devilish laugh, and was gone.

It felt different. When Peter was there—as he always had been—and even in moments when he was silent, Warren could still feel him. Now there was nothing. He felt alone. He'd summoned the experience. He'd made the decision. Yet the sadness threatened to derail him and his intentions.

A waiter arrived at that moment, young, early 20s."William" was printed on the name tag. Average height and build with the sad early beginnings of a beer gut, evidence of what employees got up to after the boss was gone for the night. Piercing blue eyes sat deep into his face, making his nose appear longer than it actually was.

Warren ordered a bowl of soup and the surf and turf with mashed potatoes. Plenty of courses, plenty of time to give Mr. Venom ample opportunity to accomplish his objective. As Warren waited for his soup to arrive, he admired the old wooden booth and its soft leather seats, which had thankfully been comfortably reupholstered, and thought about how life had brought him to this place of lying in wait for someone to poison him. It was almost funny. It did not go unnoticed either that he was sitting in a secret booth formerly occupied by the President of the United States, a man who'd only risen to that office after his predecessor's assassination. Ironic that his alter ego was responsible for the assassination of another, some would argue far greater, president.

Warren kept an eye on the waiter. You never knew who could be bought. Before Warren took his first bite of the hearty beef barley soup William delivered, he again felt his right pocket for the syringe. Still there. Safe at hand. Better still on the table, but really, how hard could it be to retrieve it if—when—the time came?

The soup was excellent, as was the house salad of fresh greens, romaine and baby spinach, plump tomatoes, cucumbers, and raw onions, which he removed. Raw onion was one of the few foods that signaled his gagging reflex. The waiter brought him a glass of Cabernet to complement his 8-oz. fillet mignon and lobster tail duo with creamy mashed potatoes. Simple, yet satisfying.

Before he sunk his fork into the steak he raised his glass to the sky and toasted his parents—and realized he meant it. Without his parents' dying, he would not be here now, sitting in this restaurant with a king's feast in front of him, endless money in his pocket, and the world at his feet. "Here's to you, Mom and Dad," he said, "I wouldn't be who I am without you." He dug into the juicy steak with a chuckle. If he was going to be murdered today, he'd prefer his steak and lobster first.

By the end of the meal, as he finished off his potatoes, Warren was slightly uneasy. He'd enjoyed a tasty dinner with no apparent unwanted side-effects. Had he miscalculated Mr. Venom's move so badly? Was there no plan to attack Warren here, now, today? Feeling like this opportunity had been squandered, possibly lost altogether, almost as relieved as frustrated, Warren put cash down to cover his bill and rose to his feet when he felt a sting behind his right shoulder.

Sonnofa– He reached over with his left hand and removed the protruding thing from his back, tearing the flesh as it came free. Warren felt the blood drip down his back. A dart. The poison wasn't in the food. It had never been in the food.

• • •

The rubbery taste he'd been expecting in his mouth all night confirmed the reality of his circumstances. He went to reach into his right pocket for the syringe as planned. Unfortunately, he found his right arm was already numb on the way to incapacitated, dangling like a wind chime. *Really? I'm going to die because the syringe I so carefully placed in my pocket will stay there while I expire? I don't think so.*

There was no time to think. He fell to the ground, pulling the tablecloth and remaining dishes to the floor with him. His previously hovering waiter was nowhere to be seen, and the booth's seclusion was effective in its privacy. On the ground, his body was seizing up. In all his reading, there had been nothing about the actual speed of the venum's effect in the bloodstream, even if he'd known how much was in the damn syringe. He had to get his left hand to his right pocket. Now. But the effort only rolled him a few inches under the table.

His heart was racing. His breathing was labored. With a final burst of effort, he cajoled the syringe from his suit pocket. Now all he needed was to remove the cap from the end of the needle. His fingers felt like lumps of clay, not the tools of dexterity they'd always been. The world began to blur and he vomited his surf-and-turf dinner. If he'd only known.... But would it have mattered? Would he still have taken the risk he'd been so sure was a calculated one? His body writhed in pain. Was he having a seizure? When the front of his pants felt wet, he realized he'd urinated. The shame, combined with his stupidity, the fact that he'd actually thought he could outsmart Mr. Venom like this, would have been amusing if it weren't for the fact that he was about to croak. And that he'd never see Vivian again.

Vivian! The thought of her brought anguish, and then a jolt of renewed fervor. He could not, would not, give up now.

The cap. Remove the cap. Stab yourself with that syringe. Do it now. Otherwise, you will never see your beloved again. You. Will. Die.

Somehow, he didn't know how, the cap was now removed from the syringe. Plunging the antivenom into his thigh was the preferred method, but it was all he had left in him to push it over to his leg and push the leg into the needle while holding the plunger in place. The shaking didn't help. It took every bit of concentration he had.

It's done, he thought. But was he too late?

• • •

The pain subsided first. Within seconds. Next came the feeling in his arm. His breath returned to normal. He rolled onto the syringe so it was under his back and stared up at the ceiling, which desperately needed a new coat of paint. The stench emanating from his own body was reviling. Still, he waited. Would Venom be content to view his kill from afar? After several minutes of playing dead, Warren decided he'd had enough and started to his knees only to lower himself to the ground again as footsteps came around the corner. He froze. Went limp. The footsteps stopped inches from his body. He heard the breath of the person belonging to the feet.

Venom.

A kick to his ribs, then another. He held his breath and prayed the vomit would keep Venom from coming in too close. Just as he was about to reconcile himself to the need for air, with one more good kick and a grunt of satisfaction, the footsteps began to recede. A door opened and closed. Warren waited. Waited so long that he thought the waiting would surely kill him since the poison had not.

Finally when he decided he'd laid in his own vomit and urine long enough, he stood up, slowly testing each leg and arm on the way. He was busy congratulating himself when he again heard footsteps. He dove back under the table and lay still again, his eyes closed. If whoever it was felt him for a pulse he'd be dead meat; it was racing that fast.

The footsteps stopped only a few inches away and a foot jabbed him unconvincingly. There was a loud sigh. And not the sigh of a waiter who'd just discovered his customer had expired after eating the dinner he'd been served. This was a different kind of sigh. The sigh of a tired, annoyed Watcher, there to clear the scene after the successful killing. A Watcher. Warren slit one eye open just enough to see that he was right—and wrong. The man was a Watcher, there to take care of business, but that man was also his waiter.

The waiter was stronger than he looked. Groaning at the smell, he pulled Warren away from the table. Warren's head smacked against the solid oak chair leg and he had to use all his will to keep from crying out. *Dead men don't cry.*

The Watcher left him there to retrieve a dolly and then strapped Warren into it. If the kid'd been even a slight bit more motivated, taken even the slightest interest in his task, he'd have known Warren was faking. But he didn't. It came to Warren that this was one Watcher the Circle should oust. The thought came unbidden. He did not want to think like *them.*

Finally, after the waiter had cleaned up the scene with a bucket of soapy water and a mop, he gave the dolly a kick to set it back on its wheels. Warren's weight sent the dolly careening to the side, and once again Warren found himself on the floor. This time with a shoulder that felt broken. He heard a groan.

The groan was his.

The waiter yelped and scooted back away from Warren and the dolly.

Warren opened his eyes and peered at the waiter. "Hey, William," he said. "What's for dessert?"

41

February, 1981 — Zurich, Switzerland

Five years. That's how long Gérard had been on this path. Learning how to extract information, training in hand-to-hand combat, weaponry, stealth. Exercising patience he never knew he had. Learning the long game. He couldn't say he was having the time of his life. On the other hand, it was exactly that. He was 25 and in more control than he'd ever been, an attribute that had eluded him in his youth.

He was in the bowels of Miss Zutter's home on a black mat circling a heavy blue bag hanging from the wall. He punched at it over and over, the sound of the glove slapping the leather echoing through the large space, which contained only gym equipment. Sweat glistened on his skin as he practiced protecting the face, bobbing and weaving in between punches. The mirror along the close wall reflected just how powerful he'd become.

Gérard felt the air move by his head. Miss Zutter, about to deliver a round-house kick to the back of his neck. Her silent approach was noteworthy, but ineffective as Gérard dodged the blow and rolled away, taking her legs out from under her with a sweeping kick.

"Excellent," she said from the floor. "I have taught you well."

Gérard did not lower his guard. His arm was cocked back and ready for another strike. He nodded.

"But it is you who have achieved so much."

Gérard was surprised by this vote of confidence. Miss Zutter was never one for compliments. He offered a hand and she took it. After rising to her feet she dusted off her clothes and straightened them. "I have news," she said.

"What kind?"

"The kind you'll like."

"I'm intrigued."

"Another mission, in Spain."

"When do we leave?"

"First thing in the morning," she said. "And not we. You."

Gérard was knocked back. "Now? Me? Alone?" He'd been waiting for this moment, but the suddenness of it left him breathless.

"Yes, you. Alone. You're ready." Miss Zutter turned to go. "Get cleaned up and come upstairs. I have a dossier waiting."

Gérard used the small shower in the basement to wash up quickly. The water dripped down his body in rivulets, changing direction with every scar it met. The one on his shoulder from the wrong end of his foster father's belt at eight. He'd needed stitches that time. Another on his abdomen where one of his foster mothers had struck him with a curling iron. He could still smell the skin sizzle as he touched the raw scar tissue. Finally, the one on his leg from the bite of that neighbor's pit bull. He hadn't walked for a week and survived only because the dog hadn't been rabid and the bite didn't get infected. He could have died, and without much notice, probably.

The scars were part of the training he hadn't known he needed, but now appreciated. It had gifted him with the ability to throw compassion out the window. To kill. To take a life without remorse. And now he was going to get to do it on his own. Put his skills to the ultimate test, and not just for some woman in a bar. A Watcher needed to be eliminated, and Gérard would be the one to take care of it.

He turned the water to its hottest setting. The water scalded his naked body, the steam filling the tiny shower stall. He stood facing the stream of water and counted to ten, then again. Then once more, until his skin burned. He turned around and repeated the same ritual. He controlled the pain, savoring the experience and compartmentalizing it. Then he turned the water to the coldest setting and again went through the same process. The extremes were painful and liberating. The icy water cooled his burned skin, while chilling him to the core. It focused him. Brought him clarity.

He turned off the water. He hadn't brought a change of clothes down from his room, so, wrapped in a towel, he ascended the stairs to the living room. Miss Zutter was waiting on her elegant couch with a legal-sized white envelope resting on the coffee table. He'd seen enough to know that white was for Watchers, unlike the blue ones designated for members.

"Meet Mr. Pérez," she said, tossing it to Gérard whose towel slipped down his hips an inch or two as he snatched it from the air. "He's located in Bilbao, Spain. Sloppy. Unreliable. Leaving traces of blood behind at several locations. Unacceptable."

Gérard leafed through the paperwork that went with

the file. "Why did this come to you?" he asked, "and not the person in your position in Madrid?"

"Good question, Gérard. However, while there are many in my position, there is only one of me. And I am the best. All the files come to me first."

"What if something happens to you?" Gérard asked. "I mean, you can't keep doing this forever."

"No, I can't. But rest assured, when I am ready to stop, or when Father Time decides for me, there are contingency plans in place."

Gérard nodded.

"Now, back to Mr. Pérez," Miss Zutter said.

"It says here that he's a father of five and supports his wife's parents financially."

"And…? Is that a problem for you?"

"Of course not," said Gérard, lamenting the slip. Rule Number 1: Show nothing.

"Good," she said. "I would not want to think I have made the wrong decision here."

"Of course not," said Gérard.

Miss Zutter let a beat go by, then said, "Your ticket and return ticket are in there, then. You have 48 hours to make it happen—and I expect you to make me proud."

September, 1983—Kanab, Utah

Peek-a-boo Gulch and Spooky Gulch made for two of the most picturesque trails in all of Utah. They could each be conquered individually, but the challenge to the experienced hiker was to tackle both on the same loop. Known for their tight enclosures and smooth carvings into orangey rock formations, inexperienced hikers often found it difficult to find stable, secure footing and to handle the ever-present claustrophobia.

One such inexperienced hiker had Dr. Vivian Chambers buckled into a helicopter and rushing to the scene of a potentially dangerous accident. Word had gotten to her small practice in town that someone had fallen into a crevasse and was in need of medical assistance. No one liked being seen as the "inexperienced hiker," but it was most often the experienced one who goaded them into doing something beyond their capacity. It was not the first time Vivian was called for such an emergency, either, and almost certainly not the last, when she would have to pack up her medical bag and climb aboard with almost no information to help her prepare.

"Same landing spot as usual, Jack?" she asked her pilot.

"You know it," he replied, his voice echoing through her headset like it came from the other end of a Campbell's soup can on a string. When the chopper touched down at their designated spot. Vivian thanked him and carefully exited. She didn't have to give him the signal to power down; he knew this would take a while.

Waiting for her was a park ranger, a tall slender man in an impeccably clean uniform complete with standard issue stetson. "Dr. Chambers," he greeted her.

"Hey, Brian. Where are we going this time?"

"Spooky, Disputed Monument lands."

"Spooky, huh? But...how…?"

Brian rolled his eyes and let out a long sigh. "I'll give you one guess."

Vivian chuckled. "Judy's at it again, huh?"

"Yup. Brought a new boyfriend for his first hike. I was standing right there," he said, gesturing to a patch of ground not far from the entrance, "when she challenged him—oops, I mean, *asked* him—if he could handle the hike."

Challenged was certainly the more apropos description. Judy Ferguson knew this gulch better than anyone. Odds were she was ready to break up with the guy, new or not. It was her signature move. Bring them here where they'd realize they couldn't keep up with her and back off of their own volition. *Poor guy. It's embarrassing enough that they had to chopper in a doctor to help him. Any minute he was about to find out he'd already been dumped.*

"Can you take me to him or am I going in alone?"

"It's all you,Vivian. You know the trail by now."

Vivian wasn't dressed in her standard white coat. Not for this call. Instead, she was geared up in her full hiking apparel complete with hydration pack and North Face footwear. Also in her pack were medical supplies for setting broken bones and treating potential infections including scorpion and snake bites. She gave a new meaning to the phrase *house call.*

There was a time factor in getting to the patient, but it didn't stop her from admiring the splendor of the Gulch. The sharp angles of rock formations that suddenly change to smooth curves. Parallel lines like age rings around a tree trunk running along the rock. The stark contrast of the colors of the amber accenting the clear blue sky.

It wasn't long before she spotted them about 50 yards away, the boyfriend on the ground clutching at his ankle, Judy pacing around him, annoyed. Hopefully the poor guy thought it was concern. But Vivian knew Judy was only peeved that she hadn't been able to go on with the hike.

"Hey, Judy."

"Chambers."

"What'd you do to this guy, huh?" said Vivian as she approached.

"Nothing. The fool did this all himself."

"Not cool, Judy," the guy said.

"Well it's true, Theo!" Judy snapped. "I'm not the one who insisted I could climb and jump at the same time."

"You did what?" Vivian asked.

"He tried to climb up one wall and jump over to the other one," Judy said. I mean, look at the grip on those shoes. I told him it was a bad idea."

Vivian agreed, but the poor guy had only tried to impress.

"It's called parkour," Theo said. "It's huge in Europe."

"I told you already, I don't care," Judy said.

Theo had already removed his shoe and sock to accommodate the swelling, which was bad, the size of a cantaloupe.

"Theo, I'm Vivian. I'm here to take a look at that leg, okay?"

Theo nodded, but winced in pain when Vivian lightly touched his foot.

"Does it hurt when I touch it here?"

He bit his bottom lip. No one likes to look like a sissy in front of his girlfriend. Or used-to-be girlfriend, anyway.

"Okay, how about when I move the foot this way," she said, angling the foot downward.

This time Theo let out a yelp of pain and bit down on the knuckle of his index finger.

"That's what I was afraid of. Theo, this is broken."

Theo groaned again, this time from exasperation, Vivian suspected, and Judy did the same, probably for a very different reason.

"I have some supplies to put together a splint for it, but we still have to get you out of here." She took her time when she spoke to him, making sure to use soft tones to calm him down as she rifled through her pack for all the required materials. "I'm going to have my pilot lower down a tether. We'll strap you into it and lift you out, get you to the hospital where they'll reset your ankle and put on a cast, okay?"

Theo nodded, resigned. "I'm going to send Judy back to talk to the pilot. You and I will wait here. Judy?"

Judy nodded and sprinted away before Theo could say anything.

He looked at Vivian. "She's gonna dump me, isn't she?"

Vivian didn't answer.

"Yeah, I kinda had that feeling."

"Listen, Theo. You're a nice kid. You'll be fine. But maybe next time you won't try so hard to impress," she said.

"So...is there a Mr. Vivian?"

Vivian was flattered, but it wasn't the first time she'd been hit on by a patient grateful for her services. It had been a while, though, and it felt good. At 40, it was bound to happen less and less. Nice that this kid, all of 25 or so, saw her as a romantic interest. Or conquest. "Yes, there is," she said. "But if I were you I'd be more worried about that ankle…." She had to hand it to him. Broken ankle and about to be dumped, he'd risked rejection for a third time in one awful day. "And Judy," she added, "I'd definitely be worried about Judy."

The two of them shared a laugh as the sounds of the helicopter blades echoed overhead. It didn't take long to have Theo tethered to the cables and brought safely to the helicopter. Vivian waved off Jack so he and Judy could take Theo directly to the hospital. She'd get a ride home from Brian, who lived around the corner from her.

• • •

Warren Nichols was now Cole Warren. He'd told Vivian he wanted to change his name to signify a new beginning. "Warren Nichols missed 16 years with you. Cole Warren didn't." Vivian admitted she didn't fully understand, but had supported him and his need for change nonetheless. After his departure from D.C., his journey to Kanab had been a long one wrought with stopovers in over a dozen small towns. Each town, a bank. Each bank, an account. Each account, a cashier's check after a total withdrawal of funds. On to the next. When he arrived in Kanab he had over 13 million dollars of the Circle's money...his money...that he deposited into the local bank. The 200-plus million that he'd given to the Circle all those years ago was well worth the 13 million he'd kept for himself. He was satisfied with the trade. He had his life back.

It had been eight years since he left the Circle and there hadn't been a trace of any investigation or search or… anything. He'd actually stopped looking over his shoulder at the five- year mark. That's when he and Vivian had tied the knot.

Five years. He couldn't believe it. And all because he'd trusted that waiter, the night Mr. Venom had come for him. Sometimes, looking back, Warren almost believed there could be a God.

He'd given the waiter the shock of his life when he'd opened his eyes and awakened from the dead. It took Warren several minutes to calm him down.

"But they're going to kill me," he said. "You're supposed to be dead. That guy...the dart...I don't understand...."

"You don't have to worry about that," said Warren, "I have a plan." Of course he didn't, he was pulling one together on the fly, but better that William didn't know that. "Try to relax."

"Relax? You've got to be kidding me."

"Well, you don't have much of a choice. I'm not dead and I don't plan to be any time soon."

The waiter pulled the privacy curtain closed around the table and sat down, still shaking. "What do you want from me?"

"You could start by untying me."

The waiter approached with trepidation, but ultimately obliged.

"Thank you," Warren said as he rose to his feet. "Tell me your name."

"Williams. Watcher Williams."

"Your real name."

He hesitated. "Duncan," he said.

"Warren," said Warren. "You might know me as Mr. Vice."

They went to shake hands, but Duncan drew back quickly. "No way I'm shaking a hand that's been lying in vomit and piss."

Warren laughed. "I don't blame you. Here's the thing, Duncan, Mr. Venom believes he killed me. That means the Circle believes that I am dead. Once this scene is cleaned up, no one will be looking for me. No one. Ever again. Do you understand what I'm saying? I can offer you $100,000 if you simply go about your job of cleaning up while I make my getaway."

"Why?"

The question was unexpected.

"What do you mean, why?"

"You're a member of the Circle. You survived. Why do you want to play dead?"

Warren looked at the kid. "Because I've had enough."

"Well, then," said Duncan, "I've had enough, too."

That didn't sound good. "What does that mean?"

"That means I want out, too. This whole thing has been a mistake. I don't want to be a Watcher for the rest of my life. But that'll mean I need to disappear, and that'll take a lot more than you're offering."

Young, but not that dumb, Warren thought. "Fine," he said. "Name your price."

Duncan named a number much higher than Warren's original sum, but set against his freedom it was a drop in the bucket.

"Deal," he said.

Twenty minutes later when the clean-up was done, "Watcher Clean," as they called it, Warren sent Duncan off in a taxi to the airport with an account number of a bank in Missouri where he'd collect his money.

Duncan rolled down his window. "Hey, you're not gonna track me down and kill me, are you?" he said.

"Kill you?" said Warren. "Not if I don't have to. You wouldn't be stupid enough to share our little secret. So, no,

I'm not going to kill you. Which is why you're going to disappear. Forever."

Duncan blanched, but then nodded, rolled up his window, and told the cabby he was ready to go. It had been that easy.

• • •

It had been a small ceremony—their wedding, that is, his and Viv's. A tent and a few chairs that staked a claim overlooking Coyote Butte. Majestic and awe-inspiring, jagged layered rock formation against the backdrop of a pink sunset. Vivian wore a beautiful white sundress and a tiara she'd made for herself out of lilies. Warren appreciated the choice, a nod to his departed parents. He did not need to tell her that his sadness around not having them there at the ceremony was more about the fact that he'd had no relationship with them other than missing one.

Stacy flew in from D.C. on a series of flights and layovers specifically designed by Warren to keep any interested parties at bay. Just in case. With him dead and Stacy and Vivian Chambers nothing more than his former housekeeper and daughter, however, he doubted there was any real need. Still, he'd rather be safe than sorry.

Miss Stacy, though, generally uncomplaining to a fault, was not happy upon arrival. "Why so many planes? A trip from D.C. to Utah shouldn't have to take three days!" Warren blamed the airline and assured her the flight back would be first class with the least amount of stopovers possible.

Miss Stacy was the only family present for both of them. She walked them both down the makeshift aisle. Arm in arm, they slowly walked over a path of rose petals to stand in front of the justice of the peace. A few pronouncements and a passionate kiss later, they were husband and wife. They didn't honeymoon right away, choosing to stay local for a while and build Vivian's practice in a small office in the center of town.

"Cole" was now the current owner and operator of Al's Auto Detailing in Kanab, Utah. His only previous job had been accomplice to 51 murders, so he'd had to find something that pretty much ran itself. Al's fit that description. Al Panzarelli was ready to retire and Cole's offered price was way above market value. Once he'd stepped aside, Cole told all the employees that he'd keep each of them on if they continued to do the job right. After a month, he'd give them all a 10% raise. He promoted the most senior guy, who had turned out to be a great manager, adept at the day-to-day running of the place. As businesses went, it was perfect. As the owner, Cole came and went as he pleased, handled the advertising and marketing materials, and hired a couple to write and sing a jingle for their radio ad. *When your car shuts down, don't wear a frown. Come right to Al's where your car's our pal.* It surprised him how much he was enjoying what most people would call the humdrum life.

Going to Utah and buying a detailing shop might not be everyone's dream, but that's what he was bargaining on. No one in the Circle would expect someone with his access to funds to live this kind of basic hand-to-mouth life. And with Vivian so happy in her new practice, things were ideal.

They were happy. They were safe. They were in love.

43

1981—Bilbao, Spain

One of Spain's coastal cities, Bilbao lies on the bank of the Estuary of Bilbao, which leads to the Bay of Biscay. Like all Spanish towns and cities, residents, young and old alike, enjoy the benefits of the siesta, a two-to-three hour hiatus in the middle of the day for lunch and rest. Such is this cultural norm that major corporations also abide by this schedule, taking the work day well into the evening, but ensuring each day's productivity.

According to the paperwork in the dossier, which he read on the train to Bilbao, Gérard had noticed a brief window of time between the school-day schedule and Mr. Pérez's work-day schedule and had packed everything he needed for the job in a standard-sized leather duffel bag with many zipper compartments. Underwear, socks, pants, a few shirts, plus the real essentials: duct tape, a switchblade knife, some rope. The rest he would procure in Bilbao.

Gérard's opportunities for a quick and efficient kill were not going to happen in a bar or nightclub. Not for this Watcher. This was a working-class family man with responsibilities. This was not someone prone to flights of fancy like an evening of drinking after work. He did his job. He went home. He helped his kids with their homework and tucked them into bed. He repeated the same thing the next day. By the second day, Gérard was bored to tears from watching the slow drip of the guy's life.

Pérez remained at home until his children left for school after siesta at 3. He wasn't due back to his job at the sales office until 4:30. A 90-minute window. More than enough time. An added bonus was Pérez's line of work. The salesman could go missing for hours at a time with no one any the wiser, all assuming he was out on a sales call.

It was all a matter of how. Specifically, how to strike without the cover of darkness. There was no time to surveil Pérez any longer, no time to establish more long-term habits or holiday plans. Gérard would have to rely on the information provided in the dossier, which indicated that Pérez always left the office promptly at 1:35 to arrive home by 2:00, home being only a short walk from the office. By the time he arrived, his wife had already fed the children lunch and sent the older ones off to play quietly or complete some school work. The younger Pérez children would be napping in their rooms.

Every day Pérez ate a quick meal with his wife, who always waited for him, choosing not to eat with the children. Then they, too, would retire to their rooms to rest for an hour or more before Mrs. Pérez got the children off to school once again. Pérez left in time to return to his office by 4:10. It was mind-numbingly boring, yet helpfully reliable. Gérard had acquired a map of the area at the train station and found the perfect location for reconnaissance, at the intersection of Calle Juan Ajuriaguerra Kalea and Ercilla Kalea, where he drank coffee and watched and waited at a small café on the corner. From that vantage he could see everything he needed to see.

Bilbao was a busy place with busy people. Apartments above the shops housed the shops' owners, similar to his own small domicile in France where he'd left Charles. He sipped his coffee slowly, mindlessly perusing a newspaper, mainly looking at the photos. French and Spanish might both be derived from Latin, but the countless dialects of Spain rendered his translative abilities almost useless. He looked for key verbs that might provide context clues. Then, above the headlines, he saw Pérez. Up close, the man looked every bit the six feet and two inches the dossier had reported, though it had not quite captured the girth. The man obviously enjoyed his food. One might argue a bit too much.

Pérez, in an ill-fitting worn gray suit, was lugging his briefcase down the sidewalk. He looked neither happy nor unhappy. Simply...resigned. For a man whose body received little care, his hair was a different story. Jet black, obviously dyed, coiffed in a studied comb-over that did little to hide his bare scalp. Thin mustache trimmed to perfection. He'd probably been attractive once upon a time, but that time was past. Pérez took no notice of Gérard sitting at his tiny round table in front of the café. Why would he? Gérard was just another tourist, unworthy of attention. Pérez couldn't possibly be much of a salesman, though, thought Gérard, with the attention to detail of a gerbil.

Gérard let Pérez pass his location on Ercilla Kalea on the way to his sales office on the next street. Gérard would have to act fast. He followed Pérez down the sidewalk, making a point to match each of Pérez's footfalls on the concrete with his own. Gérard quickly gained on the salesman, whose stodgy gait was easy to mimic. The smell of his cheap cologne was overpowering; his breathing labored.

When Perez reached Mazarredo Zumarkalea, Gérard tapped Pérez on the shoulder. When Pérez turned, surprised, Gérard grabbed Pérez under the right shoulder and forced him into the alley. Hidden from the direct sunlight, the alley was dark and dank. The red brick of the buildings looked more like purple or black. Pérez, still staggering to maintain balance, swung his briefcase wildly at Gérard. Dumb luck and the sudden darkness of the shadows connected it with the side of Gérard's head.

Gérard stumbled for a moment, but only one, and Gérard was back on Pérez before he had a chance to turn and run, what with his size and awkward movements. Gérard had him swiftly tied into a sleeper hold within seconds. Pérez fought back, grasping for purchase at anything that might give him leverage, but the more he struggled, the more quickly he lost his strength. Gérard kicked out one of Pérez's legs, which sent him crashing down to a knee. Pérez's hands clawed at Gérard's arms, scratching the skin, releasing streams of blood that ran down Gérard's forearm. Gérard barely noticed. A few short moments later, Pérez was unconscious.

Gérard released his grip on Pérez. The body collapsed to the ground with a heavy thump. Gérard moved quickly to the dumpster in the back of the alley where he'd strategically placed a wheelchair that was hidden from view by debris. It was then he realized he would have to lift this lump of a man up into the wheelchair, a task made more difficult now that he was essentially dead weight. He sighed and opened up the folded chair and set it against the wall going for leverage. He bent his knees carefully, hooked his hands under armpits, and pulled upwards. It took three tries and strained muscles before he managed to get the man's backside settled in the seat, his poor eating habits be damned. Once he'd secured Pérez in the chair, Gérard withdrew a small syringe and injected its substance into Pérez's thigh. Enough serum to keep him asleep until after dark, even for a man his size. Gérard checked his watch. 4:27, less than an hour until sunset. He was prepared to wait.

• • •

It was later than expected, after 11 pm, when the sedative began to wear off and Pérez sputtered awake at the splash of water Gérard tossed at his face. Awake, groggy, and confused from his medically induced slumber, Pérez attempted to wipe the water away, but found quickly that his forearms were tied to each arm of a wheelchair. He tried to rise to his feet, but even if he had the strength, it would do no good, as his legs were also bound to the chair. Gérard marveled at the struggle, the panic in his eyes, the muffled grunts of dread from beneath the gag, Pérez's own sock stuffed into his mouth with duct tape across his lips.

"The Circle doesn't tolerate sloppiness," Gérard said. It wasn't much of a conversation starter. If Pérez didn't know why he was there a moment ago, he did now. His eyes filled. His struggle lessened, his panic turning to resignation at the mention of the Circle. Pérez knew this was the end. He was a man, defeated.

"Is there anything you have to say for yourself?" Gérard was improvising. He had never seen Miss Zutter allow a disgraced Watcher's last words, but for some reason he felt inspired.

With a swift yank, he tore the duct tape gag from Pérez's mouth, Pérez let out a yelp. Half of his mustache was now on the tape. Gérard folded it and carefully put it into Pérez's shirt pocket.

Pérez hung his head low. No words would prevent what was about to happen. "*Zirkuluaren behatzailea naiz.*" Gérard was expecting Spanish, not Basque, but *I am a Watcher of the Circle,* was universally understood. Pérez uttered the statement more pathetically than proudly. He wasn't defending the sanctity of the Circle; he was finished. He had come to terms with what all Circle members and Watchers waited for since day one of their initiation: The ultimate sacrifice.

Gérard had to admit the man had some pride. Most men in his position would surely utter a final declaration of love for his family. His wife. His children. But no, Pérez stuck to the script. Undoubtedly, his family would be well compensated for his doing so. Gérard nodded, stepped behind the wheelchair, and slowly began to push.

It was then that Pérez seemed to grasp where they were, where *he* was, on the bank of the Estuary of Bilbao. On the edge of the bank, now, and about to head over it. Gérard felt Pérez's fear roll off him in waves.

The water of the Estuary was deep enough to handle such a deposit. But Gérard was trained well. Lungs filled with air cause a body to float. He locked the wheelchair in place only inches from the edge of the platform. Tucked inside his belt was his knife. Gérard latched onto the collar of Pérez's blazer for stability and plunged the blade through the back of the chair into Pérez's lungs.

The gurgling sound was proof that he hadn't missed the mark. Once he heard it, Gérard unlocked the wheelchair and gave it a final thrust forward.

Tumbling through the air, the wheelchair and Pérez fell. It wasn't more than 10 feet, but for Gérard watching the fall was the foreplay. The slow rotation as the chair and the man made almost a full revolution. Pérez's blazer flapped in the air. Then came the heavy splash. Submersion. Bubbles of air bursting through the surface. Reminding him of Lieutenant Martin's demise at his hands as well as his first experience with the mass drownings on the Seine. How young he'd been. How inexperienced. And, later, how negligent. Unlike then, his emotions were in check. But unlike then, he didn't want to kill Pérez out of any personal sense of revenge. He needed to, as part of his greater plan against the Circle. He watched until the bubbles were gone. Then he watched a little more. Gérard stood on the precipice of the water and extended his arms to either side. The breeze passing around him gave him a sense of calm. Satisfaction of a job well done.

After several moments of studying the water and watching for ripples, he was convinced Pérez was gone. Through Miss Zutter's contacts at the Circle's Madrid chapter he knew that the disappearance of Mr. Pérez wouldn't yield any leads or results; a missing person, all he'd ever amount to, as only an average man would. As such, the Circle would continue to live on. The hypocrisy of that realization left a feeling in the pit of Gérard's stomach that he chose not to identify.

44

January 1984—Kanab, Utah

Cole Warren came as quickly as possible. There was an accident. His wife. Vivian. On the way to a house call. A new family in town with a sick little girl with a bad fever. Vivian had fled with her bag after a quick goodbye and a smile. The woman never hesitated, thriving practice or not, especially to help a child. All he knew was that her car had skidded on a patch of ice and she'd slid into an intersection to be T-boned by a tractor trailer making its way down 89 South. She'd been wearing her seatbelt, but it wasn't enough to keep her head from smashing the driver's side window glass, and then the steering wheel…and then the front grill of the tractor trailer.

Now in the E.R. of the hospital, he had been told to get out of the way. To let the doctors do their job. He wanted to scream. When he heard the words "severe head trauma" it was all he could do to stay standing. Cole, numb to the doctors and nurses moving around and passed him, doing their best to keep her alive, remained frozen in fear, tears streaming down his face, lips trembling, fingers unconsciously spinning the wedding ring on his left hand. *Please, God, no. Please, God, no. Please, God, no.*

The hospital's harsh lighting hurt his eyes. He heard voices, but dimly, as if he were in a sound bubble, and the constant beeping of the machinery keeping Vivian alive. Had they slowed, sped up...or, God forbid, stopped? He couldn't tell. He didn't want to know. He wanted to go back to two hours earlier when he'd reminded Vivian it would be easier to tell the girl's parents to apply a cold compress, give her some Tylenol, and that she'd check in on her in the morning.

"She's a little girl, Cole," Vivian had said, her warm grin chiding him. "It's why I'm a doctor, remember?"

"Well, I know it's because you're a doctor—the only doctor around—that still makes house calls." They'd just sat down to watch *M*A*S*H*,* a show they loved watching together.

Vivian kissed him. "*M*A*S*H** can wait, not the little girl or her parents."

The remark hit home. They'd tried for a good two years for a child, but it just didn't seem to be in the cards for them. They hadn't exactly stopped trying, but had accepted the unlikelihood of a pregnancy this late in the game.

"But it's icy out there," he argued. "I don't like it."

"A bit dramatic, aren't we?" said Vivian. "It was almost 60 today, how icy could it be?"

Cole knew he'd lost the argument before he'd even begun. "It's only 23 now out there. Which usually means ice."

"You're cute when you worry too much," Vivian said. "I'll be home before you know it."

• • •

But she hadn't come home. She was here. In the Emergency Room. And she might never come home again.

"Mr. Warren. Mr. Warren, can you hear me?"

Cole turned when he heard the doctor say his name. He saw it in the doctor's eyes.

"Nooo," he moaned.

"I'm so sorry, Mr. Warren. We fought for her, we did everything we could. But...it was too late." The doctor placed a hand on Cole's shoulder, but he shrugged it off and turned away. His whole world was gone. One minute he was the loving husband of a perfect woman; now there was nothing. *He* was nothing. He'd wasted so much of his life with the Circle until he'd found Vivian again. And then forced her to move here after his escape. They could have stayed in California. They might not be together, but at least she would still be alive.

It was his fault. Her death was on him.

• • •

What do you do when your world is stripped of its purpose, when you have gone from everything to nothing in the space of a moment? When the one with whom you planned your future is gone, along with the laughter, the smiles...the arguments. No more days spent thinking about how to make his wife happy, about how to show his devotion. No reason to live.

He'd been allowed to see her briefly after they'd patched her up a bit. Someone put a hand on his arm, but he'd shaken it off angrily. How dare they think there was any solace in the world that would help? He'd sat with her as long as they let him, taking her hand in his, clinking their wedding bands together over and over. "My Vivian," he wept, "my love, come back to me. Don't leave me. Don't leave me here alone. I can't...go on. I can't go on without you."

After what felt like a long time, he'd kissed each finger, then kissed each one on the other hand. He'd kissed her forehead and her cheeks. Her body's warmth and the warmth she'd exuded had disappeared with her life force and now there was nothing but cold. Cold, sterile, death. Hers and his. Because he had no life without her. He would never be whole again.

Finally, he had kissed the tip of her nose and each eyelid before turning away...and toward the gates of hell.

45

1984—Zurich, Switzerland

Exercise was Gérard's release. He'd learned over his time with Miss Zutter that controlling what he could was the best approach to suppressing his urges, saving them for the right time. This time Gérard was on a run. He liked to do laps around the Arboretum, typically six. He was currently on number four going past the Burkli memorial. Each step helped him clear his head. Right, left, right, left. His heart rate escalated; his muscles pulsed with each stride. The sweat dripped down his temple and past his cheek. He heard his own breathing in his ears with each contact of his feet with the pavement.

He thought of the past few years. His training. His promotion, as it were. His killing of 13 watchers in four different countries. He was a robot, a killing machine that knew how to execute a plan to perfection. He was excelling beyond even Miss Zutter's expectations. She'd said so herself earlier in the week, calling him her protégé, her legacy. Very unlike the cold woman he knew only as far as she allowed.

The Arboretum was not far from the house. After his run he removed his shirt and exposed his physique, taking his time to towel off his neck and forehead, for the viewing pleasure of anyone in the vicinity. He took short sips from his water bottle as he began the short trek back. The shade from the trees overhead provided comfort and relief from the hot sun beating down on him. It was a good run, but not his best time. Not that he was looking to break records, but he liked to be consistent. Inconsistencies could be costly.

He finally reached the house and took the stone steps to the front door three at a time. He entered his key and turned, but nothing happened. He checked the key ring, making sure he was using the correct one, and tried again. Nothing. *What the hell?* Then he saw it. A blue envelope jutting out from under the door. He bent down to reach for it and saw his name, *Mr. Finck,* scribbled on the outside. Feeling suddenly vulnerable, he turned around, sat on the top step, and opened it.

Mr. Finck,

You have been a fine student and protégé. I have enjoyed our time together, but it is time for our arrangement to end. I've taught you all I know.

Contained in the envelope is your bank information. You'll be happy to see that your money has almost doubled. Your personal holdings are now over a quarter of a billion dollars. I suggest you use this money to seek out the Circle in New York. The New York chapter is the head of the beast, the flagship branch of the Circle world-wide. But you cannot just show up with a quarter of a billion dollars without drawing attention to yourself...so be smart.

Also, before you run off to America with your dreams of revenge, I have one final test for you. You have been the hunter, with prey oblivious to your existence, and you have enjoyed great success. You have shown yourself to be quick, decisive, and efficient. But to survive in the Circle, you will not only be the hunter, but also the prey. And there is only one way to prepare you for that.

For the past year I have not only been training you, I have been training my replacement. A person you have met before, even interacted with. And effective noon today, my replacement will be hunting you. In 48 hours one of you will be dead.

Good luck, Mr. Finck. It has been a pleasure doing business with you.

Panic. Fear. Adrenaline. Excitement. All rushed through his body like a freight train. He hadn't been paying attention. For years he'd been training by studying his targets, sexual conquests in bars for practice, Watchers for keeps. But he'd been oblivious to anyone who may have been watching *him*. And now someone was after him. Someone who had been studying *him* the same way he himself had studied all his former prey.

He looked at his watch. 11:39. Could he have run past his potential attacker in the park? On the walk to the house? Were they watching him right now?

So many questions, their solutions all out of reach, made his head spin. Then his training kicked in. *One task at a time. Compartmentalize.* His first task. What should it be? He needed to arm himself, but how? He had no money, other than the bank book declaring him worth more than $250 million, and he couldn't access any of it without identification. He was still in his running attire, sans wallet.

He turned back to the house, looked again at the note in his hand, and knew what he had to do. He took a large rock from the landscaped yard and hurled it through the front door window. He reached in and unlocked the door and let himself into the house. He made a beeline straight to his quarters. But they weren't his living quarters any more. All of his effects had been removed. It looked like an empty hotel room. A bed, dresser, and nightstand were all the decor remaining.

It was futile, but he checked the drawers anyway. Nothing. All empty. So his wallet and money were gone, as well as his personal belongings. He still needed to arm himself. He raced to the kitchen for the knife block and found it completely empty. He checked the drawers. Nothing but forks and spoons, not even butter knives. It was as if Miss Zutter had abandoned the house as she had abandoned him.

He raced downstairs to his training area. The majority of his equipment was still there. The heavy bag still hung. The gloves were sitting on the mat where he'd left them. In the corner of the room, where the weaponry had been, there was nothing but the bow staff, nothing more than a big stick. Not the greatest defense from whatever his would-be assassin was likely to be carrying. It would have to do. He grabbed it and bolted from the house gripping it firmly in one hand, his bank information in the other.

• • •

He had to get somewhere safe, somewhere out of the ordinary for him. If his hunter was any good, he knew Gérard's tendencies by now and would have a plan—a dossier, most likely—on what he enjoyed, where he liked to go. Gérard had to go off book and think on the fly. The bars were out; any of the bartenders, customers and bouncers could easily be his hunter. He hadn't paid them a single iota of attention in their limited interactions. But he needed money to go anywhere. He had to go back to the bank. Had had to risk seeing Miss Zutter again.

The thought stopped him dead in his tracks. *That's exactly what they want me to do.* Nothing would help his hunter more than to behave predictably. That would be Gérard's approach; he had to assume his hunter would do the same. They had had the same teacher, after all. No, he wouldn't play into their hands. He had to be unpredictable, erratic even. Instead of heading towards the bank, he took off running in the opposite direction.

His senses peaked now, each rustle of the trees, each car horn, each pedestrian he encountered sending impulses to his brain. Assessing every potential threat. He still didn't know where he was going, but it had to be far away from where his hunter wanted him to be. Not that he was being discreet: a madman running through the streets of Zurich carrying a long bamboo stick.

A Porsche pulled over about 50 yards ahead and a man got out, locked the door, and entered a tall building. Gérard followed the man inside the lobby. When the man did not turn, Gérard brought the stick to his front and executed a cross-check. Hard. The man fell to the ground, staring up at Gérard with wide, terrified eyes. Gérard said nothing, lifted the man's wallet, and left the lobby. The whole thing had taken less than 15 seconds.

Fortunately, his mugging victim had almost 400 francs on him. More than enough to procure Gérard a safehouse of sorts. Jogging now to give off the appearance of normality, even for a man with a stick, he hailed the next available cab he could. Once inside, he told the cabbie to drive to the outskirts of the city where he knew of several possibilities for cheap lodging.

It wasn't far, but he gave the driver 20 francs, telling him to keep the change. Every moment mattered. Five minutes later he had set up shop in a room no larger than a walk-in refrigerator. He had to regroup, he needed a plan, but couldn't think straight with his blood still pumping the way it was.

There was no mini-bar, so no booze. He went to the bathroom and looked around, disgusted. Rust stains covered every metal surface. The sink dripped at an incessant rate. The toilet had definitely seen better days. He turned to the bathtub, layered with a disconcerting orange residue indicating its last cleaning was probably around the time of Marie Antoinette. He turned on the water and closed his eyes.

After killing Lieutenant Martin, and embarrassing himself by making a play for Miss Zutter, Gérard had learned this tactic for satisfying his arousal after a kill, especially a drowning. He listened to the sound of the rushing water filling up the tub. He steadied his breathing. He let the water run until the tub was almost overflowing. Then he rose to his knees and submerged his face in the water, holding his breath as long as he could, then expelling all his air at once in an underwater scream, bubbles of air erupting forcefully downwards. On their way to the surface they brushed past his face, comforting and rejuvenating him.

When he emerged he was calm. Collected. Focused. Ready to fight.

If only he knew whom he was fighting.

46

January 1984—Kanab, Utah

Cole stumbled through the darkness and through the door of his home in a haze. He reached automatically for the light switch, but pulled away. Light would only make things worse. Clenched firmly in his hand was a bag filled with Vivian's belongings, her clothes, her medical bag, what was left of it, and a few folders with patient information in them. He had placed her wedding ring on his own pinky finger so he could still feel her presence. *As if.* All he had to do was look at it to feel another wave of overwhelming grief.

Dead. Vivian was dead.

As he dropped into the armchair in the living room exhausted and grief stricken, he looked around the room. Without Vivian's presence, the room was without warmth, without charm, without life. The way she'd welcome him at the door with a smile that could charm the quills off a porcupine. But as he processed his surroundings, he knew something else was different. The television. He'd left it on when he'd rushed out to the hospital, but now it was off. And he'd tripped over the ottoman at his feet, upending it; now it stood upright.

"Hello?" he called out, now on high alert. "Is someone here?"

The chair behind his desk swiveled slowly around. He saw a man, but only his outline was visible in the dark room.

He scanned the room for a weapon. "Who the hell are you? What are you doing in my house?"

The man in Cole's chair mumbled something, which didn't make sense. He quickly turned on the lamp on the side table to get a better look. It was then he saw that the man's arms were tied, his mouth stuffed with a gag. The face was familiar. Someone from the shop? A customer?

Cole realized just how stupid he was, rushing over to free this man who had somehow ended up at *his* desk, in *his* chair, when he heard the cocking of a gun.

"That's about far enough," came a voice from the shadows.

"Look, just take what you want and go," said Cole. "No one has to get hurt here."

"You think I want your things?" the voice sneered.

"Then, what *do* you want?" said Cole, his mind racing with possible reasons for this armed visitor, and options for his own survival.

"I'm here to reintroduce you," said the voice. "To our friend, here." The gun was now pointed at the man in the chair, who whimpered behind his gagged mouth.

Cole had found himself in some pretty interesting situations over the years, but this one took the prize. He wasn't thinking clearly, either, he realized. Not since—not after...not after what had just happened to his wife.

"Remove his gag," the man ordered, finally stepping out from the shadows. He was tall, about the same height as Cole, in a dark black trench coat and round-framed glasses. The guy had to be in his sixties. Cole walked toward the desk, assessing his chances at fighting the man off.

"Don't even think about it," said the man, reading his mind.

"Listen," said Cole. "Maybe you should just leave. Take your friend—or whoever he is—and go. No harm no foul. I won't report it. I have...I have enough on my mind right now."

"Remove. The gag," the man said again, more quietly, no less insistent.

Cole approached the man in the chair and did as he was told, his mind still searching for answers. After so many years he'd gone soft. Otherwise he never would have been caught unaware like this. Well, that and the fact that he'd just lost—

He stepped up to the man. The gag was a bandanna, wet from blood and snot. He didn't bother trying to untie it at the back, just slid it down to the man's neck. He'd been beaten. Badly. So badly that Cole almost didn't recognize him.

Almost.

When the man saw the recognition in Cole's eyes, he nodded weakly.

"I don't know how they found me..." he started, but before he had the chance to say anything else, his head exploded in a spattering of blood, brains, and skull. Through the ringing in his ears, Cole heard the man with the gun speak once again.

"Now, Mr. Vice," he said, "It's time for you to sit down. We have much to discuss."

47

1984—Zurich, Switzerland

Gérard had to assume the worst case scenario. His hunter had a head start and knew who his target was. Gérard didn't. Over the past hour he'd comprised a list of possible hunters from his interactions with people over the past year. The reality, though, was that despite the number of the people he considered a threat, there were countless others he hadn't even considered existed. Could any of them have been working with Miss Zutter at the same time? Hidden from view. Living in darkness. Watching from afar. Collecting information.

Being on the other side of the equation was definitely not the preferred side.

Gérard had decided on a daring approach.. He'd never be able to find the identity of this hunter in the recesses of his mind, so he wouldn't waste his time searching. The clock was ticking. He needed his hunter to make an attempt that he could defend and rebut. Gérard would not hide. He'd bait the hook with his own life. Wait for his assassin to show himself. Play into his assassin's hands.

Miss Zutter had only been training this person for a year, seven fewer than the time she'd spent on Gérard, and he was betting the guy had far less superior skills, the one real bonus he had. In a vacuum, Gérard calculated he would have the upper hand on sheer physical ability alone. The goal? Meet his would-be assassin on equal footing. And he had an idea how to do it.

• • •

There was no question that in the time Gérard's hunter had been following him, he would have clocked Gérard's preference, compulsion might be a better word, to be near the water. Gérard banked on this probable known secret between them. At the northern end of Lake Zurich was a walking path that led over the Quaibrücke bridge. From that position on the bridge he would be able to see in all directions; anyone looking for him would be easily identified. Once he knew who his hunter was, it would simply be a matter of fighting to the death.

Instead of a change of clothes, Gérard used the remainder of the money he'd stolen to purchase a gun, an American combat weapon, a Bren Ten, which fired a .40 caliber round. Short and compact, it still packed a wallop. All chrome with a partial wooden grip. A rare find in a random Zurich pawnshop, only a few thousand of them manufactured before the company went belly-up, and now one of those was hidden in the pocket of Gérard's running shorts and covered as well as possible by his T-shirt.

Cooling down after a late night jog was an easy cover to maintain. The clothes made sense for the narrative he was trying for. Gérard ran at a steady, easy pace the majority of the path to keep up his appearances with the passersby. By the time he was about 100 meters from the bridge, he slowed to a brisk walk, elevating his arms over his head as he'd learned to do to aid in blood circulation.

He scanned the bridge for anything suspicious. There were several people standing and looking out at the water. The bridge was a romantic and picturesque location. On the opposite side he saw a man proposing to a woman against the backdrop of the setting sun. Her response, clearly a yes judging by the way she leapt into the man's arms, caused the ring to fly out of his hand. The ensuing gasp and cheer by the gathering crowd was evidence of its recovery and her acceptance.

In another life, he thought, that might have been me. He squashed the thought before it gained momentum, a useless trail going nowhere.

Gérard found a bench and took a seat. Made a show of staying still, relaxed. Nowhere to go. Just a guy on a nice day taking a break. He'd been thorough with his surveillance of the running path and bridge. Anyone with a long-range weapon out in the open would be spotted, if not by him, by an innocent civilian. His attacker was going to have to do this up close and personal…and time was running out.

• • •

Time dragged on. Gérard refused to abandon his post. Like a sentry standing guard over a base camp. The sun had fully disappeared into the night sky and the moon and stars were the source of the warm light that fell. There were no signs of anything untoward on either side of the bridge. Maybe today wasn't the day. Maybe his attacker had decided not to take the risk. Or perhaps he was patient, the way Gérard had been taught to be.

After what he calculated was close to two hours he couldn't sit there any longer. His plan to gain the upper hand and force his attacker into the light had been unsuccessful. He hadn't completely wasted his time because he learned something. His attacker was patient, not one to take risks or fall victim to accidents due to opportunity. Whoever it was had a plan for Gérard. Forcing it out into the open so easily was off the table.

He'd seen neither human, animal, nor vehicle in at least a quarter of an hour. Zurich was asleep, and he should be, too. He retraced his steps the way he came, pondering the wisdom of doing the same thing tomorrow, even making a routine of it. The hotel was only a few miles away. He'd shower, ignore the tub's lack of hygiene, and eat something. He took off in a brisk jog. After all that time on the bench, it felt good to move.

Jogging at night was not relaxing. In this new scenario, no overhead lights meant potential hidden threats, not a calm peaceful night. He found himself slowing down every time he noticed a shift in the shadows on the narrow path. Rolling an ankle in this position would be bad, but becoming incapacitated as a result would make him a sitting duck for his hunter.

Another jogger appeared a few hundred meters ahead. Well, his flashlight, bouncing in cadence with each stride. Gérard moved slightly to the right on the path to avoid a collision. The runner was moving quickly. Almost too quickly. The hair on Gérard's neck stood up.

As the dark shadow of the jogger approached, Gérard, now on guard, noted his interesting arm motion, more of a shoulder rotation than a pumping back and forth. An injury? Clavicle or rotator cuff, probably, from the awkward movements. When the jogger and Gérard were only feet away from one another, the flashlight fell to the ground with a thud. That's when Gérard saw the jogger was a woman, a woman slowing down to retrieve it.

In a step he was on her, crunching her nose under his fist. It was a sound he would not soon forget. She spun back and went down with a cry of pain. He reached out for her hair to pull her back to her feet. He shoved her against a nearby tree, withdrew his gun, and pointed it at her head.

The woman looked at him, the blood dripping freely from her nose. "How did you know?" she said.

"All those sparring lessons," said Gérard. "You've been favoring that shoulder since that time I finally beat you."

"You always did like to gloat," she said.

Gérard took a good, long look at her. "Were you really going to kill me?"

Miss Zutter raised her hands to show she was unarmed. Then she slowly reached into her back waistband and took out a butcher knife. The one that used to be in the block in what was now his former kitchen. "You've always erred on the side of politeness, my dear Mr. Finck. And I've always told you it's a liability. The second you picked up that flashlight you would have been mine. I would not have hesitated."

It was true. Zutter was ruthless on and off the field of battle. Never relented, never exercised a moment's hesitation, never passed up an opportunity. If he'd learned anything from her, it was that. To strike when the moment is right. He should have killed her.

"So," he said finally, "Did I pass?"

"Your final test? No...not quite yet," she said, choking on her own blood. "I'm still alive, aren't I?"

The knee she sent up and into his crotch was a surprise. He doubled over. A solid shot to the nuts, and he hadn't seen it coming. The gun fell to the ground. She kicked it away. Gérard's face felt the force of another kick knocking him backwards. He rolled to his stomach and crawled in the direction he thought the gun had gone, searching with his hands.

"You still haven't learned that valuable lesson have you?" Miss Zutter asked as she stalked him along the path. She kicked him again in the side and stomped on his back with her heel. "Never..." she kicked him the kidneys "ever..." a stomp to the back "hesitate."

"You think your targets in the Circle will hesitate before they kill you? Before they pull the trigger, stab you, blow you up, or choke the life out of you? You won't have the time to wisecrack with them or ask them your questions. This isn't a game, Mr. Finck. If you think it is, you will be careless. Carelessness will get you killed." She aimed a heel at his face and Gérard felt its force through his teeth.

Bleeding from the mouth and tasting the dirt of the beaten-down running path, he knew his one chance was leverage. The gun was far out of reach; it may as well have been on Mars. And if he knew this woman like he thought he did, and as she was declaring she was, she was going to go for the kill. Soon. She and her knife would be coming for him.

"I am disappointed, Mr. Finck," she said sadly. "You were supposed to be special. Son of Mr. Spade. Born from the depravity of the Circle's antiquated rules. Destined to tear it down. But you're not." She looked at him disgustedly. "I've wasted my precious time on a loser."

Her words hit Gérard like a smelling salt under his nose. He felt strength he thought had fled and rose to his knees, hoping to appear as if he was begging for his life. Which, of course, he was, in a way. The glint of the blade in Zutter's hand reflecting the moonlight was all he needed to confirm that it was either die here in the gutter or find the wherewithal from somewhere to fend off his opponent.

Miss Zutter's face was hard and menacing. While he'd trained with her, she'd never been anything but cold and distant. This was whole new level. He'd been under the illusion that she'd had a soft spot for him, but he was wrong. The woman was nothing but a killer. Who this time had her sights on him.

He had one major advantage, however: He knew her. He knew her tricks, her maneuvers, her body. The way she would be going for the lungs. He'd have one chance and only one chance to deflect the blow when it came. He waited for the tell-tale twitch of her eye to know the wait was over.

Now!

He tucked his right arm in and rolled toward her with a fast kick to the stomach. The knife missed him by centimeters as it fell to the ground. He picked it up and plunged it deep into her stomach. Blood flowed, warm and sticky, on his hands. She gasped for breath, shock on her face at the turn of events.

She struggled to speak. "Well played,… Mr. Finck," she said. "I suppose you expect me...to take back...my criticism…."

Gérard smiled.

"Well, don't...hold your...breath," she said, exhaling the last bit of raspy air from her lungs. "But never forget… that you are...the one. The one...to...bring...it...down."

48

January 1984—Kanab, Utah

Deep in the recesses of Warren Nichols' mind and soul, Mr. Vice awoke from a deep slumber. Warren, paralyzed, had somehow simply obliterated from his consciousness that this day would ever come. That it was even a possibility. And, with his emotions so rawly exposed only hours before, he found he had none left for the armed man in his house. With effort, he moved his gaze to the dead man in his own favorite chair.

That's when it came to him—the man's name. Duncan. Duncan was—had been—a Watcher. The last time Warren had seen him was when he'd forced the Watcher into a cab in D.C. after the rendezvous with Mr. Venom. Set "Duncan" on his way to the airport and, presumably, a flight to Missouri.

Nine long years ago. Warren didn't know what to do. It was as if he had selective amnesia. He didn't want to remember what he'd done. Who he'd been. But the matter at hand called for action, without which he was dead. And, with Vivian gone, there was no way to stop it.

How long would it be before the dam broke...before Mr. Vice was let loose from his prison?

"How did you find me?" he asked.

The man waved away his question. "That is not important," he said, still training his gun at Warren. "What is important is that the Circle is everywhere. And that you, Mr. Vice, owe us a very large debt."

"Who are you?"

"You're right, of course. Where are my manners," the man said. "I am Mr. Black. Of the St. George Chapter. Once we found out you were here, it was my good fortune to be the Mr. Black closest to your location."

"Just kill me already," Warren said. "I don't have the stomach for this anymore."

"If I wanted to do that," Mr. Black replied, his eyes cold and threatening, "I would have waited to cut your wife's brake lines until I knew you'd be in the car with her."

Warren's knees threatened to buckle as realization set in. The Circle always got its pound of flesh. This time it had been Vivian's. Vivian...innocent, smart, capable, infinitely gracious and loving....

"You killed my wife," he said. "You...killed...my....wife." He needed a weapon. This sonofabitch was going down.

"I wouldn't take those thoughts too far," said Black. "It's about time you owned what you have done. You know as well as I do that we have rules. Sacred rules. No one gets out—no one. You broke that rule. In doing so, it was *you* who risked the lives of your friends and family. Who sent your wife to an early grave."

It started in Warren's hands, which slowly gathered into fists. Then it spread up his arms, and then up into his shoulders, neck, and head. That feeling of being taken over by a force greater than himself. By Mr. Vice. *No. There has to be another way. Vice is dead and gone. I am Cole Warren now. Owner of an auto repair shop. Husband--grieving husband of my recently departed wife.*

Warren fought for control. To concentrate, focus on the right thoughts. "Stacy?" he asked.

"Stacy?" Mr. Black said. "Oh, you mean the late Miss Chambers. Sad, really. An overdose. Heart medications are tricky that way. Such a shame. Avoidable. If only she'd been more careful."

The war in Warren's head threatened to explode like a bomb. Why not get it over with. Why not charge into the gun and feel it go off and end his life now? Why did it matter if he ever took another breath?

Why was Mr. Vice stopping him?

Vice was angry. Screaming for attention. *Warren, you lied to me!*

It doesn't matter anymore, Warren said. *Don't you get that?*

You think I'm going to let you take the easy way out – sacrifice your messy, measly, pathetic self-righteous self? Well, think again. I am here. I am back. And I...will...rise...again.

Aloud, Warren shouted over the voice in his head. "Just kill me already, Black. I'm done here. I want out. I'm finished."

Mr. Black shook his head. "My dear Mr. Vice, I wish I could oblige. But, as I said, I'm not here to kill you. You're no Mr. Spade. Your actions have not resulted in the deaths of innocent people, shining unnecessary light onto the Circle. I'm only here to bring you back. Back to serve your remaining 16 years of service. Of course there are rules against forcing you to continue to hunt after that age or that would be my recommendation. Additional years to make up for your time away. But *C'est la vie*. You have been relocated."

Vice continued to pound at him. *They killed your wife. I can avenge her. It's time to get back in the game!*

"No!" Warren shouted again.

"You're not in any position to refuse, Mr. Vice." Mr. Black said, revealing his impatience, believing Warren was speaking to him—which was not entirely untrue. "I'm not at liberty to kill you. But I *am* willing to deliver you to your new safehouse in less than pristine condition."

He lowered his gun slightly, pointing it at Warren's shoulder.

He's going to shoot us!

"No! I can't," Warren shouted. His head throbbed, shattered by a million shards of glass. He put his hands up to his ears and pressed hard against his temples.

Mr. Black sighed. Warren's shoulder felt the impact of the bullet. He fell to the ground with a hand to his bloody chest. "No. Please. No," he whispered over and over. "No...."

• • •

Nine years of involuntary isolation. That's how long it had been. Nine long years imprisoned in the body of his host. But it was all over now. Now he was free, and would never be bound by the constraints of that host again. His wounded arm was the last remaining vestige of that codependency. Its healing meant he would soon, once again, be the hunter he was born to be.

Vice rose to his feet, poking at the wound to encourage more blood to flow from what was, in reality, only a flesh wound. Mr. Black was a good shot; he'd missed the bone entirely.

"I'm waiting," Vice said. "Get on with it already. Where am I headed? That's what you said you came here for, right?"

For a moment Mr. Black's eyes wavered. Vice didn't blame him. Gone was the angry, fearful, trapped man of a moment ago. If he were in Black's shoes, he'd also be wondering who this calm, cold, collected one was who now stood before him.

"I asked," said Vice, "how much time will I have? To make my living arrangements and procure weapons?"

"You are not a new member, Mr. Vice," said Black, still shaken by the transformation, "and you've had nine years to make such arrangements. You get no additional time. Use your next furlough as you see fit. If you make it that long, that is."

"Ah, my next assignment.... Where is the dossier?"

"Impatient," commented Black. "All in good time, Mr. Vice. You know the procedure."

"I'll need the location of the safehouse, then, and an address," said Vice. Time to make up for lost time, time long overdue. Warren would never again be more than a pimple on the face of a mountain. Warren at the helm led them to disaster. Innocent people died. With Mr. Vice in the driver's seat, survival of the fittest was a certainty.

"New York City," Mr. Black said. "Tasker's. It's a bar."

Part III

49

1984—New York—Mr. Vice

The address on the slip of paper in Mr. Vice's hand guided him to a nondescript hole-in-the-wall: Tasker's Bar. His new safehouse. Already on the clock, and at a supreme disadvantage, he had his work cut out for him. He knew no one in this chapter, had no weapons, and no place to hide. He was starting over. Well, sort of.

He straightened and pulled back his shoulders to reflect confidence and strength, wincing at the pull on his bandaged shoulder wound. Formed his expression into one that said "I am here. I am Vice. I am invincible," before opening the door and going in. Everything was different, yet the same. The smells, the atmosphere...all but the faces. And a lot more of them than he'd expected to see.

He approached the bar, admiring its detailed carpentry. The bartender, a younger man, early 30s, seemed to be some kind of apprentice. Taking over the family craft? Not uncommon. Once a safehouse was established, its proprietors were known to maintain them as a matter of legacy. It looked as if Vice had arrived amidst a changing of the guard. "Bourbon," he said. "Neat."

"Yes, sir," said the young bartender politely.

"You seem young for this position," Vice said, stating the obvious, feeling things out.

The bartender shrugged. "Old man's feeling the years. Setting me up to take over." He pointed over his head at the photo hanging above the bar. Black and white, probably taken 30 years earlier. "Grandpa'll be coming down soon to make room for Dad."

Vice nodded. Each safehouse had its traditions; seemed like remembering the past was New York's. Vice nodded. All background information. You never knew what would come in handy as you hunted. But he'd have the remainder of his life to get acquainted, and time was of the essence. "I need to speak to Mr. Black."

The young bartender went white. An interesting reaction to a perfectly reasonable statement.

"Um, I…I don't think that…."

"Look, buddy," said Vice, losing patience, but keeping his voice level. "It's not rocket science. I'm the new member, transplant from D.C. I need to see Mr. Black. Now. I have an assignment waiting."

The bartender's eyes widened. "Oh...you're...you're the one…the one they found…." He stopped.

Vice waited for the boy to put two and two together. He was slow. Behind a bar was a good place for him to be. Not terribly taxing.

A few seconds went by. Vice tapped his fingers on the bar, waiting for the light to go on in the kid's head.

"Sure," he said finally, "I mean, yes sir. He's right through there."

• • •

Vice took his drink, thanked the bartender, and walked through the panel as it slid open behind the bar. *Nice. Leave it to New York to have the swankiest house.*

Once through, the action within came to a slow halt as the members assessed the newcomer, appraising the potential new target. Vice calmly ran his eyes over the room without settling, seeing what he'd expected to see. Game tables. Sumptuous leather chairs. Card tables and games. Scantily clad women—the "entertainment." And many of his fellow killers. He looked for the oldest among them for Mr. Black, but didn't spot anyone who seemed to fit the bill, so he took a seat and slowly sipped his drink. Black would have to come to him.

It was almost 10 minutes before a tall slender man approached and took the adjacent seat. Vice had crossed over into irritated impatience five minutes ago, but said nothing. Showed nothing. The man was older than Vice, with a scraggly beard that lacked the wherewithal to fill in fully, leaving patches of dry skin. Surely this couldn't be the man himself.

"I bid you good morrow, sir," he said with his hand out.

Vice shook reluctantly, nodding. He didn't like the man's approach, nor his affected speech.

"Well," the man went on, a little too loudly for Vice's comfort, "it seems before us we have a hungry lean-faced villain of the highest order. Huzzah! And your name, sir?"

"Vice," said Vice, projecting just as loudly. "Mr. Vice."

It had the desired effect. In a moment they were joined by a mountain of a man with a laugh to match.

"Don't mind Shakespeare over here," he said. "Name's Mr. Crush."

"Mr. Vice," said Vice. "Pleasure."

They shook, and in that moment he instinctively knew Crush was not his hunter. At least not at this stage in the game. Another member had stepped back from the pool table to watch the interaction, however. Average build, nondescript. Vice studied him out of the corner of his eye, the flair of his nostrils and the way he'd gone still. The idiot had enough tells to lose a child's game of poker. Either the guy was a novice or a really bad actor, it remained to be seen.

Vice went along with the conversation with the killers at his table to maintain a facade of indifference.

"Does he always speak in Shakespearean quotes?" Vice asked Crush.

Mr. Crush laughed his overly loud laugh again. "I'm afraid our Mr. Shakespeare is somewhat of a—"

"Of course not," Shakespeare interrupted, "yet wouldn't you agree that the web of our life is of a mingled yarn, good and ill together?"

The man's warmth and good humor was disconcerting. Vice wasn't a Shakespeare kind of guy, but he admired those who embraced their eccentricities. He raised his glass in a toast and finished the last of his drink, then reached for the tin of Altoid mints on the table.

"Oh, I wouldn't do that if I were you," Crush warned.

"No? And why is that?" said Vice. He didn't like being told what to do. Or not to do.

Crush shot a thumb over his shoulder. "Those belong to the Dentist."

The Dentist. Huh. Interesting.

He laughed. "And the Dentist counts his mints?"

"Go ahead, then," Crush said as a small crowd formed around him. "But don't say I didn't warn you."

The production was beneath him and Vice didn't appreciate the attention. Were they actually suggesting that taking one of this Dentist's mints could cause a problem? Well, screw that. He scanned the crowd. No one stood out. Nothing but a bunch of slack-jawed gawkers waiting for him to do something. It was now a matter of pride.

Opening the tin was easy. Seeing what was inside and reacting as if he were seeing nothing more than a bunch of little white things was not. These were not mints, but teeth. Human teeth.

The crowd erupted with raucous laughter. Vice's carefully cultivated indifference fled for a moment and he knocked over the tin, spilling a few of the teeth onto the carpet. He immediately bent to pick them up, taking the opportunity to collect himself. Still, he shuddered at the touch. He should have known. Hazing the new guy was an honored tradition in the Circle. It galled him how out of the loop he was, how soft he'd gotten.

"Nice," he said. *Ever the guy who can take a joke, that's me.*

A few of the men went so far as to pat him on the back, sending spasms of pain through his shoulder, which he did his best to hide. It was worth it. He'd been accepted into the chapter. Public embarrassment was a small price to pay to be one of the boys. Still, why would Mr. Dentist leave a box of teeth lying around? To make a statement? Or was it more personal—to show Vice that the Dentist was a formidable adversary? There was no way to know for sure.

"Welcome to New York, Mr. Vice," said a voice from the back corner of the room.

Vice turned toward it as the other members formed a semicircle of respect and waited.

Finally. The man himself.

Mr. Black waved them off. "Gentlemen," he said, "and lady," he added, nodding at the lone female member in the room, "I'm fairly certain our Mr. Vice won't be needing anymore of a traditional recruit's welcome." There were a few chuckles and the group disbanded as quickly as it had formed. While unintimidated, it had been helpful to see so many members gathered in one place, 25 in this room alone. It was the numbers *outside* the comfort of the safehouse that were more concerning.

"A word in private please, Mr. Vice," Mr. Black said, gesturing to a small, round table.

Vice sat.

Black's eyes held him with a strange depth, one that Vice couldn't quite figure, something vaguely reminiscent of compassion. Not likely in anyone who'd risen to his position in the Circle. As if he wasn't all that happy to be there. An unwilling recruit who'd lived long enough to earn his way to the top? And something else...pity. A look he hadn't seen in so long Vice almost didn't recognize it. But there was no pity in the Circle either. He must be mistaken.

"I would never say this in front of the other members," Black began, "but I was sorry to hear about what happened in Utah."

Vice was unmoved by the sentiment, given the likelihood it was nothing but pretense. What happened to Warren in Utah was over and one and no business of Black's, or anyone's, anymore. Yet Vice had to take ownership of his prior host's carelessness. He chose his response carefully.

"I broke the rules," he said. "I hold no grudges."

"That's...forgiving of you," said Black, "considering what happened."

What kind of Mr. Black is this? Why insist on a conversation that means nothing? Vice noticed a small scar above Black's chin. Presumably a battle scar from time served. He looked away. "It's important to compartmentalize what happened then, and what has to happen now," he said.

Mr. Black nodded, and reached over and patted him on the shoulder. A bit harder than necessary. "I'm happy to hear that." He patted some more, each pat more forceful than the last. Vice braced himself for what was to come. The final "pat" was not only more forceful, but purposeful, as if Black knew exactly where to land the blow—a reminder of his position. Vice muffled a grunt and adjusted his gaze back to Mr. Blacks' eyes, now cold and unforgiving, reminding him who was in charge here. Vice's shirt turned red from the blood. He nodded. *Message received.*

"Because if you think something like what happened back in D.C. is going to happen in my chapter, here in New York? Don't think for a second I won't hunt you down and kill you myself."

Vice nodded again. It was the right response. They both understood it wasn't about fear or intimidation, per se. He was hardly a new recruit who needed that kind of initiation. But this was Mr. Black, and Mr. Black needed, and deserved, his full attention. He wasn't threatening Vice, not really. Simply making a promise. In fact, the declaration made Vice feel right at home.

"This is New York, Mr. Vice," Black went on. "The flagship chapter of the Circle. And I won't tolerate any rule violations. I assume you remember the Circle's bylaws. Please recite them now."

Vice resisted the urge to roll his eyes like a third grader being chastised for pulling a girl's hair and did as he was told. "There is no escape."

Nod.

"No civilian casualties."

Nod.

"Respect the safehouse."

Nod.

"No unauthorized killings."

"Excellent," Black said. "Now that we understand each other, welcome to New York. Welcome back to the Circle." Black extended a wiry hand for Vice to shake, then reached into a satchel by his chair to retrieve a blue envelope. Vice's heart began to race. This was it!

"Your first assignment," Black said, sliding the folder over to Vice. "I'm afraid the member assigned to you has had *your* dossier for a number of hours now, which puts you at a slight disadvantage."

Vice hoped his clenched jaw did not give him away. "I think I can handle myself," he said, picking up the folder but not opening it. He would not give this Mr. Black the satisfaction.

Black nodded and sat back into the shadows. "Good luck, then, Mr. Vice," he said, "it's been a pleasure."

50

The thick mattress in the penthouse of the Waldorf Astoria was just what the doctor ordered. It wasn't his apartment from D.C. but it would easily do for the time being until he had a place he could more easily monitor. He thumbed the lip of the blue envelope but didn't open it. He had missed the texture of the thick paper in his hands. The smell of the glue that held it together. Vice imagined a Watcher painstakingly licking each one closed before delivering it to each member.

When he finally opened the seal, the details of his new target covered the pages. He was both exhilarated and disappointed. He felt he would have really enjoyed getting to know the Shakespearean member before killing him. Alas, it wasn't meant to be. *Parting is such sweet sorrow,* he thought with a humorless chuckle.

Wait. Was he reading that right? That Shakespeare lived in a village? No, it was *the* Village. There was so much he didn't know about New York City. He'd have to learn fast. Nothing like baptism by fire. The data also indicated that Shakespeare was a huge supporter of the Vivian Beaumont Theater on West 65th Street.

Ah. There it is. The reason for the assignment. The Circle's way to send him a not-so-subtle message about his wife—well, Warren's late wife, anyway. Were the pathetically sentimental Warren still in charge of their movements and emotions, just the connection to her name would send him into convulsions. Vice shook his head. *Stupid man.*

Vice studied the paperwork in the dossier and discovered that Mr. Shakespeare, known to the outside world as Glenn Burr, was a major donor to the theater whose favorite pastime was mingling with fellow thespians. There had not been a resident company there since the late '70s, however, and the theater was often rented to outside producers while they searched for a more permanent location.

Even though he itched to get back to the game again, Vice would do nothing but hunker down for at least a week. He needed to find his bearings, acclimate himself in his new city. Collect maps, train and bus schedules. Set up surveillance, identify routines, look for openings and opportunities. No one's guard was impermeable nor impenetrable. Still, he required more information, and a weapon. Make that multiple weapons.

After a long shower, a change of dressing to his shoulder wound, and a brief nap, he found himself meandering his way through the city and back to Tasker's. The young bartender was there and ready to serve. Customers intermingled with members in the front room and, while inviting, Vice needed to concentrate on the other members exclusively. He ordered a drink quickly, club soda with lime, and began sidestepping the drunken party impeding his progress to the back, where he waited patiently for the bartender to push the button and open the door. Shakespeare wasn't there, but it wouldn't be a total lost cause. Information on all members could be useful in the future. Not to mention any possible data on his target that surfaced in the process of mingling.

He eyed the room. A short yet powerful-looking man sat drinking with the tin of Altoids at his elbow. Had to be Mr. Dentist. No spring chicken, late 50s by the look of him, u-shaped balding. Round, black-framed glasses, a five o'clock shadow.

"So, molars, bicuspids, or canines?" he asked, sitting down and pointing at the tin. It was where his knowledge of teeth began and ended.

The man shrugged. "Beats me," he said.

Not the damn Dentist, then. One down, lots to go.

"Vice," he said, offering a hand.

"Belt," the man answered. "Welcome to New York."

"Thanks...Belt?" He let it hang.

"Oh, it's not what you think."

"No?"

"No. We're talking belt sander, not the kind that keeps your pants from ending up around your ankles."

Vice laughed appreciatively, delighted at how wrong he was, impressed at his competition's resourcefulness.

"You?" said Belt.

"Vice grip."

"Got it," Mr. Belt answered. "Not bad." He raised his whiskey glass in a toast.

"Thanks, likewise." Vice finished his club soda.

"What's your poison?" Belt asked.

"Gin and tonic," Vice lied. He never drank in the safehouse, never one to risk forgetting any valuable information he gained while within its walls. This was no escape for him, as it was for the other members. He hadn't joined the Circle to "feel more alive." He'd joined to kill.

There was a long pause, used to size each other up.

"So," Belt finally said, "is it true—what they say?"

Vice anticipated he'd have to answer that question dozens of times before it became common knowledge. His name would undoubtedly become the Circle's cautionary tale, as Mr. Spade had been, to all new members. To let them know what happens if you disobey the Circle's "conditions." In a way, Vice thought, he'd become a legend in his own time. Really, quite an accomplishment when you think about it. Every member from New York to Cairo would be wondering the same thing if they ever got the chance to sit in the same room with him. *Did you really escape the Circle? Did they really kill your family to force you back in?* He'd had a practice round with Mr. Black at his re-initiation, but now was his time to deliver his rehearsed speech on the matter.

"Is what true?" he said, feigning ignorance. Never offer specific details to vague questions.

"You know what I mean," said Belt. "Did they really find you and, you know"—he pointed his finger like a gun—"and—"

"I broke the rules," Vice said. "I was punished. End of story."

Belt let out a long, slow whistle. "That's fucked up, man."

"It's on me," said Vice, beginning to feel defensive. *Damn you, Warren.*

"Still, that's some cold blooded shit."

Apparently, Mr. Belt was one of those killers with a moral compass.

"Makes you think, no?" Belt continued.

"About what?"

"How the Circle is so firm on civilian deaths, but then to punish you and bring you back in, they did exactly that."

He was right. It was an obvious contradiction in the Circle's sacred bylaws. Civilians had died to punish Vice—well, Warren, really. Not that their deaths appeared to be anything but by natural causes: car accident, accidental prescription overdose. Is that where "they" drew the line? You could kill as long as you didn't hunt? And who made those decisions anyway? It was a weak justification at best, he thought.

"I guess," he said, still wary of revealing too much to another hunter.

Belt scoffed. "You're much more forgiving than I am. I'd be taking people out left and right if they did something like that to my family."

"I was wrong to leave," said Vice harshly. It was too dangerous to continue this conversation. "I knew the risks. I accept the consequences. That's all there is to it." He changed the subject. "How many members are in the New York chapter, anyway?"

"Lots. It's big. The biggest, in fact. Probably twice the size of D.C. More than 300 of us."

Three hundred members!? That was more than twice the 122 in D.C. Vice took a slow drink from his glass to process this bit of information. With so many members, he'd never meet them all. Recon was looking less and less like a fruitful activity. It made sense, though. The size of the safehouse alone was a strong indicator. Good thing not all members were seeking sanctuary at the same time.

"There must be a second safehouse, then."

Belt nodded. "This is one of three. But there is only one Mr. Black for New York, and he runs his operations through here. That's why I keep coming back to this one," he added.

"Where are the others?"

"No idea. I've never really had any reason to go anywhere else—and none of my assigned kills have been associated anywhere else, and it's been 13 years, so…not that it won't happen at some point."

Three safe houses, over 300 members. No way to gather the information he needed. He simply couldn't be three places at once. He looked at Belt. The man was sharing a lot of information. Too willingly. You didn't make "friends" in the Circle. Still, he'd learned nothing about his potential target.

Belt suddenly rose with a surprising degree of grace and saluted. "Well, I'm off," he said. "Nice t' meetcha, Mr. Vice. Welcome to New York."

• • •

With no permanent address and no time to set up traditional surveillance, Vice was left to rely on his ingenuity to secure the penthouse at the Waldorf. When he exited the elevator to the top floor he spotted it immediately. The slip of paper he'd wedged between the door and its frame just below the lowest of the three hinges before closing the door was no longer there. Sometimes the simplest tricks are the most effective—and if it was good enough for Robert Redford in *The Sting* it was good enough for him.

He stared at the paper, which had fallen to the floor. From the elevator, it was impossible to miss. Someone had been in his room. Or was *still* in his room. His target Mr. Shakespeare? Or his nameless hunter? No way to know. Vice's instinct was to go for his weapon. But of course he had none. *Stupid miscalculation.* He should have at least picked up a knife or a crowbar or something. He took a quick stock of his surroundings. A candelabrum sat on the table under the mirror in the hallway. He silently thanked the Waldorf for its hospitality. The object was heavy and bulky, but it would do the trick.

He silently slid the key into the lock and opened the door to the sound of muffled screams coming from within.

Quickly, he took stock. The room was in disarray, the curtains dangling from its rod along the large window, the glass coffee table shattered, and the television destroyed by some kind of wooden tool, still protruding from the screen. There was no denying it, a battle had been waged in his absence—and was still going on. The sounds of struggle continued. He followed the streak of blood from the tiled hallway down the hall to the bedroom. Then through to the bathroom. There was nowhere else.

He gripped the candelabrum tightly and readied his arm for a swift blow should the need arise. The bawling had died down to a whimper when he kicked in the door, sending splinters of wood into the bathroom. Sprawled out on the bathroom floor was the same man he'd identified at his initiation, the man gazing at him from the billiard table. Now near death.

Just as I suspected, he thought. At least his instincts were still intact, if not his logical brain.

The man was bleeding from the mouth and eyes with his attacker crouched over him, frozen, realizing they'd been caught in the act. The pair of forceps holding a large tooth sat on the floor. The Dentist.

Their eyes locked.

She was a vision.

The feeling that came over Vice was unfamiliar. One of only a few women in the Circle he'd ever encountered, she was also one of the most ruthless he'd ever seen.

A long pause hung in the air before all hell broke loose. The guy on the floor groped for purchase and found the shower curtain, which came crashing down with the rod still attached, but he was too weak to drum up the energy to put it to any use.

Not so for Vice. Instinctively, he brought the candelabrum down on his would-be attacker's head, taking advantage of the Dentist, who was busy flailing at the curtain that had separated her from her victim and impeded her sight and movement. The man on the floor went limp. He let go of the curtain and slumped lifelessly to the floor.

The Dentist, now free of entanglement, breathing hard, looked up at Vice. "So, now what," she said. Her eyes, large and brown, were challenging. Dismissive. As if she didn't care one way or another. *Interesting.*

Splattered with blood, dark hair disheveled, she was like a seething, disturbingly radiant Medusa. Vice reached out a foot and kicked away the tools by her side. Then, from a safe distance, he put a hand to her face to wipe away the blood on her forehead. She flinched, but let him.

"You saved my life," she said disgustedly.

"I did," he said. "But you saved mine first, whether you meant to or not." Was the excitement he was feeling evident to her the way it was to him? He'd always followed his kills in the arms of a willing sexual partner, but here was someone—a woman—who knew what it was like to hunt, to kill. For the adrenaline rush. For the thrill. He would have to be very, very careful here.

"The Circle in action," said the Dentist, getting up slowly. "It's a beautiful thing, no?"

Slowly, Vice lowered his weapon and nodded.

• • •

The Dentist allowed him to watch as she gracefully rose from the bed to shower, retrieve her clothes from the floor, dress, and reapply her makeup. Their sex had been an exercise in struggle, control, and release. At least for her. The release, that is. She seemed to take pleasure in bringing him to the point of climax with no end in sight. Finally, she'd placed his hands around her neck and smiled as he squeezed...and tightened...

and exploded.

When she finished dressing she turned and looked at him. "We'll have to do that again sometime," she said. "That is, if I don't have to kill you first."

"I suppose we'll have to see about that," Vice said. "I'm pretty sure we both earned a 48-hour furlough just now."

The Dentist turned back to him, her face hard and calculating again after their brief, if intense, interlude. "That's not true," she said. "I have plans. Big plans for the next month. And regardless of what just happened here, none of them involve you."

"I killed him," Vice said. "He was hunting *me*. That means I have the next 48 hours off. As do you...while they're locating your next target."

The Dentist seethed for a moment, and before he knew it he had a fist in his face.

Shocked despite the circumstances, Vice put his hand on his jaw. Damn woman packed a punch. "Bitch," he said with admiration.

"Screw you, Vice. You had to come home. Ruin everything."

"Hey, don't get mad at me," he said. "It's on you. You got distracted, gave me the perfect opening."

"I wasn't distracted. I got interrupted. Then you swoop in like a vulture, steal my kill."

"Maybe if you spent less time pulling teeth and more time killing you wouldn't have found yourself in this position."

"They need to feel the pain," said the Dentist.

Vice agreed. Their rituals may be different, but he might be able to learn a thing or two about pain and suffering. He was also fascinated by her attitude towards the Circle, and her victims. She was here to inflict pain, intense amounts of concentrated pain, pure and simple. The killing was almost an afterthought.

He nodded. "We do what we have to. To survive."

The Dentist considered the clock high on the wall. After some mental math, and another long look at Vice's naked form, she said, "The Watchers will be here in less than 15 minutes…you have 13 to prove you can keep up."

• • •

Twelve minutes and 43 seconds later they were both dressed and leaving the penthouse. Vice had a small cut along his cheek in addition to the one on his bottom lip, due to a parting shot that was just beginning to clot. The Dentist was limping slightly from her battle with the dearly departed Mr. Fuel, and sporting the imprint of Vice's fingers around her neck.

The elevator arrived as they did. A member of the cleaning staff with the name tag of "Johnson" exited and went past them without a glance. They stepped into the elevator and turned to the front just in time to hear him swear when he saw the wreckage at the scene.

The elevator doors closed. Vice looked at his watch for confirmation. Yup. He'd been a member of the New York chapter for less than a day and he'd already earned a 48-hour furlough. Not bad. He slid his gaze over to the Dentist, who focused straight ahead and tapped her foot as if willing the elevator to move faster.

He allowed himself a small smile. This feisty killer wasn't a furlough girl. A play thing. She was his equal, carrying herself in a way that was both beautiful and toxic. This was a killer who carried around a tin container of the teeth of her fallen victims, likely calculating who was next on her list, just like he was. She understood his life. Especially the simple yet complicated life the Circle provided.

There was a danger here. Mr. Vice didn't love; the mere thought made him shudder. That's what mortals like Warren did. And besides, it had nothing to do with Vice's life, his work. His *needs*. But somehow he knew he'd have to tread lightly.

51

The Dentist

Stupid. Stupid. Stupid! The Dentist cursed herself as she jabbed at the elevator button for the lobby of the Waldorf Astoria. She'd succumbed to her carnal desires with this new Mr. Vice, had become involved with another member. She'd been careless. And now she had to worry about whether or not this Mr. Vice could be trusted to keep their…activities… to himself, or if he would use them to besmirch her stellar reputation as a ruthless killer.

She glanced up at him, a good five inches taller, and in that short moment she knew she had nothing to worry about. He gave himself away. When word got to New York that Mr. Vice, *the* Mr. Vice, would be joining their chapter, the Dentist had scavenged for information about him. What she'd found was a man who was stoic with his approach to the Circle, patient, meticulous, and highly effective. But there, in that elevator, when she looked at him out of the corner of her eye, the slightest of curls sat at the corners of his lips. Good, she thought. The stud had an ego. She could use that.

To most women a small smile from a man like Vice would send butterflies fluttering. But the Dentist saw an opportunity. She would be the Alpha here. Dictate terms and develop guidelines for whatever this relationship of theirs would become. In the end, there was no doubt she would hold his very life in her hands. She would make him hesitate when he used to be confident. Question everything he knew to be. He'd fallen victim to a woman's charms once before, and it had cost him that woman's life. That was his weak spot.

She pushed the stop button and the elevator jerked to a halt.

Vice started. "What are you—?"

"Shut up," she said, and reached for him where it mattered. Immediately, he went hard in her hand. She shoved him into the corner and heard his grunt of surprise, pain, and anticipation for what was to come. When her free hand withdrew a switchblade knife from her pocket to press the blade against his throat, he gasped again.

"Let me make one thing clear, Mr. Vice," she said. "If word gets out about what just happened here, two things will happen. One…."

He was breathing heavily. "You think I'd say anything to—"

"Don't interrupt me," she snapped, and moved the knife towards his open fly. "Now, as I was saying…. One, nothing will ever happen between us again. Two, I will kill you. Damn the rules of the Circle and damn what happens to me, I *will* kill you. And it won't be a fast death. It will take hours. Days. And I will enjoy every second of it."

She looked down and saw that his erection had intensified. In all her years, no man had ever been able to handle her in the bedroom. Her desires were never fully quenched, she was always left needing more than her partner was capable of, or willing to do. She thought about how she'd even paid for it a few times, but always with disappointing results. Was it possible this was the man who could change that? Provide the animalistic, salacious, one might even say sadomasochistic experience she—and perhaps he—craved?

In the end, though, it really didn't matter. This was about playing the long game, the one that resulted in her survival and, most likely, inevitably, Vice's death. She'd be the first Ms. Black in the Circles long and storied history. A legend in her own time. For that to happen, it was near certain they would end up pitted against each other. Simply, she would have to kill him before he killed her.

In the meantime, she'd make that decision as hard for him as she could by doing what she did so well.

Knowing it would only arouse him further, she opened the fly of his briefs and placed the cold steel of the blade against erection. "Do I make myself clear?"

"Crystal," replied Vice through gritted teeth.

"Good," she said. She closed the knife and put it away, then turned to reactivate the stalled elevator, pressed the button for three, and watched as he fumbled to cover up their indiscretion before anyone else entered. She planned to take the stairs. Only the Watcher had seen them and that's the way she wanted to keep it. On the third floor she got out.

"11 p.m.," she said, "your place. Have the Grand Marnier waiting."

Mr. Vice

Mr. Shakespeare, aka Glenn Burr, was an impressive specimen. Not the caliber of the Dentist, certainly, yet impressive nonetheless. Shakespeare ate, drank, and breathed theatre, like a walking course in stage history. The Vivian Beaumont was between productions, but that didn't stop their in-house thespian and biggest benefactor, a secretly thwarted actor himself, from his regular visits to hobnob with the performers and directors and impart his vast stores of wisdom. No one at the theatre deigned to suggest otherwise.

"Remember," Burr said as he concluded today's lesson to a group of up-and-coming actors who endured his endless lectures for the occasional kernel of actual payoff, "Screen acting is about subtlety. One raised eyebrow or clenched jaw tells a tale. But the stage," he paused for dramatic effect, "the stage is about grand subtlety. Your raised eyebrow may intoxicate those in the front row, but what about your audience in the balcony?" He paced the stage and projected his voice. His gestures became more grandiose and animated. "What about the last row? How will they receive your words? Your actions? Will they simply accept or will they resist in search of more convincing? Once you find your own way to master the grand subtleties then you, my friends, will command this stage. This. Very. Stage."

The young actors applauded diligently. This was nothing they hadn't heard before, but they'd been taught well. Without money, there would be no theatre and no jobs. Backstage, Vice was tempted to clap along, but he'd found a good location in the shadows he wasn't about to jeopardize. The heavy black curtains that hung from the lofty rafters created ample cover for stealthing. The intricacies of a theatrical production never ceased to amaze. So many moving parts, theoretical and literal, that went into a production. He made a mental note to attend some good theatre from now on during his next furlough.

The acting troupe slowly disbanded, a couple hanging back to place themselves at Mr. Burr's feet. *Everyone needs a rich benefactor, right?* Vice waited patiently for the great man to drink in the accolades. Why not? After tonight, regardless of the intended chosen play, he would not be this cast's mentor. When the last actor had finally departed, Burr stood quietly on the stage, unaware this was to be his last dissertation.

The light panel was just to Vice's right. In the past when Burr finished a class, he'd always come straight backstage to shut off the lights. Tonight, for some reason, he didn't. Vice waited, but the only sound were Burr's footfalls, which were already fading. The damn man was leaving the theatre! It was an unexpected turn of events.

Vice thought quickly. Why would Burr do things differently today? There was no obvious reason. It could be nothing. He could have forgotten the lights. Someone else might be returning to the theatre.... Anything was possible. But today was obviously not the day. It was time to get himself out or risk losing his anonymity.

Exiting stage right through the dark shadows led him to the nearest exit door. Just as he had the thought that it was deadly quiet in the theatre—too bad it wasn't due to the result he'd been going for—when something struck his right leg. He fell to one knee, howling at the throbbing pain, and looked up. No. It couldn't be.

Yet it was. Mr. Shakespeare was wielding a crowbar and readying for the next blow. Vice went flat and rolled, but still absorbed a vicious blow to the ribs. "'We must have bloody noses and crack'd crowns, And pass them current too!'" quoted Shakespeare, who knew he had the upper hand.

Vice, taking advantage of the dark, managed a chop to Shakespeare's knee before the next blow hit. Shakespeare buckled and fumbled to right himself, losing the crowbar in the process. It clanged onto the ground and rolled away. Unfortunately, not toward Vice.

He sensed Shakespeare's indecision. Go for the crowbar or enter into combat without it. Before he had a chance to act, Vice latched onto Shakespeare's head and forced a knee into his face. Then again. Three consecutive blows smashed Barr's nose so far inward he'd be lucky to sneeze ever again. Not that Vice planned to let him survive.

Shakespeare kept coming. He blocked Vice's next attempt with his hands and connected with an elbow to Vice's jaw. Now it was Shakespeare's turn, delivering several blows to Vice's head and face. Vice was able to wiggle an arm free to deflect the next one, using Barr's own momentum to force him onto his stomach as Vice rolled away. Vice grabbed a hold of Shakespeare's arm in the process and twisted it behind his back as he rose to a standing position. With his heel he stomped down on Shakespeare's back, while ratcheting his arm further behind. He did not stop until he heard the pop as it dislocated.

Vice dropped Shakespeare's arm, now useless, and repositioned himself for another attack, which came before he had a chance to distance himself enough to ward it off. He might not have the use of an arm, but this man was a formidable opponent. Shakespeare's knife cut through the air, slicing Vice's chest and shoulder, narrowly missing his face and neck. Vice was recoiling again from the sting of the gash when the second one came, this time penetrating his shoulder blade. This can't be the end, he thought. I can't die this way... at the hands of the Shakespeare killer. I can't.

"'There are few die well that die in battle,'" Shakespeare quoted breathlessly, left arm dangling from its socket. If he didn't get out of the way, Vice thought, weakly straining to find purchase behind him— But it was too late. By the time his hand had landed on the lever, the one he believed—he prayed—controlled the ropes coiled on the backstage floor, Shakespeare had made another cut to his forearm.

Bleeding and weak, Vice chastised himself for his hubris. Thinking he was ready to hunt so soon. Not that he'd had any choice. Still, here he was, about to die. That is, unless he had something to say about it.

Shakespeare was breathing heavily. It seemed he was weakening as well. Vice knew he'd only get one chance. It was risky, but he didn't see any other way out.

"You thought you could ambush me? In *my* theatre?" Shakespeare panted. "You are a fool! And I...I will 'fight till from my bones my flesh be hacked.'"

The knife came down again, but this time Vice was ready. He dodged the blow, taking Shakespeare down with him to the ground where Vice would have more of an advantage. Or at least more than he'd had before, which wasn't much. The thick rope at his side was soon wrapped around Shakespeare's neck like a python. Instinctively, he let go of the knife to alleviate the pressure on his windpipe. That's when Vice threw the lever.

It only took a few seconds before gravity released the sandbags hanging from the rafters. They came raining down and Mr. Shakespeare was snapped upwards by the rope attached to his neck. Vice didn't hear his neck break, so he held on until the end came. He looked into Shakespeare's eyes and nodded. *Battle well fought.*

Shakespeare blinked once, quoting his beloved Bard of Avon one last time, "'My soul...is in...the sky.'"

And it was done.

53

1985 – Gérard

Richard Osterman, Benjamin Sanders, Marcus Cobb, Leonardo La Strada, and Thomas Brown: board of directors for Atlantic Express LLC, a shipping company specializing in everything between Europe and the Americas. The funny thing about AE was that they had been operating since 1978 and were well known in the shipping community, yet owned no freighters despite leasing space in ports in every major city from the Mediterranean to the Gulf of Mexico.

Another interesting bit of news was AE's sudden merger with World Ocean Network to form WON. It was this buyout that brought to light even more interesting information about its board members. It seemed that although Osterman, Sanders, Cobb, LaStrada, and Brown owned various beautifully maintained properties around the world, not a single employee from gardeners to valets to chefs or anyone else could ever testify having seen one of their employers in person.

It was a tragedy when their private jet disappeared en route from their central offices in Lisbon to the Cayman Islands, all five men, as well as the crew of three, perishing somewhere south of Bermuda. Conspiracy theorists emerged from every corner of the globe touting definitive proof of the existence of the Bermuda Triangle, of extraterrestrials snatching humans for experimentation. Tragedy and conspiracy: what the world most loves to consume. The victims' photos—all middle-aged white men in suits—ran in newspapers everywhere around the world for weeks before the story died a slow death. That is, until one day when questions turned to suspicion when a dogged journalist discovered that, upon the death of the five men, the legalities required for the merger to proceed fell to one single man. The founder of Atlantic Express LLC.

Gérard Finck.

When Gérard conceived of his plan it was with a rare kind of pleasure. To fool one or two people? Easy. To fool the world? Positive proof of his superior intellect and abilities. Gérard's fictitious board members had many differences, but one major similarity: physically, in reality, they were all Gérard Finck. Painstaking disguises—a cleft chin here, a plumper nose there; male-pattern baldness here, a full head of jet-black hair slicked back Wall Street style there—made for easily forged identifiers like licenses and passports. He'd assigned each man a personality, an identity, along with a signature, which he applied liberally whenever required. People were stupid when it came to money, to earning it. They really didn't care where it came from. Who cares if you never see your boss as long as his name is on your weekly check?

Gérard's meticulous planning had managed to convince the world that not only had five board members no one had ever met existed and were to be mourned, but that he was now the inheritor of a fortune worth three quarters of a billion dollars.

It wasn't the world that needed convincing of his wealth, however. Gérard had a different audience in mind. Somewhere in the world, the Circle was watching. Every move he'd made in his life since the day he'd learned of the Circle's existence was predicated on that basic premise. He was counting on it.

He remembered his training, and its abrupt, unceremonious conclusion. He could still feel his reaction when Miss Zutter had pulled him in close by his shirt. Could still remember her final words, her final intake and exhale of breath as he did as he'd been trained to do—as *she* had trained him to do—plunging his knife into her lungs to seal the deal and tossing her over the railing into the river like the carcass of a dead rat. "You are the one," she'd told him at the end. "Bring it down."

The loud splash was bittersweet. He'd felt an emotional attachment to Miss Zutter. Despite their complicated relationship, he'd felt she deserved a different kind of sendoff than the same one she had offered all her vanquished foes. One more worthy of her contribution to his existence. His rebirth from unripe murderer to trained assassin. But no matter. As she would have said, "Dead is dead."

And he was doing what he was meant to do. He was taking down the Circle.

If he'd learned one thing from his years of training with Miss Zutter, it was that the Circle always needed two things: more funds and more members. By publicly inheriting that money, a solitary man with no living family, no children, and new to the United States, Gérard knew he was sending up a flare. All he had to do was wait for them to come to him.

There was no doubt that they would; it was just a matter of time.

And if there was a second thing he'd learned from Miss Zutter, it was patience.

• • •

It didn't take long. A matter of months spent studying and living the easy life of a handsome bachelor about town in New York. His French accent drew the ladies like dogs to meat, an apt description if Gérard ever heard one. They found him exotic, cultured. And, compared to the boorish Americans he met on a daily basis, he was.

Then, finally, Gérard knew he was being followed, or "tailed," as they said. Watched. Alone in his palatial apartment he spent many hours wondering who trained these Watchers, and who was cleaning up after the sloppy ones. The one assigned to Gérard for example, who seemed unaffected by Gérard's knowledge of his intentions.

Unless the guy really didn't know how inept he was. Gérard acted his part to perfection, just a regular guy in the Big Apple, presumably one who had no knowledge of a club for wealthy and bloodthirsty assassins operating beneath the surface of polite society. Again, he reminded himself to have patience. Identifying his own Watcher before the time of contact would be unwise.

• • •

It's one thing to tell yourself to be patient and quite another to do it. Another month went by until Gérard's penchant for patience grew so thin that it was no more than a thin line in the sand. It was time to speed up the process, cross that line. He'd grown tired of the patterns he'd concocted for easy tracking by the Circle. He'd wanted to seem reliable, predictable even.

If the Watchers hadn't pegged his behaviors by now, they never would. Besides, he was bored.

Finally, after four months of waiting, he gave himself the gift of the go-ahead while on the way to an appointment at Shangri-La Spa on East 84th and 3rd for his weekly massage. After rounding the corner of 3rd, Gérard turned and quickly pressed up against the building to wait. Three or four seconds later, the Watcher turned the corner, too. Directly into Gérard's hands.

"Who are you," Gérard barked, the man's lapels in his hands. "Why are you following me?"

The man, struggling to free himself from Gérard's grip, managed only a few grunts before Gérard slammed him against the wall.

"You've been following me all day," he said, as if he'd just noticed. It was one of the Circle's ongoing conundrums. The organization's need for new, rich members was insatiable, given its high rate of attrition. But wealth did not equate to prowess when it came to the hunt...which only increased the chances of the Circle's survival as rich, inept members died shortly after entering the hunt, leaving their multiple millions, or billions, in the Circle's treasury.

"Mr. Finck, if you'll permit me," the man stammered.

"How do you know my name?" Gérard demanded. The charade was already irritating. Playing dumb was not something he enjoyed.

"I'll explain," said the man, "but you'll have to let me go first."

Slowly Gérard loosened his grip on the man, keeping him close so he wouldn't bolt. "Well?"

"My name is Smith," the man said. "I...I have been sent by some very important people. To talk to you about an exciting proposition."

"Proposition? Important people? What is this all about? Tell them to make an appointment like anyone else."

"Smith" collected himself as best he could. "We're a *private* club, Mr. Finck. We cater to men of your...stature. We think you'd be a perfect fit for our exclusive membership."

Gérard paused to give the impression he was intrigued at such an offer. "I'm listening," he finally said, "but this had better be good. I don't like being followed."

"Oh, it's good, alright, Mr. Finck. In fact, I think you'll agree it'll change your life."

54

The Dentist

The thing about the long game is that it's...long. At the conclusion of her first encounter with Mr. Vice they had developed a sort of shorthand risk assessment to determine if/when it was safe to meet.

In the past, recons were reserved for prey. Between the weeks after their first meeting and the period during which time Mr. Vice had offed Mr. Shakespeare and had his 30-day furlough, they hadn't seen each other once. By her design. There were no coded messages, purposefully leading Vice to believe that there was no convenient time for them to safely meet. Stringing Vice along was intended to intensify his desires for when they finally did have the chance to meet again. And with him out of the picture for a while, she'd been able to press pause on the long game and keep tabs on her own target, Mr. Mercy, and enjoy the hunt.

• • •

Mr. Mercy had owned a construction company, the largest one in the city, prior to joining the Circle, and was aware that it was more his fighting spirit than his financial worth, far less than the Circle's average, that had made him a valued member. It had become both a joke and a matter of pride: *Don't get killed by the peasant.* Mr. Mercy played along. Being cast as the underdog had its benefits.

Many Circle members maintained their day jobs, as did Mercy, whose values around "an honest day's work" fell somewhere lower than remarkable, as opposed to his quest for personal power. Sure, the Circle had its fingers in every pie in the civilized world, but power wielded over anyone, in whatever context anywhere, was another feather in one's cap.

Through her binoculars, the Dentist spotted Mr. Mercy at one of his construction sites off Arthur Kill Road on Staten Island. It was just after dusk and getting dark fast. He was walking the perimeter and talking with another man in a hard hat. She inferred from their gestures toward the empty lot that they were discussing a new property that was to be built.

The Dentist had gone with all black, and accessorized with a small, black duffel bag which contained several implements of pain and torture. She watched as Mr. Mercy and his associate shook hands and parted ways, the associate oblivious to her location only yards away as he walked to his truck and departed.

Mr. Mercy headed for the construction trailer. It tickled her no end the way "the peasant" seemed to love to work when she herself would rather play—and be played—when she wasn't engaged in the hunt. There was no one else in the vicinity or inside the dark trailer. Once inside he'd be trapped.

It was just a matter of her getting there first.

It was almost too easy. She slipped inside quickly before Mercy had even rounded the trailer to climb the stairs to the door, smelling the sweat and dirt and testosterone she imagined was typical of sites like this. Men. So full of themselves they could never foresee the possibility of being bested by a woman. It was her greatest weapon.

The disorganization within was evident even in the muted light. Blueprints rolled up in tubes, hard hats, and overflowing trash cans welcomed her. She positioned herself in the darkest corner of the trailer, nearest to Mercy's desk. It wasn't the best cover, but it would do. It was all about the element of surprise, and, until he turned on the lights, she'd have the upper hand. She pictured Mercy scanning the perimeter for threats before entering. Having left the trailer with Hard Hat Man so recently, it was unlikely he'd expect any trouble once inside.

• • •

The Dentist woke him with a slap across the face. Then another. He was groggier than she had anticipated after injecting him with her own special solution, just enough to put him out and keep him out while she secured him to a chair with zip ties and placed a dental gag in his mouth. To receive maximum enjoyment from the kill, he needed to be alive and fully conscious. What would be the point otherwise?

When he came to, Mercy assessed his circumstances, coming to a fast understanding. She had to give him credit. His recoil, while instant, was already resigned, as if he knew the outcome. Which, of course, he did. The panic would come later.

She wore a clear face shield with a pair of magnifier glasses resting on her forehead, ready to start the game. It was when she took out her favorite pair of oral extraction pliers that Mercy's calm demeanor fled and fear took over. How nice it would be to bottle up that kind of fear and take it home to experience again later.

She smiled. "Welcome to my office," she said. "I'm going to take a good look in that mouth of yours. Don't bother resisting. Because if you do—well, it won't be just teeth that I pry from your mouth. Nod if you understand."

Mr. Mercy nodded.

"Good," said the Dentist. "Hold still, now." She poked around with her sharpest pick for a minute. "Tsk-tsk, Mr. Mercy. I see you haven't been brushing very well around the gum line," she chided. "Plaque...decay...you should be ashamed. That's what's causing your halitosis, you know." She shook her head. "I suppose there *is* one way to fix the problem, though, and, fortunately for you, I'm just the gal to do it."

Mr. Mercy's eyes grew bigger and rounder with every word she spoke.

The Dentist spent the next hour utilizing every tool in her professional kit. Between Mercy's agonizing cries and her own satisfaction—well, the results were gratifying.

Before she left, the Dentist performed her next-to-last act of dropping four of Mr. Mercy's teeth into her Altoid tin. She'd need a new one soon. This one was almost full to the brim. "That sound you heard, the crunch," she told Mr. Mercy (they said people in a coma might be able to hear people around them, right? and he'd probably like to know), "was actually inside your head. The jawbone carries sound directly to the inner ears, bypassing the ear canal completely. So even if your ears were blocked, you'd hear it. Fascinating, no?"

She didn't wait for an answer.

She roused Mr. Mercy just enough to let him know his

time had come, removed her fine pointed extraction forceps from her bag, and jammed it into his neck. His life was extinguished in less than a minute.

The Dentist packed up and turned to go. "No mercy for Mr. Mercy," she said, and smiled.

55

Gérard

Finally.

Inside the belly of the beast.

It was like coming home. If there was such a thing.

Smith led him through a virtually empty bar—it was still early—to a back wall, which slid open to reveal some kind of VIP lounge. Gérard took in the atmosphere. It was well maintained, orderly. Other than the hungry, empty eyes of its members, it might have been any gentlemen's club. Indeed, cigars, games of skill and chance, women of the night...all there for the taking. Miss Zutter would have been sorely undervalued in such a place, he felt sure.

"Mr. Black will see you in the back," Smith said, pointing. "I'm afraid this is as far as I can take you. Best of luck, Mr. Finck."

Gérard gave a brief nod for his safe delivery, but Smith was already slipping back through the invisible sliding door. Once he was gone and the door had closed behind him, it was as if the room had taken a breath but had yet to exhale. Silent, oppressive. Despite Gérard's confidence, he felt beads of sweat forming on his brow. That's when it struck him. These men were his future victims. With the thought the moment passed, he moved in the direction he'd been advised to meet Mr. Black. As he took the first step, the room became animated once again. A man came toward him. "Mr. Finck, I presume," he said.

His smile, soft and welcoming, was at odds with his eyes, which were cold and calculating. This was not the Mr. Black Gérard had been expecting, yet there was no doubt that the scar across his chin and over his right eye suggested he'd seen battle and survived. Many, many times. He wouldn't be a Mr. Black if he hadn't.

"Thank you for accepting the Circle's invitation," Black said. "I realize the cloak-and-dagger approach may seem somewhat over the top, but we are a clandestine society, as you have been made aware."

How would this supposed recruitment go, Gérard wondered. Many of the Circle's members were involuntary, forced into "membership" by circumstances or simply the promise of their bite of the apple. Since Gérard fit into neither category, already wealthy and already powerful in his own right, how would they play this game?

"Yes," he said. "It was, shall we say, off-putting. I found myself intrigued, however, which is why I am here."

"Come, then," said Black, "have a drink with me. There's a lot to discuss." He nodded to one of the girls who scampered off as fast as she could given her mile-high footwear, and returned with two cocktails as they settled into their chairs at the table in the back corner.

Black took a sip of his drink and invited Gérard to do the same. "I understand you enjoy a Sidecar, Mr. Finck, so I had our bartender mix one up for you. I hope this one meets your approval."

Gérard didn't like to drink, didn't like the feeling of not being 100% in control of his mind and body. But he'd made a point to manufacture a signature drink to order at each establishment he frequented for Mr. Smith's—and the Circle's—benefit. It seemed to have worked. Surprisingly, the blend of cognac, cointreau, and lemon juice was becoming an enjoyed indulgence rather than part of his cover. He hoped the sugared rim made him appear less intimidating than your traditional Scotch or Bourbon might. You never knew what detail might be important for onlookers.

"You know what I drink?" asked Gérard, feigning displeasure tempered by humor.

"I do hope I haven't offended you, Mr. Finck," said Mr. Black. "It is nothing insidious, I assure you. But our organization is an exclusive one, which is why we take such diligence in knowing as much as we can about anyone we might choose to invite into our inner sanctum. That way we ensure the best fit for our little club."

Interesting that Black wasn't hiding his interest, laying out his cards, so to speak. Gérard decided to go along by raising his glass to Black and taking a nice long draw of his cocktail, which was superior to any he'd had before.

"I see you appreciate fine liquor," said Black. "We stock our bar only with the finest spirits in the world—all free of charge with membership of course—and our bartender mixed yours with a nice Remy Martin, 1738."

That's his pitch? Lure me in with outrageously expensive booze, usurp my fortune, tell me I'll be hunted for the rest of my life, and am lucky to be so anointed?

"Of course, there is more to our organization than fancy drinks."

Okay. Now we're getting somewhere.

"As I said, Mr. Finck, we've been watching you. I won't deny it. And we also looked into your background. What we've seen is someone who's lost a great deal. No father. Mother lost in the Paris riots. Foster care, juvenile detention. Then a period where, interestingly, you were apparently missing in action altogether. Homelessness can be devastating for a young man such as yourself." When Gérard said nothing, Black continued. "God only knows what you had to endure. And then, just as you have clawed your way to the top, you lose your entire board of directors in a tragic plane crash."

Gérard was relying on his acting credibility as he responded with practiced looks of shame, shock, resignation, devastation, embarrassment, and grief. "I get it," he said, "You've done your homework. What does this have to do with me joining your…'little club'?"

"Let me be frank, Mr. Finck," Black said, as if it were a new approach. "You strike me as a lonely man…no, not lonely. A solitary man."

"I keep to myself," Gérard said coldly, "if that's what you mean."

"An excellent way to put it, yes.... But there's something missing, isn't there?"

"Missing? What do you mean?"

Black said nothing. He reached under his chair and retrieved a manila folder, which he placed on the table. Gérard had been waiting for this moment for a very long time, but what he saw still came as a shock. Photos. Lots of them. His exit file from juvenile detention. Details of his torture of the animals at his previous foster homes, the strangulation of his foster father with the vacuum cleaner cord, his time locked up in prison and the damage he'd done while inside. He shouldn't have been surprised. He knew the Circle's reach was limitless. Still, seeing it all there in black and white was oddly disturbing.

"So...?" he said.

"Please understand, Mr. Finck. We don't judge you here. That's not who we are."

"Okay," said Gérard slowly. "Who are you then…?

Black nodded. "Mr. Finck, your life would be quite different if you did not feel ashamed of these actions. If you knew they were the actions of a survivor, a true winner. What would you think then?"

Time for some belligerence. "What are you talking about? I do my best every damn day to forget that part of my life. Now you want me to…to what?Appreciate it? Embrace it?"

"Exactly!" Black said. "I couldn't have said it better myself. Embrace it, Mr. Finck. Every other member here has done exactly that. They embrace their carnal instincts, and they act on them. That's what I'm offering to you. A chance to live the life you've been wanting to live since you were a boy. Live like there's no tomorrow. Live like each moment could be your last.

"To live...for the hunt."

• • •

Gérard relived the final moments of his conversation with Black as he left to return home for the evening. Their discussion, during which Black had outlined the Circle's credos, had lasted longer than he'd thought, but he decided to walk rather than take a taxi to give him time to think.

"Be assured, Mr. Finck," he'd said, looking at Gérard long and hard. "There is great freedom within this society's protection. The freedom to give into your deepest, darkest desires."

Gérard had nodded hesitantly.

"Good," said Black. "Because with that freedom, however, comes certain constraints. Lines that may never be crossed."

Gérard knew what was coming. It was time for the showdown, and it had to be convincing. "I'm not sure I understand after all," he said.

"Oh, I think you do," said Black. "This organization is called the Circle. As a member, you are quite simply above the law. There is no reprisal. Ever. You will hunt to kill, and be hunted by your peers in the most fulfilling game of cat and mouse that has ever been conceived."

"Hunt...to kill?" Gérard repeated, as if his heart weren't beating wildly.

Black nodded. "That's right. Kill, Mr. Finck...or be killed. Naturally, there *is* one catch."

The line had been baited and cast. He was about to be hooked. Gérard played dumb. Again. "Catch?"

"It's nothing, really," said Black. "Our all-inclusive membership offers you everything you've ever wanted in return for one thing—well, two really. Your money, and your loyalty. Add your fortune to the Circle's coffers and follow our rules and there is no end to what you will do, what you will have, what you will experience."

Gérard went to rise from the table as if affronted. "You want my money? That's what this is about?"

"Mr. Finck, I assure you, your money is inconsequential compared to our organization's net worth. But membership has its price. Police, judges, politicians, doctors, reporters.... they don't come cheap. We could not have existed for as long as we have without spending a lot of money keeping ourselves out of the public eye. It may be our choice, but murder is still very much frowned upon in society today."

"And what if I say no?" Gérard asked.

"This is America, Mr. Finck. You are free to do as you please. But understand that in order to keep our organization a secret we are willing to do what is necessary."

"Is that a threat?"

Black shrugged. "Merely a statement of fact. Decline our offer if you wish. Go on. Leave and live a long, dull life. But let me be very clear. A single utterance of this club or what goes on, to anyone, will have serious consequences."

It gave Gérard great satisfaction to prolong the moment indefinitely. To watch Black sweat, twist in the wind for a few moments. His pitch had been commendable for its threats, both veiled and unveiled, but nothing he'd said was new to Gérard. He finished his drink slowly, as if considering the "opportunity" offered.

Then he put out his hand to shake Black's. "How can I say no?" he said.

Black had proceeded to go over the "details" of membership, including the parameters of the safehouse, the rules of killing, furloughs, and the like. Gérard would have his "official initiation" in the morning with several current members. He would receive his first dossier at that time. When he'd stood up to go, Black smiled another cold smile that did not reach his eyes.

"You've made the right decision, Mr. Finck," he said. "Welcome to the Circle."

56

In only a handful of days Gérard had already acclimated to his new role as an official hunter of men. Now, when he strode into the VIP parlor at the New York safehouse it was with a different air. He'd been masquerading as a bumbling novice the first time, like the infamous Scarlet Pimpernel who'd played the part of a shallow marauder while saving lives. Not that Gérard planned on saving any lives. Still, he liked to think of himself as a mystery man with a license to kill. If they only knew he'd been *dying* for this moment for years. Taking out Mr. Fall had been just the beginning of what he expected to be a long run. Long enough for the Circle to collapse in a heap of dead bodies.

Word had gotten back to Tasker's faster than he'd expected. Greeted as if he were a celebrity on the red carpet, he closed his eyes and made a mental note of the smell of success around him. The expensive cigar smoke. The clashing aromas of various colognes. The booze. He opened them again, and saw the faces of his enemies: smiling faces, minds plotting his destruction.

Gérard took note, too, of Mr. Black's raised eyebrow, as if asking how on earth this pompous, wealthy nobody had taken down one of the Circle's best hunters. Gérard looked back. Underestimate me at your own risk, he thought. Exactly as I planned.

A powerfully built man, a disturbing reminder of Gérard's own father, or at least his memory, joined Gérard and offered his hand. "Congratulations on your first kill," the man said, squeezing Gérard's hand with a tight grip. His voice was quiet, reserved, as if he had great secrets to share, and could be trusted with the secrets of others. Gérard smelled the scent of caution. He might be tempted to share too much with this man, whoever he was. "It's significant. Everyone remembers their first."

Gérard again took note of the man's firm grip. "Thanks," he said.

"Tell the tale!" came a voice from the crowd.

The tale?

"Most members believe it customary to share the details of the battle with fellow members," said the man, who hadn't yet revealed his name. "But then, you wouldn't know that, would you?" he said to laughter. Gérard felt himself feel unsure for the first time. Supposedly, these were his new clan, his brethren. Yet they were killers first. Divulging details could be dangerous.

They were waiting for him to speak. Finally, he said, "Well, once I'd located his apartment, I picked the lock and hid in the bathroom. Then I killed him when he came in." Seeing the look of disappointed expectancy, he added, "Um,

I drowned him. In a pool of his own blood." Gérard held his breath. Would that be enough to satisfy them?

From the back came a disembodied voice. "Breath of fresh air, if you ask me. Short and sweet. Just what we need around here—not another stuck-up asshole, am I right?"

There was a slight hesitation before the faces around him relaxed, and Gérard took in a breath. *Good. They were letting it go.*

"Three cheers for Mr. Finck," said the voice, "who needs a name!"

"Mr. Tiles?" "Mr. Lock?" "Mr. Blood?"

"No, no, no," Gérard's new "friend" offered, silencing the crowd. "I think it's obvious. It has to be...Mr. Pool."

Three cheers later, it was official. Mr. Pool had been fully accepted into the Circle.

• • •

Finally, Gérard turned to the man who'd named him. "And you are…" he said, waiting.

"Mr. Vice," he said.

He was aptly named with that grip. "Did I hear correctly—that we have a woman member," he asked, hoping the blood would circulate in his hand again soon.

Vice nodded. "There are a few in this chapter," he said. "But underestimate them at your peril."

Gérard flashed back to his training with Miss Zutter, as ruthless as they come. "Understood," he said.

As if on cue, a woman appeared, stepping away from the group. Gérard felt his chest tighten. This was no arm candy for the members' pleasure. This woman was sheer elegance wrapped in a bow of stunning beauty. Her olive skin spoke of a European heritage, softened in the smoke-filled room. Her brown eyes were liquid pools. Gérard cleared his throat.

"Welcome to the Circle, Mr. Pool," said the woman, offering her hand. Gérard felt the calluses against his palm and felt the electricity of her touch. Mr. Vice was right. This one was danger personified.

"Thank you," he finally said. "Ms...."

"They call me the Dentist," she said.

The Dentist. How delightfully terrifying. Her stock in his book rose yet again. "I can only imagine why." Gérard said, laying on his French accent and placing a delicate kiss on her hand. "So gallant, Mr. Pool," she said with a smile. She reached into her tiny handbag and held out a small tin. "Care for a mint?"

57

Months had gone by since his initiation. Gérard was enjoying his time in the Circle, much as he'd enjoyed anywhere else in his life the last few years. He was among his own kind for the first time, and killing for a living was everything it was cracked up to be. He'd successfully hunted and killed nine members in all so far, so efficiently and effectively that he'd spent more time in the field researching his next kill than anything else. Not like other members who vacationed at resorts, traveled for pleasure, and continued to lead multimillion-dollar corporations.

Not Gérard. He'd developed a mutually distrustful "relationship" with the Dentist and Mr. Vice, whose company he enjoyed. It's not as if he'd ever had real friends, aside from Miss Zutter, who was arguably not at all in the same category. And being friends with killers was reassuring as well as nerve wracking...exhilarating.

Regardless, she'd been the only one who had seen him for who he was, and now he had a circle, no pun intended, of, if not friends, compatriots who shared a common goal. He could be who he was meant to be. Who he was made to be, without fear of exile. In the Circle, they were all equals...until death interceded.

With 17 days remaining on his most recent furlough, Gérard was sitting in his favorite chair in the safehouse. The Dentist, the object of his unrequited lust, was on his left; Vice across from him. They were holding drinks and watching Mr. Vice light up a new cigar. It was a rare sight. Mr. Vice was avidly health conscious. "*Thunderball*," he said.

"Seriously?" snorted the Dentist.

"Come on," said Gérard, "really? *Thunderball* is one of the worst Bond movies ever made. You're kidding right?"

"Not at all," Vice replied. "Sean Connery, Adolfo Celi as Largo. Claudine Auger as the exquisite Domino..."

"I'm not about to be swayed simply because she's French, you know," said Gérard.

"No?"

"No. Bond doesn't even kill Largo. Domino has to do the dirty work." He looked at the Dentist. "No offense, my love."

She waved him off. "None taken."

"Dirty work?" said Vice. "He fights off three or four guys while steering a boat that's speeding out of control. I'd say that's something."

"In a ridiculous wet suit, I might add," the Dentist offered.

"Name one that's better, then," Vice said.

"*Dr. No, Octopussy, Moonraker*," said the Dentist.

"*...Diamonds Are Forever....A View to a Kill, The Man With the Golden Gun*," Gérard said.

"*From Russia With Love!*" the Dentist continued.

"Okay, now you're just naming all of them," complained Vice.

"Exactly," said Gérard and the Dentist at the same time.

"Because they're all better than *Thunderball,*" she added.

Gérard clinked her glass. "I'll drink to that."

Vice shrugged and took another long drag from his cigar. Gérard also had never had these kinds of mundane conversations with people he considered equals. If this was the kind of friendship he could have in the Circle, it was enough for him.

He took a glance at his watch. Approaching midnight. Yawning, he excused himself. "It's that time," he said.

"So soon?" asked the Dentist.

"He knows I'm right, that's all," Vice said with a laugh.

"In your dreams, Mr. Vice," said Gérard, "in your dreams. But this conversation is *not* over. Consider this *to be continued,* Thunderball." He turned to the Dentist, placed a delicate kiss on her hand. "*Au revoir, mon amour.* Until anon."

A moment later Gérard waved goodnight to the bartender. "Hey, your favorite James Bond movie," he called, "quick."

"*Octopussy.* Of course. Why?"

"Oh, no reason," said Gérard with a chuckle, and exited the safehouse.

He was down on the ground before he knew what hit him. Surely not an attack. He knew better. He was on holiday. Plus, there was no followup, nothing else coming his way. Knife drawn, Gérard spotted the culprit. Some dumb idiot, a jogger out for a late-night run with a flashlight, also on the ground.

The man sat up. "Wow. I'm so sorry," he said. "I guess I wasn't looking where I was going." He dusted himself off and inspected himself for any injuries, then turned to Gérard. "You okay, man?"

Gérard nodded. The jogger was likely more bruised than Gérard, whose t-shirt was torn, forehead bleeding lightly. "Looks like you took the brunt of it," he said.

Now the man nodded. "Should have been more careful." He bent to pick up the flashlight. Instantly Gérard was back in Zurich, the night he'd killed Miss Zutter. The night she'd left him with her final words: Bring it down. Gérard realized he'd let down his guard. Sure, he was hunting and killing, but was he making any attempt to take down the Circle? No. He was enjoying himself far too much for that.

The thought caused Gérard some consternation. How could he allow himself to be so caught up in the clubhouse camaraderie that he'd forget his mission? A few months with a few killer friends and he was ready to shrug off the commitment—the vow—he'd made so long ago. Disgusted with himself, he snapped at the jogger. "Next time, then, I suggest you watch where you're going, you little prick."

The man, shocked, stepped away with his hands up. "Okay, sorry, man. Relax. I'll just go…." and then under his breath "Asshole."

"Really?" said Gérard. "Relax? Asshole? You could have hurt me."

"But I—"

The jogger did not have a fighting chance. Gérard was on him before another word left his mouth, pummeling him, pounding his face, arms, and head until he was a bloody pulp. The man's breath was ragged.

Gérard looked around. It occurred to him, a little late perhaps, that he'd just killed—or was about to finish killing—a civilian, and in plain view of the safehouse. Totally against the Circle's rules. He sighed.

Dragging the man's body into an alley, appreciating the darkness, he located a brick and finished the jogger off with a final blow to the head.

But now the mess was his to fix.

• • •

An hour later, he'd taken care of it. All he'd had to do was call on his good buddy Smith, the very Watcher that had aided in his recruitment, and politely ask for his help. Unfortunately, Smith hadn't seen it that way, so it had taken some coercion. Still, Smith had a family, and once Gérard had sufficiently threatened them, his darling wife Rachael, his daughter Penelope, Smith had capitulated soon enough. Gérard required assistance getting rid of the body. Smith, actively bemoaning the situation ("Mr. Pool, you have no right to contact a Watcher. It's against the rules. If Mr. Black finds out he'll have our heads," blah, blah, blah), ultimately agreed. Together they removed the jogger from his temporary coffin in the trash can where Gérard had stashed him, loaded him into the trunk of Smith's tiny two-door Mazda, and headed for the river. Again Gérard was reminded of his own humble beginnings. How far he'd come.

For a Watcher, Smith was decidedly weak-kneed, belly-aching as they'd lifted the body out of the car and dumped it in the water. How could someone be a Watcher with such a weak constitution? Gérard turned away as Smith vomited his dinner into the river.

"Well done, Smith. Well done." They both knew what he really meant was, *You did the right thing and if you say a word to anyone I'll kill you...and your family.*

Smith had offered one final statement of disapproval. "Just so you understand, Mr. Pool. This was completely against protocol. I will stay silent for my family's sake. But if I ever see you anywhere near them I'll report this whole incident to Mr. Black, at which point you will be finished."

Gérard nodded as if he understood the warning, but a lowly Watcher like Smith was nothing more than an inconvenience.

"You have my word," Gérard said. He offered his hand, and when Smith took it he squeezed down hard, mashing

Smith's fingers together. Pool raised the tire iron and struck Smith on the side of the head and continued blow after blow until Smith had been tenderized like a slab of beef. The sound of blunt metal on flesh was intoxicating. Finally Pool did the same to Smith as he had done to the jogger. He punctured Smith's lungs and tossed him over the railing into the Hudson.

One night, two deaths: a Watcher and a civilian.

Gérard Finck's war on the Circle had finally, officially, begun.

58

1987—Mr. Vice

Vice prided himself on his discipline. For that reason, he made no effort to contact the Dentist; in fact, rarely spoke to her alone, not even at the safehouse. He led a lifestyle that had been designed to be self-sufficient—and so did she. Their tryst might have been a one-time deal. It wasn't. But he'd have been good with that, too.

Months had passed between their first and second encounters. Almost a full year between their second and third. He'd stopped counting the months eventually, but she was never far from his mind—or body. He smiled to himself behind his newspaper in the safehouse and crossed his legs.

"Weather looking good this week, Mr. Vice?"

Suddenly, there she was. He didn't look up. It was her first reference in ages to him about the weather. It was their code. Sunny = I'm willing to see you; Cloudy = Not. Simple. Effective. Annoying. At least to him.

"Looked a little cloudy today," he said mildly, "but tomorrow looks like sun, and lots of it."

• • •

The Dentist

They would meet at his place, not the Waldorf like last time. The Dentist studied her reflection in the mirror and chose the leather choker with the spikes on it over another one less flashy. It had been a while since they'd met and she wanted to make a statement. Not a word had been uttered in the safehouse about a possible connection between her and Mr. Vice, which was exactly the way she wanted it. Plus, when playing the long game, you occasionally have to let the mark win. It didn't hurt that the sex was incredible.

She arrived at his place, spotting the top-notch security system that had been installed since her last visit. High-tech, state-of-the-art. Inside the modern decor, lots of blacks and grays and glass, like the enormous dining room table, drew the eye. Either he had a good one himself or had hired a damn good designer. She'd have to ask for their contact information.

The evening and following morning went as she'd planned. She allowed him to think he led the way now and again, but every move was calculated. By her. They broke from their version of sex, which included lots of bondage and pain followed by lots of release, only for food and hydration. Their preference tonight was what the experts were calling auto asphyxiation—and they were becoming expert at it. The only downside was knowing at any moment it could all come to an end. Not from the choking, although that was certainly a possibility, but by her "lover" being disposed of. She'd never find another so compatible, so willing to follow her lead. On the other hand, knowing she herself might be the one to end it added just enough spice to the mix for a nice ironic twist. It seemed it was true: That which we create inevitably destroys us.

• • •

Mr. Vice

Vice came to while feasting his eyes on the Dentist's curvature in the glow of the dawn. For a moment there, just a moment, thinking about their latest episode, he felt something like... fondness...creep up to him and tap him on the shoulder. He gave himself a hard mental slap. Vice felt no fondness. Vice felt nothing of any kind. He was unstoppable. Impenetrable. A fortress.

And yet....

There was something about her. Oh, he was aware he might find himself choking for real—forever—the next time. That she'd look him in his eye as he took his last breath and let him know she'd won their little game. But he couldn't help himself. These stolen nights—along with the thrill of the hunt, of course—were what kept him going. One of them would surely end up dead sooner rather than later, and, frankly, he thought that was precisely what kept the Dentist coming back for more, but still he couldn't stop. It was unsustainable and he knew it. The rules they'd set up were in place for a reason. He knew he'd have to kill her at some point, and before she killed him. And he knew he wouldn't hesitate to do so. He also knew the inverse was equally true.

He rose from the bed and made his way to the bathroom. The sound roused her. She rarely said much the morning after.

They didn't talk about the Circle; another of their rules. The pretense that they were simply partners in a sex game helped them keep up the pretense within the Circle. Who knew what the repercussions would be if word got out of their collusion?

"What's your clock?" he asked her. One of the few Circle related questions they allowed themselves.

She glanced at his watch lying on the nightstand. "Nineteen hours," she said. "You?"

"Twenty-eight."

She rolled back over for a few more minutes of sleep. At least that's what he supposed. You never knew with her. It was rare that she even stayed until the morning, usually out the door once they were physically spent and he was still asleep. It would not be wise to divulge anything personal and, with no Circle talk, they were limited to communication via bodily contact. Transactional sex. He preferred it that way.

Didn't he?

He looked back at her. "Why a dentist?" he said.

"Wha—?" she mumbled into the pillow.

"A dentist. Why'd you become a dentist—a real one," he said. "Everyone hates the dentist." It was a break of the rules, sure, but maybe this time....

"That's why," she said, surprising him, "exactly. *Because* everyone hates the dentist."

When she didn't go on, Vice began to think she'd gone back to sleep, but then she propped herself up on her elbow and covered her body with the bed sheet.

"I don't get it," he said.

"Why would you," she said. "It was stupid." It was the first time he'd ever seen her the slightest bit unsure. He waited. Gave her space. Afraid she'd close up again.

She laughed suddenly. "I was going to change that. Can you believe it? I wanted to make it better. So kids like me wouldn't hate it so—" she stopped. "Hey, you know what? Forget it. This conversation is over. Done. We said no questions." She got up to dress.

"We said no questions about the Circle," he replied.

"New rule, then. No questions. Ever. About anything."

"Not fair," he said.

"Tough," she said, jaw clenched. "If that's the way you feel, then maybe this whole experiment of ours has run its course."

The words were a gut punch, as he was sure she had meant them to be. Had he really crossed the line? It was true, members rarely talked about their former lives, and Vice had never been one for small talk—or cared about anyone enough to ask—but surely, given the circumstances...

With that sentence she finished getting dressed and gathered the rest of her things. "Good-bye Mr. Vice."

"See you out there, Dentist," he said.

"No," she said, "you won't. You'll never see me coming."

59

Gérard

Almost a year had passed without a word from anyone within the Circle regarding Gérard's actions, the ones that had led to the deaths of the jogger and Watcher Smith. This gave Pool both comfort and confidence. He'd taken care of things. He had no reason to fear retaliation for stepping so clearly out of line. He also came to the conclusion that he had been patient long enough.

That night, Gérard, in a cashmere winter coat and gloves, stood above two men in the walk-in refrigerator of an abandoned restaurant. Incapacitated and shaking from the cold, the men were stripped down to their underwear and zip-tied to the arms and legs of wooden chairs. Mr. Crush and Mr. Belt. Two of the more seasoned veterans of the Circle. Right where he wanted them. *How the mighty do fall.*

Only minutes before, Gérard had interrupted the attempted assassination in progress. Mr. Crush, armed with a hand drilling hammer, waiting in the darkness for Mr. Belt to arrive. Unfortunately for him, Gérard, armed with a cattle prod, made contact first, tasing Crash until he lay drooling on the floor. Gérard had dragged him into the freezer and begun his vigil for Belt.

Mr. Belt was the building's owner, on his way over to perform a standard sweep of the facility for a prospective client. By Circle standards, he was respected, but approaching retirement, and members were waiting to see if he'd become one of the next Mr. Blacks. Why these members chose to maintain "careers" when all it did was compromise their own safety was beyond the scope of Gérard's understanding, but it wasn't his problem.

Belt stepped off the elevator and was cattle prodded before he'd had the chance to realize something was wrong. Pool then dragged him to the cold refrigerator to join his buddy.

"Not a word from either of you?" Gérard began. "I was certain you would at least wonder why you are here...why *I* am here." Pool teased the men with the cattle prod, sliding it up and down their arms, activating the trigger to send sparks into the air.

Their defiant silence impressed him, but angered him more. He held the cattle prod up to Crash's heart. "Really, gentlemen? Nothing to say? You're not curious why I've strapped two fellow members to chairs in an abandoned restaurant?"

"Fine," said. Crash, finally. "What the hell is going on here, Mr. Pool? You and I both know you have no business with me. I'm here for him." He angled his neck toward Belt who rolled his eyes at the obvious. "No hard feelings, old friend," Crush added.

"No, of course not," Belt said with a sigh.

"And I know you're not the one after me," Crush continued to Gérard, "because that's Mr. Spider, I had him figured out days ago."

"And you're not *my* target either," Belt said. "So, Mr. Pool. We ask you again. What the hell is going on here?"

Gérard smiled.

"You have no right being here Mr. Pool," Belt said. "There are rules against this."

"He's right, Pool," said Crash. "Let us out of here before you get us all killed."

"Before *I* get you all killed?" Gérard sneered. "What are you talking about? That's what we all signed up for, you idiots. To kill or be killed."

"That may be," said Belt, "but rules are rules. For our safety and for the integrity of the hunt."

Gérard scoffed at the superiority of these men. "You talk about integrity? The second we are informed we are not permitted to hunt whomever we want, whenever we want, the Circle's so-called integrity goes out the window. The Circle is nothing more than a bunch of hypocrites."

"You're wrong," said Crush, "the Circle is everything. It's life and death."

"Life and death is nature," said Gérard, "and nature follows no rules. Nature just *is*."

There was a moment of silence. "So what's your plan, then?" asked Belt. "You kill us both. And then what?"

"Then I've made my point," said Gérard. "Proving that I can kill whomever I want without consequences."

"You won't get away with this, Pool," said Crush, "you'll be discovered. It's mad—and inevitably doomed."

"How?" said Gérard, seeing realization hit both men, "you'll both be dead."

"The Watchers," Belt said desperately. "They probably already know he came here for me. They're undoubtedly on their way."

"Watchers," said Gérard. "I don't fear the Watchers. I'm happy to kill anyone who stands in my way."

Crash and Belt exchanged sideways glances.

"Besides, by the time I'm done with you both it will look like a fight to the death that went wrong. No one will investigate; it will just be another tragedy at the hands of the Circle." Pool lowered his voice. "Which means I get to keep on killing. Rules be damned."

Gérard leaned in closely so they could feel his breath upon them. "Or," he said, "I can execute you both and send a message: There is a traitor in the Circle and there is no safe haven."

Gérard took out his pistol and placed the barrel against the side of Mr. Crush's head. Crush closed his eyes, his breath releasing rapid puffs of vapor into the cold air. Pool cocked the pistol and fired. Crush recoiled from the sound. It took him a moment to realize he was still alive, yet covered in blood. Then he saw Belt, now minus most of his head.

"You're crazy," Crush cried. "You're not making any sense. Look, let's talk this over, okay? I can help you—"

Gérard pulled the trigger and Crush joined Belt in a death slump.

Gérard laughed. "You just did," he said, "more than you know."

60

Mr. Vice

This assignment was as inevitable as the sunrise. He already knew everything he needed to know about his target. In a solitary moment he questioned the timing, but dismissed it just as quickly. The Circle was the Circle, unforgiving and all consuming. There was no time for reminiscing on past escapades, even as recent as a few weeks ago.

The evening was not perfect, however. It was not his preference to hunt in the rain, his one superstition after the weather played a part in his sloppy termination of Mr. Glass. He'd lost his footing twice during their battle and vowed never to allow mother nature to interfere with his work. One made one's own luck in this business, and anyone who thought different was delusional.

Disguised as a custodian, entry to the office, if the face makeup and prosthetic nose were successful, would not be a problem. No one ever suspected cleaners—faceless drones of little consequence—of anything. Still, it would not do to underestimate the prowess and drive of the object of his assignment.

The Dentist was just like him. A planner. Undoubtedly, contingency plans had been set in place should security be compromised. Vice continued to puzzle over the need of some members to slave away at day jobs. As if the pretense of a "normal" life still held some lure, some possibility that they, too, were normal. Did that make all members psychopaths? Leading one life to the world, and leading an entirely different one behind the veil of normalcy? Vice shook his head at himself. Philosophizing was never helpful and was, in fact, irrelevant. All members hunted. All members killed. The whys and wherefores? Who cared?

He pushed his trash cart, equipped with a mop and broom, along the long carpeted hallway. The walls were painted a nice soothing taupe, as if a wall color—or the abstract art hung on them—could ease a distasteful visit to the dentist. He wheeled past several other office doors until he came to the one with a placard that read "Dr. Samantha Nolan, DDS" on it.

He'd known her name, of course, since receiving her dossier, but this glimpse into her other life was fascinating to him. The choices she'd made to create her daily environment. Images of dancing teeth with smiling toothbrushes. A large cork board with dozens of drawings, seemingly produced by patients, children, thanking their dentist. A box with toys sat in the corner, holding action figures, stuffed animals, and a couple of puzzles. The sound was off, but on the TV mounted on the wall the Coyote chased Road Runner in an endless loop.

You had to appreciate the irony. The Dentist, his former lover and current target, one of the most ruthless members of the Circle in recent memory, specialized in pediatric dentistry. He'd probably never know why she continued to practice, but that didn't matter either, now that she was about to die.

In her brief moment of vulnerability, he'd learned that she believed children should not be afraid of the dentist. But that could not be the only reason. Then it came to him. What better place to hide than amongst children? The Circle's mandate made innocent civilians off limits, and children are the epitome of innocence. Any member would be risking an awful lot attempting an on-site assassination here. She'd constructed a virtual second safehouse, the brilliant bitch.

The waiting room was empty, not unusual for this time of day, and it looked as if all the staff had gone, too.

He calculated his odds. Was she in her office—or somewhere else? What were the chances that another hunter was there hunting *him*? Vice's meticulous research and planning lead to his cardinal rule: to always to know two things before launching an offensive; 1) the member assigned to him, in this case the newest member Mr. Night, and 2) the member his target was assigned to kill. In this case, Mr. Lion. This ensured he was as prepared as possible. There were only three other members who would have any viable reason to be in this office. One of them, Mr. Lion, was seriously off limits since he was not, directly or indirectly, Vice's target—this time.

He decided to check the examination rooms first, each of the first two doors were open and ready for cleaning. He emptied the trash in each one as he went, listening for sounds. When he got to the final room he hesitated. The door was partially closed.

Vice swung it inward, ready to fight.

• • •

"Wait!"

Vice was stunned into silence. *Pool?*

Mr. Pool was on holiday after killing Mr. Saw only a few days before. Except he wasn't. He was here.

"What are you doing here?" he whispered. "I thought you were on holiday."

Pool didn't answer. Too late, Vice saw his arm raise and felt the shock of the cattle prod.

61

The Dentist

The Dentist heard the thump from her private office in the back of the facility and cocked her head to listen. Another thump, louder this time. During the day she used the office close to the examination room, but after hours she retired to her "little sanctuary" in the back that she kept locked at all times. Not even the staff had a key. She'd been feeling a little under the weather recently, and liked to use the space to freshen up in between patients. Another thump. She got up, her senses alert. Since everyone else was gone for the day, it was either the janitor, which would be unusual since his hours generally started at 10 p.m., or someone who shouldn't be there.

She shrugged. Now was as good a time as any to kill Mr. Lion. She crept down the hallway until she identified the source of a new sound, which was definitely one of her drills, coming from the room around the corner. For the first time in a long time, the Dentist felt confused. Why would someone trying to kill her announce himself with the loud screech of a drill?

Armed with the small pistol she kept in an ankle holster, she turned the final corner. A custodial cart sat just outside the storage room. The janitorial services always started at the top of the building and worked their way down. Even if the guy had completed his rounds upstairs early tonight, there was no way he'd be here before 10.

Heart pumping, she saw a light from under the door for Exam Room #3. A drill went on. None of this made sense. Why would a hunter make noise? Hunters prided themselves on stealth. Unless....

She stopped and slowly pushed open the door. Muffled groans came from the room that soon increased to screams along with the sound of drilling on bone. If this wasn't the Circle, it was something else. Something that should not be happening in her office.

Mr. Vice was strapped into the patient's chair. Bloody. At the intrusion, all movement halted and two sets of eyes, one terrified and in pain and the other surprised, looked up. The silence felt like it stretched on for a long time, but had to have been only a second, as the three assessed the situation.

She was in a strong position with a gun in her hand. But who to aim for—who to kill? Where was Mr. Lion? Vice was here, predictably, but the Mr. Lion she'd studied wasn't this brash. This sloppy.

And Mr. Pool? What was he doing here?

Again, nothing about this situation was making sense.

Only two Circle members were currently authorized to kill her during this cycle: Lion and Vice. Vice, she assumed, was here to kill her. Lion was nowhere to be seen. But, even though Mr. Pool was on furlough, he was absolutely here in her office. Which meant only one thing: a clear breach of the Circle's mandates was underway.

"Stay right there, Mr. Pool," she said. "This is not your kill. What are you doing here?"

"Hello, my love," Pool said, "delightful to see you."

She cringed at the endearment. "I said, what are you doing here? You're on furlough. You could be executed for this."

"For what exactly? For killing this member when it's not my *turn*?" he said. "Do you realize how ridiculous that sounds?"

"Rules can't be broken, Pool," she said, pointing the gun at his chest. "Everyone knows that. It's what keeps the Circle intact."

Pool smiled. "Exactly," he said deliberately. "Yet, they didn't seem to do much for Mr. Crush or Mr. Belt, did they?"

The Dentist's eyes widened. "That was you?" she said.

"A thing of beauty, it was, too. You would have enjoyed it."

"But they weren't assigned to you. You had no right!"

"No right!?" Pool demanded. "And just what gives anyone the right to tell me what to do and when? They both were ready to die for the Circle. I simply...let them. An organization of ruthless killers abiding by ground rules is a farce, and all its members are hypocrites."

"Without rules, there is chaos!" the Dentist fired back. She may not care one way or the other about Vice's survival, but like hers, and all the other Circle members, his whole existence was based on following the Circle's laws. They were licensed to kill because of those rules, and she'd be damned if someone was going to shit all over them. "And repercussions." She raised the gun, which had lost some height during their little discussion, once more.

"Oh yes, the punishments."

"Yes, the punishments! The legend of Mr. Spade reminds us that civilians can never be harmed. His story," she said, pointing to Mr. Vice, "reminds us all that there is no escaping the Circle. Are you so willing to find out what the punishment will be for an unauthorized kill?"

"Do I look like I am scared? You think that the legend of Mr. Spade scares me?"

She looked at him. He didn't look in the least bit afraid. Why not? Mr. Spade's story scared everyone. Keeping civilians off-limits was what made the Circle such a success. Members abided by that rule; it's what made them cautious. The death of Mr. Spade was one of the most important deaths in the Circle's history. "It should," she said.

Pool raised his hands, which were covered in blood. Vice wasn't moving, but his eyes were watchful. Seeing as he was strapped to the chair, he was helpless. "The legend of Mr. Spade," scoffed Pool, "is what made me. Do you hear me? It made me what I am today."

He had to be crazy. "What are you talking about, Mr. Pool?"

"You can drop the 'Mr. Pool,' nonsense," he said, taking a slow calculated step towards her.

"Don't come any closer." He stopped, but was still too close for comfort.

He clenched his teeth. "Let me put it simply so you will understand. Mr. Spade and his story? It is the reason I am here. Why I sought out the Circle. Why I kill."

"But—?"

"My name is Gérard," he said. "Gérard Finck. And Thomas Roche—your Mr. Spade—was my father."

• • •

She must not have heard him right. Spade...*the* Mr. Spade... Mr. Pool's *father*?

"You heard correctly," said Pool, as if reading her mind. "The Circle claimed my father for violating their so-called rules. They took him from me, the very day my mother was murdered in the streets of Paris. All because of the Circle's rules. And now I am here to take the Circle down....one rule at a time." He came a step closer.

"I said, don't come any closer," the Dentist said. "I'll shoot."

"People will die," he continued, not heeding her warning. As if possessed. "Members, Watchers, civilians. I am coming for everyone." He tossed a look at Vice. "It was supposed to be him first," he said, "but I don't play favorites. So it looks like you'll be the Domino to his Bond after all."

She went to pull the trigger, but in her hesitation Pool found his opening and struck her with an uppercut right under the jaw, smearing Vice's drying blood across her chin. The gun went off, grazing Pool's ear. Pool leapt at her, tackled her to the ground, halfway between the exam room and the hallway. Her gun skidded across the floor. She needed a weapon. But what? The janitor's cart was the only thing in the vicinity. Feigning fear, she crab-walked backwards. There. On the bottom shelf. A box cutter—no, a carpet knife. It would have to do.

Pool kept coming, his eyes glassy, his mouth smiling. The Dentist made a half roll toward the cart, plucked out the knife, rolled back over and stabbed at Pool, who deflected the blow easily. His smile got bigger. He was *enjoying* himself.

Well, she could relate to that, couldn't she?

Pool had the advantage. He kicked her in the kidney and then kicked the knife out of her hand. It didn't go far, but too far to do her any good. She drew up her arms to protect her face, but couldn't protect the rest of her at the same time, and Pool pummeled her abdomen with his fists. Unable to catch her breath, her hands came down, she watched him draw back his fist…

...and the lights went out.

● ● ●

The Dentist came to with Pool's hands tightly wrapped around her neck and squeezing the life from her body. Her hands, however, were free. She clapped them at his ears, hard, giving her just enough of an opportunity to deliver an elbow to his face. She felt around for the carpet knife, but her hand met nothing but the tile floor and spilled blood.

With a growl, Pool countered with a punch to the bicep, shooting a sharp pain up her arm. She recoiled, and spotted the knife, wedged under her patient's examination chair.

Pool saw it, too.

Together they dove for the blade. In a swift motion, the Dentist swiped at it and swung it towards Pool, penetrating his calf. He looked at it incredulously for a second, then went to yank it from his flesh. No way she was going to let that happen. She lurched on top of him and sent the blade deeper. Pool screamed, and she took her advantage by beating his face and upper body with her fists. Pool blocked one of the blows with an arm, but not before the Dentist had again sunk the carpet knife, this time into Pool's thigh.

Another howl of pain from Pool morphed into an unexpectedly harsh rage-fueled blow to her face, and she was knocked to her back. She watched as he crawled toward the door. If he did not attend to his wounds, he could bleed out before she'd finished with him.

She rose to her hands and knees. And slipped on the slick floor.

When she looked up, Pool was gone.

62

She retrieved the carpet knife and returned to the chair to investigate Vice's injuries. Groggy from the battle, she struggled to gain her footing as she inspected his body for life-threatening wounds. Satisfied she found none, she addressed his mouth, shaking her head. Obviously, Mr. Pool had no dental training and the drill had done a number on Vice, who had clearly gone into shock, but was breathing.

"Vice," she said into his ear. "Wake up. We need to talk."

She waited. Vice groaned just as she realized what she was doing. Mr. Vice was there to kill her. *Her.* If she woke him up, she'd be back where she started. Well, almost.

Pool had interfered with Vice's plans, but if not for his flagrant breaking of the rules, she or Vice, or both of them, would surely have died this very night.

It would be simpler to finish the job here and now. Earn her holiday. No one would be the wiser. There wasn't a single Watcher out there that would know the difference between her dental expertise and that of some amateur.

She felt nauseous suddenly, and turned to vomit into the corner of the room. Disgusted with herself and her normally strong constitution, she reached for a paper towel and gained her composure. Why not kill Vice now? To hell with Mr. Pool and his crazy agenda to take down the Circle. Or...save Vice and inform Mr. Black that Pool was a traitor with a plan to bring about the demise of the Circle.

What would Vice do? Would he have followed through on his kill? What will the Circle do if I bring Vice back to the safe house? What could *they do? Is it my responsibility to let my fellow members know about this new threat? Am I my brethren's keeper?*

Whatever her decision, it would irreparably shape her future in the Circle. She tightened her grip on the carpet knife.

• • •

Vice came to with a start. His tongue explored his mouth and tasted blood. He turned his head and spit out a mouthful. The Dentist was there.

"So," she said. "You're alive."

He tried to speak clearly, but his mouth wasn't working right. It felt like it had been jackhammered. "Whaa—?" He looked down. He was fastened to the chair. Not good. Not good at all.

"Calm down," the Dentist said. "You know I didn't do this. Not my style. You'll have to trust me."

Unable to formulate words, all Vice could do was fight his restraints.

"Stop it, Vice," she said. "If I wanted to kill you, you'd be dead already. I'm going to let you go. But you have to calm down and listen."

He spit some more blood and then started again, enunciating as best he could. "Wha' the 'ell is 'appening? How did 'ou 'et me in this chair?" he heard himself mumble.

"I told you, Vice. It wasn't me. It was Pool. Don't you remember?"

Why was he so muddled? Why couldn't he think clearly? Vice took a long second to consider what he'd just heard. "Nice try," he said, his words still muddy, but somehow understandable. "But 'ool's not assigned to either of us. Just 'et it over 'ith. You earned it."

"Sonofabitch, Vice. Listen to me. I told you it wasn't me. I didn't do this to you. And while I'll probably regret this decision for the rest of my life, no, I don't plan on killing you right now."

"What? Why?"

"Because. You said it yourself. Pool wasn't assigned to either of us, but here he was ready to kill you and me without thinking twice. I can't let that stand, and neither can you." She paused to gage his response. What did she expect him to say? "So...even though you tried to kill me today, I'm giving you a break. Letting you go so we can stop him. For the greater good."

• • •

The Dentist understood his hesitancy. She prided herself on being one of, if not, the most ruthless member of the Circle. Showing mercy and turning down an easy kill and 48-hour holiday undoubtedly looked inconceivable from his perspective. He was looking her up and down, taking in her disheveled attire and the bruises forming on her arms and face. "Wha' 'appened to you?"

"Pool happened," she said. "That's what I'm trying to tell you. Now do you want me to get you out of these things or not?"

At his reluctant nod, she unbuckled the belt-like fasteners, designed to keep children from thrashing about during treatment. She preferred not to use them on the kids, but sometimes it was necessary to get the job done.

Once out of his shackles, she helped Vice rise to a seated position.

He looked at her. "So," he said, wincing at the effort, "'ow's about a little 'ental work before we 'it the road?"

63

She cleaned up Vice's mouth as much as possible, gave him some pain killers, and promised to do some more damage assessment and repair as soon as possible. When they got to Tasker's, they were both worn from the short walk and leaning on each other for support. The bartender took one look at them and hit the button to open the sliding door to the back room.

The room was very quiet as they made their way to the back corner to Mr. Black's table.

"Well, don't you two make quite the pair," he said.

"Mr. Black, I'm afraid there's... a situation you need to be aware of," the Dentist said.

"Clearly. Do I need to point out how unusual it is for you to be coming in together?"

"No sir, Mr. Black. But the circumstances required—it's just that there's been a heinous rules violation. And it involves Mr. Vice. Involves both of us," she amended.

"What has he done?"

"It's not what he's done. It's what's been done to him. To us. By Mr. Pool."

"Is that right, Mr. Vice?" Black asked.

Vice nodded.

"What's Mr. Pool got to do with this?" He reached down below his chair to remove a folder. The Dentist couldn't see anything but a web of connecting names. Surprised by this unlikely act, assuming it was the flow chart of each Circle member and their respective targets and hunters, she took note of this invaluable fact.

"Mr. Pool attempted to kill Mr. Vice as he was..." she hesitated.

"As I was attempting to eliminate my target," said Vice, still mumbling, but more coherently than earlier.

The Dentist nodded.

"Are you telling me that Mr. Vice was there to kill you?" he said, "and Mr. Pool stopped him?"

"Not exactly, sir," the Dentist said. "Mr. Pool was there to kill us both. He told me so before we fought. He's defected, sir, says he's forsaking the rules and will be coming after us one by one until—if—we catch him." She paused. What was the straightest line through the maze of a story she had to tell? "Apparently, sir, he is the son of Mr. Spade."

Mr. Black's eyes darkened and his body tensed. "Say that...again."

"The legend of Mr. Spade," she said. "It's not a legend. It's true. And Mr. Pool is his son. Mr. Pool has planned for years to infiltrate our ranks, looking for vengeance."

Black shook his head as if that would help him grasp the situation more clearly. "And Mr. Vice here?" he asked her.

She'd been anticipating this question, but still hadn't come up with a better response than the truth. She sighed. "I could have killed him—and been well within my rights. But there's no honor in that, no integrity. Mr. Vice might have killed me today, or I could have killed him in the scrum. But Mr. Pool should never have been involved in our business. Those are the rules of the Circle. Rules I value. *We all* value. The rules that keep us from devolving back into a primitive existence. I wasn't about to allow Mr. Pool to do that to us. We are better than that."

Mr. Black looked at her. "While I do not require a lesson in the Circle's bylaws," he said, "I do appreciate your point, Dentist, and can only hope all of our members are as dedicated to the Circle as you are." He turned his attention to Vice. "It seems you are the catalyst for all sorts of mayhem, Mr. Vice. You bring with you the story of your loved ones. Then you become the potential victim of the son of one legend only to become the first member ever saved by his would-be-target. Quite an accomplishment, wouldn't you say?"

Vice was doing his best to look Black in the eye, but appeared too tired to manage it. Black was right. It was true. Vice was the first of his kind. The Dentist wondered if he'd be honored...or condemned?

"Fortunately, the Council meets tomorrow," Black went on. "I'll bring this situation to them and see what is to be done. In the meantime, Dentist, Mr. Vice, not word of this to anyone."

"But Mr. Black, with all due respect, sir, the other members need to know. About Mr. Pool, that is," said the Dentist. "He's injured and will be looking for medical attention. If we all band together we can—"

Mr. Black put up a hand. His voice went hard. "I will inform the other members when I think the time is right. Watchers, too. It will take some time. I advise you both to stay in the safehouse until further notice to ensure the highest level of security until this is all sorted out. I'm sure the Council will make short work of this...intrusion...and we will all be back to normal in no time."

"And us?" Vice managed.

"You two are removed from active duty for now, a move only involves informing two members as opposed to the entire chapter. The bartender will see to your wounds. Now, go."

The two of them got up from their seats, feeling each and every ache and pain. They relocated to a separate corner of the parlor, furthest away from the action and commotion to which they had grown accustomed. They took seats and waited silently for the bartender to appear.

When Vice spoke, the message was soft but clear. "Thank you," he said, "for sparing me."

• • •

Mr. Black had had the back corner sectioned off with a dark, heavy curtain. No members were permitted into the area until his completed conference call with the Council. When he opened the curtain, he spotted the Dentist and Mr. Vice where he'd left them, asleep in their respective chairs, bandaged and looking like the walking dead.

"Miss Dentist, Mr. Vice," he said, tapping each of them on the foot to nudge them awake, "I have word from the Council."

"And?" said Vice, his mouth like a bag of dry leaves.

"Dentist, you are to be commended for your actions last night. Both for the gallant effort you showed in battle as well as your decision to rescue Mr. Vice. You have therefore been granted an extended furlough."

"But what about Mr. Pool," she said. "What are we going to do about him?"

"I would ask that you show some patience and allow me to speak. That member has been disavowed. As such, his given Circle name is never to be spoken again. From now on, he will forever be known as the Fink. His access to our funds have been terminated and safehouse privileges revoked. New bank account cards and numbers are being distributed to every member in every chapter around the world as we speak to ensure the Circle's protection." Mr. Black paused, then said, "Members of the Circle have not been told the details involving you two, and we'd like to keep it that way. With all due respect, Mr. Vice, if word gets out that you had been spared, it could ruin both yours and the Dentist's reputation within the Circle. In fact, it may be in your best interest for one of you to request a chapter transfer."

"I'll go," said Vice, almost before Black had finished his sentence. "She shouldn't have to uproot her life because of what she did. Besides, I should be dead anyway. No sense in sticking around here."

He felt the Dentist still. She obviously wanted to object, but knew Vice was right. There was no way she would want the good deed she'd done to derail her status in the New York chapter—or get her exiled.

Mr. Black nodded.

"I guess I should get going, then," said Vice.

• • •

The Dentist waited. Vice was gone, but Black had not dismissed her.

"Is there something else, sir?"

"As a matter of fact...." he said. "As I said, we are grateful for your swift action and sacrifice on behalf of our organization."

She sensed a *but* coming.

"But unfortunately, something *has* come to our attention. You may be aware that one of the Watchers' jobs is to collect blood samples at each scene, to ensure that no civilians have been injured during a kill."

Uncomfortable where this was going, she said, "Sir, it's a room where I perform oral surgery It's quite possible my staff didn't scrub down the—"

"No, no, no. Nothing like that. I'm not accusing you of anything. What I'm more interested in is this." He held out a few sheets of paper, stapled together.

"What's that?"

"That, Ms. Dentist, is a report of your blood sample. Showing that *you* are with child."

64

Mr. Vice

He looked at the apartment he'd called home. Not much to see. A bunch of interior designed cold abstract art and little else to show who lived here. It meant nothing to him. He'd leave it where it was for the next tenant. He'd left Tasker's for the last time only hours before, resigned. It was for the best. Sticking around now would be difficult, like he'd been stamped with the proverbial scarlet letter just to mock him. He could hear the whispers. *Fraud.* In his own mind they'd already begun.

The stigma of being a living legend who'd tried to escape the Circle once before and would soon be known as the one who'd been spared by his own would-be target was more embarrassment than he could bear. The change of scenery would be good for him. Where would they send him? He'd already washed out of DC, and now New York. Which meant there was only one way to go, and that was down. To some inconsequential chapter somewhere full of nobodies. Though that might not be so bad. Once he'd proved himself worthy again by adding to his long list of kills, he'd rise easily. Too bad he hadn't been able to add the Dentist to the top of that list.

He walked by a mirror and recoiled at his reflection. Mr. Pool had done some damage. The bartender had supplied him with more pain killers, but his tongue kept poking around as if it couldn't stay away from the jagged teeth and deep crevasses where the drill had done its worst. He'd need some good dental work right away if he intended to be seen in polite society. Wherever he was.

More than his mouth, however, it was his ego that hurt. How could he have been so blind not to have seen through Mr. Pool, his former comrade in arms? He'd been right under their noses, plotting and scheming since his arrival, and no one—not even Mr. Black—had harbored any suspicion. What did that say about Vice—about the Circle? That it could be infiltrated like that. And to think that, at least in the context of the Circle, they'd been friends, kindred spirits.

A hoax. All of it. He'd been played. Expertly, impressively, played.

He recalled one of their earliest conversations that upon review had an entirely different meaning. "Isn't a 30-day holiday too long?" Pool had asked. "Why wait? Why not go right to the next target—and the next?" Vice had seen it as the eagerness of a novice. He couldn't have been more wrong.

The phone rang in his hollow apartment. Only the Circle had his number.

"Mr. Vice?"

"Mr. Black?" Usually Watchers called, never Black himself. "If you're wondering, I'm just about ready to leave. Once I get my transfer, that is."

"Save your energy, Vice," said Black. "The Dentist has opted for the transfer. We're granting it to her instead of you."

"She did what?"

"You heard me. Your status has not changed."

Why would she do that? She'd be viewed by Circle members as a hero. Unless she felt the way he did—like a fool for not seeing through Pool's act. But would that be enough to push her away from New York altogether?

"Consider yourself inactive until you hear otherwise," Black continued. "Rest up, Mr. Vice. The Circle will handle the Fink."

The line went dead.

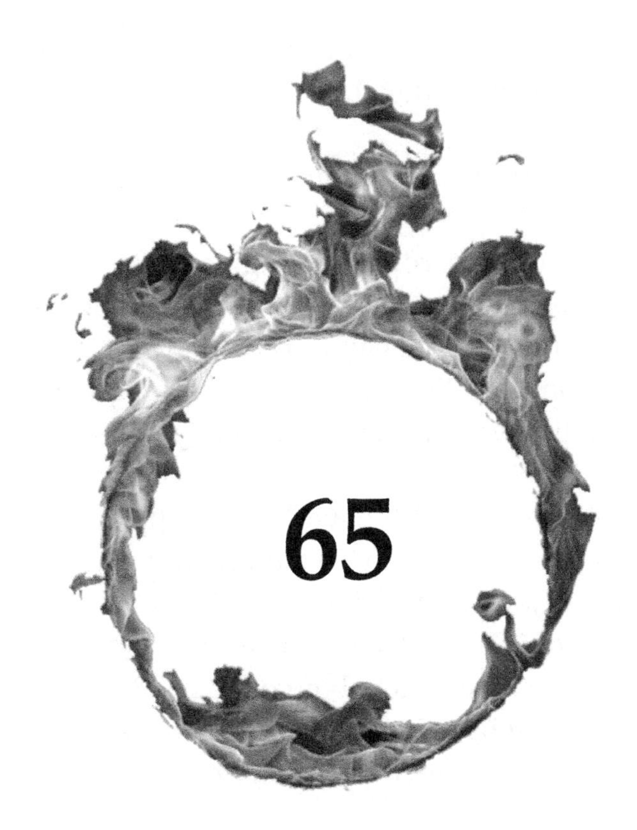

1987—Pittsburgh—The Dentist

She had done the math. She had been to the doctor. She was with child. Pregnant. Knocked up. She was going to have a damn baby. In less than seven months. No wonder her stomach had been off lately.

"So it would seem," Mr. Black had commented tactfully back at Tasker's three days before her descent into exile.

She'd asked him exactly what that meant for her continued membership in the Circle. It was the first time she'd ever seen Mr. Black discomforted. "Well," he said, " I am sorry to have to say this...you have been an invaluable member from your very first day of initiation...but…."

"Sir, please. Just cut to the chase," she said.

"Yes. Of course. You understand that members are free to do as they please. But this—situation—has never arisen before."

She said nothing. *Let him stew. It's their own damn fault for being so sexist.*

"Yet, as I'm sure you can imagine, there is no possible way that a pregnant woman can function as an active member of the Circle. The Council has agreed. Many would argue that there is an innocent life you will be carrying within you at all times. Killing you would mean killing the—that innocent life."

The dentist felt as if the world had toppled and crushed her. "What does that mean? What are you saying? Are you telling me I'm...out...out of the Circle?"

Mr. Black sighed. "There was a reason that I made the decision to offer transfers to both of you." He waited. "As of this moment, you have been released from the Circle. You are free to have your...to give birth...and do as you wish for the rest of your life."

"Wait, I don't understand. There *is* no out. We all know this. Mr. Pool—"

"The Fink."

"—Yes, the Fink. He and I fought over upholding these same sacred rules."

Mr. Black shrugged. "And yet you have been...let go, also according to the rules. Go, take care of things."

The bastard couldn't even speak the words.

"Keep it, if you want. There will be no ramifications from the Circle. Or give it up for adoption, rejoin the Circle in another chapter when you're ready—or when the Council decides you are ready, I should say. One way or another, your time in New York is up. As far as the rest of the members are concerned, you have simply taken a transfer."

Her first thought was that she needed a drink. A strong one. Then she remembered that such everyday luxuries were no longer an option. How could this be happening? How, after so many years, after all she'd done and all the places she'd been, all the men she'd been with, could something like this happen to her? Years of patience and practice and honing her craft and living by a set of rules that allowed her to harness her innermost desires. Gone. For what? A few nights with…*him*.

And why hadn't he been dismissed—set out to the curb like so much expendable trash? She could tell you why. He was a man. It was that simple. The world of patriarchy had once again reared its ugly head of sexist decrees. This was Vice's damn baby, too. Why should he be given a free pass and she a life of...ugh...*motherhood.* She shuddered.

Adoption. Black had said she could return if she put it—she refused to give it a gender—up for adoption.

No, wait. They can't force me to have this thing. But before she could speak Mr. Black handed over a bank book and a few more papers.

The Dentist scanned them quickly.

He nodded. "Ten percent of the fortune the Fink brought to the Circle. The Council felt it was...appropriate."

Another awkward pause.

She bit her lip. *This isn't fair*! She didn't care about the money. She tried again. "You can stop this," she said. "Put me on an extended holiday."

"It's out of my hands now," Black said, already standing up as if to dismiss her.

"It's not! I can get rid of the—it—and be back in action in less than a week. If I found this out before the Circle did, who's to say I wouldn't make this exact decision anyway?"

"We don't deal in hypotheticals," Black said.

"This is outrageous! How many of these men have fathered children while serving the Circle? Do you even know? How many of them were forced to leave as a result? Obviously, our Mr. Pool—*Fink,* that is—was the result of one of those indiscretions."

"And look where that's landed us," Black said, putting up his hand and signaling the end of their discussion. "I'm not saying this is fair, but it's been decided. There's nothing I can do."

She stood still and said nothing.

"This is farewell," Mr. Black said again, "from the Circle."

Finally, dismissed, she turned away.

It was all Vice's fault. And Pool's for screwing everything up with his demented plans for vengeance. Her blood was boiling. Vice would pay. Pool would pay. The Circle would pay. The Circle had made her; the Circle would have to face the consequences of its actions.

66

Good day, Mr. Black –

It's time I reached out to you. You once knew me as Mr. Pool. Now you call me the Fink, which I find both apropos and amusing. In my former life I was Gérard Finck. One letter changed me from gullible mark to miscreant. You sold me on the Circle in a single afternoon, remember? In one short conversation you convinced someone you had just met to offer up his fortune and become a killer. And you didn't think twice. As easy as "Would you like steak or fish?" I bet you thought your recruitment skills were what took me in, but in fact your arrogance blinded you from the truth.

You see, it wasn't by chance that I found myself in New York with hundreds of millions of dollars.

I have the Circle to thank for that money. Well, the Circle and my father, who did a splendid job siphoning off millions back in his time, investing it in a Swiss bank. That's where I met Ms. Zutter. She trained me, turned me into a weapon that would wreak havoc on the Circle. Do you want to know her dying words to me? "Bring it down," she said. And that's just what I plan to do.

Of course, the Circle has stolen my fortune. But I might check my bank records if I were you. Don't worry. I've taken only a fraction of what the Circle is worth. And it's more than I'll ever need to hunt down each and every member until there are none left for the Circle to carry on.

You see, Mr. Black, I'll never get tired. I'll never rest. I'll always be in the shadows, like a coiled cobra ready to strike. Your members will live in fear, ever wondering when their day will come. And when it does, if they'll be ready for me.

More members will die. More Watchers will die. More civilians will die. Starting with the ones you see every day. Have fun watching them drop like flies around you.

– The Fink

67

Mr. Vice

Mr. Vice walked into Tasker's hoping the trepidation he felt didn't show. His physical injuries had healed, he'd had his teeth and mouth tended to (although he was still on a soft diet), but he'd been having nightmares that signaled he still had some significant mending to do on other levels.

Primarily, he questioned how he'd be received. How much did the other members know? How many of his "old friends" would still be alive and active? By now, word of the Fink's taunting letter had made its way to every member from New York to New Delhi. The Circle was in crisis mode. What was supposed to be an easy fix had already turned into a global problem. The Fink could literally be anywhere. The general consensus was that his letter was "mostly true" — that

New York was still his base of operations and his top priority was to inflict the most damage where he was most comfortable.

Mr. Black was coming under fire from the Council as well, and, as such, things around the safehouse were doubly tense. The mere fact that members were feeling the pressure from the Council was telling, too, since all Black communications with the Council were supposedly highly secretive. The word was, as impossible as it seemed, that Mr. Black was becoming unhinged, akin to King George III after losing the Colonies. Delusional, accusatory. Of everyone who came into the parlor. There was chaos where there had once been order. Vice was about to find out if that was true.

Mr. Night walked past him with a brief nod of wary acknowledgment at Vice's return to action. Vice had to physically stop him in his tracks to talk to him. "What's going on around here?"

"You haven't heard?" Night asked in disbelief.

"Heard what?"

"You've been gone a long time; a lot's happened."

"Spit it out already."

"Mr. Pool went rogue. Turns out he's the one who killed Mr. Crush and Mr. Belt a few months back. Then got into some big fight with the Dentist that ended up getting her shipped out of here."

This conversation was revealing in a number of ways. For starters, Vice had no idea that Pool had been involved in the deaths of Crush and Belt. Word had only been that it was a botched attempt resulting in two deaths instead of one. Secondly, it seemed there were members of the New York chapter who didn't know of his own involvement in the Pool/Dentist saga.

"Crush and Belt?"

"Yeah, then the Dentist. He sure knew how to get our attention."

"But that was months ago. Why does everyone look so frantic now?"

Night looked at him and lowered his voice. "There's more," he said reluctantly. "Pool sent a letter to Mr. Black not long ago. His manifesto, if you can call it that. Turns out he was the son of Mr. Spade…as in *the* Mr. Spade, from the stories. He only joined as some revenge mission to bring the Circle down. From within."

"You're kidding," said Vice, choosing to keep his knowledge to himself.

"That's not all," Night added. "This letter says he's coming for every member, every Watcher. Even civilians. And that there's going to be some kind of aggression directed at us."

"What? When?"

"No one knows. It's bad enough that we have our own assignments to take care of, now we have to be on the lookout for Pool at every turn. Holiday or not."

This visit to Tasker's had turned into an invaluable one. The magnitude of an attack on the Circle itself was momentous. If anyone had the audacity to pull it off, it seemed it would be the vengeful Mr. Pool. Terrorizing members in their element was one thing, but an attack on the safehouse was entirely different—just what Pool would be looking to do. But how brazen would he get? Would he have the audacity to come back into the safehouse himself to confront his former cohorts?

• • •

There was a thundering crash from beyond the parlor walls. Vice and Night reached the sliding door in time to see a taxi cab barreling through the wall. It was mayhem. Members frantically searching for a way out or dragging their injured bodies away from the wreckage. The elderly bartender slumping lifeless, sandwiched between the taxi and the bar; another member crushed beneath the tires.

"Oh my God," said Night.

Vice shoved him aside and began escorting people to safety. Mr. Brick, a new member, had been in the bar retrieving a drink. He looked a little worse for wear, but unscathed. Vice helped him to his feet and pointed him in the direction of the door.

That's when the first shot came. Mr. Brick dropped to the floor, shot through the neck. Poor guy never had a chance. The shots were close range. Sure enough, a figure in military garb, complete with tactical gear, field protective mask, and ear protection appeared holding a handgun as the dust was still settling. Vice dove for cover, but knew he'd been spotted, and the bar stool offered no protection whatsoever from a bullet.

"Come out, come out, wherever you are," called the man.

All it would take was one shot to take the guy out. But weapons were *verboten* in the Circle's safe houses. Always had been. So far, no one had thought far enough ahead to foresee this kind of intrusion.

Pool. It had to be.

In one hand he held the gun; in the other was a strange device like a gun with no trigger. Like a joystick from an arcade game, topped with a small dish-shaped object.

Vice pushed the curtain aside. "Pool?" he said. "You sonofa—"

Suddenly Vice and everyone around him was screaming and covering their ears. Pool had triggered the device in his hand, which was emitting a high-pitched, deafening screech of sound. "Thunderball. How nice to see you. How do you like my new toy?" Pool's voice sounded far more sinister through the protective mask. "Effective, right? Got a buddy in R&D at a weapons manufacturer. Guy told me what it did, but who knew I'd have such impressive results?"

Vice felt something drip down his neck. Blood. From his ears. He tried to move, but his equilibrium was off and he was hit with a bout of vertigo.

"I'd stay put if you know what's good for you," said Pool. " Not your time…yet—and the Dentist isn't here to save you." He looked around. "I'm here for someone else at the moment."

"Do you realize what you're doing?" Vice shouted. The ringing in his ears was so severe he couldn't hear his own words.

With his hand held ready to trigger the device for another shock of sound, Pool stepped over the debris and the bodies to what had been the bar's sliding door, now just a piece of fragile wood hanging on its hinge. He kicked it in with his heavy boot. A couple of brave members went to stand, but Pool pressed the trigger and they fell back to the ground as their eardrums were attacked by the splintering noise.

They watched as he proceeded to the back where Mr. Black was lying on the floor holding his ears.

"Well," said Pool. "What have we here? It's our fearless leader." He kicked Black in the gut and then hammered the pistol down on his head. Black passed out.

Pool turned to the room. "Not so fearless now, is he, folks? So, here's how it's going to go. I'm taking him out of here. With me. If anyone dares to follow us, Black dies. If anyone attempts to leave this room I will know, and I will be in range to press this trigger until your ears burst."

He removed some thick rope from the sack strapped across his shoulder that he positioned under Mr. Black's armpits to drag him away. Most of the members in the Circle were powerfully built, but Pool acted as if Black—a tall, well-built man himself, was no more than a sack of rice.

"And don't worry gentlemen... you'll each get your chance at me," he taunted as he left the room. "I suggest you prepare yourselves."

Vice couldn't help himself. The bastard's confidence was off the charts. He lunged.

Pool laughed, and triggered his sound mechanism again. Immediately Vice fell to the floor, blinded by the pain of the ultrasonic weapon. "While nothing would make me happier than finishing what I started, Mr. Vice," Pool said, "I'm afraid today I have other plans."

68

To the New Mr. Black –

Welcome to New York, and congratulations on your new post. Navigating the aftermath of my last visit was no easy task. But you handled it with grace and poise, so for the Circle to award you this position was a smart move. I am sorry our paths never crossed during my time as an official member, but if I had been stationed in your chapter, I believe we may have gotten along very well. I just hope this promotion doesn't feel like an empty gesture, considering what happened to your predecessor.

I'm pleased to say that the last Mr. Black suffered greatly. I want you to know that. He was my recruiter, you know. It's funny, actually. All those years as an active member he was sharp as a tack. But alas, somewhere along the way, he'd lost a step or two. His skills deteriorated and people died. It's a damn shame, don't you think?

A few aspects of the current situation are interesting, though. For starters, you were appointed the very next day, which, even I must admit, is pretty cold. He was the Mr. Black of one chapter of a global organization, not president of the United States, yet was replaced so easily. Which brings me to my second item: Did the Circle even bother to search for him? For an organization specializing in hunting and killing, one might be surprised by the lack of pressure after a terrorist infiltration where its leader was kidnapped. Does it not seem strange to you? No pressure. None. At. All.

I reminded my Mr. Black of that fact each and every day that I held him. That he had already been replaced and that no one was coming for him. Despite his position, despite his adherence to the rules for his entire tenure with the Circle. You left him for dead without even the slightest hint of concern. Shameful? I should think so.

Which leads me to something I wanted to share with you right away—hence this letter. It was a revelation really. You see, Mr. Blacks are under the illusion they have power and control when, in actuality, they have neither. They are prisoners. Just like the rest of the Circle's members. Maybe even more so, given their endless days spent in the safehouse, confined in a life never to be lived on their own. It's forced retirement, that's what it is, without even the decency of the cheap gold watch and the option to live out the rest of one's days with dignity.

At initiation they make it sound like surviving to the age of 60 is a tremendous feat, an honor, but it's not. If joining the Circle is a death sentence, becoming a Mr. Black is a life sentence. Forfeiting the right to hunt means surrendering any semblance of freedom you ever thought you had. A position of power like that should carry tremendous gravitas. But Mr. Blacks like you are simply appendages of the Circle, nothing more. Appendages that apparently grow back if severed. You're living proof of that, aren't you? You are now the warden of this backwards prison, where everyone else is free to leave but you must obediently stay like a dog in a cage.

You do have my pity, Mr. Black. After all, I am not without empathy. You might be interested to know that I still have some business to attend to here in New York before I take my skills on the road, so I'll be seeing some of your members very soon. Which, of course, means, you won't be.

Enjoy your prison, however long it lasts.

– The Fink

Mr. Black stuffed the letter back into the envelope that bore his name. He buzzed with anger and something else he dared not name.

"Attention everyone," he announced from his back corner of the parlor. The general hum in the room died down instantly. "There are a few things I need to say that I'm afraid are long overdue.

"You don't know me," he started, trying to hide the shaking of his hands by putting them in his pockets. "My former chapter called me Mr. Blade. I don't have history with any of you the way my forerunner did. With him, you talked together, celebrated together, laughed together, I assume, all in this very parlor. But that does not change the fact that, due to the terrorist attack on our institution a few short weeks ago, I find myself here as the new Mr. Black." He paused and looked around at the faces of the members. "I'm honored to be here with you, but I have to say that I'm disheartened by the circumstances that brought me to this position. You all served under my predecessor. And while you undoubtedly had your share of disagreements, I've come to realize that each and every one of you always respected his authority over this chapter. What happened to him was... inexcusable...unforgivable, and left the Circle with many unanswered questions."

He paused again. "Until today."

There was a murmur as the members gathered closer to hear what Black had to add to their paltry knowledge of Pool's actions.

"Before I share that information, however, first a bit of good news. Thanks to our well-placed assets at the *New York Times,* the *Daily News,* the police department, the District Attorney's and the Mayor's offices, our status as a clandestine organization remains intact." Sighs of relief echoed through the parlor. "Unfortunately, with the good comes the bad," he said, holding the envelope high over his head. "I've received correspondence from the Fink."

The room fell silent.

"It seems, at least according to the Fink, my predecessor, your former leader, is dead."

There was a collective, if small, gasp. It wasn't as if the members expected any other outcome.

"I took this position," Mr. Black went on, "because I am the appropriate age, but also because I wanted to be here. With you. During this trying time in our storied history. Please, rest assured I will do everything in my power to keep you all abreast of the whereabouts of the Fink. My goal is to keep you, and the integrity of your respective hunts, intact.

"It is for that reason I am informing you of the contents of this letter. The Fink claims to be remaining in New York, at least for the time being. He also claims to be on the hunt for each of us. And given the obvious, I deliberately say 'us' here. So keep your guard up, even if you're on holiday. As we all know, the audacity of the Fink knows no limits."

69

1989—Mr. Vice

The serenity and the solitude sword fishing brought Mr. Vice was a welcome change to the hustle and bustle of the big city. His boat wasn't extravagant like some of the others that were docked at the West 79th Street Boat Basin on the Hudson, but it was just right. For him, anyway.

It had been two years since the attack on Tasker's but a sense of normalcy had finally been restored. As he gathered his fishing gear and loaded up his food supply he contemplated all his experiences over the course of his time with the Circle. How much he had changed. He thought more about himself as a person. He thought about Warren and their struggles. He'd named his boat "My Better Half"—a tip of the cap, as it were, to Warren's influence on his life, on his existence. The name fit right in with so many of the boats in the Basin named for "other halves," like the innocent "My Darling Jennifer" on his right to the borderline offensive "She Loves My Dingy" on his left.

After shutting Warren down so completely for so many years, it was the first time he'd really thought about the possibility that he'd been imposing on Warren's life as opposed to the other way around. Warren had always been the obstacle he needed to overcome—to rule, control, and destroy, but in these private moments he realized that he may have needed Warren more than he realized. Warren was his polar opposite, the nemesis seeking to undermine his very existence, yet Warren had also been weak, painfully so, which made him easy to disdain and disregard. It was a mystery to Vice, therefore, that he was thinking that Warren's company might be welcome at a time like this, rocking along with the water on a beautiful afternoon. It might even be pleasant.

His next thoughts came as unexpectedly as the ones before. Could he and Warren have coexisted? Were they not two opposite sides of the coin? Was it possible for a killer mentality to exist alongside an innocent one, one with morals with which most of society would agree?

All this philosophizing was interesting, he supposed, when one had the time, but the answer was still a hard no. The unfortunate conclusion was that they never could, would—or should intertwine. This body was Warren's, but Warren had created Peter and Peter had become Mr. Vice for a reason: To fill the cataclysmic void in his life left by inattentive, unfeeling parents. That fact alone was enough to convince him that the two would never have been able to share control of the vessel he, Vice, now inhabited.

Having lost contact with the Dentist also supplied some additional perspective. He didn't love her—what was love anyway but a pretense to ensure entrapment and dependency?—but he would be lying if he did not admit to missing her company. And not only their stolen moments. She was as close as Vice had ever come to a friendship, although he suspected it fell into the same category as "love." Still, it came with another unexpected pang, which he laughed off. Then there was Mr. Pool himself, whose defection and insurrection had caused the Dentist's departure.

Once again, Warren floated by in his mind, asking him to remember the loss he'd suffered when the Circle took his wife. Really, when you looked at it from a certain angle, Warren wasn't so much weak as broken. Like a fragile baby bird after a tumble from its nest. All he needed was Vice's help to build him back up again. Sure, it'd require some deliberate spoon feeding, but....

Vice sighed and shook his head. Enough philosophizing. Time to head below deck.

• • •

With nautical maps and charts spread out before him, Vice was planning for the voyage ahead. Twenty-nine more days of holiday since Mr. Carbon's timely demise the day before. It would take him a little over a week each direction, leaving him 13 days to fish and explore the Gulf. He'd make it 10, just to be safe, to leave him time to decompress and regroup after the holiday before jumping back into action.

The boat undulated beneath him, the wake of a much larger vessel departing the marina. "No Wake Zone" signs were clearly posted; apparently the entitled captain felt they didn't apply to him. Vice took one last look around the cabin. Satisfied, he powered up his motor and slowly made his way out of the Basin.

• • •

The spray of the Husdon river on his face came as welcome relief. Rejuvenated, he headed to the tip of Manhattan where Lady Liberty struck a pose off in the distance. Though he swore no allegiance to this or any other country, the pull of her magnetism was undeniable.

Casting a quick eye about the boat as he regularly did, he spotted a buoy off the stern that would need retying if he didn't want to lose it. He shifted the engine into neutral and moved to remedy the situation. A quick retie of the knot ensured it wouldn't come loose again. It was then he realized the buoy was only the beginning of his problems.

"My Better Half" had been compromised.

"Nice day," said a voice behind him.

Vice slowly turned and put his hands up. Good manners when the guy in front of you is holding a harpoon gun squared at your chest. "Fink. What the hell are you doing here?"

"Not so happy to see me, then?" said the Fink.

"Not happy to see a delusional, psychotic killer of innocent civilians on my boat? Why would you think that?"

The Fink's grin disappeared. "Spare me the ethics lesson, Vice. This is a war, plain and simple. Your so-called innocents? Nothing more than casualties of that war, like any other."

"But civilians—"

"Civilians get caught in the crossfire all the time, Thunderball," said the Fink, cutting him off. "I'm disappointed. I thought you were smarter than that."

"You attacked the bar to get to the parlor," said Vice. "That's not war, that's murder."

The Fink laughed. "That's good, Vice. Really. Calling what I did murder, but what you do for a career 'hunting.' Give me a break. I mean, honestly, what did you think was going to happen to a 'secret society' that operates in plain sight, a bar the only thing between its members and the public, when I came along?"

"I guess we all know the answer to that now," Vice said, "don't we?"

The Fink nodded congenially. "Goddamn right we do. Their blood isn't on my hands. It's on the Circle's. The Circle's very existence killed those people. I was nothing more than the bullet in their decades-old gun they never had the courage to fire."

Vice shook his head. "Know what I think, Fink? I don't think you're any different from the rest of us. You're just hiding behind some backwards logic you devised to justify your actions. And I think you're crazy. The Circle gave us everything we ever wanted. We have money and power and the freedom to live the lives we wanted. What's the point of all this?"

The Fink looked at him. "I've never understood why you were so loyal to an organization that hunted you down and killed your wife just because you chose to leave. You loved her. They killed her. And yet you came running back. You think *I'm* crazy? What does that make you?"

When Vice didn't answer, the Fink went on.

"You're the worst kind of Circle member," he said. "You're nothing but a lemming. So afraid to stand up for something that you can be led into doing anything."

Vice's stomach was in knots. Warren's loss of Vivian felt like a lifetime ago. Yet now, on top of the Dentist's departure—and due to the Fink's prodding—it was rearing its ugly head. "Point the finger at me all you want, Fink. It doesn't excuse what you did."

"Sometimes doing what some might consider unforgivable is the only way to stop the indefensible."

Vice took a long look at the sharpened harpoon pointed at him. "Tell me, is there any point to this discussion, Fink? Because if you're going to kill me I'd prefer you got to it already."

"Believe me," said the Fink, "I'd love to accommodate you. Nothing would give me greater pleasure. But hear me out. The Circle took your wife from you. And her mother. Just like they did my father. No one knows suffering at the hands of the Circle more than we do. *You and me.* You should be on my side, not theirs. Take a good look at what I'm trying to accomplish here. Join me and we could bring the whole organization down. Make them pay for what they did to us. To your family. To mine."

• • •

"Well," said the Fink after a couple of moments went by, "I don't have all day. What's your answer?"

Vice considered the harpoon, the horizon, and, finally, the look in the Fink's eyes. What he saw there surprised him. It wasn't the look of a man who'd lost his grip on reality, but the pleading eyes of a man yearning for...acceptance? ...absolution? What did it mean? He shook his head to rid himself of such a flight of fancy. This was an insane killer, not some poor schmuck looking for a hug.

"So, what," he said, "you expect me to join you—trust you? How could you possibly think that was an option?"

"You're still alive, aren't you?"

Vice conceded the point. "But how long will it stay that way? Until our first disagreement? Then what?"

"Mr. Vice," the Fink said, "you must know that you're special. You are just like me. A kindred spirit. That's why we're here out on the Hudson together and you have not been dumped overboard like chum."

"Harpoon is a nice touch," said Vice. "Good time for another screening of *Thunderball*, realize you were wrong."

"I highly doubt that."

Vice lowered his hands for the first time since the Fink had emerged from below deck. "Which reminds me," he said, "Why are you asking me to join you now, when almost two years ago you tased me with a cattle prod, strapped me to a dentist's chair, and tortured me with a drill?"

The Fink laughed. *Laughed.* "Can't a guy have a change of heart?"

"Pretty big change of heart, wouldn't you say?" said Vice, relaxing his body and taking a couple of steps toward Pool. "But, the thing is, I had a feeling you might be visiting me, and here you are."

The Fink's expression shifted and he trained the harpoon at Vice's chest. "I guess that makes you a prophet," he said.

Vice nodded. "Your flair for the dramatic precedes you."

"Guilty as charged."

"Which is why," said Vice, "I removed the firing pin from that harpoon gun."

Pool's eyes went wide. He fired. *Click.*

His eyes quickly darted to the trigger and then back to Vice who had already made up the ground between them. The Fink lifted the harpoon but was too late. Vice lunged at the Fink, tackling him to the deck. The harpoon gun skittered away and down the narrow steps leading below deck. Their bodies collided in the confined space. They traded punches until the Fink managed an elbow to Vice's face and a hard shove back, giving him enough space to regain his footing. The men stood toe to toe, breathing heavily. The Fink reached into his pocket. The knife was small, but sufficient to do plenty of damage.

"A fight to the death seems fitting, doesn't it, old friend?"

"I'm not your old friend," growled Vice, dodging the slash of the knife and the backhand that followed. With the Fink off balance, Vice kicked him in the chest and sent him back to the deck. The Fink quickly rose again, the knife still clutched in his hand.

"You're sloppy today," Vice said, taking a fast fist on the jaw but missing the knife's trajectory. The Fink had speed, but was impetuous, at least in circumstances where his plans had gone awry. Vice would take advantage of the weakness.

"Bastard," said the Fink, coming at Vice again with the knife, which he deflected by forming an X with his arms

At least he thought he had. The burn in his chest said otherwise. And Pool was coming again.

This time, Vice was ready. Ready and truly pissed off. Feigning serious injury, when the Fink closed in Vice swung around and drove a knee into his back. The knife slashed Vice's cheek, but he hardly felt it. The Fink turned around. This time, the tip of the blade penetrated Vice's flesh a few centimeters and Vice let out a slight yelp. With the adrenaline boost he drove a knee to the Fink's stomach and diverted the knife from his body. The Fink blindly swiped backwards as he fell and the attack sliced a gash across Vice's arm. Vice hurried to his feet to gain some kind of level ground back.

Off in the distance, Vice saw a large boat speed by, maybe 100 yards away. Too far for anyone on the boat to see what was happening, but convenient just the same.

"So," Vice said, breathing heavily, "I'm thinking maybe you were right."

"Too late, Thunderball," said the Fink, tightening his grip on the knife. "That ship has sailed."

"You know," Vice said, "I really hate that nickname." He gauged the boat's distance. A minute at most and they'd pass by causing what Vice hoped would be a wake to end all wakes. *Thank goodness for idiots.*

"Life is full of disappointments," said the Fink, moving in yet again.

Ten seconds. Keep moving.

Vice took another step back.

Five.

"Stay still and fight like a man," said the Fink.

And....

SLAM. The wake crashed against "My Better Half's" port side and the Fink lost his balance just as Vice had hoped.

Unfortunately, he fell on top of Vice.

The sting of the blade cut through his flesh just under his armpit. Vice heard the Fink's grunt as it did. Then a slurping sound as the Fink yanked it out and drove it into Vice's abdomen. He looked up into the Fink's face. Time slowed. Would this be the end? Would Vice die on a boat in the middle of the Hudson River?

"Had enough?" the Fink gasped. "I can finish you off now or leave you to bleed to death. Your choice."

He had to get the knife out. It was his only chance.

"I'm done," he said.

The Fink nodded and leaned back.

With every bit of stamina he had left, Vice pulled the blade from his stomach, knowing that if he didn't staunch it soon, he'd bleed out.

The Fink took a second or two to register what he'd just seen, inviting Vice, barely strong enough now, to push the Fink to the deck and put the knife to his throat. The Fink went still...and smiled.

Vice was the larger man, but incapacitated by pain and blood loss. The Fink was younger and relatively unhurt. He rolled to the left, causing a stream of blood to appear on his neck from the swipe of the knife, before head-butting Vice with a loud crack.

Vice felt his nose explode.

The Fink wrenched away. Vice tripped him and the Fink went down. Vice's hands went around the Fink's neck, squeezing and squeezing until his eyes bulged.

Trembling and turning blue, the Fink reached up with all the energy he had left and poked his fingers into the knife wound under Vice's armpit. Vice was too weak to absorb the pain and finish him off. The last thing he saw was the Fink staggering overboard.

70

2001—Mr. Vice

Every time he picked up the letter, it burned another hole in his hand. He shoved it back in the drawer of his desk. Not that he was sentimental. Yet his new role in the Circle, a promotion to Mr. Black, was hardly something that happened every day. Only a week since the letter had come, too, so he supposed adjusting to the fact was to be expected. Although who could deny it was his own doing—and his alone—that had brought him here. That it was his destiny.

He'd done it. Survived to 60 despite Warren's defection and the Council's disapproval. At some point, feeling magnanimous and to compensate for his mistakes, he'd offered to put in a few extra years. Now, looking back from this advanced age, that wasn't so smart. Fortunately, they'd declined his offer...and now this. Mr. Black. Of the New York Chapter.

Some might say it was lonely at the top. Death being the only constant, almost none of the members he'd known through the years were still around. And only one of the few still knew of his rescue by the Dentist and her resulting transfer.

Vice did a search as soon as he had access to the Circle's full database, but had found no record of the woman who'd been his perfect match. Mean, dogmatic, sadistic, and manipulating. Just like him. It was as if she had never existed. Which really left only one possibility. That she was dead. In this case, "transfer" had been nothing more than the Circle's code for termination. Helping him had gotten her killed. The guilt was both unexpected and warranted.

The stalwart Mr. Lion was his one remaining colleague. Since Pool—the Fink—and the Dentist were gone, he'd become the closest thing to a friend Vice had in the Circle. And now that he was no longer a hunter, nor would ever be hunted again, and there was no chance the two would ever find themselves on opposite ends of a blue envelope, friendship was more than the vague concept it had always been.

That was when it had occurred to him to make Lion his second in command. As a member, Lion knew everything. He'd been part of the chapter's illustrious and infamous history. In a position of authority, Lion would be beholden to uphold the Circle's code of silence related to all things Dentist and Fink related. Lion hadn't hesitated, and agreed to allude to certain past "indiscretions" to keep new members on their toes, but that would be all. Mr. Black would never speak of the Fink—or think about the Dentist—again.

• • •

Hello there, Thunderball—or should I say Mr. Black?—

It's been a while, though I have to say it feels like only yesterday that we engaged in our...melee. So sorry I left prematurely...I bet you thought I'd perished in the river that day, or hoped I had, anyway. You know what they say: lose the battle, win the war. Bringing down the Circle took precedence over our own little skirmish, much as I regretted it at the time.

And now look at you. Another Mr. Black who's killed himself all the way to the promised land, despite such colossal failures. I wonder how many new recruits it will take before those stories die. Will you share the legends of Mr. Vice, of the Dentist... of me? Oh, don't you worry, my lips are sealed. My beef was never with you, per se. Although...we both know that you are now a figurehead in the organization I vowed to bring to its knees. Such a complicated blend of the paradoxical.

Rest assured, however, I am not interested in your newer members, such as Mr. Cufflinks or Mr. Chemist, at least not yet. Though this Mr. Fingers character intrigues me, as I'm sure he does you. So similar to our old friend the Dentist, no? Kill trophies, and all.

I'm sure you've heard, New York isn't the only branch of the Circle I plan to disrupt. There's no hurry; another day, another death, that's my motto.

Take care, old friend. You haven't seen the last of me.

It had been twelve years of silence. Vice had almost—*almost*—convinced himself that the Fink was gone forever. It had always bothered him that the traitor's body was never found, but each year had lessened his concern. Yet, here he was again, as only a James Bond villain would, rising from the dead once more. As the new Mr. Black, he had two questions: How long would it be before the Fink finally struck again and would his first target be equal to the task?

EPILOGUE

2016 – *Pittsburgh* – *The Dentist*

Mother,

I've done it. I'm sorry I didn't write sooner, but I didn't want you to try to talk me out of it. I know you won't approve, but I felt like I didn't have a choice. It went just as you told me it would. They couldn't resist my money, were drawn to it like a moth to a flame. I didn't say no. And now I am a full-fledged member of the Circle.

I know what you're thinking, that you didn't want this for me. That I'm risking everything. That I'm acting foolishly. But I'm not, Mom. These are the very people who cast you aside like you were nothing – and after you – YOU – had saved them.

They should be held accountable.

Like I said, I don't want you to worry. When the time comes I will be able to cross that line. I have no problem with death, and the whole blood-and-guts thing...well, let's just say I have an iron stomach. And you know I can take care of myself. If the time ever comes that I can't, well, I want you to know that I'm doing this for you. Because I love you, and love that you chose me. You could have destroyed me or left me or given me up to return to the game, but you didn't. That decision held you back. That's why I plan on making it right. I will *make it right. No matter what it takes.*

I'll write again when I can. No emails. The Circle has evolved and its reach extends farther than it ever has before. I love you, Mom. Please, don't worry about me. Like I said, I can take care of myself. In fact, I already have.

The Dentist took two mints from her Altoid tin, securing one in between each set of molars. A comforting habit. Tears of pride and shame dripped down her face as she read her son's letter. She knew Kevin better than anyone. Despite what she had just read, he was no killer, and even less of a hunter. Like all parents, she'd questioned her parenting, every decision she'd ever made. But in this case, each decision had contributed to, culminated in, this. She should never have shared stories of her past. She should have trained him in the art of self-defense and war. But she hadn't. In believing she could keep him safe, she'd done him a grave disservice. Now it was unlikely he would survive the year. It would take a miracle.

She plucked a tissue out of the box and dabbed at her eyes. Such devotion and commitment to doing the right thing was also a testament to her as a role model. A single mother who had raised a fine, young son on her own.

Still, she held in her hand what she suspected might well be his final communication. Visions of all the hunters she'd ever known in her time in the Circle paraded through her head. No one, not even the Fink, had managed to bring the organization down. What monsters were waiting to end her son's life now? Or, even worse, what kind of monster would he become if he *did* survive?

She'd willingly spent more than two decades tending to her son's needs, putting the Circle away in a small section of her mind, taking it out only occasionally for the fond memories. There was one thing she knew, however. It would not matter how old she was, nor how strict the Circle's rules, the reckoning of the member who killed her son, now Mr. Dart, would be slow, painful...and satisfying.

ACKNOWLEDGMENTS

This book would not be possible without the love and support of my amazing family. My wife, Maria, you are my rock. Thank you for who you are to me and our family. For reading each and every one of my chapters, revision after revision, and offering your honesty each time. For my beautiful daughters, Mallory, Jocelyn, and Emilia, thank you for being the lights in my life. You make me so proud each and every day and I love you more than you will ever know. Thank you for your infectious enthusiasm for life and always putting a smile on my face. My father, Stan, thank you for being my number one supporter in everything I do. Greg, Danielle, and my beautiful nieces, thank you for your love and support. Mom, I miss you every day. Thank you for looking over us all.

Special thanks go out to Brian and Neva. Thank you for pushing me to keep writing, and for your relentless efforts to get my books into the hands of as many people as possible. I am truly grateful for your friendship. It's only a matter of time before *The Circle Saga* ends up on HBO Max. To my editor and part-time therapist, Heidi Connolly: once again you've helped me take my ramblings and create something of which I'm truly proud. Thank you for your insight, your diligent work, and for helping me grow as a writer. I am truly blessed to have found you all those years ago. To my Beta readers, Raquel Gifford, Alexis Perry, Anna Mungo, Colby Bettley, Garrett K. Jones, and Jamie Wickam: your feedback and honesty have helped make this book the best it can be. I'm so grateful to have you in my corner and honored to call you all my friends.

To an idol of mine, Samantha Downing. I cannot begin to express how meaningful your words of encouragement have been to me. You took a chance on an independent author and I will never forget your kindness.

To my fellow indie authors out there, including my friends Stormi Lewis, Santana Saunders, Garrett K. Jones, EJ Yerzak, Lance Karlson, KT Lyon, Brianne Davis, Kim Catanzarite, Quinn Noll, and countless others. Thank you for your camaraderie. Self-publishing is hard, but with such a great collection of people supporting one another, the process is made exponentially better. Keep churning out your amazing work. When one of us succeeds, we all succeed.

#SupportIndieAuthors.

To my loyal fans and the #Bookstagram community. Thank you for welcoming me into the fold with open arms. I started from nothing and now have the love and support of so many amazing people. Were it not for your warm reception of *The Circle*, we may never have learned of the Legends that preceded it. #TheCircleIsReal

To my Markham Warrior family, thank you for not judging me too harshly based on the content of these books.

• • •

This book is a byproduct of the COVID-19 pandemic. While I'm thrilled to have had the time and opportunity to sit down and write it, I'm deeply saddened by the toll the coronavirus has taken on all of us. My heart goes out to anyone that suffered a loss during this time. I would like to offer my profound thank you to all of the front-line workers, doctors, nurses, police, fire, EMTs, military, and anyone whose job was deemed essential for our daily lives to continue.

You are the real Legends and your efforts and sacrifices will not be forgotten.

ABOUT THE AUTHOR

LEGENDS OF THE CIRCLE is the latest installment in Stephen J. Galgon's world of **THE CIRCLE**. He began his writing journey at Fairleigh Dickinson University where he received his bachelor's and master's degrees and completed **LEGENDS OF THE CIRCLE** while teaching middle school virtually during the COVID-19 pandemic. When he's not writing or teaching, he is active in fundraising for the National Brain Tumor Society. Steve and his family live in New Jersey where he is currently at work on the next exciting chapter in The Circle saga. He enjoys interacting with fans and invites you to follow him on Instagram **@TheCircleIsReal**.

Made in the USA
Middletown, DE
21 January 2022

58205348R00229